HIGH ACCLAIM FOR *THE PLAINSMEN*
SERIES BY
TERRY C. JOHNSTON

Two-time Golden Spur Award nominee and winner of the Medicine Pipe Bearer's Award for *Carry the Wind*

"JOHNSTON KNOWS HIS MATERIAL!"
— *Washington Post Book World*

"HALLELUJAHS FOR TERRY JOHNSTON. *SIOUX DAWN* IS REMARKABLE. I HAVEN'T SEEN ITS EQUAL."
— Will Henry, *Golden Spur Award-winning author*

"This is true masterful storytelling at its best! . . . Judging from the excellence of *Sioux Dawn*, I cannot wait for the rest of them to come out!"
— John M. Carroll, *renowned historian, member of the Order of Indian Wars and the Custer Battlefield Historic and Museum Association*

CA

D0172783

Continued . . .

CALGARY PUBLIC LIBRARY

OCT   2012

Praise for previous books by
TERRY C. JOHNSTON

"JOHNSTON'S WAY OF TELLING HIS STORY
WILL CAPTURE YOUR IMAGINATION!"
—*Guns & Ammo*

"Memorable characters, a great deal of history and
lore . . . and a deep insight into human nature."
—*Booklist*

"Gutsy adventure-entertainment . . . larded with
just the right amounts of frontier sentiment."
—*Kirkus Reviews*

"Johnston's books are action-packed . . . .
lively, lusty, fascinating."
—Colorado Springs *Gazette-Telegraph*

DON'T MISS BOOKS 1 & 2
OF *THE PLAINSMEN:*
Sioux Dawn: The Fetterman Massacre, 1866
*Red Cloud's Revenge: Showdown on the Northern
Plains, 1867*

THE PLAINSMEN SERIES BY TERRY C. JOHNSTON

Book I: Sioux Dawn

Book II: Red Cloud's Revenge

Book III: The Stalkers

Book IV: Black Sun

Book V: Devil's Backbone

Book VI: Shadow Riders

Book VII: Dying Thunder

Book VIII: Blood Song

Book IX: Reap the Whirlwind

Book X: Trumpet on the Land

Book XI: A Cold Day in Hell

Book XII: Wolf Mountain Moon

Book XIII: Ashes of Heaven

Book XIV: Cries from the Earth

Book XV: Lay the Mountains Low

Book XVI: Turn the Stars Upside Down

THE STALKERS

THE BATTLE OF BEECHER ISLAND, 1868

TERRY C. JOHNSTON

St. Martin's Paperbacks

NOTE: If you purchased this book without a cover you should be aware that this book is stolen property. It was reported as "unsold and destroyed" to the publisher, and neither the author nor the publisher has received any payment for this "stripped book."

This is a work of fiction. All of the characters, organizations and events portrayed in this novel are either products of the author's imagination or are used fictitiously.

THE STALKERS

Copyright © 1990 by Terry C. Johnston.

Excerpt from Black Sun copyright © 1990 by Terry C. Johnston.

Cover art by Frank McCarthy.

All rights reserved.

For information address St. Martin's Press, 175 Fifth Avenue, New York, NY 10010.

ISBN: 978-0-312-92963-3

Printed in the United States of America

St. Martin's Paperbacks edition / December 1990

20 19 18 17 16 15 14 13 12 11

with admiration I dedicate
this novel of the Indian Wars
to Fred H. Werner,
the Beecher Island historian
who taught me how it really happened!

The fighting was of the closest and fiercest description, and the Indians were under the fire of one of the most expert bodies of marksmen on the plains at half pistol-shot distance in the unique and celebrated battle. The whole action is almost unparalleled in the history of our Indian Wars, both for the thrilling and gallant cavalry charge of the Indians and the desperate valor of Forsyth and his scouts.

—Cyrus Townsend Brady

We are beyond all human aid, and if God does not help us there is none for us.

—Major George A. Forsyth
on the island,
first day of the siege

. . . *Several years later I met one of the younger chiefs of the Brule Sioux . . . who wished to talk to me about the fight on the Republican. He asked me how many men I had, and I told him, and gave a true account of the killed and wounded and I saw that he was much pleased. He told the interpreter that I told the truth, as he had counted my men himself; and for four days they had been watching my every movement, gathering their warriors from far and near. . . .*

I then questioned him regarding their numbers and losses. He hesitated for some time, but finally told the interpreter something, and the interpreter told me that there were nearly a thousand warriors in the fight. . . . Regarding their losses, the chief held up his two hands seven times together, and then one hand singly. . . .

"That," said the interpreter, "signifies the killed only. He says there were 'heaps wounded.'"

Just as he started to go he stopped and spoke to the interpreter again.

"He wishes to know whether you did not get enough of it," said the interpreter.

"Tell him yes, all I wanted," was my reply. "How about yourself?"

As my words were interpreted he gave a grim, half-humorous look, and then, unfolding his blanket and opening the breast of his buckskin shirt, pointed to where a bullet had evidently gone through his lungs, nodded, closed his shirt, wrapped his blanket around him, turned, and stalked quietly from the tent.

—Major George A. Forsyth
Harper's New Monthly Magazine
June 1895

Author's Foreword

I think we should take a moment to talk of a few things before you, the reader, jump into this novel with both feet. Just to give you a sense of what it is you are about to read.

This, above all, is the story of a time and characters largely forgotten with the pace of our comfortable, relatively untroubled lives. What strikes me as a shame is that even most of those who have a speaking acquaintance with the long struggle to open the West really know little or nothing of this nine-day battle and siege on a dry, obscure riverbed island, somewhere in the trackless Colorado Territory, much of it still unmapped at the time of this story—1868.

In a study of the era of the Indian Wars, again and again one runs across instances of small groups of determined defenders holding out against overwhelming odds of screeching, equally determined horsemen. Perhaps by now you have read *Red Cloud's Revenge,* so you understand a little about desperate men surrounded and fighting for their lives in both the Hayfield Fight and the Wagon-Box Fight. Men who were prepared to sell their lives as dearly as possible before the enemy overwhelmed them.

Across the years, I have found in my reading of the history of the Indian Wars that time and again in every one of those skirmishes and battles I run across references that clearly and unequivocally state that the white men thus surrounded and desperately fighting for their very lives nonetheless stood ready to take their own lives at a moment's notice should the fight be lost and the red onslaught breech the walls of whatever fortress the white men had chosen for their final stand.

Time and again in the writing of the Old West, one runs across the well-considered, oft-repeated, and most-popular old saw that in the end a white man must take his own life before he was captured alive by a band of hostile warriors. For, to be taken prisoner simply meant unspeakable agony and torture. A slow death.

No death for a hero.

But the reader must stop, and consider the nineteenth-century mind of those who ventured beyond the confines of just what scant civilization the West offered at the time. We are asked to consider that it was the last *brave* act of desperate, overwhelmed, and very courageous men *to take their own lives.* So in any group of fifty "hardy frontiersmen," one will find stories of both the brave and the cowardly. Tales of those ready to die and those pleading to live, penned down on an island in the middle of Cheyenne hunting ground on the Central Plains. Without hope.

This story of the fight for Beecher Island: human conflict, and pathos and passion—white men and red alike colliding on that far-flung, unknown prairie riverbed beneath a cruel late-summer sun on the high plains. Warriors time and again hurling nothing more than their naked, brown bodies against the fiery muzzles of the white man's powerful carbines. Eventually four white men flung themselves against the tightening red noose around the island, volunteering to try to escape from that siege, each one of the four hoping to carry word to the outside world of the horror and desperation of those survivors he had left behind.

Fifty hand-picked frontiersmen, chosen a'purpose to engage the cream of Cheyenne cavalry on the Central Plains— no better or more exciting a backdrop for our cavalryman-turned-plainsman once more—Seamus Donegan (*Shamus* as the Irish pronounce it).

The writer of historical fiction assumes a perilous task: While he must remain true to history, there are the demands of fiction pressing the novelist to pace, dramatize, capsulize, omit. So with not only the battle and siege of Beecher Island studied and restudied, the site visited and walked over, a sense of place and time finally in my grasp—the story of those nine long summer days in 1868 all but lay before me. I had only to let the soldiers—Major Forsyth, Lieutenant Beecher, Sergeant McCall, and scouts Sharp Grover, Jack Stillwell, and John Donovan, all actual participants of that tragedy—tell their tales.

Into their midst ride my two fictional plainsmen: Seamus Donegan and his uncle, Liam O'Roarke, galloping across these bloody pages stirrup to stirrup with the likes of Forsyth, Beecher and the rest.

To write this work of history, I relied on many sources, a few of which I'll make mention. The first three I called upon most heavily, drawing much of the human element of the story as those were three firsthand, primary accounts (the first two by participants of the battle and siege, the third by the leader of the army column to rescue Forsyth's fifty frontiersmen).

Maj. George A. "Sandy" Forsyth did not publish his story of Beecher Island until more than a quarter-century had passed. In an 1895 issue of *Harper's New Monthly Magazine,* the major wrote the piece upon which I draw extensively not only for its rich detail, but for its chronology and its view of some of the primary characters as well. True to the sort of man that he was and had proved himself to be, not only in the Shenandoah Valley during the Civil War but on Beecher Island too, Forsyth chose a simple, yet eloquent title for his story: "A Frontier Fight."

Cyrus Townsend Brady's *Indian Fights and Fighters* continues the tradition of firsthand accounts by recounting the story of a civilian hired on by Forsyth—a young man not yet twenty who had come west from New York City for excitement, clean air, and unparalleled vistas. His recollections are but part of what actually occurred during battle and siege, and through them we see that young Sigmund Shlesinger got much more than he had bargained for when he migrated to the Plains intent upon finding adventure.

Every bit as exciting for me was the drama attending the dash to rescue Forsyth's fifty. How fitting it was that one of the major's old friends and Shenandoah comrades should find himself already in the field, perhaps the closest column to that island where Forsyth's men sat huddled, waiting out the days of rancid horsemeat and sand-seep for water. Capt.

Louis H. Carpenter's own account of his two-day race across the rolling prairie at the head of his H Company of Negro "buffalo soldiers" to lift the siege is told in his own words, "The Story of a Rescue," which appeared in the 1895 *Journal of the Military Science Institution of the United States, vol. XVII.*

To gain some insight into the Indian side of that long struggle, I relied on two sources. The first is one I have used repeatedly in the first two volumes in this series: George Bird Grinnell's *The Fighting Cheyenne.* For although we know much more of what happened on the island itself from the recollections of the white men, there was high drama and tragedy attending the loss of Roman Nose's powerful war-medicine moments before he was to lead his warriors into battle against Forsyth's scouts. No Shakespearean tragedy can elicit finer emotions than this tale of that great war-chief's eventual decision to ride into the face of the white man's guns, singing his death-song, stripped of any spiritual protection.

I was able to learn much of the participants and the mood of those Cheyenne bands that summer of 1868 through the story of Charlie Bent as told in George E. Hyde's *Life of George Bent, from His Letters,* published in 1967 after Hyde's extensive research and cross-referencing.

From the scouts' firsthand accounts, mingled with the Indian accounts of their massed charges and eventual abandonment of the siege, I moved to more modern-day renderings of the story. James S. Hutchins's chapter on "The Fight at Beecher Island" in *Great Western Indian Fights* gives us a capsulized and readable version of the story highlights, in a well-researched and thoughtful presentation.

When one is writing of the fighting Cheyenne on the Great Plains, he would be remiss if he did not consult Donald E. Berthrong's *The Southern Cheyenne,* published in 1963.

Yet with all these volumes at my fingertips, it was the work of one man above all whose story of Beecher Island made sense to me in a way no other writer's had. Greeley, Colorado, historian Fred H. Werner has invested a lifetime in pursuit of truth while debunking much of the myth that is so often taken as the story of Indian Wars of the West. This lifelong journey has proved a labor of love for him. Fred has invested not only his time but his own money as well to self-publish his many volumes in his "Western Americana Series," dealing with the drama of clashes from the Dull Knife Battle, to the pathos of the Slim Buttes Battle. It was to Fred Werner's volume, *The Beecher Island Battle,* that I found myself returning again and again throughout the months of study and writing, referring repeatedly during each of my visits to the battle site itself.

Perhaps now you will understand why this work of historical fiction is dedicated to historian Fred H. Werner, with my sincerest appreciation for his keen scholarship and my gratitude for his reading the final manuscript in hopes of purging it of errors. Should any still exist, blame not Fred Werner.

Still, as a historical novelist, I assume a task beyond the mere *retelling* of history. For in picking up this volume, you, the reader, demand of me to add something that history alone can't convey to most folks: a warm, throbbing pulse that truly allows you, the reader, to *relive* the bloody, tragic, but always exciting history of the winning of the West.

All that remained was for the novelist in me to flesh out the drama of Beecher Island: that stalk, battle, siege, and rescue.

This dramatic story chronicling the clash of cultures across a quarter-century will actually take over the next half-dozen of our years to relate. We began *The Plainsmen,* our account of this epic struggle of the Indian Wars, with that story told in *Sioux Dawn* of a bitterly cold December day in 1866 as Capt. William Judd Fetterman led eighty men beyond Lodge Trail Ridge and into history. *Red Cloud's Revenge* carried on the bitter contest waged on the Northern Plains along the Bozeman Road during a summer of blood. Now, with *The Stalkers,* we find ourselves more than two years into this captivating era, a time like no other, a time that would not come to an end until another bloody, cold December day in 1890 with another massacre along a little-known creek called Wounded Knee.

The fever of that quarter-century made the Indian Wars a time unequaled in the annals of man, when a vast frontier was forcibly wrenched from its inhabitants, during a struggle as rich in drama and pathos as any in the history of man.

Into the heart of the red man's paradise of the Central

Plains, both government and entrepreneurs alike were thrusting the prongs of their railroad and freight roads. To protect both the settlers on the Kansas plains and travelers alike, the army erected its outposts: Forts Harker and Hays, Larned, Dodge, and Lyon. And, far out on the Federal Road to Denver, Fort Wallace.

Here, where Major Forsyth will receive word that a warm trail beckons him. At Fort Wallace, Forsyth's fifty begin their stalk. To think of it, riding as one of only half-a-hundred riflemen, following the trail of those most feared warriors on the Central Plains, proven warriors who had taken scalps at the Platte River Bridge or the Fetterman Massacre.

Fifty of you, against who knows how many you would face. . . .

There can be no richer story than to peer like voyeurs into the lives of those half-a-hundred who volunteered to stalk the Dog Soldiers, volunteered to put their lives on the line for the men and women left behind. So it is we are left to wonder, as only a reader in the safety and comfort of his easy chair can, if we too would have measured up with the gallant defenders made to bleed on that island stinking with rotting horse carcasses, wide-winged buzzards hovering overhead. Would we have possessed the grit to stand in the face of charge after charge of Roman Nose's hundreds, stand and stare down the muzzles of our Spencer carbines as the brown horsemen came screaming down that dry riverbed?

It's important too that you realize you are *reliving* the story of real people. From Gen. Philip H. Sheridan, Maj. George A. Forsyth, and Lt. Fred Beecher . . . to civilians like Jack Stillwell and Sigmund Shlesinger (both only nineteen years old), crusty frontiersmen like old Pierre Trudeau, or simply hardy settlers like John Donovan wanting a crack at the Indians. Not to forget all the faceless others who hugged their rifle-pits, silently followed Forsyth's orders, and waited beneath a hot sun across nine grueling days in September 1868. Indeed, you are reading a story peopled with flesh and blood that walked and fought, cried and cheered on that hallowed ground now swept clean beneath the relentless march of spring floods and prairie drought.

So it is that good historical fiction fuses the fortunes, adventures, and destinies of numerous characters. Glory-seekers and murderers, settlers and cowards, army officers and soldiers (like Captain Carpenter's "brunette" orderly, Reuben Waller, one of those Negro soldiers who would gladly accept the danger inherent in the rescue of those white men slowly dying on that murderous island). Remember as you read—these were actual, living souls striding across that crude stage erected on the high plains of western Kansas and Colorado Territory . . . all, save two.

Into their midst, I send my fictional characters, Liam O'Roarke and his nephew, Seamus Donegan—late of the Union Army of the Shenandoah, cavalry sergeant turned soldier of fortune, having sought a change of scenery in the West, and some escape for his aching heart. With each new volume in this "Plainsmen" series that will encompass the era of the Indian Wars, you will follow Seamus as he marches through some of history's bloodiest hours. Not always doing the right thing, but trying, nonetheless, for Donegan was no "plaster saint" or "larger-than-life" dimenovel icon.

History has itself plenty of heroes—every one of them dead. Donegan represents the rest of us. Ordinary in every way, except that at some point, we are each called upon by circumstances to do something *extra*-ordinary . . . what most might call heroic. Forget the pain, the thirst, and hunger on that sandy island as each man wondered when it would come his turn to die. Forget the blood and vomit and maggot-ridden wounds stinking each man's nostrils.

Each of us does what he must in the end.

That's the epic tale of the fight at Beecher Island. If you will listen carefully now, you'll hear the grunts of the lathered horses and the balky mules straining to carry their riders to the island in the pre-dawn light . . . the eerie, humanlike cries of panic as each animal went down, killed by the Indians in those first frantic minutes or sacrificed by the scouts themselves. You can hear the cursing of frightened, wounded men or the silent cries of those who fell wordlessly, dead before they hit the sand.

Listen upstream, and without straining you'll hear the screeching war-cries of Indians and the pounding of two thousand pony hooves. And if you're lucky, and can sense the throb of your own blood at your temples, you might even overhear the prayers of the man in the rifle-pit next to yours, prayers mingling with the smothered screams of those slowly dying.

Sniff the air—you'll likely smell the burning fragrance of gunpowder or the stench of your own blood slowly cooked as it drops from your wounded head into the overheated breech of your Spencer carbine . . . while you wait for the next rattle of gunfire from the Indian snipers clustered among the swamp-willow on the bank, wait with the others for the hair-raising thunder of Indian pony hoofbeats bearing down on you in a glittering spray of sand and creek-foam.

The fight for this unnamed strip of sand happened. This story needs no false glamour, no shiny veneer of dash and daring. What has through the centuries been the story of man at war—of culture against culture, race against race—needs be told without special effects.

There's drama enough for any man across those nine bloody days on the Arickaree.

Yet, the story of Beecher Island is really a very old tale indeed, my friends. A tale whose time for telling has come at last. I've done my best spinning the whole-cloth of that story in these pages.

None alive can say if I've succeeded or failed . . . save for those ghosts still haunting the sage-covered, umber ridges overlooking that wide scar of sandy riverbed—ghosts both red and white who alone lived and perhaps died during those desperate days when Roman Nose's Dog Soldiers and Pawnee Killer's Brule Sioux flung themselves against fifty scared yet courageous men, men determined to hold out against all odds.

—Terry C. Johnston
Beecher Island Battleground
Colorado Territory
September 17, 1988

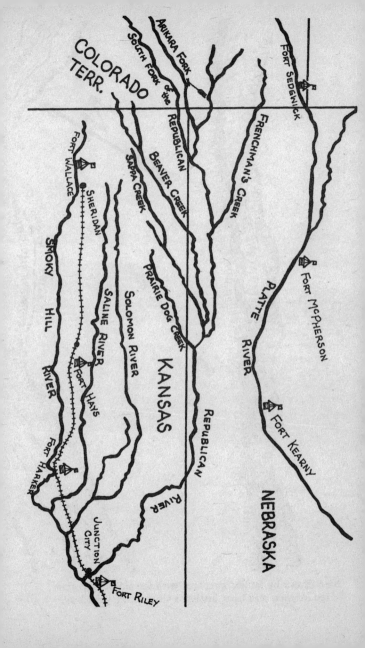

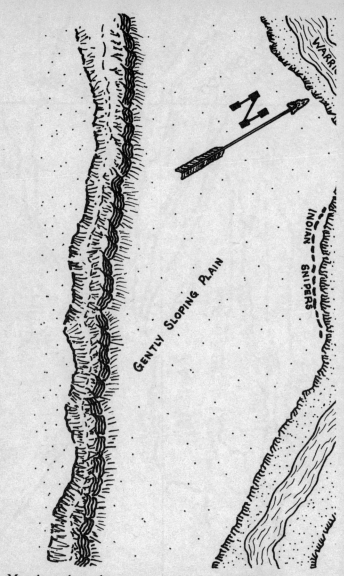

Map drawn by author, prepared with the aid of Historian Fred Werner, and from firsthand visits to the battlefield.

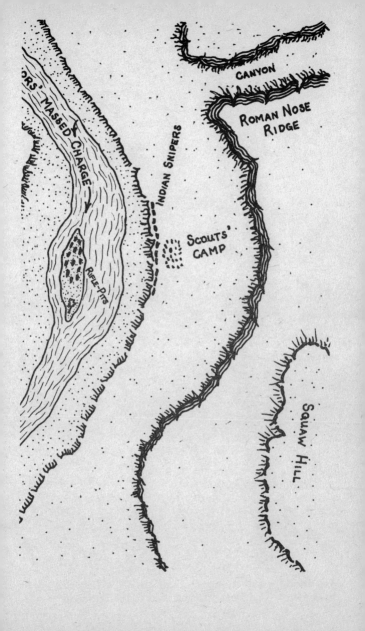

Prologue

"I don't figure this got nothing to do with you," the sergeant growled, his red-rimmed eyes glaring harshly at the civilian striding up to the hitching post. He reminded the newcomer of a skinny wolf.

"None o' your business, stranger," echoed a second soldier.

A third dressed in dirty army blue lunged up, shoulder to shoulder with the first. "You heard the sarge here," he spat. "Best you g'won your way now, sonny. Afore you get hurt."

"Not so sure it's me what gets hurt here," the tall Irishman replied, the hint of a smile spreading his dark beard. Almost a head taller than any of those five soldiers now crowding him at the hitching post, he gazed down at the shiny, blood-smeared face of the Negro soldier sprawled in the dust of what Fort Wallace, Kansas Territory, called a parade.

"A mick, he is, boys!" the sergeant roared upon hearing the stranger speak, his reedy laughter goading the other four shouldered close round him like a pack of wolves with a downed buffalo calf in sight. "As if there ain't enough of 'em in this goddamned man's army . . . we got loudmouthed ones wearing civilian's clothes, too!"

"Sarge—this'un makes out like he owns them army britches!"

The older sergeant's eyes narrowed, studying closely the patched and worn Union britches the tall civilian sported. Complete with yellow stripe down the outside of each leg.

"Cavalry, was it, Irishman?"

"Aye," he answered, taking one step back as two of the leering soldiers slowly flanked him.

"That's horseshit if I ever heard it!" the sergeant spouted. "Ain't an Irishman been borned what can straddle a horse long enough to be a cavalryman!"

The five roared with crazy laughter.

The Irishman swallowed the knot of pride hot in his throat and lunged, snagging the soldier inching up on his right. Flinging him back against three others, the stranger spoke it as calmly as he could. "Like I said when I walked up on your little party here . . . your fun's over, sojurs. I asked you polite to quit jobbing on the darkie here."

"Oh, he asked us polite to quit jobbing on the darkie, was it now?"

"I suppose you sojurs wanna dance?"

"And what army impostor would be asking me now?" the sergeant snarled.

"Seamus Donegan . . . formerly of the Army of the Shenandoah," he answered. "And by the looks of your dirty uniforms . . . you all must belong to the Seventh Cavalry I hear so much about . . . from Julesburg on south."

"Heard about us, he has?" roared one of the corporals as he scuffed backward and grabbed a handful of the dirty blue blouse worn by the Negro soldier on the ground, yanking the bloodied man to his feet. "Have you heard we don't take to these here darkies the army sends out here to fight Injuns as well?"

"Heard your regiment's led by a man named Custer," Donegan replied. "Word has it up to Laramie that Custer got himself in trouble having some of you nice fellas shoot deserters this past summer."

"Any man deserts General Custer deserves what he gets!"

Seamus smiled. "I was there when that curly headed sonuvabitch strung up some Johnnies at Front Royal in the Shenandoah—"

"You called Custer a . . . a sonuvabitch?" the sergeant roared, spittle flecking his cracked lips.

"Figured I had to get you fellas riled up some way. Let's *dance!*"

With the last word off his tongue, Donegan swung his big

right hand in a might arch, scooping the sergeant off the ground. Before the soldier landed in the dust, Seamus's left fist jabbed the man rushing his flank. As quickly, he flung his boot at another before dancing backward, both fists up before his face, shoulders hunched and bobbing as the five soldiers assessed their three casualties in those first few seconds.

Stunned, the sergeant brought his fingers to his mouth as he sat sprawled in the dust. The fingers came away stained and damp. With a tongue he rocked some loosened teeth. "You stupid bastards—tear his eyes out!"

The three soldiers who were still on their feet charged him at once, swinging wildly with all they had. Backward Seamus pedaled, jabbing and swinging when an opening came. Bobbing right, then left, as fists shot his way in a blur or dirty fingernails clawed for his face.

From the corner of his eye he saw two more soldiers in dirty blue tunics bolt from the shade of the nearby porch, on their way to help their kinsmen. The sergeant clambered clumsily to his feet, charging back into the fray.

"Now you'll pay for sticking your mick nose in where it don't belong!" the sergeant roared.

Five of them descended on him at once. Pinning down his arms so that Donegan couldn't swing. He sensed the blow coming more than saw it, the great, white scar along his back gone cold, prickling with warning. Then recognized the metallic clunk of the pistol-barrel against his skull. A glancing blow, but enough to jar him to his boots. Enough to bring him to his knees.

"Now we'll show this big-mouthed bastard what the Seventh Cavalry does to them that talks bad about the general!"

Seamus gazed up through the meteors in time to see the play of October sunlight glint off the knife-steel twisting in the sergeant's hand.

"What say we cut out his tongue, Sarge?"

"Good idea. Teach this mick not to talk bad 'bout Custer, won't it?"

The sergeant no more than got it said while hauling down on Donegan's chin whiskers, intent on opening the Irishman's mouth, when a black hand swept round the soldier's neck, yanking the sergeant off his feet. Seamus figured that was his cue.

Two of the soldiers imprisoning Donegan made the mistake of lunging to help their sergeant.

Wrenching his left arm free as the pair pulled away, Donegan put that powerful oak-rail arm and mallet-sized fist to work. Swinging it across his body with sudden effectiveness, the first soldier stumbled backward. Stunned, holding a hand to a nose spurting bright gouts of blood.

That left hand pistoned back and jabbed the second soldier, who waited too long to make his move. Petrified too long as he watched his friend back off bleeding, he himself crumpled backward into the dust as the Irishman's quick left jab cracked against the side of the soldier's head.

Whirling, Donegan was pleased to find the mouthy sergeant had his own problems. In one hand the sergeant still gripped his knife. While the other clawed at the black arm clamping his throat in a vise, barely dangling the soldier above the ground. Above the clamor, the sergeant struggled to growl orders for the four soldiers to come to his aid. His voice no more than the squeak of a field-mouse caught in the jaws of a trap.

The sergeant's four gallant rescuers pummeled the black soldier from all sides. Swinging, yanking, wrestling to free his death-grip on the sergeant and his knife. Tiring of the struggle, one of the four freed the mule-ear, army-issue holster at his right hip and cleared his pistol, swinging it overhead toward the shiny black face.

Hurling forward, Donegan caught the hand before the pistol cracked into the unsuspecting skull. He wrenched the soldier round, stared a moment into the surprised eyes, then jabbed his fist into the face, blood spurting from his nose.

Stumbling over the body as it sank to the trampled dust, Seamus dug his fingers into the hair of two more attackers, trying to yank them off the black soldier. They only yowled in pain. One lashed out with a dusty boot. Both hands still in their hair, the Irishman cracked the heads together like a hickory axe-handle whacking the staves of an oak water-keg. They crumpled without protest.

He turned in time to see the last of the rescuers dig his fingers into the black soldier's eyes, pulling the darkie off the sergeant. Gasping for air, one hand clawing at the neck of his sweaty tunic, the sergeant fought to breathe, his eyes bulging. Then turned in one swift motion, bringing the knife into the air once more as he lunged up the Negro soldier's back.

Donegan caught the arm from behind, clutching the white wrist in both of his hands. Wheeling beneath his own arm, the sergeant brought a knee violently into the Irishman's groin. Seamus stumbled back a step, then a second, as another blow came his way. Yet he refused to release the knife hand. The sergeant connected with a third boot.

A rush of gall and puke flung itself against his tonsils as Seamus sank to his knees. Almost more pain than he could bear. Watching the sergeant through the sweat dripping in his eyes. A swirl of dust around them all. Faintly heard, the murmur of voices ringing from all directions. That knifeblade glimmering in the bright autumn sun here on the far western plains of Kansas.

The knife falling toward him like the streak of a meteor . . . a streaming sliver of sunlight off the blade, like that dusty trail smeared behind a falling star against a prairie night-sky. . . .

A gunshot cracked through his pain.

The crack of a pistol.

"Hold it!"

That stopped the knife-hand in its fall.

Seamus glanced up at the sergeant, recognizing in those red-rimmed eyes the look of an animal suddenly caged. Something dark and dangerous shut off behind those whiskey-soaked eyes. Again the pale saber scar along his back warned the Irishman. He whirled around, staring into the muzzle of another pistol held by a soldier with a smashed and bloody nose. The lower half of his face glistening pink in the midday, October sunlight.

"Belt your weapons!"

He watched the pistol tremble for a breathless moment before the soldier dropped his arm, and reluctantly stuffed the weapon into the holster on his right hip.

"I don't have enough to worry about here," said the same deep voice, drawing closer. "Cheyenne and Sioux tearing up the tracks . . . Kidder's men got theirselves butchered . . . I can't keep the mail-lines open to Denver—and now you boys get yourselves all oiled up and jump this civilian and one of Carpenter's brunettes!"

Seamus clambered to his feet, studying the big-framed soldier striding up at a ground-eating gallop. A thick shock of hair atop his head, wild and unruly, and now slightly flecked with gray. Shiny teeth in a neat row beneath the iron-colored mustache, waxed and curled at the ends.

"Sergeant of the guard?"

"Yessir."

"Bring those others over here until we make sense of this."

"Yes, Captain."

"Give me your knife, Larson."

"Captain . . . weren't our fault——"

"That was an order. Gimme your knife!"

"Yessir."

The officer turned on Donegan. "Who are you, and what business have you here at Wallace?"

Seamus took a moment in answering, dusting the front of his sweat-stained shirt. "Donegan." He looked squarely in the officer's eyes. "Seamus Donegan. Come here looking for word of me uncle. Heard at Fort Hays he might be here."

"A soldier?"

"No, Cap'n. Civilian. Scout, so I'm told. Working for you."

"This uncle of yours has a name, I take it."

"O'Roarke. Liam O'Roarke."

"Indeed, he is a scout for us. Or"—the officer paused—"I should correct myself. He was a scout during Hancock's summer campaign."

"He's not here?" Donegan asked, craning forward anxiously.

"Not any longer, stranger," the officer replied. "With Hancock's campaign over . . . Colonel Custer brought up on several serious counts of courts-martial . . . the army let its scouts go for the coming winter."

"Let him go?" He bit his lip. "Where? You hear where he was heading?"

"Hold on, stranger. O'Roarke said he was heading over the Rockies to spend the winter in the City of the Saints."

"City of the——"

"Salt Lake. Brigham Young. Mormons," the officer instructed impatiently. "You heard of Mormons, haven't you, stranger?"

He shook his head. "No."

The officer sighed. "You will out here. If it ain't Cheyenne stirring up trouble . . . it's Mormons migrating to their beloved City of the Saints. Or on the road east to sell their goods. And if it ain't Mormons . . . it's soldiers like these with too much time on their hands, jumping Carpenter's brunettes. I wish Bankhead would get Carpenter and his darkies transferred outta here," he muttered.

"What would he be doing in the City of the Saints?"

"Not that I have anything against Negras, you understand," the stocky officer explained, still deep in his own thoughts. "I was born in Virginia and raised out Missouri way—fought for the Union, mind you. A Union man tried and true——"

"Captain—what would Liam O'Roarke be doing in the City of the Saints?"

"O'Roarke? Why, probably looking for work."

"Work?"

"Brigham Young always has something for a man to do on the other side of them mountains," he said wistfully, pointing off to the west beyond Fort Wallace's pink-limestone walls. "Any man that's good with a gun and can stay atop a horse at a full gallop. I hear he calls that bunch of renegades his 'Avenging Angels' . . . Danites. Damn—but there's times I wish I had a few like them myself. If I only had some that were good with a gun and could stay nailed in the saddle at a full gallop—"

"How do I get there . . . to this City of the Saints?"

The captain laughed. "You aren't going there now, stranger. Unless you're planning on taking the long way around. Them mountains out there would chew you up this time of year . . . spit your bones out come spring. What's left of you, anyway. Wouldn't be a scrap of meat left after all those winter-gaunt critters get through with you."

Then suddenly, the officer clamped a hand on the Irishman's shoulder.

"Best you stay on this side of them mountains for now. Come back here in the spring . . . early summer. Liam O'Roarke will return here then as well."

"Back here?"

"He knows I've got honest work for him next year," the captain replied. "Another summer. Another campaign against these infernal Cheyenne. Keeping the wires up and the telegraph open. Pushing the railroad to Denver. Honest work for a scout . . . not like working for Brigham Young."

Seamus watched the captain direct the guards off to the stockade with the grumbling, cursing soldiers. "I'll be back . . . come spring."

"Suit yourself," the officer muttered, reluctantly tearing his eyes off the far western mountains. "Now you"—he flung his voice at the black soldier—"get your ass back to Carpenter's camp and stay there! For your own good!"

"Yessir! Cap'n, sir!"

"Hold on, sojur," Donegan ordered. "I'll walk 'long with you." Then he turned back to the officer just starting back to the shade of his post commander's office.

"Say, Cap'n, I want to thank you for your help . . . the information on my uncle."

The officer stopped in stride, turned. "Quite all right. I'd appreciate a return of the favor by you taking yourself and the darkie out of here. I don't need any more excitement this week."

"Did not catch your name, Cap'n."

He smiled beneath that bushy mustache, pushing a shock of dark hair from his eyes. "Benteen. Fred Benteen. Don't believe I caught yours."

"Seamus Donegan."

"Been nice talking with you, Donegan. Best now that you make yourself scarce before any more of these drunk, sullen soldiers take a carving knife to you."

"See you come next year, Cap'n Benteen."

Seamus turned back, finding the Negro soldier awaiting him.

He ground his dirty kepi hat between his two huge, black hands, both scarred with light-skinned tracks. "Wanna thankee, sir."

"No thanks needed. You're a freedman, aren't you?"

His shiny face bobbed up and down. Flinging drops of sweat. "I am."

"Hot enough to boil the fat off a flea, sojur." Donegan started off. He watched the sullen, glaring faces of those soldiers lounging in knots round the parade, faces filled with distrust and downright hatred for the black soldier at the Irishman's side.

"I'll go back to my unit now."

"Think I'll walk you there," Seamus replied, nudging the soldier off. "Not much of a happy place, this Fort Wallace."

"Thank you again . . . for coming to help me with them boys hacking on me. I owe you one, Mr. Donegan."

Donegan smiled, slapping the soldier on the back as they trudged toward the far side of the parade. "Call me Seamus, sojur. What's your name?"

"Waller, sir. Given the slave name of Reuben. Took my old field-boss's name after my master was killed in the war . . . when I run north to fight in the war on the Union side."

"Reuben Waller, is it?" Seamus said with a grin, gingerly feeling the growing knot at the back of his skull. "Glad to meet you, Reuben Waller."

Chapter 1

"What you make of that, Sam?"

Sam Marr turned, staring up the side of the hill where another civilian employee of Fort Phil Kearny's army labored among the timber above Pine Island in the middle of Big Piney Creek.

"Looks to be traveling alone, don't he?" A second woodcutter inched up beside Marr, asking his question as all work on the slope ground to a halt.

"Let's hope he is, boys," Marr, a Missourian, replied with a drawl that had all the warmth of a cheery firepit on a winter's evening. "This ol' body of mine doesn't need it any more bullet holes."

They watched the lone horseman halt upslope. Then slowly raise his right arm in signal.

"Halloo!"

With the lone stranger's holler, most of the civilians looked again at one another in disbelief. One of them nervously levered a shell into the chamber of his Winchester repeater. Sam braced his hand out, forcing the man's rifle down.

"I got more reason'n any of you to be jumpy, boys," he whispered gruffly now. "I say he's a white man——"

"Shit, Sam!" one of the workers growled. "Ain't no white man gonna be coming up outta the Peno."

"That bastard's riding outta Injun country——"

"——crawlin' with Sioux and Shians!"

Marr took two steps forward and turned on the others.

"Let's be hospitable, boys. But keep them fingers near your triggers."

Sam cupped a hand at his mouth. "Halloo! Come on in, stranger!"

He watched the man's eyes as he came on slowly, easing his pony down the slope. Long ago, Sam had learned to watch the eyes. Even more important than watching a man's pistol hand. These eyes talked nervousness, while the stranger's face tried to display calm detachment.

"You're from Dixie, aincha?" the horseman asked, his hard eyes center-firing on Marr. He stayed atop his pony.

The horse-breeder in Marr saw the animal was badly in need of a curry. No saddle poking up beneath the greasy trade-blanket neither. Sam's eyes narrowed. The horseman's Southern accent came more as an affront than did his question.

"Missouri."

He nodded, those red-rimmed eyes bouncing finally over the others. Marr couldn't help feeling a bit of relief that those dark, marble eyes flicked to someone else for a moment.

Killer's eyes, he thought to himself. *Cold, downright, blooded killer's eyes.*

"Missouri, eh? I spent some of my time in——"

"What brings you down outta Sioux country?" asked one of Sam's companions suddenly, made bold by the wizened stranger who looked more in need of a meal than did a stray trail-dog.

His eyes flashed a moment. Then cooled before he opened his mouth, showing more of the browned, rotting teeth. He spat a stream of warm juice into a patch of melting snow left on the hillside by yesterday's first storm of the coming winter. "Come down from Fort Smith, I did." He leaned forward on the pony. "Watched all the way for Injun sign. Nary did I see one of Red Cloud's boys."

Marr watched the tobacco juice hiss into the soft October snow. "We figure they still licking their wounds from the fight we give 'em couple months back." When he looked up, he found the horseman's eyes narrowed on him.

"You there?"

"I was," Sam answered. Something eerie and chilling

about the man had sent a single drop of cold spilling down Marr's backbone.

The stranger only nodded at first. Then finally leaned back on his trail-weary pony. His shoulders sagged a bit. "Won't be staying here, fellas. Moving on. Just looking for a fella . . . friend of mine. Irishman."

One of the boys turned to Marr, whispering. "He talking about Donegan, Sam?"

Marr watched the stranger perk up, his jaw jutting.

"That's him," he replied. "The Irishman. Named Donegan. Knowed him up at Fort Smith. Heard he come down here." His eyes darted anxiously. "He . . . he around here someplace?"

There it was. Bigger than life. Sam Marr felt it crawl round his belly. But before he could let the others know of his suspicions, slow-witted Silas Heeley blurted it out.

"Ain't here, stranger. Donegan ain't. Come through here, on his way down from Smith, all right. Heading south to Laramie. Going on to Kansas from here, weren't he, Sam?"

Marr turned from Heeley's open, blundering face to find the stranger coldly waiting for Sam's answer.

"That where my friend went . . . Sam?"

"Yeah. Went to Kansas. Some reason you're looking for the Irishman, stranger?"

"I owe 'im, friend."

"Card game, I bet," Heeley said.

He smiled. "Might say that, yessir." He nudged heels into his pony.

Marr snagged the pony's rawhide bit with a hand. " 'Fraid you didn't tell us your name, stranger."

He smiled as he gently used the muzzle of his brass-tacked Winchester to nudge Marr's hand from its grip on his pony. "Didn't."

"And your business?"

"Finding the Irishman."

Marr was forced to step back out of the way with the others as the ugly cayuse carried its owner on down the hill and across the Big Piney.

"You ever see a rigging like that on a white man's horse before?" Sam asked the group.

"Never," replied one of the workers. "That was out-an'-

out Injun. No two ways 'bout it, Sam. And them britches, that shirt he wearing . . . and capote he got tied behind him. Injun doin's."

"Figured that," Marr replied, eyes locked on the stranger's back. "Seamus Donegan never been the luckiest man playing cards I know of."

"Maybe he run off last summer owing that stranger," Heeley said, puffing his chest out as if he had just read the tea-leaves at the bottom of a soothsayer's china cup.

Marr wagged his head, watching the stranger nudge his pony into a lope, bypassing the wood-road that would take him to the fort, instead turning south on the Bozeman Road. Toward Fort Reno. Fort Laramie. And all points south.

Kansas.

Sam sighed. "I'll wager it ain't money that renegade bastard's out to collect."

Jack O'Neill swiped a dirty sleeve across his mouth. From his mustache and beard hung bits of the slop the bartender in this piss-hole of a saloon called a two-bit meal.

It wasn't that a woman's scream was all that unusual. Hell, the chippies who worked places like this accepted that they'd get knocked around a bit in their particular line of work. So, hearing a woman scream a bit from the back where three slick-worn saddle gals plied their trade from tiny cribs wasn't anything new.

He went back to eating, and nursing the two fingers of what passed for rye in this part of the world.

Jack had had much better in his time. But sadly, that was a time both come and gone.

Son of a Southern plantation owner who again and again slipped down to the slave-quarters to take his pleasure, mulatto O'Neill had quickly become his daddy's pride and joy. From knee-bouncing child, to under-wing favorite, Jack's mama always said she was proud Mr. O'Neill done right by her boy, even if he couldn't do right by her.

Then the Yankees up north started rattling about wanting to free the slaves. And a young man barely twenty and helping his father run his Georgia plantation couldn't understand why that man Lincoln and the rest were hollering about taking a man's slaves away from him. From the way things looked to young Jack O'Neill, his daddy's slaves had everything they could ever want. Besides, there wasn't much beating going on neither.

Ebenezer O'Neill had proudly bankrolled his own company of Confederate volunteers and set the plantation womenfolk to sewing butternut uniforms so that when the family patriarch had marched away that day in late 1861 at the lead of his private army, he left young Jack behind to see after things until he should return at the head of a victorious Southern army.

That damned war anyway, Jack brooded again. Had a way of changing everything . . . for everybody.

His daddy never came back. But the Yankees come, and they took the plantation when Jack couldn't pay taxes. No wonder. The help all run off, up north and God knew where. No one tending field. No money neither. What paper script they had wasn't worth wiping his ass with in the outhouse back of the big-house.

Jack O'Neill wandered west in the early spring of 1867.

A big, strapping mulatto nudging shoulder-close to thirty years, Jack had adapted as he always knew he could. Working for a short time on a dock in Independence, Missouri, before he hired on to drive freight for the railroad. K-P. Like a second daddy the Kansas Pacific had become for the man who followed orders, stayed out of the way of others. And watched his money when he came to town.

Drop his wagon off to have it loaded for a return trip while he walked down the muddy, slushy streets, looking. Maybe spend a little of his money for something hot to eat. A little more for a few drinks like daddy used to pour from cut-crystal decanters back . . . hell, it hurt Jack to think about it.

But O'Neill always saved a little something for the chippies. Lord, was he happy the first time he found out at least one of them girls who worked the back didn't mind having herself a black man . . . at least a half-black man with a little money to jingle in his pocket.

Emmy was her name. And damn, if that didn't sound like her scream now.

Jack looked up over the lip of his bowl, staring round the murky, lamplit room that reeked of urine and dried blood and red mud melting into stinking puddles on the pounded-earth floor. With all the snow building up on the roof this February, no small wonder it leaked here and there.

Seemed to him just about every man there was staring at him, all of them listening to Emmy scream. Their faces dumb with curiosity, or fear. Beyond the back door that led to the cribs, the noises grew louder still.

Sounds like he's cuffing her, his warm, dulled mind thought, working its way through the rye, nuzzling the thought the way a child will curl up with a favorite scrap of blanket.

Then he heard furniture scraping and banging against the thin, pine-plank walls. Starting to rise from the table. All six-foot-some-seven-inches of thick, sinewy, rope-muscled frame. His skin beaded with diamonds of sweat, warmed with the sheet-iron stove at the corner, the pale lamplight giving his skin the color of old butter-scum set out too long in the springhouse churn.

Halfway across the floor, Jack suddenly wondered what he was doing, heading like he was for that shabby door hung like a limp, broken shutter on the servants' quarters back home. Slap-banging, that one back home would always batter the side of the house in a storm. Then as he stopped, not sure what to do . . . when the sound of it crawled up from the bitty-bottom of his spine and liked to knock the top of his head off.

Never heard nothing like that, except when they gelded the colts.

Emmy was no longer just screaming. That screech meant something terrible had happened back in that crib the girl called her home.

Funny the easy way the door came off in his big hand as he yanked it out of the way, shouldered left, then found the latch to Emmy's room with both big hands. Jack threw his weight against it. The door ripped back, sending splinters into the room as his eyes struggled to focus in the cloud of coal-oil and tobacco smoke.

A strange and awful, wild stench stung his nostrils as he leaped into the room, eyes squinting, searching for her.

"Jack! *Jack!* He'p me . . . oh, God!"

She loomed out of the yellow haze. Naked. His eyes went

to hers. Hers both bloodied and bruised. Puffy lips spouted flecks of crimson as she tried to talk. Frantically, he fumbled to make sense of it. Looking at the rumpled bed, the rickety nightstand toppled nearby. The place a shambles. With one hand she covered a white breast. A tiny stream of red pushed between the fingers she held against her freckled flesh.

Then Jack was ashamed to look at more of her nakedness. That dark, curly triangle of hair at her crotch. Where she clamped the other hand as she slowly sank to her knees in a puddle of blood.

"Oh . . . God—he cut me . . ."

As Emmy collapsed to the side her hand fell away, revealing a butchering that no man could heal. Purple gut spilled forth from her belly, just above the dark, moist, shining triangle mat of curly hair.

"Who cut you——"

"He did!" shouted a voice behind him.

Jack jerked his head around. Suspended behind him in the doorway must have been a half-dozen faces, all gone white and wide-eyed. One of them pointed to the far wall.

Through that yellow haze and wild stench that was as thick as gut membrane he would slash when butchering cow buffalo, Jack O'Neill caught the filmy movement toward the tiny window that led to the alley. And he realized suddenly what the wild smell was. Remembered it from times he had bumped into them on the streets of these far western towns. It was the wild, bear-greased stench of an Indian.

Jack lunged for the Indian's shadow, slipping in Emmy's blood. Landing on his knee with a loud grunt and scrambling again on his hands to the window. He caught the man's ankle in one big paw, yanking the moccasin back into the room. The killer turned like a wild thing, hissing and snarling like a trapped animal. Jack jerked back, startled. It was not for the wide, white eyes of the man, nor the seething hiss between his teeth like something cornered crazed. But, this was a by-God white man!

No Indian a'tall.

And the white man still held the long, graceful knife in his hand. Still sticky and damp with Emmy's blood as he waved Jack back.

"She ain't even good as a 'Rapaho squaw . . . that slut!" the man drawled.

Jack figured him for no-good white . . . from the South, same as him. O'Neill squatted there, stunned, not believing any of this had happened. Not to him. Not to Emmy——

"Squaws know how to make the poking fun for a man . . . this'un started screaming just when I was having fun. Sluts like her don't matter anyhow. Don't deserve to live noway. Woman can't give a man his fun—she gonna get stuck!"

He whirled into the tiny window again before Jack clambered off the floor. The mulatto grabbed for a foot again. He was too late in letting go as the knifeblade slashed back at him. Across both wrists.

Sharp as daddy's razor . . . he remember thinking, pulling the arms back, looking at the purple-white of bone. Blood spurting from the clean slices.

Outside he heard the killer drop to the snow and mud with a drunken grunt. Moccasins sloshing away across the sleety puddles . . . then the snort of a horse and the clopping of hurried hooves.

"Jack?"

He turned, finding two of the men crammed in the tiny crib with him now, kneeling round Emmy. He crawled across the slickened floor to her side.

"Jack? You there, ain't you?"

Lifting one of her hands against his rough cheek, he felt tears begin to fall.

"Cain't see you, Jack?" She whimpered, more weakly now. "I don't wanna go . . . oh, God—he hurt me!"

The big mulatto shouldered one of the men aside as he cradled the whore across his legs, clutched her to his breast.

"Always promised you'd take me away from here, Jack. Denver——"

"I'm here to do just that now, Emmy. Whenever you're ready."

"S-soon, Jack."

He gazed up at the anxious faces crowding into the room, the murmuring lips of those explaining what they had seen to those come too late. Then he realized his blood was mingling with hers.

And knew there no longer was anything keeping him here among these whites.

Time it was that he should find his own kind. Back to what was left of home.

Emmy dying in his arms. Her blood and his on this dirt floor. Killed and cut by a white man dressed like some wild, savage, killer Indian. And talking like Southern slave-hating trash.

Oh, for the love of a whore . . . time for Jack to go home.

Chapter 2

*T*he cruel March wind hurled itself through the plank door with the half-dozen soldiers pushing into the Shady Rest, nothing more than a watering hole squatting here in Hays City along the Smoky Hill River. Three miles west where Big Creek flowed into the Smoky Hill, Fort Hays itself stood like a prairie-dog town on the flat prairie in that same brutal wind, reminding Seamus Donegan that winter was far from done with the Central Plains.

Eighteen sixty-eight was little more than two months old. The buffalo grass gone brittle and winter-dried. Beyond Hays City, the prairie lay sleeping beneath a coating of frozen sleet and snow. Outside the Shady Rest, those rutted mud-wallows the citizens of Hays City charitably called their streets had to be negotiated by the unwary stranger or drunken customer leaving any one of a string of watering holes and smoky cribs where a man could buy himself a bottle of bad whiskey and an ugly woman to share it with.

Seamus drank his whiskey alone.

Sucking at the lip of his cloudy glass, the Irishman delicately ran his tongue across a missing chip. And drank deep of the familiar smells of the Shady Rest. Spilled whiskey and ale. Urine and dried blood. A good mix of mule-skinners' unwashed anuses and soldiers' sweat. Struggling against it all the heavenly perfume of plug burley and the lilac-watered chippies who peopled places like this on the far-flung distant prairie of Kansas's Smoky Hill country.

Women and watering holes. The first to arrive after the soldiers and the railroad.

He barely listened as the noise at the bar rose, then fell, while glasses filled, then emptied. An ebb and flow of sound washing about him like the waves of that ocean separating him and his beloved Eire. A stinking, rat-infested English ship had carried him to this new land, away from the grave of his father and the home of his mother.

Much, much better it be, he brooded, *better to forget that cursed ship brought me to Amerikay——*

"I'll be damned," a voice roared above the clamor.

A hand landed on Donegan's shoulder.

Whirling about, Seamus recognized, through the fog that had been his most of this past winter, a familiar face.

"Seamus Donegan, ain't it?"

His eyes watered in the smoky haze of the barroom. The figure swam before him a moment. Then his focus cleared. "Sharp? That you, Sharp Grover?"

The man dragged a broken chair to the table and straddled it beside Donegan. "All winter you been punishing that saddle varnish they proudly call whiskey here, eh?"

Attempting to steady it, Seamus held his hand out. Instead, the hand trembled slightly. He hid it in his lap. Out of view. And smiled at the older plains scout. "Ain't been much else for a man to do in a hole like Hays, Sharp."

Grover wagged his head. "Used to better in your Boston, is it, Irishman?" He sipped at his whiskey. "Damn—this stuff wash the varnish off my tonsils!"

"Good, ain't it?" Seamus held his chipped glass up in toast.

Grover clinked his up against the Irishman's. "Damn right, Donegan. Here's to green-up."

"Aye. Here's to spring."

They drank in silence for some time while Grover watched Seamus peer into his amber whiskey, the color of pale tobacco-juice.

"How'd you fare the winter, Irishman?"

"Cutting wood. Teamstered between here and Harker a few runs when the blizzards shut down the roads and no one else dared make the haul. I took their money—and the gamble as well."

"You're a man likes a gamble, is it?" Grover asked.

Christened Abner at birth, his father had hung him with a name that suited the youth better when it was discovered the boy could shoot sharp. Born in the East, Grover had come to the plains with his parents at an early age, growing up on the border of the frontier where he learned to speak a fluent Sioux. He was pushing the downside of his forties as he sat across the tiny table this winter night. Shorter than Donegan, he was spare in build as well, yet most men gave him wide berth. Knowing not only that his mother's French-voyageur blood had given him its hot courage, but most had learned of his recent return from Turkey Legs's camp, a journey that had cost the life of Grover's partner, Bill Comstock.

"Aye, I gamble," Seamus answered. "If the stakes are fit . . . and I'm not staring a hold card. You have something on your mind, Sharp?"

"It can wait," he replied. And poured them each another into the dirty glasses.

No less than Gen. Philip H. Sheridan himself had dispatched Grover and Comstock to Turkey Legs's village, north on the Solomon River at that time, to find out the mood of the Sioux. Rumors had it that the bands would be taking war to the plains again come green-up. Turkey Legs's war-chiefs had professed a hollow friendship for the whites, yet insisted the two scouts leave their camp. Seven warriors left the village, explaining they were there to escort Sheridan's emissaries safely some miles from camp, when the Sioux suddenly swung about and fired on the white men, hitting them both in the back.

Comstock fell, dead instantly. Behind the body the wounded Grover huddled, opening up on the warriors with his repeating carbine. The warriors fell back to the safety of some trees, where Grover held them at bay until darkness drenched the sky.

Bleeding heavily, Sharp stumbled off across the prairie, eventually making his way on foot to Monument Station on the Kansas–Pacific Railroad. He was bandaged there, then placed on the train to catch a ride as far west as the rails allowed. Alone, he had reported in, telling Col. Henry C. Bankhead, commander at Fort Wallace, about the murder of his partner.

In those early post-war years on the Central Plains, there were five army scouts whose names brought admiration from the civilians they protected and the officers they served: William Cody, Dick Parr, Liam O'Roarke, Sharp Grover, and William Comstock.

That had been the toughest part of walking out of that wilderness on foot for Sharp Grover. Knowing that now there were four.

"Heard someone talking 'bout you last week," Seamus said, easing his glass to the table. "Said you was wounded by an Indian bullet."

"I was," he replied, then sipped at his whiskey. "I heal fast."

Seamus saluted with his glass. "I suppose out here a man has to heal fast, doesn't he?"

"Was a cold one this year." Sharp sighed, changing the tune.

"Be glad when winter lets go this land."

The dark eyes of the prairie scout narrowed. "You ready for some honest work, Seamus?"

He perked a bit, one eye squinting at his table-mate. "Honest work, you claim? And what would that be, coming from a stinking mule-lover like you?"

Grover laughed and slapped Seamus on the shoulder, then poured them each another round from Donegan's bottle. "Word has it all the way from Little Phil's headquarters that we'll be moving out again this spring . . . soon as freeze-up breaks."

"Sheridan, eh?"

"Yep. He's bound and determined to punish the Cheyenne and Sioux since he couldn't whip 'em last summer."

"Hancock and his God-a'mighty self, Custer . . . neither didn't make Lil' Phil proud, did they, Sharp?"

"If you're a man for taking another's advice, Irishman— best you keep your voice down about Custer in these parts. This is the general's country . . . and his soldiers' as well."

Seamus chuckled. "Learned how Custer's sojurs watch out for him last fall over to Wallace. Funny thing, though—the Boy General hisself is taking holiday back in Michigan, I've been told."

"Every word of it true."

"The army gave him a year's vacation, Sharp. Shooting deserters like they was Johnnie prisoners."

"Take my word for it, Irishman. Hays isn't the place to be hacking on Custer."

"Sounds like you're a fast friend of the general."

He shook his head. "I'll just figure that's the whiskey talking, Irishman. I work for the man a'times. Work for the army as well. And the pay's good. Out here, a man learns fast he don't bite the hand what feeds him."

Seamus finally grinned, and held up his glass in salute. "You're right, Sharp. I'll keep Custer to meself."

"Besides, Irishman . . . you might soon be working for the army as well."

He cocked his head. "I had my share of whipping mules through snow-drifts. Don't figure to——"

"Their money saw you through the winter, didn't it?"

"Waiting for my uncle 'swhat I'm doing here."

"Drinking it away?"

"Don't see any reason why a mule-whacker can't keep a belly full of this puggle, do you?"

"No, I don't." Grover leaned back in his chair, the fingers of both hands laced atop his belly covering the greasy gray tapestry of his brocade vest. "But, a man wants to step up in the world . . . a man what don't wanna always work on the south side of a northbound mule—that man gonna have to back away from the bottle ever' now and then."

Donegan eyed him. His foggy mind working it over and over as he repeatedly licked his cracked, raw lips. "You got something on your mind, Grover. Better you spit it out. I ain't of a mind to dust it off for meself."

"Short of temper, are you, Irishman?" he said, then laughed loose and easy.

"Might say that," he growled, his dark head slung between his shoulders.

"Cheer up, Seamus. I get that whiskey soaked out of your system in a few weeks, we're gonna make a army scout out of you."

"Ain't in no mood to have any man hacking on me. That includes you, Grover."

He wagged his head, pushing himself away from the table, and stood. "So be it. If that's the way you want it. Thought I might do something to help you out—give you a job to count on while you wait for Liam."

Seamus glared up into the murky lamplight at the plains scout, startled. "Liam . . . Liam O'Roarke. That's right."

"I remembered you're his nephew."

"I . . . see." He looked back at his whiskey. Suddenly his stomach lurched sourly. And Donegan remembered he hadn't eaten in the better part of a week.

"What I seen, you can ride a horse better'n most men . . . and I'll teach you to read trail sign sooner'n you can——"

"Don't do me no favors, Grover," he snapped.

"Excuse me," he replied after a moment, taking a step away from the table, appearing to fight down the impulse to stomp away. "I got you confused, Irishman. Got you confused with someone who really needed at least one friend."

He never looked up from his whiskey. "That's right. You got me confused. Don't wanna work for the army. I'll sit right here and wait for O'Roarke, biding my time."

"You do what you will, Irishman," Grover said as he lashed up the leather whangs on the front of his greasy, buffalo-hide coat. "You get yourself dried out and ready . . . come look me up. Me or the lieutenant I'll be riding with come green-up."

"Humph!" Seamus growled. "Small chance of me doing that. Thankee for your kindness all the same, Grover."

"Come see Lieutenant Fred Beecher . . . or me, Irishman. You get your head cleared of that poison. That whiskey, and whatever else's eating a hole in your privates."

Donegan listened to the aging scout shuffle away, back to the bar, where Grover rejoined the soldiers he had accompanied to the Shady Rest. At the bar a noisy reception greeted Sharp.

"Beecher?" Donegan repeated the name under his breath as the strong brown liquid hurried past his lips.

Lt. Fred Beecher . . .

Chapter 3

"*I* came south to fight the whiteman," the tall Northern Cheyenne warrior boasted. "Not run from him."

"We are not running from the whiteman," protested Tangle Hair, a headman among these Cheyenne on the Central Plains. "We must protect our villages . . . women, children, and the old ones."

"Perhaps you have grown old as well," the tall one snapped. He slowly twisted some strands of light hair between his fingers. The hair was not his.

Roman Nose enjoyed displaying his colorful trophies from the fight for the Northern Plains. Hair of gold and that touched by the red of a setting sun. Strands of curly brown the color of mud in a buffalo wallow, and that hair of black-skinned white men the color of a buffalo bull's hump with the coming of winter. The corners of his large mouth turned upward in it characteristic thin-lipped sneer as one of Tangle Hair's compatriots rose to the bait.

"Long ago we decided our warriors would do our fighting," Running Elk spoke evenly, knowing that it perturbed The Nose that he was not provoked to anger. "There have been too many empty lodges, too many motherless children for any man not to remember the lessons of Sand Creek . . . don't we remember the lessons of Pawnee Fork last summer?"

Roman Nose let fall the auburn hair that hung beside the quillwork sewn down his arm, glaring at the Cheyenne chief across the smoky firepit. "Yes, my friend—I remember well the lessons of those who would listen to the words of the whiteman treaty-talkers and their women-killer soldiers."

Of a sudden, the diabolical grin stretched into a smile, startling the others. His gleaming teeth more wolfish than friendly, eyes like cold obsidian chips, The Nose realized he had once more caught these chiefs unawares. Just when they thought they had him sorted out.

"It is right, what our chiefs say. Right that the villages should stay far away from these soldiers and their forts. It is for our warriors to take the battle to the whiteman."

Around him arose a brief muttering of assent as more of the Cheyenne chiefs agreed. Suspiciously.

"Surely," Roman Nose continued, "our warriors can raid the roads that take the whitemen west. Lay siege to the camps where stay the men who plant the iron rails for the puffing-smoke horse. Our scouts will tell us where and when the whiteman gathers to follow us. So that once more we can disappear like a puff of breath-smoke in a winter wind."

"Perhaps our brother Roman Nose sees the merits of protecting our villages, while continuing to strike back at the whiteman and his soldiers?" asked old Two Crows, one of the acknowledged leaders of the plains Cheyenne.

He nodded. "I do, Uncle. Last summer I watched Red Cloud's Sioux and Cheyenne slowly strangle the life from those three forts the whiteman had built along his medicine road north into the land of the Sparrowhawks."

"Where the whiteman scratches at the ground for little yellow rocks!" injected White Horse, laughing, his ample belly wiggling.

"Where they go for yellow rocks," Roman Nose agreed, "but instead find *red* death."

"Yet, even before the first snow fell last winter in the *Drying Grass Moon,* word came from the northlands that Red Cloud and Crazy Horse had not been victorious when they attacked two forts along the whiteman's road."

Roman Nose slowly shifted his eyes to Tall Bull. Near his right hand, The Bull was not a man given to many words. When he spoke, it was with wisdom, and always struck straight to the heart of a matter.

"Yes, Uncle. The words of Tall Bull are always straight.

Too many of our warriors, Sioux and Cheyenne and Arapaho all, fell from their war-ponies . . . to rise no more."

"It was said the whiteman made medicine over his guns."
Sioux chief Turkey Legs finally entered the debate.

"The whiteman made no medicine," Roman Nose
sneered. "He has rifles that shoot many times before reloading. We too will have these rifles one day soon."

"Until then?" Tangle Hair asked.

"We must continue to strike the whiteman wherever we
find him—stealing his powerful weapons until we have
enough of his repeating rifles that we can successfully attack
his forts."

"Roman Nose will stay in this southland for the coming
summer?" Running Elk inquired.

The Nose smiled, knowing The Elk was attempting to put
him on the spot. "Yes, Uncle. I will remain with your bands
here in the south for the summer. And . . . I will lead our
warriors in our raids on the whiteman's roads and camps
and settlements."

"Yes!" Two Crows cheered. "The white peace-talkers
guaranteed us rifles and bullets in the shipments he would
bring us under last winter's peace-signing. The rifles have not
come." His eyes grew cold. "Someone must pay."

"Let all whitemen pay," White Horse replied. "When we
receive our weapons from the peace-talkers, we can once
again hunt buffalo . . . and whitemen as well."

"Forget buffalo this year, my friends." The Nose raised his
voice above the noisy clamor, quieting them all. "Forget having our young warriors follow the shaggy beast this summer.
Instead, we leave the hunting of buffalo to the women and
old men . . . to the boys. Instead, the men of our bands will
hunt bigger game."

"What . . . what is bigger than a buffalo, Roman Nose?
What could be harder to bring down than a full-grown bull
in his prime?" asked Turkey Legs.

The Nose rose slowly to his feet, all six foot, three inches
of him, taller than every other man in each of the gathering
bands of Cheyenne. "This summer we hunt a worthy foe.
Come the short-grass time, *Shahiyena* will stalk the whiteman!"

* * *

"By damn, I want that red bastard's scalp myself!" Lt. General Philip H. Sheridan roared, banging his meaty fist on the tabletop. His black bush of a mustache all but covered his mouth below the hawk's-beak of an Irish nose.

Maj. George A. Forsyth watched the papers and maps and dispatches scatter as his commander whirled into the horsehide chair behind the desk. Handsome, curly haired "Sandy" Forsyth had been with Sheridan since the bloody days of '64 in the Shenandoah Valley. In fact, Forsyth carried the reminders, puckered scars left behind by four rebel bullets he had earned himself in the final year of the war. One of three leaders who more than any others had earned the unbridled respect and trust of the little Irish bantam-rooster who commanded this Department of the Missouri. Without reservation, Sheridan trusted George Armstrong Custer, Wesley Merritt, and Sandy Forsyth.

Custer had been there to accept the rebel flag of surrender at Appomattox Wood. Made possible by Sheridan's daring and magnificent ride that saved the day at Winchester. At Phil's side had galloped George A. Forsyth.

Sheridan's three commanders had brought Phil his victory in the Shenandoah. And in so doing, Sheridan had handed Ulysses S. Grant his victory over Robert E. Lee's Army of Northern Virginia in turn.

"We'll find where Roman Nose is, Phil—and if I have to cut his hair off with a butter-knife myself . . . by God—I'll do it!"

"That's the spirit, Sandy." Phil whirled back round in his chair.

The two of them alone in Sheridan's spartan office here at Fort Leavenworth on the plains of eastern Kansas, Forsyth knew the short, dark-haired Irishman realized this battle for the Central Plains was not his to fight. Sandy knew the gauntlet was being passed to him.

"Custer's not here to do this," Sheridan muttered to his papers, not raising his eyes.

"You have me, Phil."

Only then did the general lift his bearded face and stuffed a match-stick between his meaty lips. "I may need him yet."

George felt the heat rise from his collar. He hadn't been as fortunate as had the "Boy General" during the recent rebellion. Never in the right place at the right time. Yet, Forsyth remained certain that he was every bit as good as the younger, more impetuous soldier spending a year's hiatus in Monroe, Michigan. "But, Custer's been . . . court-martialed for a year, Phil. Won't be back till late this fall."

Sheridan motioned Forsyth to sit. "Don't get me wrong— it's not your ability versus Custer's, Sandy. It's simply . . . this job is shaping up to be more than what any one man can handle."

"How's that, sir?"

"From everything that's been hitting us since last spring," Sheridan began, walking over to the office window to gaze out at the Leavenworth parade, "I'm beginning to think I've got to fight this war on two fronts."

Forsyth joined Sheridan at the window, where he stared out at the hot parade baked by an early August sun. This summer of '68 had proven itself to be one of record heat . . . with no end in sight.

"I have an idea what you mean," George replied. "Though we know the Cheyenne are striking at our settlements here in central Kansas, still reports have it there are others, proving that two separate groups are involved in all the raiding."

Sheridan turned, smiling. "Right. The Southern Cheyenne and Kiowa coming north across the Arkansas from The Territories."

"And, the Northern Cheyenne and their Sioux allies raiding south, coming down across the Republican."

"You've got it, Sandy. Lieutenant Beecher's scouts have found out that much, by God."

"And a helluva lot more, Phil." Forsyth slipped a cheroot from a pocket, dragged the match-head across the windowsill, and lit his thin cigar. "Beecher's done one masterful job with those plainsmen he's hired. Problem is, he doesn't have enough of them to watch the movements of all the bands, both north and south of the K-P's line."

Sheridan wagged his head, jamming the stump of his well-chewed cigar back between his teeth. He ran a meaty hand over his thinning hair, short-cropped and newly graying.

"Telegraph Beecher for me, Sandy." He continued gazing out at the glaring parade.

"You want him to come in, sir?"

"No. Just inform Fred that you and I are considering hiring us . . . say, fifty first-class frontiersmen. Men good on horseback and good with a gun. Not like these recruits they're sending us out here to wear a blue uniform and eat army chow."

"Fifty, Phil?"

"Volunteers. Tell Beecher to start sniffing around for the best he can hire."

"As civilian quartermaster employees?"

"That's right," Sheridan replied. "That way we can pay them top dollar, to get the best manpower there is to offer on the plains right now."

"Why fifty, sir?"

With his tongue, Sheridan shifted the cigar stub thoughtfully. "Tell Beecher I'm thinking about sending his plainsmen out in pairs . . . each pair assigned to follow a band . . . dog its trail, and when they find a band—report back to Wallace or Harker . . . wherever. Then the army will take over from there."

"You'll have army detachments attack the villages, General?"

"That's right. Way I see it, Beecher's plainsmen won't have to do a lick of fighting. Just some sniffing around and some tracking."

"They'll find the enemy camps. Then our soldiers will do the rest."

"You've read my mind, Sandy."

Forsyth swallowed, took the cheroot from between his teeth, and licked his lips. "Uh, General."

"Yes?"

"May I impose on you to read my mind, Phil?"

The shorter Sheridan turned on the stocky Forsyth, almost toe to toe with the square-jawed thirty-one-year-old major. Phil laughed easily, slapping a hand down on Forsyth's shoulder.

"Hell! That's always been the easiest thing to do with either you or Custer."

Forsyth nodded. "You understand then, sir?"

He laughed easily again as he strode back to his desk. "Go on now, Sandy. Send that telegraph to Fred Beecher. Let's get this campaign rolling before another month goes by."

Forsyth stopped by the door, his hand on the cast-iron shuttle latch. "You'll give me a piece of this, General?"

Sheridan nodded, his back to the major. All the time his eyes narrowed on the wrinkled map crookedly nailed to the wall behind the general's chair. "Sandy, I'm beginning to think I want to hammer these red bastards with the best Phil Sheridan can put in the field. That means getting Custer back sooner than any one of us had planned."

"Custer?" Forsyth asked, his throat constricting.

Sheridan turned. "He'll be my pincer in the south, Sandy."

"And . . . and me, General?"

The general smiled. But it did little to relieve that anxious, cold stone in Forsyth's gut.

"You, Major . . . you can plan on getting yourself a good piece of the action if you want it." Sheridan turned back to the map, running a stubby finger west along the route of the Kansas Pacific tracking the flow of the Smoky Hill River . . . past Fort Harker and Fort Hays . . . into the rolling wilderness of the Solomon, the Saline, and the faraway Republican.

"Action? Finally fight some Indians, General?"

Sheridan looked over his shoulder at Forsyth, smiling. He nodded. "If Fred Beecher and his plainsmen can find 'em, Sandy—you all can fight 'em."

Forsyth saluted smartly. "Thank you, General! Thank you——"

"Get that goddamned message keyed to Beecher now," Sheridan said as he dropped to his chair and tugged to loosen his damp collar. "What I wouldn't give to be sitting with Bill Sherman right now, Sandy. Up in Chicago, feeling those lake breezes blowing in my window."

"Yessir. I'll get this off to Fred right now."

Forsyth watched Sheridan turn his chair round as the general went back to studying his map, only the top of his bristling head showing.

Minutes later, Sandy found himself pacing, filled with anticipation as the telegraph clerk tapped out the message Forsyth had scribbled on a pad in the key-shack on the far west side of the parade. The major stopped, the clicking of the key fading in the background as he stared out onto the rolling Kansas prairie where afternoon hung on forever and the whole world shimmered beneath a hazy mirage, giving the land a look of make-believe. A dreamlike quality that suddenly captured and took hold of Maj. George A. Forsyth.

Running a pale, damp hand through his long, wavy brown hair he kept neatly parted on the left and swept back like a dandy's behind each ear, Forsyth ruminated on what beckoned to him from beyond those far hills. And what had brought him to this moment.

Last fall on Medicine Lodge Creek near Fort Larned, nearly five thousand Indians had gathered to talk peace with the white man. Cheyenne and Sioux, Arapaho and Comanche. Even the feared Dog Soldier bands from the south and Roman Nose of the Northern Cheyenne. In return for the promise that the Cheyenne would remain on their reservations in The Territories south of the Arkansas River, the tribes were promised shipments of annual annuities to include food, clothing, blankets, and some trade goods. More important was the matter of weapons and ammunition the warriors demanded were necessary to their annual hunts for the nomadic buffalo.

In anticipation of the gifts, the Central Plains had quieted for a time with both the coming of the promised annuities and that hard winter of 1867–1868. But by April Lt. Frederick Beecher, working out of Fort Wallace at the far western border of Kansas Territory, reported finding evidence of large Sioux and Cheyenne camps.

None of the tribes was staying within the confines of its assigned reservation. Civilian scouts and interpreters confirmed for the army that the Cheyenne were moving northwest. Word had it the old chiefs were hoping to avoid contact with whites, both settler and soldier alike.

But by May 19 young Cheyenne warriors had attacked a trader's store at Fort Zarah on Walnut Creek near the Arkansas. Seven days later Forsyth and Sheridan received a report that a civilian wagon train bound for Denver had been attacked on the Smoky Hill. That meant one thing—the warriors were migrating north. Not only had they crossed the

Arkansas, but they had marched right into the heart of the Kansas Pacific construction and wagon-freight route of the Smoky Hill Road west to Colorado.

Daring the white man and his soldiers to punish them if they could.

Report after report had clicked over the wires from Fort Wallace. Beecher kept Sheridan informed that many of the attacks were most probably the work of young warriors out to prove themselves, perhaps for the first time. But as a consequence of these spring raids, the army denied the Cheyenne their shipments of arms when the annuities were finally handed out in mid-July at Fort Larned.

Sandy remembered Beecher's terse dispatch informing Sheridan the Cheyenne had proudly refused their entire shipment of annuities if they were not given the arms and ammunition they had been promised the previous fall.

Just days ago in a long message, Fred Beecher had ventured a rare opinion, yet one shared by and gathered from a consensus of the plains scouts the lieutenant had working under him on the far Kansas frontier. Beecher did not believe the Cheyenne wanted to start a general war.

Something inside Sandy Forsyth hoped fervently along with Beecher that a major war with the Cheyenne was not being ignited in the West.

Yet a part of that thirty-one-year-old soldier who stood staring at the sun setting beyond the rolling Kansas prairie land itched to have just one crack at the Cheyenne, the feared Dog Soldiers.

Perhaps, if he was lucky, even a crack at Roman Nose himself.

Chapter 4

"*W*hat's your name, son?" asked the hard-eyed, thirty-year-old sergeant named William H. McCall, perched behind the wobbly table set in the shade of a Fort Harker awning, some halfway between Fort Riley and Fort Hays on the Smoky Hill Line.

"Stillwell, sir," he answered, his voice cracking. He had prayed it wouldn't.

"Your full name."

"Jack Stillwell." He watched the hard eyes narrow, the pen poised unmoving above the sergeant's leather-bound ledger.

"Your *Christian* name, son."

"Simpson . . . E. . . . Stillwell, Sergeant."

The soldier smiled. "That's better, son. Now, how old are you?"

Jack swallowed. This was every bit as hard too. The others behind the sergeant at the table had stopped and were staring at him. He could hear the whispers behind him in the long line stretching back into the shade. Someone was joking about his curly hair belonging on a girl more than it belonged on someone joining Forsyth's scouts.

Stillwell sensed the drop of cold sweat slip down his spine like January ice-water. Another soldier leaned over the sergeant's shoulder and asked the same question again, with a quiet, reassuring voice.

"I've heard you've done some scouting for the army before, Jack Stillwell. But, we still need your age, young man.

For the record . . . and to be certain you're of age to join up with my expedition."

Jack knew who the young, sun-bronzed lieutenant was. No one needed to tell him here stood Fred Beecher, Civil War hero and chief of frontier scouts for none other than Phil Sheridan himself.

Stillwell straightened. "Nineteen, Lieutenant Beecher."

The lieutenant straightened as well, smiling. "Very good, Jack." He presented his hand. They shook. Beecher had no way of knowing how Stillwell's knees rattled beneath his canvas duck britches. "You're officially a part of Forsyth's scouts. Give the information to Sergeant McCall here, and he'll get you squared away. I'm glad you're riding with us."

"Thank . . . thank you, Lieutenant. Can't figure how to show you what it means——"

"You'll have a chance soon enough, Jack. Show me by keeping your nose clean till it's time for us to march to Fort Hays. There we'll finish hiring our entire complement and be on the trail to Wallace."

"I'll be glad to be back in the saddle myself, Lieutenant," McCall advised. "Chasing the Cheyenne, that is."

"Let's hope it's not like chasing the wind this time, Billy."

Stillwell watched Beecher turn and disappear back through an open doorway. He figured it was cooler in there. Maybe not. There wasn't a breeze stirring anywhere here on the Central Plains. Hotter than any man alive could remember it getting out here. He thought again how lucky the Dog Soldiers were, riding their quick ponies in nothing but breechclout and moccasins——

"——ask you again, Mr. Stillwell . . . are you providing your own mount?"

"Yes . . . yessir. Sergeant . . . yes, I am," he answered nervously, hearing the snickers rising behind him from the long line of volunteers waiting to enlist in Forsyth's scouts.

"Sign here . . . on this page." McCall turned his ledger book around, facing Stillwell, and indicated a line for the new recruit's signature.

Jack carefully formed his letters. Then considered it a moment. He had forgotten to draw a line across the one upright stick-letter. He was always forgetting to do that. Again he considered the words. They were just as much hen scratchings. But his mama had taught him to write that much. Even if he couldn't read what it said. He was sure all those scratches amounted to Simpson Elmore Stillwell.

"You're now a civilian quartermaster employee of the United States Army, Mr. Stillwell. No rank."

"None of us wearing uniforms, Sergeant?"

"Only three will wear uniforms. Major Forsyth. The lieutenant in there," McCall said, throwing a thumb back into the cool shade of the room where Beecher had disappeared. "And, myself." He smiled. "Your sergeant."

"Yessir. What's pay?"

"Since you're providing your own mount—seventy-five dollars a month. Fifty if we provide for you."

"If . . . if my horse is . . ."

"If your horse is killed, Mr. Stillwell—the army will repay you full value for the animal."

He liked the sound of that. Loving his horse the way Jack did. Seeing him through these last two years the way the animal had.

"And, the army will provide full rations, equipment, and weapons for you. Forage for your mount."

"Weapons?"

"Spencer . . . seven-shot repeater, Mr. Stillwell. A Colt's army revolver as well."

Jack knew the pistol. Heavy things they were. Big too, clamped in a small hand such as his. But, Stillwell fired a weapon with the best of them and rarely missed his mark.

"Should I bring along my own blanket, Sergeant?"

"If you need more than the one I'm assigning you."

"Summer nights can get cold . . . west of here, sir."

McCall smiled that warm, brown-toothed smile again. Jack decided he liked the sergeant. Liked those eyes that warmed with every smile. It seemed his whole face warmed in fact. "You slept out on the prairie a time or two, Jack?"

"I have, sir." He swallowed. "I'll take your blanket and keep mine along as well."

McCall nodded. "Smart lad. But, best you travel as light as you can. And I hope your mount's a strong one . . . as Major Forsyth is a fighter and he says we'll make a fast march of it. General Sheridan figures it may take until first

snow for us to catch the red bastards . . . but the major's
the sort who won't stop until the job's done."

"I'm glad to be part of this, Sergeant."

McCall presented his beefy paw to Stillwell. "Glad you're
with us, Jack. Go with Culver here . . . he'll show you
where you can draw your truck and rations."

Jack saluted self-consciously. "Yessir."

The sergeant saluted in turn. "That's the last one of those
you'll get out of me, son. No need me getting one from you."

"Thank you, Sergeant."

The cackles and laughter of the older men drifted away
behind Stillwell as he followed a civilian into the sunlight
and across the parade.

"We're leaving tomorrow for Fort Hays, you know."
George Culver struck up with a bit of conversation.

"No, sir. I didn't."

The thin rail of a man stopped, turned. Presented his
hand. "Name's G. W. Culver, that is."

"Jack Stillwell."

"I know."

"Yessir."

"Don't have to call me 'sir,' neither." Culver strode away
again. Jack figured he was expected to follow.

"Major Forsyth's gonna hire thirty men here, then head to
Hays."

"Why only thirty, G. W? Thought he needed fifty."

"Does need fifty."

"But, he's got more'n that waiting in line back there
now——"

Culver stopped again, his scuffed boots kicking up a small
shower of dust that sparkled in the mid-morning sunshine
that foretold another steamy day on the plains. "Listen, Stillwell. The major ain't just picking any nit, prick, or stillbirth
walks up to that table, you see."

"Nosir?"

"No, he ain't. He and the lieutenant hisself both watching
the men from the window of that room behind McCall's
shoulder. Beecher comes out if the sergeant's s'posed to hire
a man."

"Like he done to me . . . right?"

Culver grinned a tobacco-stained smile. "Right, boy. Lord

knows what them army fellers see in a young'un like you."
He wagged his head, sucking on his tongue in critical ap-
praisal of Stillwell. "Likely as not, if you don't run the first
time you come eyeball to crotch with a Cheyenne . . . your
kind'll just piss your pants!"

Jack felt the first twinges of shame as the older man
turned, laughing hysterically at his own humor and strode
on beneath the sunshine. Then came the anger. And Jack
swallowed it down, staring at Culver's back, a splotch of
dark sweat stained between the older man's shoulder blades.

"By dámn," Jack whispered, his fists clenching, "I won't
run . . . and I never been known to piss my pants neither.
Goddamn you, Culver. Goddamn all you sonsabitches. I'm
ever' bit as good as any man of you. And I'll show you that
come the time them Cheyenne wanna fight 'stead of run."

He nodded his head once, as if convincing himself of it.
And followed George Culver toward the quartermaster's depot.

"By damn," Stillwell repeated, softer now, for he was
thinking on his mother back to home, "time comes . . . I'll
stand with the best of you."

"Damn right, I'll ride with you to Wallace," Seamus
Donegan agreed, staring up through the murky haze of a
Hays City saloon at the civilian scout standing over him.
"Thanks for asking."

Sharp Grover dragged up a chair, sitting across the table
from Seamus. He slipped the glass from Donegan's hand and
tossed the whiskey against the back of his throat. "You'll
owe me for this one, Irishman."

Donegan's eyes narrowed. "Never will forgive me for me
drunken rage last winter, will you?"

"That? Shit!" Grover roared as he poured himself another
drink into Donegan's glass and threw it back. "That was
over the minute I walked away from you far as I was concerned. Man wants to punish himself in the cups as bad as
you was doing . . . not my place putting a halter on him."

"Army work taking you to Wallace?" Seamus asked after
he sipped slowly at his whiskey.

"Yes," the scout answered. "And no."

"You're a puzzlement, Sharp Grover. Far be it from me to

try sorting you out. Just as long as I've got me your company on the trail."

"Still set on going there to wait for O'Roarke to return from the land of Deseret, eh?"

"Aye. I talk to every one who comes here if they've heard tell of Liam showing up at Fort Wallace. It's go there, or I go to work laying track to work me own way west."

"Got an easier way to make a living, Seamus."

"Working for the army?"

Grover rocked back on two legs of his chair, his thumbs stuffed in the pockets of his greasy, round-collared vest. "Been all right to me, it has."

"Some men don't mind having any kind of work, I suppose."

Grover chuckled at that. "And here you sit, all high and mighty, eh? That it, Donegan? 'Bout starved yourself when you wasn't froze up last winter . . . chopping wood, driving mule-teams to Harker and Dodge . . . anything for money to drink on, right?"

Seamus eventually smiled. "You got me to rights, Sharp. Man does what he has to, doesn't he?"

"Want work?"

"Got something on your mind, don't you?"

"Just asking if you want work."

"Spit it out."

"Army's looking for scouts——"

"There you go again. You tried that on me last winter," Donegan snapped, irritated as he cut Grover off. "Didn't work then either. No scouting."

"Major George Forsyth can use a man like you. Good on a horse."

"Lot of us come out of the war what can ride a horse, Sharp."

"Not many can track well as you, Seamus. Shoot center either, forked on a horse or planted on foot."

"What's this leading to?"

"Told you. Army's hiring."

"Means nothing to me."

"Forsyth is putting together a company of fifty scouts. He and his lieutenant—one I told you about—fella named Beecher, already hired thirty men out of Fort Harker."

"And?"

"They come in here last night. Figure to fill out the fifty here."

"I won't be one, if that's your angle, Grover."

"Pay's good."

"Army work's not."

"You sure you don't want to walk on over with me and sign on?"

"You're going with this Forsyth?"

"Major's already counted on me. I had no choice, Seamus."

"See what I mean about the army, Sharp? Man doesn't have much say-so, does he?" Donegan saluted the scout with a shot of whiskey, tossing it back, then wiping his lips with the sleeve of his dirty shirt.

"Well, can I at least count on you riding along to Wallace with me?"

"When you leaving?"

"Day or two at the most. Major finishes out his brigade of plainsmen—we'll be marching."

"I'll be ready, Sharp."

Grover scooted his chair back, a hand on each knee, staring at the whiskey bottle a moment. "Some news you might think worthwhile, Donegan. Seems Major Forsyth is leaving one slot open for an old friend of mine, someone he's picking up at Wallace. Telegraphed ahead to have Colonel Bankhead hold the scout there . . . wait for Forsyth to arrive."

Seamus squinted as the tobacco smoke clouding the room singed his eyes. "Major must want this man in a bad way."

"The fella's one of the best scouts in my book."

"You know 'im, you said."

"I do. Major Forsyth is marching to Fort Wallace . . . expecting to find Liam O'Roarke waiting there."

His throat constricted on that shot of whiskey he had just thrown back. Donegan sputtered. Wiping his chin. No longer did the big Irishman have the full beard he had worn since the middle of the war. Now he sported a full mustache curled at the ends and clean-shaven cheeks. But on his chin he boasted a sporty Vandyke, trimmed neatly of late. Wet with whiskey at the moment.

"Liam? Liam O'Roarke?"

"I know of no other scout with that name out in these parts, Irishman!"

"Your rag-tag band of civilians going to Wallace to pick up O'Roarke?"

"Major Forsyth read the telegram this morning from Wallace. Said Liam should be there . . . waiting his arrival by the time we get in. Word has it, O'Roarke can't wait, Major said—what with the Cheyenne raising all kinds of hell west of——"

Donegan suddenly grabbed hold of Grover's hand, shaking it. Then nearly knocked over the whiskey bottle as he rushed to jam the cork in the neck before stuffing it in his coat pocket. Grover was laughing as Seamus picked up the full shot and drained it before the Irishman enthusiastically yanked the army scout toward the door, sweeping chairs aside.

"Gawddammit, Sharp Grover! Will you hurry up! That Major Forsyth of yours best not have all his recruits signed on before I get there . . . or I'll be one to skin you alive!"

Grover stopped dead in his tracks at the door while Donegan plunged on into the August sunlight. "This mean you're joining us?"

"By damn—if Liam O'Roarke's going to ride with Forsyth, it's for certain Seamus Donegan will as well!"

Chapter 5

"*H*ow do you spell that?"
"S-H-L-E-S-I-N-G-E-R."

"And your first name?" asked the soldier with chevrons on the sleeves of his damp shirt.

"S-I-G-M-U-N-D."

"Got a horse?"

"No, sir."

"Sign here. Then go with Issac there and he'll get your gear assigned."

"Thank you, sir."

"Thank Major Forsyth, Mr. Shlesinger. He's the one said hire you."

Bob North watched the young man nod his head and without reply follow the civilian named Issac into the bright light of the Fort Hays parade.

"Name?"

"Smith."

Sgt. William McCall halted his pen and gazed up at the man before him. "Smith ain't a very common name down South, now, is it?"

"Got a problem with the name my dear departed daddy give me, Sergeant?" North made it sound as sweet as molasses on johnny-cakes.

McCall smiled. "No problem . . . Smith. Got a first name?"

"Bob." No lie this time, but sweetened every bit as much by that tobacco-stained smile of North's.

The white man-turned-Arapaho-renegade had pulled in here at Fort Hays late last night. For the past hoary winter and the better part of hellish summer, North had been stalking the ghostly trail of a particular tall, dark-haired Irishman who rode a monster of a gray horse. Trouble was, until of late Bob North had been inquiring as to the whereabouts of a *full-bearded* Irishman.

Only two suns back at Fort Larned had he learned there was just such a fella working out of Hays. A ways up north.

The renegade had scrambled into the saddle and had not climbed down until he reached Fort Hays. Cursing both that nameless Irishman, along with the hole in North's belly the Irishman's bullet had made better than a year and a half ago on a cold December day up the Bozeman Road.

North never had been one to loosen up on a grudge, especially when he had been nursing it through two long prairie winters. Hatred of that caliber was sure to keep any man warm.

Not finding the tall one when he had scoured Hays City, North rode out to the fort. It was there among a swelling group of civilians lounging round the post that the renegade thought he had at last found his man. Only to discover he was about to lose the Irishman every bit as quickly.

Didn't take long for the sweet-talking Confederate to talk a loose-tongued soldier into spilling it all. In horror North learned that some damned major was leading those rowdy civilians on west with him to Fort Wallace. From there, word was they'd be tracking Cheyenne.

That bit of news caused one hell of a chuckle for the Southerner. These fellas—most of them dressed like dirt-farmers—tracking Cheyenne?

About the time North himself had bid farewell to the Big Horn country, he learned Roman Nose had already headed south from Red Cloud's land—last *Drying Grass Moon* it was . . . October. Crossing the plains of Colorado Territory and into Kansas, the white renegade had followed rumors the Cheyenne war-chief was himself leading the parties who were wreaking such havoc on settlements and the K-P's track's end, every chance they got to attack freight-haulers and harass small details of soldiers.

So Bob North had had himself a good laugh on that—

damned funny notion too . . . knowing a warrior such as Roman Nose was not about to let himself get tracked by the likes of these sod-busters.

Why, some of 'em look like their mamas was wiping their noses just last . . .

"You fight for Lee himself?"

McCall's question snapped North's thinking back like a hard, sudden tug on a rawhide rope. "Yeah."

McCall leaned back in his chair. "Lord, did you boys in the Army of North Virginia make things hot for me a time or two." And he smiled.

North grinned in return. Things were going well. Then a thin, cadaverous officer appeared, almost out of nowhere, and looked over the sergeant's shoulder.

"You made it here just in time . . . uh, Mr. Smith," said the officer. "I'm Lieutenant Fred Beecher. Second to Major George Forsyth."

"Yessuh."

Beecher eyed the side-arm slung at the front of the new-comer's hip. "You any good with weapons?"

He snorted. "Lieutenant Beecher, is it?"

"Yes . . . Beecher."

"Well, now, sir. I reckon I'm better at this pistol than just 'bout any of those fellas over there." He flung a thumb back toward the various groups milling in the shade of Fort Hays's quartermaster depot. "I'd dare say I'm better than your best, it comes down to a match of it. Who is your best, Lieutenant . . . say, that tall one over there—with that pretty beard of his?"

"Donegan?" Beecher replied, eyeing the distant group. "I figure he may be about as good as most. But, I'd put my money on old man Farley over there . . . alone with his boy, Hutch. Either one the man to beat."

"Donegan, you say?"

"No, I said old man Farley was the best shot going with us."

North shook his head. "That tall one with the pretty beard. Name's Donegan?"

"Yes," Beecher answered, his eyes going back to McCall. "Mr. Smith, I'll sign you on—if you can take orders."

North turned back round, reluctantly tearing his eyes

from that Irishman . . . named Donegan. Smiling, he said,
"Yes, Lieutenant. I understand the taking of orders, sir. Sergeant here . . . and yourself too—look like good men to
ride under."

He watched Fred Beecher eye him a little harder, then
soften as the velvet-lipped compliment worked its magic.

"Sergeant McCall here will get you commissioned. You
showed up just in time. I have one more slot to fill here . . .
then we're on our way to Wallace come morning."

North grinned, those teeth of his once more shining like
pine-chips. "I always was a lucky sort, Lieutenant."

"Helluva time for the major be saddling us up," growled
the stranger with a drawl as he threw the saddle he had
stolen at Fort Lyon atop the saddle-blanket on his pony.
"More likely it's time for a man to find himself a piece of
shade. Hear you're called Donegan."

It was nearing four in the afternoon on 29 August. Saturday.

Seamus Donegan nodded in reply as he looped back the
cinch for his Grimsley saddle, then patted The General on
the neck. The animal that had carried him through the last
year of that bloody war back East sensed some of the Irishman's anticipation. He nuzzled Seamus on the back of the
shoulder as Donegan walked round to the newcomer.

"Name's Seamus to me friends." He held out his hand.

The stranger grinned widely inside his patchy, unkempt
beard. "Seamus Donegan, is it? How-dee-do! I'm Bob Smith,
Seamus."

"You done much of this scouting before?"

He wagged his head and spat a stream of juice into the
powdery dust near the pony's hooves. "A little while I was
galvanized up to Reno on the Bozeman."

"Fort Reno, was it? You was one of the Confederate war
prisoners who come out here to fight Injins, eh?"

"Appears I ain't quite had my fill of killing the bastards,
don't it?"

"Maybe we'll both be lucky, Bob—and we won't see a
warrior's feather or smell a squaw's fart on this ride with
Forsyth."

The stranger laughed loud and hard, almost doubling over

as he slapped his knee. "Damn, if you Irish boys don't have a way of saying the damnedest things to make a fella bust his gut, Donegan."

"Told you, Bob. My friends call me Seamus."

"All right, Seamus. Care if I ride with you?"

"Be my guest, friend—I figure the major'll have us march column of twos."

"Be obliged, Seamus. I'll mess with you if you don't mind——"

"Mount!" bawled Sgt. William McCall.

It sent a familiar chill of anticipation right up Donegan's neck. His scalp prickled with an old, comfortable excitement as he settled in the Grimsley atop The General.

"About-face!" McCall hollered. "For you civilians who don't know any better—bring your goddamned horses round to face me in a line!"

As Seamus gently reined The General about to face the sergeant, that long, thick, saber scar on his back went stone cold. Donegan looked over his shoulder as Smith drew alongside, smiling. Seamus was certain he had just been told something, warned of something deadly. Ominous. But, for the moment chose to shrug it off. The Southerner wasn't all a bad sort. About ten years older, but a friendly cuss as well.

For a moment Seamus hunched his shoulders in hopes of shaking the ghostly cold nagging that strip of white flesh across the great muscles of his back. Maj. George A. Forsyth reined up before the fifty scouts there on that hot, dusty, treeless parade at Fort Hays.

"Gentlemen, I'm glad to be the one leading you. Into what, none of us know. General Sheridan himself has agonized over these depredations of the Cheyenne and their hangers-on. But this entire department has been assigned no more than twenty-six hundred men, both mounted and foot, to police a vast area. So it was we determined the need to enlist a fast-moving force of civilian scouts the likes of which this country has never seen."

Not considering himself a part of Forsyth's scouts, Donegan did not join in the cheers that rocked over most of the others. Beside him, Bob Smith turned, nodded, and grinned. He too refrained from joining in the high spirits of the rest.

"If we rode out in any greater numbers, we would not be

able to move as fast as need be . . . as fast as our enemy. Anything smaller than this fifty—and we would be too tempting for a small war-party to ambush us. As it is, I am in hopes of finding our enemy, causing him to turn—and fight."

This time Seamus could not help but be stirred. Some of the old sensations rumbled through the bowels of him. Once more he was among fighting men. Not reluctant recruits or martinet officers. These frontiersmen and the three soldiers —fighting men all.

The General pranced a moment, perhaps sensing the same shift in the air as did Donegan. Snorting. Pawing with a hoof. Anxious for the trail and what would next be required. Seamus patted the big gray's neck, calming the animal.

"Simply put, gentlemen—our job is to track the war-parties responsible for the thefts, rapes, kidnapping, and murders on this frontier. And if need be, our job requires us to kill Indians. So—by God—I plan on scalding the bastards good!"

A shrill rebel yell burst from the throat of Bob Smith. Others as well noisily hooted in anticipation of settling old scores with the Indians.

"By the time we strike the Saline tonight, Sergeant McCall will have you men organized as a unit of cavalry. You'll ride, mess, sleep, and fight in platoon. Do not be confused because you have been hired as civilian quartermaster employees. The army is paying good money to each man of you to perform under my orders. If you fail to understand that, I would prefer that you stay behind rather than to cause the death of one of your fellows."

Donegan found Smith grinning at him. The former Confederate nodded as his azure eyes went back to Forsyth. Eyes as cold as chips from a blue china plate.

"General Sheridan has seen to it that you men will not be found wanting for the best of firepower. One hundred forty rounds for your repeating Spencer. Another thirty rounds for your percussion Colt's pistol. Sergeant McCall has equipped you with mess equipment and tack. Anything more you better leave behind. An extra few pounds on this ride might just kill your horse . . . or you."

Forsyth drew in a deep breath, then settled himself atop

his McClellan saddle. The fort fell silent. At least a hundred soldiers lounged in the shade of buildings surrounding the flat, dusty parade, watching the show. Here and there a horse snorted or pawed, tails switching to shoo nagging flies. A man slapped at one of the huge flies landing on the back of his hand. But, for the most part, the place fell as quiet as the passing of the summer sun.

"Sergeant McCall," Forsyth said dramatically as he reined to his left, "let's go find us some Cheyenne."

"You heard the major!" McCall bawled. "Left face! Front by column of twos! At a walk . . . *forrard—h-o-o-o-o!*"

Clumsily, the citizen soldiers turned their mounts and straggled into something like a column of cavalry. Many of the men recalled familiar commands of years gone by, yet painfully fresh in both mind and soul of a fighting man. Behind Forsyth followed some fifty of those who had served one army or the other across four bloody years, men now like thousands of others flocking to the frontier when they found nothing they could go home to.

For sure, Donegan thought, most of these had fought in the war—had some action under their belts. And some even looked as if they might be seasoned plainsmen. Good at tracking Indians. Experienced at fighting them as well.

As soon as it had been made known that this troop of scouts was to be organized back at Fort Harker, Forsyth had been buried under applicants. Many of those lounging about the fort as frontiersmen would often do, waiting for work of one color or another. Others came in as word spread, men who might have a personal debt to settle with the Cheyenne —knowing a friend, perhaps a relative, who had suffered at the hands of the raiding war-parties igniting the Kansas plains. The major had skimmed the cream at Fort Harker.

When he had moved west to Fort Hays, Forsyth found the news had raced there before him. More than a hundred men of all breeds waited a chance to sign on. From them, Forsyth had chosen but twenty. Still he had one to pick up at Fort Wallace in the days yet to come.

The brigade would travel fast and light. As McCall had told them, "Not stringing no baggage train ahind us. We'll carry what we need on our horses, boys."

As the dust of the Kansas prairie stung his nostrils, Donegan recalled how the sergeant had chuckled, then continued.

"I'm in charge of four of the ugliest mules you'll ever see. Trouble is, them Jennies're prettier than a lot of the chippies some of you bastards been sleeping with! Them four mules is our whole pack-train. Most of it ammunition. I'll have food for your gut, bandages for your wounds, and salve for your saddle-galls. Yes, by damn—bacon, beans, biscuits . . . and bullets, boys! That's all we're taking this ride out!"

Besides the four thousand extra rounds of ammunition, those four pack-mules also carried some medical supplies for Dr. John Mooers, in addition to extra salt and coffee. A few camp kettles and six shovels completed the pack-train's load. Each man carried his own seven-day rations in his own haversack slung to the back of his saddle. Not much more than each scout's own dry rigging, perhaps a change of shirts.

"Light and lean," Donegan mumbled once more.

Perhaps as well as any man on this march, the big Irishman knew the plains Indian. He was not alone in considering the warriors the finest light cavalry the world had yet seen mount a four-legged animal.

"The major's got to travel light and lean to ever entertain a hope of catching those h'athens—much less a hope of getting them to fight on his terms."

Seamus rode on, the Confederate at his side whistling one mountain tune after another. And all the while the Irishman cursed himself.

Bacon, beans, biscuits . . . and bullets. By the saints! It appears Mither Donegan's first-born son is back in the army!

Chapter 6

G eorge Forsyth had taken his men north by northwest from Fort Hays as the sun climbed high in the sky that thirtieth day of August.

Early the morning before, he had been handed orders from Sheridan.

> *Fort Hays, Kansas*
> *August 29, 1868*
>
> *Brevet Colonel George A. Forsyth,*
> *Commanding Detachment of Scouts:*
>
> *I would suggest that you move across the headwaters of Solomon to Beaver Creek, thence down that Creek to Fort Wallace. On arrival at Wallace report to me by telegraph at this place.*
>
> *Yours truly,*
> *P. H. Sheridan, Major General*

From the Smoky Hill country, the major steered his brigade of scouts toward the Saline River in that bracing, clear air of the plains. No more than an hour out of Hays, Forsyth spotted his first antelope of the trip on the distant, rolling hills. More of the white-rumped creatures joined the first, curious as to the long column of riders crawling across the brown, shimmering plains beneath a midday sun.

At noon they halted to rest the animals and gnaw on their "tacks," the hard bread, while coffee boiled. By the middle of the afternoon Forsyth figured no man with him could fail to understand they were at last beyond civilization. At the Saline late that night in the first drops of a drizzling rain, he quietly informed the scouts they entered the land of the Cheyenne.

Most of the civilians went about their mess as cheerfully as possible in the cold mist. Few of them had stayed atop a saddle for this long in many a month. Blisters, sore backsides, or just plain fatigue were commonplace as the camp settled itself for the rainy summer night.

Sgt. William McCall assigned duty to rotating pickets at Forsyth's order while coffee brewed over small, red-pitted fires that twinkled as merrily as the stars overhead.

"Major."

"Billy," Forsyth replied, nodding to McCall as the sergeant settled beside his firepit.

Experienced plainsmen all, they started each fire at the bottom of a hole scooped out of the sand. In that way, a wandering warrior would not easily spot the glowing fires, until he would be practically upon the camp.

"You get the feeling we're chasing the wind, Major?" McCall whispered as he accepted a steaming cup of coffee from Forsyth.

George smiled, drinking from his own cup before he answered. "They're out there, Billy. If I don't find them, I've got a feeling the bastards will find me."

McCall blew steam off his brew. "Have me the same feeling. Us . . . or them. No matter—there'll be a fight of it."

Forsyth held his cup on his thigh and gazed past the cottonwood and willow. Somewhere to the northwest in the inky blackness of that prairie night. "The Cheyenne are waiting for us, Billy. They know we're coming. Sooner or later, they knew someone had to come."

"They know, sir?"

He nodded, his eyes coming back to rest on McCall. "August 12: seventeen killed . . . August 14 on Granny Creek: another murder. Twenty-eighth: eight more on North Texas, three on Two Butte, two on Pond Creek. Between Kiowa Station and Fort Lyon itself: five more killed . . . I could go on."

"I understand, Major. They're gouging you, begging someone to come out and dance, aren't they, sir?"

Forsyth nodded as he rose stiffly, the kinks in his legs once more knotting up as the prairie's warmth where he had been sitting quickly escaped into the cold of summer night. "Billy, I've waited the better part of three years for a chance like this."

"So had Fred Beecher, Major."

"I know. Yet no man will ever understand how it feels to watch Sheridan give the cream of the action to Custer. Or to that aide of his, Crosby. Sheridan even gives his own brother——"

"Your time's come, sir."

"Yes, my time has come, Billy. I'm ready to dance with Roman Nose."

Silently Forsyth turned and slipped into the darkness, his eyes adjusting to pick out the lumps of sleeping bodies among the saddles and baggage on the ground. Out near the pickets, he stopped and loosened the buttons of his fly. It felt good, this. His kidneys got a damned hard pounding all day.

As much as he had wanted this assignment, George Forsyth realized it would be many days before he would once more be saddle-fit, truly ready to take the hammering of the trail. He turned, gazing at the dark lumps, men rolled in blankets, most paired back to back to share their warmth.

And he shuddered.

Knowing these men didn't have an idea one what they were heading into. While most of his volunteers had fought in the war, and a few had skirmished with Indians here on the plains of Kansas—a melancholy Forsyth figured that not one among them understood what might be asked of them in the next few days.

Truth of it was, he and Beecher were heading into Cheyenne country come morning, fixing to stir a big stick in a hornets' nest.

Their second night out of Fort Hays, Seamus Donegan lay awake for the longest time, listening to the musical snores of other men, the whispers of the nearby pickets, and the gnawing of the animals on the brittle, sun-cured grasses where they were hobbled. That first night he had fallen into his blanket, exhausted from Forsyth's relentless march. But after two full dawn-to-sundown days of straddling a saddle, Seamus had been relieved to find some of the old familiar exhilaration that came from the fatigue.

As the sun had sunk in the west, Sharp Grover had signaled the column from a far hilltop. From there, the scouts had recognized the inviting ribbon of water glittering in the twilight a few hundred yards away. The South Fork of the Solomon River. From what some of the Kansas men were saying, seemed like the major was aiming them straight for Fort Sedgwick with this northwest trail he was cutting into Cheyenne country.

"He's got orders to turn back to Wallace once he hits Beaver Creek," Grover explained to Donegan in a harsh whisper during that third day's ride.

"You think he'll do it?"

"Do what?"

"Point us back to Wallace."

"You must wanna see this uncle of yours something awful, Irishman."

"I do. My mither asked it of me."

Grover had nodded without more reply and reined away for the rest of the day. But Seamus could still not help thinking that George Forsyth had a burr under his saddle-blanket, bound and determined to march his men into a fight. And he recalled the major's own words that last night at Fort Harker.

"You men have been hired to fight Indians. To kill as many as you can."

Before they kill us, Major? he asked himself now as Bob Smith hollered beside him, pointing to a far knoll in the rolling swales of land that reminded Seamus so much of the Atlantic Ocean and that cursed ship that years ago brought him to Amerikay's shores.

Forsyth ordered old man Trudeau to spell Sharp Grover, sending Sharp back to the column. Trudeau loped off, joining Grover on top of the knoll. Neither of them rode down the slope. Instead, they waved the column on.

What greeted the command when they crested the knoll was something most men of the day had never before seen, and lived to tell of.

Forsyth peered at the sun. "Late enough in the day, Sergeant. We'll order a halt here."

"Yessir." McCall turned his horse as Forsyth walked off, talking in low tones to Fred Beecher. "Dismount! Water 'em quickly, boys. Supper's up to you. Light 'em if you got 'em. I'm gonna take me a shit."

Donegan chuckled along with most of the others as he slid from the saddle. Once The General had been watered and hobbled in a nice spread of grass beside the mouth of Sappa Creek, Seamus had him some boiled coffee and fried pork. Deciding to return for beans later, the Irishman wandered fifty yards from camp to the bank of the North Fork of the Solomon. Here Sappa Creek flowed clear and cool into the bigger stream.

And here he stepped cautiously into the ghostly remains of a Cheyenne sundance arbor.

With the setting sun casting long, blood-red shadows from the west, the upright poles encircling the tall center pole reminded Donegan of the skeleton of some huge, prehistoric beast. Halting at the base of the center pole where lay four painted buffalo skulls, he stared into the growing twilight of the Kansas sky at the tatters of rawhide thongs still tied to the top of the monstrous pole.

"The bastards hang themselves from that pole."

With the sound of the voice, Seamus jerked around, his heart in his throat. Having believed he was alone, in a place both savage and sacred at the same time, he was unnerved to find that the Confederate Bob Smith had crept up on him soundlessly while he had been standing in awe of the structure.

"Hang themselves?"

Smith pointed an index finger at each breast. "Medicine men cut under the muscles. Slip a twig under the muscle and hook up the young bucks to those long rawhide whangs."

"Then what?"

Smith snorted and knelt, his fingers playing with the designs in earth-paint on the forehead of a skull. "Then the sonsabitches dance round and round and round . . . yanking back on those rawhide cords all the time."

Seamus winced. "That all?"

"That, and the drumming. Like to make a man go out of his mind—they drum for four days straight."

"How long the men hang and pull on the cords?"

"Long as it takes 'em."

"To do what?"

"Get a vision of something powerful. Or pull free."

"Rip their muscles?"

Smith rose, kicking at the buffalo skull. "Yep. Tear 'em to hell sometimes. Awful scars."

"You seen it, Smith?"

The Confederate nodded and turned away with that tobacco-stained smile of his. "Gotta go. Show up for my guard-duty, Donegan."

Seamus listened as the man scrunched across the hardened earth, then turned to stare at the tall pole once more. Funny thing about it, Smith kept on talking as he climbed the hill to camp.

"Way things look to me, them Cheyenne was making powerful medicine here, Irishman. They fixing to do some mighty big hurt to somebody now."

"Who?" Seamus asked as he turned back to the knoll. "Who they fixing to hurt?"

But he found the hillside empty. Except for a scut of cold wind that announced the sun had abandoned the sky and the ghostly shadows bleeding into the moccasin-hammered sand. The hair stood up on the back of his neck.

Seamus figured he had the answer to his question.

Continuing northwest, Forsyth led his fifty across the North Fork of the Solomon. By sundown of the fourth day, they had finally reached Beaver Creek at the spot where Short Nose Creek emptied into the Beaver. It was here they camped and when the mess-fires were warming kettles of coffee, and the smell of roasting bacon drifted on the cool breezes, the major called the men together.

"I want to speak to all of you for just a moment, and thought this would be the best time before Sergeant McCall has to assign his pickets for the first watch. With the sun setting and the horses watered, I won't have another chance to talk to you before morning."

Seamus listened as someone muttered grumpily behind him, and others shifted nervously from foot to foot.

"I've got to tell you, I'm disappointed, men."

There, Donegan thought to himself. *Forsyth's admitted it.*

"Disappointed we didn't see a single Indian for our trouble. So, although I would rather plunge ahead . . . keep going straight on toward the South Fork . . . the Delaware or Arikaree Fork of the Republican—I've got my orders from General Sheridan. We're turning south in the morning."

"South, Major?" asked someone behind Donegan.

"Yes. My orders read that I'm to push on to Fort Wallace and await word from the general there."

"We're marching to Wallace in the morning?" asked another voice.

"With first light," Forsyth answered. "Sergeant McCall, I want the men up at four-thirty. Cold mess done by five. See that we're marching by five-thirty, Billy."

"Yessir," he replied and saluted.

"You men are dismissed. Get your supper down, and into your blankets as quickly as possible."

Seamus turned into the throbbing body of scouts breaking apart to the individual mess-fires. As he settled to his haunches beside his own fire-pit, the familiar voice settled nearby.

"Reckon I heard the sound of disappointment in the major's voice back there."

He glanced over at Smith. "He might just well be the only one, me friend. Looked to me like everyone else be glad to have 'em a stopover at Wallace."

Smith slurped at one of the juicy plums the men had pulled from the trees that abounded along Short Nose and Beaver creeks. On a nearby gum poncho lay bunches of wild grapes some of the scouts had picked and rinsed off in the creek for evening mess.

"I get the idee you're the one happier'n all the rest to be heading to Wallace."

Seamus smiled. "I am."

Smith slipped a long, thin-bladed knife from under his coat. For the first time, Donegan caught a glimpse of the porcupine-quilled scabbard that hung from the back of the

Confederate's belt. Smith sliced off a portion of the pork side-meat dripping into the low flames of their fire. For the longest time, Seamus watched the Rebel eat, smacking his lips and wiping the grease in his beard and hair. Sucking at his dirty fingers as if they were sugar-cane after every bite.

"That an Injin knife?"

"What knife? Oh, this'un here? Yeah. Here, have you a lookee-see to it."

Donegan felt the balanced heft to the sleek weapon. The hardness of the steel. "Knife and sheath come to your hands together?"

"This ol' thing? Nawww. Ol' poxy squaw made this for a old knife of mine. I come on this not long back, Irishman."

"Didn't look like it was a h'athen's weapon."

Smith laughed crudely, sputtering round his greasy chew of meat. "Shit-fire, Irishman. That's a woman's knife. I got me the gawddamned thing from a chippie while back."

"She give you this knife?"

"You might say she gave me that knife. Yessir. You might just say that now."

Chapter 7

"What's eating a hole in your belly?" Sharp Grover asked, scratching his cheek where the skin lay freshly bared of whiskers. He, like many others in Forsyth's detachment, had taken advantage of a shave compliments of the Fort Wallace barber after arriving on the fifth of September.

Three days ago.

Seamus had just stormed out the door of the post commander's office as he had many times in the past three days, bumping this time into the old scout responsible for Donegan coming to this part of Kansas.

"Still not a shadow of him, gawddammit!" the Irishman spat.

"O'Roarke?" Grover asked, stepping alongside Donegan in the sunlight.

"Who the hell else you figure I'm waiting for?"

"You sound testy as a sore-assed bear, Seamus." Grover slapped him on the back. "If it helps, you aren't the only one getting sore waiting for Liam O'Roarke. The major had been fixing to be long gone from here by now."

"Where would Forsyth go?" Seamus asked.

"I s'pose back there." He pointed. "East. Along the Solomon and Saline where the Cheyenne been raiding. Damn," he muttered angrily. "I was the one myself what told Forsyth and Sheridan I figured the Cheyenne for heading this way."

"Round here?"

"Not really," Grover admitted. "More north." He jutted

his bare chin in the direction. "Up yonder on the Republican
. . . where the bastards usually go to hunt this time of
year."

"Thought we looked up there, before coming in here."

"We did . . . that's the mystery of it, Seamus." Grover
wagged his head, staring at the ground.

For a moment, Seamus felt sympathy for the scout. "We're
both in a bad way, Sharp. I can't figure out what's become of
me uncle . . . and you can't figure out——"

"What's become of Roman Nose!"

Together they laughed spontaneously, pounding each
other on the shoulder. With relief, Donegan sensed part of
his tension free him.

"What are the chances Forsyth will march without
O'Roarke?"

Grover studied the Irishman quickly. "Slim."

"Then it appears I've got me something in common with
the major. I'm not about to budge till Liam rides in. And
Forsyth won't ride out until Liam's shown up." He saw
something on Grover's face that he could not decipher. "You
got something in your craw that you haven't begun to tell
me, Sharp."

Grover stared over the western wall of Fort Wallace, the
falling prairie sun casting a red light on the pink-limestone
walls. This setting, at this time of the year, ignited the place
with a strange fire.

Astraddle the Smoky Hill stage and freight road stretching
between Kansas and Denver, the fort had proven itself the
most active of outposts in recent months. Both it and Fort
Lyon, to the southwest along the Arkansas, had suffered the
brunt of Cheyenne attacks as civilian traffic plied its way into
Colorado Territory.

As commander of Fort Wallace, Col. Henry C. Bankhead
oversaw the operations of four companies of the 5th Infantry
and one of the Negro 38th stationed at this far western outpost. From time to time, the fort would entertain elements of
both George Armstrong Custer's 7th Cavalry, as well as
companies on detached service from the "Brunettes," Negro
10th Cavalry. In addition to their normal duties of patrolling
a vast amount of prairie real estate, Bankhead's soldiers were
responsible for guarding the many stage-line way stations or

"ranches," often called upon to escort the coaches themselves.

Grover reluctantly stopped, grabbing Donegan's arm.
"Listen, Irishman. I owe it to you to tell you. The season's
late."

"What are you trying to say?"

"I'm saying if O'Roarke was gonna show up . . . he'd of
come in last spring after the mountain passes broke."

"You . . . you don't think Liam's coming—do you,
Sharp?"

Grover's eyes hugged the ground. He shook his head.
"No, Seamus."

Donegan grabbed Sharp's dirty vest in one big hand.
"Why didn't he come, Grover? You aren't telling me everything, dammit!"

"I've just heard stories across the years, Seamus——"

"What kind of stories? Something about O'Roarke?"

He wagged his head, tried out a grin as Donegan released
his grip. "No. Tales coming out of Deseret."

"What the devil's *Deseret?*"

"Utah Territory. Where the Mormons set up their own
private kingdom."

"That's where Liam went to winter—right?"

"Yes. And that's why I don't think you can count on him
coming back."

"All of it, Sharp."

"Men who go to work for Brigham Young's band, what
the Mormons call their *avenging angels* . . . those men
don't often leave that bunch."

"I was told that this Young was just hiring guns. Nothing
more than——"

"There's a lot more to it, Seamus. The Mormons—he runs
'em."

"This Brigham Young?"

"And he pays good for protecting what he figures is his."

"Bodyguards, is it? Well, many a boy from County
Kilkenny spent a year as a papal guard for the Pope——"

"Young ain't the Pope, and his band of 'Angels' ain't just
guarding their Prophet."

Something struck him of a sudden. Like the heel of a boot
to the side of his head. Grover had a roundabout way to him,

sneaking around in the brush rather than diving head-first at something. But, it was finally coming clear. Like silt settling to the bottom of a prairie pond after a storm had passed. Eventually leaving the surface clear.

"Them hired guns of Brigham Young's——"

"Seamus, it's the same vigilante bunch tried to arrest Jim Bridger better'n fifteen year ago now."

"Arrest Bridger?"

"Young wanted him out of the way," Grover tried to explain. "Young sent a hundred of his Danite bunch out to capture Bridger. Never found ol' Gabe . . . but they wrecked Bridger's place. Burned half the fort Jim had him there. Then rode east to where Jim had a ferry on the Green. Killed Bridger's men there——"

"In the name of God!"

"Now you see." Grover sounded excited. "Young done it all in the name of his god."

Seamus wagged his head. "You're telling me Liam's mixed up with this bunch . . . and ain't likely to return?"

"There's no way O'Roarke had anything to do with Young fifteen years ago. But, that Danite bunch is a strange and tight bunch—they're not likely to let your uncle just waltz out of Deseret on his own hook. He'll know too damned much."

"Unless . . . Liam's got smart since he grew up," Seamus said, watching the last fiery lip of a red sun ease beyond the western edge of the world. "And give that murdering bunch slip."

When Donegan finally gazed back at Grover, Sharp said, "I don't want you counting on nothing when it comes to O'Roarke."

"The major is, ain't he now?"

"Yes, but——"

"Good enough for Forsyth to count on it coming true . . . good enough for Seamus Donegan to pray on it as well."

"I suppose that's what I'll have to do, Colonel," George Forsyth agreed reluctantly. He waved the paper in front of him that moments before had been handed him by the com-

mander of Fort Wallace. A messenger had just come in from
the settlements to the south.

"I'd send my own troops, Forsyth—if I had 'em to send,"
Henry Bankhead replied bitterly. "But I've got Captain Gra-
ham out with his company of Brunettes chasing a couple
dozen warriors now who we figure sacked a supply train
coming in on the Denver Road."

"And you told me you've already sent Captain Carpenter's Brunettes out to trail another war-party of two hundred."

"Their trail pointed west," Bankhead explained. "Carpenter has his hands full—those warriors are driving better than
twelve hundred head of cattle, horses, and mules before
them."

"A trail headed north and west, Colonel?"

Bankhead eyed the young major. "Very possibly, Forsyth."

George sighed, kneading one fist inside the palm of his
other hand. "Just not mine to play out, so it appears."

"Don't feel like your luck's run out, Major."

Forsyth flung the message on Bankhead's desk. "That
messenger just handed you this letter from the governor of
Kansas—asking your help in protecting the settlers down in
the Bison Basin. I suppose I'll take my scouts down there
and see what we can scare up."

"I heard Crawford's resigning as governor," Bankhead remarked. "He's raising some companies of Kansas volunteers
on his own to get the frontier quieted down."

Forsyth wagged his head. "Farmers. And storekeepers.
Out trying to do the army's work."

"Phil Sheridan doesn't have enough men to cover this territory. So if the army can't protect the citizens . . . then
God bless the settlers for protecting themselves."

He gazed long at the aging Bankhead. "Strange for an
army man to say that."

Bankhead pressed his lips in a thin line before he spoke.
He pointed past Beecher and McCall, standing by the door,
outside, beyond his office walls at the limestone buildings of
Fort Wallace. "Just what the hell have you got out there,
Major? Are any of those men riding with you soldiers?"

Forsyth finally wagged his head and snorted. "I suppose

not, Colonel." He sank into a chair near Bankhead's desk. "You're right. Phil Sheridan's only done what he had to do."

"If there aren't enough soldiers, Major—then hire some civilians to kill these Indians——"

"Colonel Bankhead, sir!"

Forsyth turned suddenly, as did they all, when a young soldier tore through the open office door, waving a flimsy telegraph.

"Gimme that!" the colonel ordered. His weary eyes crawled over the document for a moment before he handed it on to Forsyth.

When George had read it, he stood and passed it along to Fred Beecher. Sergeant McCall craned his neck over the lieutenant's shoulder as they studied the telegraph together.

"That telegram is what you've been waiting for, Major Forsyth."

He smiled at Bankhead. "By damn, it is, sir!"

"You'll go tonight?"

He shook his head once. "No, sir. Sun's already setting. We'll march before sunup. I couldn't get this rag-tag bunch pulled together to get very far with what light's left us."

"With your permission, I'll pass word, Major," McCall said.

Forsyth saluted his sergeant enthusiastically. "Certainly, Billy. Let the men know we're riding before first light."

They watched the sergeant dash from the office into the fading light watering down the Fort Wallace parade into twilight.

"What about Governor Crawford's appeal, gentlemen?" asked the frantic messenger, who had ridden all the way up from the settlements of the Bison Basin.

Bankhead turned on him first. "This telegram gives the major a fresh trail, Mr. Flanagan. Better that Forsyth follows a fresh trail than mere ghosts on the wind."

"Ghosts on the goddamned wind!" Flanagan roared, then suddenly composed himself. "Then, I can tell Governor Crawford that the army assigned to Fort Wallace will not protect the settlers——"

Bankhead pounded his desk, clearly frustrated with week after week of chasing ghostly war-parties while the death-toll continued to rise. "Dammit, Flanagan! You tell Crawford what the hell you want. He's no concern of mine."

The civilian fumed silently a minute more, then slammed his dusty hat atop his head. "Good day, officers." He stormed toward the door.

"Mr. Flanagan?"

The civilian halted at the open door, turning to find Forsyth addressing him. "What is it, Major?"

"You're welcome to ride along with my scouts."

"Now, why would I want to ride with your men, Major?"

George felt his eyes narrowing into slits. "Just in case you really are serious about getting a chance to kill some Indians."

Flanagan's own fiery eyes flared at Bankhead before he wheeled about, sputtering incoherent chips of words, and tore into the twilight.

"This is great news, Major." Beecher turned from the door.

"What do you make of it, Fred?"

Beecher scanned the telegram. "Civilian freighter's train . . . the warriors jumped them in camp on Turkey Creek near Sheridan . . . killed two Mexican teamsters and ran off eighty head. It has all the marks of a big war-party."

"Do you figure we can track them back to their village?"

"We jump on this at dawn like you say, Major—we'll stand a good chance of catching the culprits."

"No more ghosts, Mr. Beecher."

"No, sir." And young Fred Beecher's bearded face grinned widely.

"How far is Sheridan, Colonel?"

Bankhead turned, considering the crude map nailed behind him. "I'd say fifteen to twenty miles."

"More like fifteen, to my reckoning," Beecher admitted shyly. "I've covered that ground a time or two before, Major."

Forsyth nodded. "You and Billy McCall will see to it that our bunch is fed and watered well before four A.M. This time I'm not about to let this war-party of murdering bastards disappear like ghosts."

"No, Major," Beecher replied, his young face lighting with that cheery smile of his, "no more ghosts!"

Chapter 8

*H*e couldn't believe he was sweating. Not as cold as these summer nights got out here in western Kansas. Once the sun went down, a man could find himself chilled to the core.

So why the hell was he sweating?

Another drop of moisture tumbled down Bob North's spine. A narrow river of cold between the cheeks of his ass. Waiting here in the dark was enough to give any man the willies, he decided.

Yet, the darkness felt like a comfortable old coat to him. Like an old friend, if not accomplice.

Back three days ago now, Major Forsyth had led him and the rest into this piss-poor excuse for an army fort. Once again Bob North wondered how in hell the Confederacy had lost the war to such a rag-tag, poor-digger outfit like this here Union army. From the looks of things, these soldiers were going to have themselves a time of it holding back the Injuns—here, and up north in Red Cloud's stomping ground.

That's just what those Sioux and the rest been doing up there too. Stomping. Beating hell out of them soldiers every turn. Time had come, Bob North to do the same with a certain Irish fella.

Pains weren't all that sharp no more. Like a dull burning now. But, North's belly still troubled him. Lot of the time, he found it hard to keep his food down. Not that he figured he had a hole in his stomach. Just that whatever that bastard mick's bullet hit, it sure didn't take much to North eating at all. So he kept his belly quiet with whiskey. Much as he could stomach and not puke up. Kill the pain. Dull the remembering. Soothe his fears about waiting here in the dark way he was.

Waiting for the Irishman come out for his night-time stroll and stop by the slip-trench before he headed back to that low-roofed limestone barracks where Forsyth's scouts bedded down. Lord, was that Irishman a creature of habit. What with riding alongside Donegan for the past nine days, North figured he had the Irishman down like a boar-hog going into rut. Leastways, the mick always come here for a pee late after moon-rise. Just before he went to his blankets.

He heard voices. Two men outside the low wall, muffled a bit beyond the unroofed latrine. But muffled or no, one of the voices was the Irishman. A set of footsteps moved away without any more said. A second set of steps pushed into the moonlight and shadow of the latrine.

North chuckled to himself. Fitting that he should do here what he had long been planning for the mick. In this place that stank like hell, he was going to send that big bastard straight back to hell itself.

He waited, fretting. Hoping the footsteps coming to a rest in the shadows over the slip-trench were in fact the Irishman's. North inched along the wall, hugging the shadows as if they were the only safe places for a soul as dark as his.

Squinting, the renegade regarded the bulk of the man making water in the trench. He couldn't be sure. The shadow looked big enough to be the mick. Still . . . Then the man began to whistle a lively Irish melody. North was sure enough for killing.

Water splashing in the smelling trench, his head held back as he regarded the stars above in the night-sky, North's victim never knew what hit him until the renegade was on him. He started a turn as the Confederate looped a left arm up and worked the long knife-blade in under the ribs.

What frightened North most was the bulk of the man, the way the muscles came suddenly alive like cat-gut drawn taut on a fiddle, making it hard for the knife at first. But the renegade drove it all the way to the hilt the first time. Feeling the warm gush of sticky blood burst across his fingers. He pulled the knife free and shoved it in again, a rib higher this time. Feeling his victim jerk, trying to kick, mumbling and biting beneath North's hand.

They fell over together, landing at the edge of the damp trench in the foul, wet sand where the stench hung strongest and gravity was slow in working its duty.

His free hand came off the man as they scrambled. North's cheek landed in the sticky sand. Growling a whispered oath, he turned, eyes squinting in the dark, spotting his victim crawling to hands and knees. The renegade hurled himself on the bleeding, mumbling form once more. Plunging the knife again and again into his victim's back. Until all fight went out of the body and sank with a grunt in the sand.

North stood, triumphant, gasping for air. His hands dripping with the man's blood. As his breathing slowed, became more regular, the renegade listened to the night for more footsteps and other voices. When he was assured no one was coming, Bob North drove his heel into the big man's body, rolling him off the side of the shallow, sandy trench into the foul muck.

His victim made no sound landing at the bottom, save for the splash as the huge weight plopped into the thick moisture.

Stumbling back into the shadows, he caught the wisp of voices approaching. They stepped close, turned along the wall before moving away once more into the darkness.

North swallowed down his heart. Then knelt beside his victim. Quickly he sliced round the skull and yanked off the scalp with a soft, sucking pop. Only then did he drive the thin-bladed knife several times into the damp sand, clearing it of blood and gore. North carefully slipped it into the porcupine-quilled sheath at his hip, then stuffed the warm, wet trophy inside his long handles, careful not to smear too much blood on his shirt.

Puffing his chest like a banty rooster, Bob North began to whistle happily as he strode out of the shadows onto the Fort Wallace parade. He'd slip out when he could. Head east, maybe. Perhaps come nightfall tomorrow.

Might even have to give some thought to heading back up the Bozeman Road. Heard tell there wasn't much left down south to go back home to now anyways. And from what he'd seen of white whores, they wasn't nowhere near as much fun as them Arapaho sluts. Mayhaps, Bob North cogitated, he should strike his stick for the north country again. With the Irishman dead at last, it had come a time for celebrating.

And what better way to celebrate than with a brown-skinned Arap squaw who knew how to please a hungry man?

Jack O'Neill had never eaten puppy before. Hell, since he had been captured by these Cheyenne late last winter, the mulatto had been doing a lot of things he had never done before.

Like sleeping with one squaw after another. Ever since the time he had headed back home on his own for Georgia, and two mornings later awoke to find a dozen warriors circling his bedroll, Jack had discovered he had a real knack for this Indian talk. Not a day had gone by that he didn't pick up a whole slew of words. Pointing out some object to a child, perhaps to one of the squaws who seemed to dog his every step round the nomads' village.

Being late summer like it was, near as he could figure from the heat and all, the village had once again swelled in numbers after the sundance to begin its annual migration following the buffalo herds along the Republican. Funny thing was, much of the time Jack was just about the only man left in camp. If a person didn't count the boys too young for vision-quests and the men too old for war.

At first, a lot of things had been funny. And had made Jack laugh out loud. The way a few of the warriors who had captured him not far out of Fort Lyon had licked their fingers and rubbed on his honey-colored skin. Some of their attempts to rub his color off had actually tickled O'Neill. Then the squaws started tickling more than just Jack's flesh. Any one of these women knew more about love-making than a whole slew of whores working the cribs back there across the river from Fort Lyon.

At times he remembered Emmy, and how that white woman was the first to love an outcast named O'Neill. He had cried often at first, much of the time when he rutted with the squaws. Each warrior who gave his wife to Jack explained that they wanted his blood in their people . . .

wanted the wife to conceive and carry a child fathered by the
honey-colored giant.

Still he cried for Emmy much of the time while doing his
business. Then laughed when he was done and catching his
breath. Never before had Jack O'Neill had so much honey
on his stinger.

As each day passed, he had grown to accept the tribe as
his own folk. What with his daddy dead somewhere back
east. And his mammy killed when Sherman's deadly army
burned its way across Georgia. But after so many years of
wandering, Jack had found Emmy. Sweet Emmy, who gave
her warm body to him night after night and didn't care if the
lamp was lit. Poor, sweet Emmy—nearly cut in half by that
half-Injun bastard . . .

Again and again Jack had pushed the terrible image from
his mind. Coming to accept that the one who had killed his
Emmy was no Injun after all. Coming to accept as well that
these *Shahiyena* were no savages over the weeks and months
he had slept and ate, played and fornicated. And learned to
ride and fight like *Shahiyena*.

In the last few weeks, Jack had thought more and more
that come next sundance time for these people, he would
hang himself from the huge center pole. His feet would
pound the ground in an endless dance round and round to
the throbbing beat of ear-numbing drums and soul-stirring
voices all a chant from the fringe of the huge arbor.

Weeks ago when the tribe had halted for many days to
celebrate the sundance, O'Neill had first believed the young
warriors who pushed the sharp skewers through their chest
muscles were simply working themselves up into a frenzy for
war. Only of late did he come to accept that the sundance
was what the squaws claimed it to be. The young men had
offered themselves to the sun in thanks for the buffalo and
the nomadic life of The People, thanks for another year of
freedom. Despite the troubles caused by the white man.

O'Neill brooded on that a lot lately. The white man always
come in to frig things up. It wasn't only for the black man;
he was stirring shit with the red man too.

Jack figured he just might found himself a home.

And thought again of the sundance. All those young, glistening naked bodies sweating as they pulled on the rawhide

tethers tied to the center pole. Yanking and dancing round and round staring wide-eyed at the hot sun until in a wild explosion of frantic revelation the warriors ripped their flesh and fell free and bleeding. Many laughing. Some silently crying. Tears of joy coursing down every man's face. For they had each and every one stared into the face of their Everywhere Spirit and come away blessed.

O'Neill wanted that. As badly as anything he had ever wanted, as much as he had wanted to have his daddy come riding back up the lane to the big-house after the war, as much as he had wanted to take Emmy back to that Georgia plantation with him. But knew neither of those dreams would never come true for him. Jack wanted to stare into the face of the god that drove these beautiful, simple people back and forth across the plains, from creek to river and beyond again, following the big, shaggy beasts, in pursuit of the old way of life before the white man came to frig it up and stir the shit with a big stick.

Jack wanted to see the god. Like all the rest of the young warriors. Roman Nose himself. Who fell from the flesh-tearing, babbling dry-mouthed about the coming war with the white man. Told by the Everywhere Spirit that he would find his vision-place on a sandy island in the middle of a river . . . somewhere on the plains they roamed. His thick lips flecked with foam, The Nose had risen from the ground pounded smooth by bare feet, and swore he had seen his medicine place.

Then turned, finding the wide, white eyes of the mulatto staring into his from the fringe of the sundance arbor. And said to the only man who stood every bit as tall as Roman Nose, "My medicine place will be for you as well, Black Jack. There, in that day yet to come—we both will find the answer to what troubles our hearts."

Gnawing at a strip of half-cooked meat along a rib-bone, Jack remembered the wild look in Roman Nose's eyes as he had spoken for the first time to the mulatto prisoner adopted into the Cheyenne tribe. In those eyes were acceptance, and a recognition that the two of them would share some secret discovery come the time The Nose found his sandy island on that unnamed river.

O'Neill had found himself a home. Food anytime he

wanted to eat. Women ready for his randy dance of love every time Black Jack wanted to wet his stinger. And, come a time, there would be some white men to kill with Roman Nose.

For the one the Cheyenne had come to call "Nibsi," there would come something to ease the pain of Emmy's remembrance. Some blood atonement for all the hurt caused a man raised up learning not to hurt a living thing—a man who now had learned what it meant to thirst after the blood of woman killer.

Never before had Black Jack O'Neill felt so free. So alive. With such power pulsing through his body. For the first time he understood what the Cheyenne meant when they talked about powerful medicine.

With his own, Black Jack knew as certain as the sun would rise, come morning in its own time, that he would one day have his hands round the throat of the woman killer.

Come that day, the mulatto swore he would rip the white man's throat out with his own teeth, then drink of the bastard's blood while he slowly died.

Chapter 9

*T*hey moved quietly about beneath the bright summer stars flung over the dark prairie here at the end of the world.

In and out of the mess-hall where the sweating cooks had coffee brewing and hard-tack frying in fragrant bacon grease for those who wanted to eat.

Others made their first stop a hurried visit to the corner of the small compound, there to stand or squat over the slip-trench latrine. Finished, they leisurely strode away from that stinking hole.

In the dark, the crowd at the hitching rails planted before Wallace's cavalry stables swelled as one after another ventured into the lamp-lit shadows of the stalls, there to locate his mount and saddle, blanket and bit. Outside again at the rail, most of them quietly grumbled about the goddamned hour or the lousy coffee or their bowels giving them fits with the alkali water. Some, like Seamus Donegan, silently worked over The General, petting, blanketing, patting, buckling, stroking, cinching. He stuffed his hand into a dirty coat pocket and pulled out a handful of sugar he had stolen when the mess-cooks weren't looking.

The big gray nuzzled the Irishman's hand there under the starlight of the Kansas sky. Big eyes 'volving, watching shadows move across limestone buildings. Ears twitching with the snorts of animal and the mumbled curses of men. Nose swelling with the smell of familiar things, the smell of newness to what was yet to come. Seamus left the horse ground-hobbled.

Scratching at his chin whiskers, Donegan quickly strode back toward the mess-hall. No sign of the soldiers yet. He had time for another cup of that poor excuse for coffee. Still the best he had tasted this side of a little shack outside of the stockade at Fort Phil Kearny.

Better than a year and a half now since you . . . held her, Seamus.

And in thinking of Jennie, knew how a man's arms could ache for a woman. Not just any woman. Like most men, he had been in need of just any woman more times than he dared count. But, when he could not help himself and ended up thinking on Jennie, Seamus knew how empty a man could feel in there where few, if any, ever see.

Steaming tin in hand, he stepped outside into the chill pre-dawn dark, squatting against the limestone brushed egg-shell white beneath a sinking moon and starlight. Here in the darkness this west Kansas post looked a bit more military, perhaps more imposing than it did in the light of day. Two limestone buildings squatting among the rest, slab-sided cottonwood. And out there in the middle of the parade stood the flagstaff.

Quite possibly the tallest thing between here and the high mountains separating him and Liam O'Roarke.

Seamus nursed his coffee as he watched the others go about their business here before marching out. A few noisy, loudmouthed ones. But most of these citizen-soldiers, these paid mercenaries, kept to themselves, and kept quiet. Like him, in their own thoughts in these minutes before they would ride out onto the plains that knew no roads and few trail, to track some scalp-hungry young bucks until . . .

None of them had a good idea when they would see so much as this fort again and call it civilization. Something down inside each man standing here on the edge of riding out into the prairie darkness following a blood-trail always knows there will be some who will never come riding back. And in his own way, each man prayed as he ate, pissed, saddled, or hung back in the shadows, alone with his own god.

"Draw your seven days' rations here, boys!"

Donegan recognized Billy McCall's voice as the sergeant emerged from the lamp-lit rectangle of mess-hall doorway.

"Seven days, Sarge?"

"That's right," McCall answered a faceless scout shoving into the mess-hall.

"We'll be back here by time we run out?"

"Just draw your rations and dream of fragrant mule-steaks roasting over a buffalo-chip fire, mister," McCall snorted.

As he rose, back against the limestone wall, Donegan's ears pricked with the sound of something new. The hair on the back of his neck stood, skin going cold. A new voice come marching across the parade moonlit and shadow-streaked. Faint at best, but a new voice nonetheless, walking between two others, all three heading for the mess-hall. Back-slapping and laughing among themselves.

As the trio threaded their way through the tangle of horses and men at preparation for the march, reaching the greasy-yellow rectangle of door-light, Seamus inched up to get a better look. And to listen closely. A few more words, and he was sure. No mistaking the tongue of the mother-country. And his mother's eyes.

One step and Seamus moved into the light. "Your name O'Roarke?"

The big man was graying at the temples, lines in his face like a war-map. He eyed Donegan down, then slowly up. "I am Liam O'Roarke. Who'd be asking?"

"Just a nephew's been looking for your worthless, bleeming carcass . . . a promise made to his mother who's dying back in County Kilkenny."

The last word landed on the bystanders' ears at the same time Donegan's fist connected with the older man's jaw. O'Roarke backpedaled a few steps into the moonlit darkness, men scampering backward round him, their roughened morning-voices suddenly pumped louder, prodded, more excited. Behind him Seamus heard wooden benches hurriedly scraped across the rough planks of the mess-hall floor. He knew they were all leaving their breakfast behind, bolting out the door to see this.

And his gut warned him this would be a long morning. What, with the way his long-lost uncle had taken Seamus's best shot and still stood. It was going to be one hell of a long morning.

Liam strode back into the yellow doorway light, his bearded jaw cradled in one hand, working it back and forth like a slow, methodical steam-piston. When it appeared to work well enough, he dropped his hand, smiled, and asked.

"By the saints—li'l Seamus, is it?"

Donegan flung the right arm at that shiny casement of grinning teeth. It felt as if the solid meat of that arm he hurled had been battered aside by a hickory axe-handle. Yet he did not have much time to ponder the pain in the battered arm as O'Roarke flung it aside, for Liam's right fist plunged into the smooth washboard of Donegan's belly. Driving the last little ounce of morning air from the nephew's lungs.

He stumbled backward to the hoots of the scouts crowding in for a closer look at the scuffle. Whistles and shoving, cat-calls and wagers. Something sure to awaken a sleepy pre-dawn unit of crude frontiersmen on the verge of riding out to seek their own valley of death.

As he slowly caught his breath, his bugging eyes rising to look his uncle over, Seamus realized just how big a mouthful he had bitten off for himself. If ever there was a man bigger than himself at lowly Fort Wallace, it was surely this Liam O'Roarke. He understood again where he came by his own size. His mother's side of the family. The brawling O'Roarkes of Ballinrobble. And what Liam might give up to Seamus in all those years like a wide gulf yawning between them, Liam gained back everything and more in the experience only years on the prairie and among the far mountains would bestow upon a man.

"You always was one to try a leg up where you shouldn't, li'l Seamus!" Liam roared, laughing.

Donegan sucked wind, readying himself. "By the love of God . . . I've been praying for this day, you bastird!"

He came in low, finding his uncle immediately crouching. Seamus feinted with his right, saw Liam's head moving left, then jabbed with the surprise fist. A glancing blow only, bouncing off O'Roarke's thick shoulder before it connected with the side of the uncle's head. The hardest head Seamus had ever made the mistake of connecting bare knuckles with, that is.

Cradling his left fist in his right, Seamus took one step, then a second, backward as Liam advanced, grinning toothily. Shoulders hunched, his neck disappearing in the process. Head dodging behind the wheeling fists.

"Your mother ever tell you 'bout my love of a good round-house, Seamus?"

"No, no——"

"Always looked forward to the day we'd have a go at it ourselves . . . you and me, Nephew."

"You weren't there to meet me——"

"These were the best fists in County Tyrone, Seamus. Always figured they'd get me a job one place or another." He swung, connected on Donegan's jaw, snapping his nephew's head back. "Funny how things work out. Me, Liam O'Roarke . . . making a living with me wits and not me fists!"

"Glory, you pack a wallop!" Donegan wagged his head clear and set his feet. He swung as Liam opened his mouth to go on.

It was a doozy. Stunning the taller, heavier, older O'Roarke right where he stood, overconfident of his Queens-bury abilities. Gingerly, Liam touched a finger to his oozing nose, feeling his upper lip puffy already as he spat loose some flecks of crimson foam.

"Sweet Mither of God!" he roared, wiping his bloody hands off on his sweat-stained calico shirt. "You're good, Seamus. I've not had me this much fun . . . since I knuckled me way out of Deseret! C'mon, boy—let's make a dance of it, shall we?"

"Dance, my arse, Liam O'Roarke—you'll eat dust before you'll ride out of here upright with me."

Liam jabbed. Donegan ducked, and could not get out of the way of that ball of fire hammering his belly once, twice, and a third time before O'Roarke grabbed hold of Seamus's hair. Yanking his nephew's head back, he smiled, spitting his words past the swollen lip and blood streaming from the broken nose.

"Ride where with you, Nephew?"

"We've got to go east . . ." Seamus sputtered, the pain rising from his hammered belly like gall rising to burn the back of his throat. "A ship."

"Ship off to where?"

"Town Callan, you bastard!"

"Home to Eire? Why there?"

"Your sister, bleeming idjit! She's . . . she's dying."

Liam flung Donegan backward, watching the younger man stumble over some crates of ammunition and sprawl in the dust before the mess-hall.

"Dying?" He shook his head as if measuring it. "There's no way she can be——"

"Wrote me. Begging me to find you both. Bring you home."

O'Roarke took three long strides so that he stood over the young Irishman. And stared down at his nephew. "I'll not go back, Seamus Donegan. There's nothing for me there."

"Your sister——"

"Another woman, like me own mother . . . every bit and true like our mother she became. And I'll not let another woman control me like I did those two, Nephew."

Donegan scooted backward in the dust, out from under the tall man. "It was like a vow . . . a prayer of hers——"

Suddenly Liam landed atop him, one knee on his chest. "Tell you what, boy. I'll go back with you . . . soon as we finish this little job for the major."

"I mean to have no part in his fight."

Liam filled his huge hands with Seamus's shirt, lifting him from the ground. "I do, Seamus. And a good fight it will be."

"We go now." Donegan tried to make it sound as forceful as he could, staring into the face that had changed over all those years. But the eyes had remained the same. Enough of that face as well, a face he had grown up with across the seasons in County Kilkenny. And those eyes that had wept at the side of that dark hole the day his mother's two brothers had buried Seamus's father.

"One way or the other . . . I mean to take you back——"

"What the blazes is going on here?"

Seamus turned, finding Major Forsyth shoving his way through the knot of spectators.

"Liam." Forsyth almost gushed with the word. "Bankhead told me you wandered in here in the wee hours." Then he looked at the bloody Donegan as well. "Explain this,

O'Roarke—why you're up to your old ways . . . beating one of my men."

"Good to see you, Major," he began, hoisting Donegan to his feet, dusting the young man's clothing. Liam held out his hand to Forsyth and they shook.

"I'm waiting, O'Roarke."

"Just a bit of a donny-brook, Major."

"Between you and one of these men? I can't take the chance of any of you fighting among yourselves . . . not with the job we have——"

"Major, please," Liam cooed, the gray hairs in his mustache curling upward. "Wasn't beating up on one of your men."

"He most certainly is one of my——"

"One of your best scouts, Major. This is Seamus Donegan . . . me blooded nephew."

"You . . . your nephew?"

"Sure and begora, Major," Liam chimed. "We was . . . just having us a bit of a family squabble, 't was."

"Dammit! With one of the colonel's own soldiers getting himself killed a night ago over in that latrine—Bankhead's nervous as a hen about to lay. And you come in here blooding this ground——"

"That weren't none of my doing, Major. Wasn't even here."

"Damn well I know you weren't!" Forsyth snapped. "Your kind of work it was, Liam. The knife. The poor man's scalp ripped off—like an Injun himself. Or . . ."

"Or, you're saying," O'Roarke interrupted, "the work of a half-wild army scout?"

"I don't know who or what, Liam. All I know is, I've got Cheyennes to stalk. And you can hunt them with me if you're a mind to taking orders."

"I'm of a mind to take orders from you, Major Forsyth."

To Seamus, the words of his uncle sounded as if they had come from the mouth of a contrite schoolboy caught roughing up the younger lads on the school-ground.

"I'll have none of this scrapping on this ride, O'Roarke. Save it for the Cheyenne, damn you!"

"The Saints preserve me if I ever go again' you or your orders, Major."

"Be more than saints you'll have to worry about, Liam—I catch you flogging a man with your fists again." Forsyth turned, finding McCall.

"Goddammit, Billy!" He began pushing his way through the crowding spectators. "Get these men saddled up! We've got some murdering Cheyenne to track!"

Seamus turned back as McCall ordered the rest away to their mounts.

"You've got a horse, Seamus?"

He jerked back round to stare into Liam's face. "I do."

"Bring 'im with you, boy. You'll ride with Liam O'Roarke. And we'll talk of old times, you and me will. Talk of mending broken hearts as well."

Chapter 10

$\mathcal{I}$f he lived through the coming hunt, Jack Stillwell brooded, he would see his twentieth birthday this autumn. If he didn't—well, it had been nineteen years of fun as it was.

Time and again he tried to swallow down the fear-tinged excitement that puckered his bowels and twisted his stomach into such tight knots that he hadn't been able to eat breakfast that morning in the darkness before they climbed into the saddle. Not a chance to climb out for a bite yet either. No matter. Jack was certain if he had tried to eat then as now, for sure he would lose it all on the side of the trail Forsyth was racing down to reach Sheridan, Kansas, some thirteen miles northeast of Fort Wallace.

Where the Cheyenne had just killed two men and run off with some stock. Providing the major and his scouts a clear trail to stalk.

Straining to make out the changing countryside in the murky, pre-dawn light, Jack was soon heartened to see the sun rise in the east, red as a buffalo cow giving birth. That sun hung barely three fingers above the horizon when Forsyth's scouts pounded into the little settlement of Sheridan, on the north fork of the Smoky Hill River. For a moment in time on this expanding frontier, Sheridan would enjoy its singular status as the farthest advance of the Union Pacific track.

Outside the tiny settlement on a stretch of some marshy

grassland, the scouts found the smoldering ruins of several wagons.

As he led his horsemen off the hills toward the scene of the Cheyenne attack, a few riflemen ventured cautiously from the doorways of pine-slab shanties several hundred yards away. They set up a lusty cheer upon recognizing the fifty as white men. Led by three uniformed soldiers. A few slowly made their way toward the teamsters' camp where the Cheyenne had killed two Mexican drivers.

Both bodies had been butchered and scalped, and still lay in the grass beside the charred wagons. Stripped of all clothing, their arms slashed four times and thighs opened up like a hog's neck, from hip to knee. Eyes gouged out and tongues cut off, each replaced with a shriveled penis, the scrotum like a dark pendant on their battered chins. Stripped of dignity in their violent passing.

Jack Stillwell forced the bitter gall back down his throat. He had nothing else in his belly to come up.

"Never seen how a Injun cuts up a man, eh?"

Stillwell gazed over at the old man, Pierre Trudeau. And finally shook his head, still unable to speak.

"Won't be your last, eh?" Trudeau clucked. "You do to suck it down. These two past praying over now."

Jack watched the old frontiersman nudge his horse ahead, worming through the others who ambled about the charred wagons.

"You! All of you—stay back!" Forsyth hollered, standing in his stirrups.

"You boys'll ruin the tracks!" Sharp Grover screeched, waving the scouts back to the far side of the battle site. "Leave me something to read, dammit!"

Dropping from his horse and ground hobbling it with the rest, Stillwell hung close behind Forsyth and Beecher, listening as the two picked their way across the trampled grass. Then finally worked their way up toward the far hill where Sharp Grover was down on his hands and knees. Crawling back and forth, back and forth, until he raised his head, noticing Forsyth and Beecher. He smiled.

"You got it sorted, have you?"

"Could be, Major." Grover clambered to his feet and dusted his hands. From a pocket he took the remains of a plug, bit it in half, and shoved the leaf-burley to his cheek like a squirrel storing nuts.

"Sergeant McCall, I want you to go back and get some of those cowardly railroad workers to work, digging graves for these two. We won't be here long, but I better see them buried before I'm gone."

McCall had saluted and gone down the slope before Grover began to explain.

"Ground's soft, Major. Wagon ruts cut it up pretty good all round here. Supplies coming in. Truck going out."

"What you make of it, Sharp? A big war-party hit this place?"

He pursed his lips a moment. "Wasn't a big one, Major. Lots of tracks . . . but for all that I gone over the ground, I can't make the group any bigger'n twenty—maybe twenty-five at most."

Forsyth squinted at the trampled, broken grass leading over the slope and out onto the distant prairie. "You're sure about that, Sharp. Sure all this was done by twenty-five warriors."

He nodded. "Near as I can make it. They weren't a real war-party. Been more of 'em had it been a bunch of bucks out on a hunt. This was just a bunch of youngsters letting the wolf out to howl, Major. Have themselves a spree. From the looks of things, they rode in from the east."

"The . . . the east?" Forsyth sounded more astonished than before. "How can that be, Sharp? Few days back we came in from——"

"Most likely, the bucks was trailing us, Major. We've been bedded down at Wallace for several days. And most like this little war-party crossed our trail back east a ways. Likely they was following us when they come on track's-end here."

"And had themselves their spree," Fred Beecher grumbled.

Grover gazed at the lieutenant. "You see most of these prints are different. Many as they are, all round here, as they rode down and shot up the teamsters' camp—we only got twenty-five to track, Lieutenant."

"I only need one, Sharp," Forsyth said before anyone else spoke. "Only one—if he'll lead me to the rest."

"Major!" Sergeant McCall shouted as he trotted uphill.

"Got some of the other drivers digging the graves now." He huffed up to the group, catching his breath. "They tell me the warriors came out of the east, off those hills there, riding straight down for the teamsters' camp. But the drivers evidently put up enough of a fight of it that the warriors let off their attack after a couple hours, and scared off the stock instead."

"Good," Forsyth answered. "It will give me more to track."

In silence, Stillwell watched them all turn their heads up-country, eyes following the wide, well-beaten path through the tall, browning buffalo-grass. The downtrodden trail across the soft, marshy ground made a distinct shade of brown from the grass on either side of it. A path as plain as the scars on the back of Jack's hands, the Cheyenne trail could be read by a schoolmarm just off the train from Toledo.

"Go gather the men, Sergeant," Forsyth said suddenly as he turned, flinging his arm to shoo McCall on his way.

Jack loped downhill behind the sergeant, where he caught up his horse and milled in close with the rest of the scouts as Forsyth came to a halt in their midst.

"Sharp, I want you and Lieutenant Beecher to ride the point."

"We've got something to track now, Major!" Beecher cheered. About half of the scouts shouted in encouragement with the lieutenant.

"Damn right we do, Fred. We're not letting this trail go cold on us now. Those murdering bastards left their tracks behind for me to follow. We'll ride this bunch to the end of the earth if we have to."

Jack watched Forsyth turn, sweeping up his reins. "Saddle up, boys. There's a lot of daylight left us. And we're going to use every minute of it to cut down the Cheyennes' lead."

The major waved Grover and Beecher ahead, then followed at fifty yards while the scouts roughly formed their column of twos as they loped their way into the rolling hills.

"Major find these Cheyenne, no?"

Jack once again found Trudeau, the old frontiersman, beside him.

"I s'pose that's what he's counting on."

"And you, young one? What do you count on?"

Jack gulped, looking back over his offside shoulder at the tiny valley buried in the swales of tall buffalo-grass where lay the two butchered bodies and the wisps of greasy smoke hung on the dawn air.

"I count on finding them Cheyenne too, Pierre."

Trudeau winked at Stillwell, then turned away chuckling like a mad rooster who believed not a word of it.

Hell, Jack thought. *I don't believe it either. All I count on is to keep from wetting my pants when we find Forsyth's Cheyenne.*

Just keep from soiling my britches.

As soon as the men had packed the mules and Beecher inspected their loads, Forsyth once again sent Grover and the lieutenant out on the point. First to follow the trail they had dogged all day yesterday after leaving the Sheridan outpost, until it grew too dark and the major was forced to make camp. Around a few small fires the men had boiled coffee and chewed on their raw bacon before curling up in their blankets. A few of the scouts had done without, falling asleep almost where they struck the ground as they slid wearily out of their saddles.

For only a moment, Sharp Grover had been concerned about those few among Forsyth's scouts who were green to this much saddle-work. The whole bunch of them were at it before dawn the day before and not down on the ground again until twilight had swallowed the prairie.

And now, a handful of hours later in the gray light of predawn, the major had Sharp pushing ahead as soon as there was enough light to follow the trail.

Once the sun rose behind his right shoulder, the old scout began to grow more and more certain of it. And sure that the major would not like hearing the news he had to bring. Though he believed what he had seen with his own eyes, Sharp nonetheless waited to tell Forsyth until they halted for a noon rest.

He strode up to the major through the knots of scouts talking excitedly of overtaking the Cheyenne, preparing themselves for the possibility of a fight. Sharp shoved his dusty hat back, showing a stripe of trail-dust halfway up his forehead. "Major?"

"Sharp," Forsyth cheered, squinting into the bright sunlight. He patted the grass beside him and offered a chunk of pork. "Have a seat."

"No thankee, Major. Et my own yonder." Sharp settled, then sighed. " 'Pears the bucks are heading northwest, like they were following a compass."

Forsyth finished his bite of bacon. "To the Beaver?"

Sharp nodded. "Looks like it." He watched Beecher scoot in closer to join the conversation. "From there to the forks of the Republican."

"Cheyenne country, Major," Beecher added quietly.

Forsyth nodded, looking back at Grover. "Something's worrying you, Sharp."

Pursing his chapped lips, Grover spat it out. "Trail's growing dimmer and dimmer."

The major looked at Beecher. "You read it that way too, Fred?"

" 'Fraid so, Major. Appears the warriors are dropping off here and there. Makes it harder and harder to read the trail. Man has to keep looking ahead of him quite a ways to get an idea where it's heading."

Forsyth sighed. "Not good news, is it, fellas?"

"Didn't wanna have to tell you."

"One good thing about it, Sharp," the major cheered. "They know we're back here, on their tails. And we must be getting close or they wouldn't be dropping out, would they, boys?"

"I suppose you're right, Major," Beecher agreed.

"You figure on going on like we are?" Grover asked, rolling a sprig of buffalo-grass between his lips.

Forsyth scrambled to his feet slowly, stretching some kinks out of his back. "I don't have a choice. We'll follow this trail until it gives out."

"You turning back if it does?"

Forsyth eyed the bunch that had been gradually gathering round him. Then his eyes fixed on the wolf-faced Confederate who had drawled the question.

"No, Mr. Smith. I won't turn back. Chances are, we'll cut another trail sooner or later by heading northwest into Cheyenne country. And that new trail will take me where this one won't. Right to the main village."

"The main gawddamned village, Major? What happens we run into fifteen hunnert the sonsabitches? We being the ones get rubbed out?"

Forsyth snorted angrily, his eyes glowering at the Southerner. "You hired on to fight Indians."

"Fight 'em, Major. Not get kilt by 'em!"

There was a patter of some nervous laughter to Smith's rejoinder.

"Each of you was given a new pistol and a new repeating rifle. Those weapons make every man jack of you equal to ten times your number in Cheyenne warriors. Don't let your fears run away with you, fellas. If we come eye to eye with Roman Nose's murderers, we may not be able to whip the whole damned bunch——"

"That's just what I'm 'fraid of, Major!" Smith whined.

"Mr. Smith, I spent a good portion of the war following a man you Southern boys came to hate, General Sheridan. And let me tell you that to Phil Sheridan, the only thing that counts in warfare is results. Success, gentlemen. Now tell me how we're to defeat the Cheyenne if we don't fight them. Eh? We may not be able to whip Roman Nose, but by damn those bastards won't defeat us!"

"Hear, hear!" Beecher cheered, raising a fist to the sky. "Here's to giving Roman Nose a sound whipping, boys!"

"By Jesus, we've got to find the bastard first!" Liam O'Roarke hollered above them all.

"Suppose you start earning your keep, Liam." Forsyth stepped up to O'Roarke. "Ride on up there with Beecher and Grover . . . let's see if you still have the eyes for this job, Irishman."

"Wondering when you'd be giving this leprechaun the pleasure, Major! At your command!" He snapped heels together and saddled. "Lieutenant? Mr. Grover? Let's find these red h'athens for the major here—what say?"

Beecher rode off with O'Roarke. For a few minutes Grover hung back among the scouts as the rest climbed aboard their mounts.

"Major, remember my suggestion?"

"I certainly do, Sharp." Forsyth turned in the saddle.

"Sergeant McCall—form up a dozen of your best men. I want to use some outriders. Sharp believes we have reason to be on our toes now, riding this far into Cheyenne country as we are."

"Certainly, Major. I put six outriders on each flank of our march."

"Splendid, Billy." He turned back to Sharp. "Better?"

Grover smiled. "Yes, Major. With your outriders now on our flanks, the Cheyenne can't jump us so easy."

"But I'm almost willing to risk that, Sharp," Forsyth replied. "Sheridan granted me a roving commission. I'm not locked in. It's the hostiles I need to find. But, if they find me first . . ."

"Major Forsyth, I figure with some fifty men riding with you, there's no way the Cheyenne will let you catch up with a small war-party on the prowl."

"What do you mean, Grover? I've made up my mind to find and attack the Indians, no matter what the odds."

"Just what I mean . . . the Cheyenne will let you follow the trail they want you to follow."

"And . . . if I follow the trail they want me to?"

"It won't mean you finding the Cheyenne."

"No?"

"It'll mean Roman Nose closing the back-door on that trap he has planned for us."

Chapter 11

*T*hree days ago Seamus had grown weary of this chase. Up before first light every morning. Out of the saddle long after sundown. Often too weary to do much more than rub down The General with a handful of dry grass, hang the blanket off the Grimsley, and stuff a bite or two of bacon and hard-tack down his gullet. Most nights he never waited for coffee to boil. Much less having any time to talk with Liam O'Roarke.

Donegan's uncle was one of the first out in the pre-dawn darkness, and one of the last ones back in come twilight's hand across the land. Never leaving much time to talk. To say what needed saying. To heal the wounds left festering through these years. All Seamus wanted was to see this hunt done as quickly as Forsyth would have it. Over and done with, only then did Seamus figure he could find the truth behind the answers Uncle Liam had reluctantly given him.

Now nearing late afternoon on the seventh day out of Fort Wallace, 16 September, Seamus let his mind rove over the long days of Forsyth's march as easily as his eyes roved across the brown and umber plains rolling like an endless, swelling sea-desert, and he adrift upon it with memories of that cursed ship that brought him to these shores.

At dawn on the twelfth, O'Roarke, Beecher and Grover had led the scouts north from the banks of Beaver Creek, a tributary of the Republican River. Northwest still. They were fortunate those first few days out of Sheridan, running on to antelope and buffalo from time to time to supplement their diminishing store of beans, bacon, and bread.

By the afternoon of the thirteenth, Sharp Grover's eyes had found sign of a faint trail. Forsyth and Beecher determined it was better than nothing, so they put O'Roarke and Grover on the scent. The spoor of the Cheyenne led the frontiersmen across Short Nose Creek, the stream old Pierre Trudeau said the Sioux had long called the Prairie Dog.

The next morning, the scouts continued following the wisp of a trail toward the dim, hazy line of green in the shimmering distance.

"That'll be the Republican itself," Jack Stillwell piped up.

"How you know?" Bob Smith asked caustically.

"Heard Grover and the rest talking 'bout it during the noon stop. He and that big Irishman figured we was getting close," Jack replied, his eyes flicking to Donegan as he said it.

"Them two ought to know, Mr. Smith," Seamus declared, wishing it were so. He wanted something cool to drink. Not the tepid, brackish water grown warm in his canteen, rocking as it hung from the saddle.

Up ahead from the hoof of every animal rose a yellow dust, spinning into the late sun like golden cobwebs. Alkali enough to eat a man's eyelids off, and as fine as baby talc.

"I eat any more dust on the bleeming trail," Donegan joked, "I'll have enough to apply for territorial status meself!"

Yet more than something cool and wet, Seamus hungered for shade. Just a little piece, where a man could close his eyes for a wink or two without having to doze off, listening to the sound of squeaking saddle leather and bit-chains, the curses of men and the complaints of balky mules.

"What day you make it, Irishman?"

Seamus eyed Smith, calculating. "I make it the fourteenth, me friend. Looks to be we're stopping for a spell."

"Times like this, Irishman—I wonder why I wasn't a foot soldier."

"Can those dogs of yours stand it better than your arse?"

" 'Bout now I'm willing to give 'em that chance!"

Seamus dropped wearily to the ground along the bank of the Republican with the others.

"Break out, boys! Ten minutes to water. Drink enough to go on but don't make them mounts loggy!" McCall barked his orders.

After patting The General a moment, Donegan pointed himself away from the rest of the group toward an inviting thicket of willow and alder. Just the spot where the horse could drink of the cool waters in the Republican's south fork, and he could close his eyes in the shade.

Finding his way blocked by the tangle of willow, Seamus moved on upstream a few yards and again attempted to force his way down to the bank. Frustrated and struggling, the Irishman finally studied the thick copse of alder. Willow branches had been tied together with rawhide whangs, forming a crude dome on which someone had laid drying stalks of the long swamp-grass bordering the Republican.

He dropped to his knee and inspected the ground. A piece here and a piece there, some threads had been snagged from the wool blankets thrown over the entire structure for protection against night winds and sudden rain-showers. In a crude circle the grassy floor itself lay trampled.

Seamus sniffed the grass. The same smell of greasy hides and smoked skins that he had learned to identify with Jim Bridger on the trek to the Crow almost two years past. Much the same smell of the Crow lodge where he had slept the winter through with Eyes Talking.

"Liam!"

He watched O'Roarke turn, then amble over. "I been meaning to talk with you, Seamus. Believe me, there's much to tell——"

"It can wait for now, Uncle." He stepped back, pointing. "Have you a look at what your nephew found."

Liam immediately went to his knees, inspecting it. Then forced his way through to the bank, crouching as he searched for prints. When he came back, his grin was as big as the bells of St. Mary's.

He slammed young Donegan on the back. "Good work, lad! Damned good work!" Liam leveled his voice at the main bunch spreading out to find themselves bits and pieces of shade downstream.

"Major Forsyth! Bring Beecher and Grover with you . . . on the double!"

The trio trotted up, followed by a growing crowd of the interested.

"This will just about make your day for you, Major," Liam piped up.

Forsyth and the rest inspected the place themselves. "Good God, O'Roarke! This can't be that old. The grass is still fresh on top."

O'Roarke smiled. "Thank me nephew, Major. He found it." He laid a huge arm round Donegan's shoulder. "It's him you'd be thanking."

Forsyth nodded to Seamus, but his eyes went back to Liam. "Tell me what this means."

"You're right that it's fresh, Major." Grover got to his feet from his inspection of tracks and the willows. "I figure they used it last night."

"Last night?" Beecher roared. "You hear that, boys?"

There erupted a spontaneous cheer from the scouts assembled at the fringe of the creekside willow.

"Last night, Major," Grover went on. "I figure two of 'em. How you set with that, Liam?"

"Two of 'em it is, Grover. Appears they're on foot. Crossed the river. Heading north."

"Right where we thought they'd be all the time, fellas," Forsyth chimed in.

"Where you was counting the bastards going, Major," O'Roarke added.

"These two left here at dawn today?" Forsyth asked.

Liam nodded. "I figure so." And he pointed to the trampled grass leading from the shelter to the riverbank. "Appears the tracks were made only this morning before the dew dried off the grass. But I'll know for certain when we've been on their trail a wee bit more."

Forsyth grinned. "What we waiting for, gentlemen? We have a trail growing warmer all the time. What say we put some more ground behind us before the light's gone for the day?"

With a little grumbling from the men, McCall set the columns back to the march. The eagerness of some to find the Cheyenne was rewarded a scant two miles farther when Grover found the campsite of three mounted warriors. Ashes in the firepit proved that the three had spent last night warming themselves round this fire.

Now the major had five to track. The first pair had in all likelihood hooked up with the trio not long after leaving the Republican. The trail showed that two of the war-ponies were carrying an extra burden as the warriors pointed their noses ever north by west.

Not long after leaving behind the small ravine where the trio had slept, smaller trails began to converge from both northeast and southwest. Across the hours of that fourteenth day of September and into the next, the scouts watched in eerie silence as the trail widened beneath the relentless summer sun, a trail taking on a life of its own.

Wider and wider it became a well-scoured road that led up to the forks of the Republican River, fording to the north bank, then continued upstream. A large pony-herd as well as stolen cattle were being driven along with the march. Hundreds of travois poles had scarred the earth in their passing. And the unshod hooves of burdened ponies told of many families now joining their warriors.

Some of the men began to murmur among themselves that this wide, well-beaten trail of women and children might not be so good an omen after all. Now with their families joining them, the warriors were forced to slow their march. Which meant Forsyth's scouts would in all likelihood catch them much sooner than expected. Most sobering of all, with their families soon to be threatened by the fifty, in all probability the warriors would turn about and fight all the harder.

Muted talk rumbled round the small fires that night. As he soaked his hard-bread in his coffee, Seamus refused to join in arguing among the scouts. He lay warming his blankets between Smith and Stillwell by the time Liam O'Roarke returned from Forsyth's fire.

"You 'wake, Nephew?"

"Barely."

Liam quietly pushed his huge frame beneath his blanket, inching backward until he lay against Donegan, so the two would share each other's warmth.

"Tomorrow we march down into the valley of the Arickaree, young Seamus."

"Aye," he replied groggily.

"Grover and Beecher both been arguing with me." Liam went on to explain quietly as the camp began to snore around them. "They said we'd be in the valley of Delaware Creek. I told 'em they was daft. It's the Arickaree we'll see tomorrow."

"Does it make any difference, Uncle?" Seamus inquired, closing his eyes at last to the spinning stars in the night-sky overhead.

After a moment, Liam answered. "S'pose it doesn't make a tinker's difference, Seamus. Whatever name a man chooses to put on that stream, make no mistake of it—we'll be in the very gut of Cheyenne hunting ground."

O'Roarke said no more. And within moments, Donegan was surprised to hear his uncle's throaty snore. Just as he was closing his eyes once more and for good, he was greeted with the quiet, Southern drawl from a bedroll close by.

"G'night, Seamus Donegan."

The next morning, the scouts again took up the well-beaten trail, watching as more and more smaller trails converged with the widening road. The grumbling among some of the scouts grew in volume.

By noon-halt of the fifteenth, a small self-appointed group approached Forsyth and Beecher, demanding an audience for their grievance. At the same coffee-fire sat Grover, O'Roarke, and Seamus Donegan.

"Major, we'd have a word with you," announced the spokesman as the group ground to a halt behind him.

"Smith, isn't it?" Forsyth asked, taking a blade of dry grass from his sun-chapped lips.

"Yeah. Me and the others," he began, flinging a thumb over his shoulder, "we been talking."

Forsyth inched off his elbow and slowly stood. "I figured you had, Smith. Last few days, in fact, you've made yourself a real pain in my saddle-muscles. So, what have you boys got to say?"

"If we keep following this village, we'll be staring some pretty nasty odds in the face, Major."

"I won't argue with you there, Smith."

The Southerner's eyes narrowed as if he believed he had the major to his way of things now. "There comes a time they decide to attack us with them odds, no way our bunch can make a decent show of it."

"I see."

"Happens we don't think you do see, Major." Smith plunged ahead. "Men like us don't mind fighting Injuns . . . maybe even dying. What troubles us most is that we won't make a good show of it. And sometimes, what matters most to a man is that in his dying . . ."

"——he makes a good account of himself, Mr. Smith?" Liam O'Roarke suddenly entered the conversation.

The Confederate's eyes snapped down to the Irish scout. Harsh and cold blue chips lit with some inner fire. "Damn right," he barely whispered.

"Gentlemen," Forsyth said as he took a step toward Smith, "the decision has been made. I'll remind you I'm in command here. But if you care to listen, I'll explain for all of you."

The major waited a moment longer while more of the civilians came to a rest around Smith's group. He took the blade of grass from his bleeding lips.

"You fellas are assuming no more risk than I am. Or Lieutenant Beecher. We'll all sink or swim together. Beyond that, I remember no man among you being forced to march up to the recruiting table and give his mark in signing on. Any of you forced against your will?"

Forsyth waited an appropriate time, his eyes slewing the bunch. Seamus found that few men would look the major in the eye.

"For the most part, fellas—we're here. In the heart of Cheyenne country. And since we're here, there is less danger to going on, staying on the heels of a village that from all indications knows we are following it."

"I think it's time we turned round!" Smith suddenly barked. "Turn round and head back to Wallace while we still can."

"Head back to Wallace?" Sergeant McCall exploded as he leaped to his feet. "The red bastards would jump our tails!"

Smith turned on him. "Let the army do the Injun fighting!"

"That's what you was hired good money to do—seventy-five goddamned dollars a month, Smith!" McCall roared.

"And me? A sergeant like me mucking in the same shit as you—I still draw my shitty twenty-three dollars, month in and month out."

The Confederate smiled. "It's your army, McCall. I didn't fight for Lincoln's Union."

"Gentlemen." Forsyth stepped between them as the sergeant was about to lunge for the rebel. "Most all of you served one side or the other during the war. So you'll know in your gut just how important it is that you obey my orders at this point, deep inside enemy territory."

Seamus listened as more than half of the scouts grudgingly agreed.

"I'm of a mind to release those of you who don't want to continue," Forsyth admitted. "But, my conscience would bother me, knowing the odds against you making it back to Wallace now that the bands appear to know we're on their trail."

"Some of us take our goddamned chances of it."

The major wheeled on the Confederate. "You don't have that choice, Smith! I simply won't release a man among you . . . because at this point it would be as good as signing that man's death-warrant."

Chapter 12

*T*here were none braver than he.

Though not a chief, Roman Nose stood before his people as an acknowledged leader in war.

In this *Drying Grass Moon,* he listened to the excited voices announcing the approach of Sioux riders, coming hard from the southwest.

A strange direction, he considered. To come riding hard into this Cheyenne village along the Arickaree, skin lodges breasting against the summer sky, huge pony herds dropping fragrant offal on the surrounding prairie, watched over by young pony-boys. Three of the youths came tearing into the village carrying the news of the Sioux riders, their small, brown feet hammering pony ribs into a frantic race.

Upstream from this Cheyenne camp stood two large villages of Brule Sioux under the bellicose Pawnee Killer. It was The Killer himself who had rubbed up against George Armstrong Custer's 7th Cavalry one summer gone now, when the short-grass time made the Lakota war-ponies sleek and fast. Now the Brule had joined the Cheyenne, mostly Dog Soldiers under Tall Bull and White Horse. Nearby camped a small band of Northern Arapahos who traveled in the shadow of Roman Nose.

The bands had come one together with the rest to hunt buffalo here, where the great herds gathered in the great valley of the Plum River, what the white man called his Republican. Last moon, while celebrating their annual sundance on a tributary of the Plum called Beaver Creek, roaming scouts from the villages had reported spotting Forsyth's plainsmen. From that point the bands quickly migrated to the northwest. *Surely,* the tribal leaders debated, *if we have seen white scouts on our trail, close behind will come the long columns of soldiers.*

Aggravating, yes. On came the small band of white men, like a persistent badger intent on clawing his prey from its hole. Following . . . forever following.

"They have entered this valley?" Roman Nose asked the first young Sioux horseman who galloped to the center of the Cheyenne camp.

The youth nodded, breathless still. Explaining that he and a handful of others had been out for several days with a larger war-party of Sioux, they had decided to turn back two days ago, intent on returning to their village. On their way across the plains, the young warriors discovered the dust rising above Forsyth's command in the shimmering distance beyond the dry, rolling hills.

"You are sure these are whitemen?" Roman Nose inquired, his eyes narrowing beneath the heavy brow. "Sure these are not your buffalo hunters?"

The hands of the young Sioux flew before him as he spoke in sign. "These are not buffalo hunters. This is a band of fighting men. All carry many weapons. On strong horses. With only four pack-animals."

Roman Nose glanced quickly at the swelling crowd of Cheyenne warriors gathering round him in the morning light. "How is it they did not see you?"

The hands signed again. "We rode wide around, Roman Nose. And once out of danger, far beyond the hills where the whitemen marched, we raced back here with the news. Now we must go tell Pawnee Killer and the rest."

"Wait," The Nose signed. "I will go with you as well. This is momentous news for us all. Sioux and Cheyenne must once again talk of battle with the whiteman."

Around them all the Cheyenne and Dog Soldier camps came alive as they waited for ponies to be brought up, the entire village throbbing to the exciting news of the whitemen coming. A force small enough that this time every warrior knew they would not merely protect their villages while women, children, and old ones escaped onto the prairie as they had done when Long Hair attacked last summer.

This time, the men exhorted one another, *this time we will attack and wipe these half-a-hundred off the face of The Mother of All Things.*

Turning from the tribal leaders to the milling crowd of onlookers, The Nose found the one as tall as he.

"Nibsi!" he shouted.

Immediately the big mulatto knifed his way through the throng to stand before the war-chief. "You call," he replied in his unsure Cheyenne.

Roman Nose smiled, the wide, white teeth glimmering in the mid-morning sunshine. "The others you see preparing for war. I will go counsel with the Sioux of Pawnee Killer so that we can move in force to attack."

"Do I come with you this battle, Roman Nose?" Black Jack inquired, his honey-colored face beading with anticipation.

Roman Nose laughed lustily, head thrown back. "Yes, Nibsi! This time you ride with Roman Nose. It is as I saw in my medicine dream at the sundance on Beaver Creek. You and I will together make this valley our medicine place."

"Our medicine place," Jack O'Neill repeated, as if enjoying the taste of those words on his tongue. "The . . . the white man comes?"

"Many," he answered. "Half-a-hundred. Some are wearing scalps that soon will hang from your belt."

One hand Jack laid on the butt of his old percussion pistol. The other rested on the wide belt-knife given him by an affectionate squaw. His eyebrows newly plucked, his cheeks clean-shaven and as smooth as the inside of Emmy's milky thighs, Jack O'Neill's face lit up with a strange light. "My first scalps! *Aiyee-yii-yii!*"

"Prepare yourself, little brother," Roman Nose advised as he turned away. "I will return soon to lead our warriors in the slaughter."

As the acknowledged leaders of the Dog Soldiers, White Horse and Tall Bull led the way to the Sioux camp with the young Sioux warriors in the lead. Roman Nose rode behind them all.

"Make ready!" Pawnee Killer shouted, standing outside

his lodge when the delegation rode into camp, announcing the presence of white men. "No more shall we wait for the soldiers to find and surround us as did Long Hair last summer, burning our lodges and winter meat. This time we attack the whiteman!"

Instantly the Sioux camps buzzed with the electricity of the news. While the Cheyenne delegation joined Pawnee Killer for a brief meal, the young warriors in all camps stripped off their hunting clothes and donned their finest war regalia. At this warm season, most wore nothing more than moccasins and breechclout. Yet what marked each individual's battle costume was not the clothing, but rather the headdress or simple hair-covering, perhaps the body and face-paint, or those decorations now lavished on a favored warpony.

Small, fleet, wide-chested little cayuses that would now carry their owners into battle as the Sioux and Cheyenne butchered that small band of white men foolish enough to ride into the steamy gut of Indian hunting ground.

Instead of the white men stalking the villages, Forsyth's plainsmen had become the quarry.

By the time the masses of Sioux had dressed and made their medicine, assembling to ride south where they would join with Cheyenne warriors, the sun had fallen past midsky. A young, flat-nosed warrior announced their readiness at the doorway of Pawnee Killer's lodge.

"We ride!" the Sioux chief exclaimed, indicating the time had come for leaving.

The immense Brule village hummed and shrieked with activity as the war-chiefs emerged from The Killer's lodge. Young boys still scurried here and there, bringing war-ponies in from the herds.

Women chattered loudly, no one in particular listening, as they brought forth the weapons their men would use. Out into the sunshine of this battle day came the short horn or Osage-orange bows, skin quivers filled with long iron-tipped arrows fletched with owl feathers. Axes, knives, and war-clubs—some stone, others wood, a few nail-studded like archaic mace. Long, grooved lances, many more than ten feet long, tiny grooves radiating from the huge iron spear-points to drain a victim's blood. Here and there, the afternoon light glinted from a firearm, either pistol or rifle. White-man weapons bought with blood beyond the Lodge Trail Ridge when many of these same warriors had butchered the hundred-in-the-hand.

Last into the light of a battle day were the shields, pulled ceremonially from their hide wrappings by the women. Gently each wife smoothed feathers and tiny brass cones, brushed a finger over the magic symbols painted across the bull-hide surface, stroked the tiny weasel skull or a badger jaw, elk milk-teeth or a buffalo scrotum. Potent totems. Powerful medicine evoked come this time of war. Come now this time to slaughter the half-a-hundred.

As the ponies were brought up to the Cheyenne delegation, Roman Nose turned slightly, greeted with the fragrance of stewing meat and fry-bread pungent on the afternoon breeze. As was custom at this time of year, the women cooked outside, usually beneath a hide awning, so that the interior of the lodge was not heated beyond anyone's endurance.

What he saw as he stood there beside Pawnee Killer's lodge caused The Nose to feel his throat constrict.

Three squaws huddled round two steaming kettles where they had boiled the hump-meat the Sioux chief had just served his guests. A third kettle crackled with spitting grease, where the women fried their bread made with flour stolen from raids on the white man's roads and settlements.

The big Cheyenne's eyes narrowed as he was handed the reins to his war-pony. He watched the old Sioux woman repeatedly pull the fry-bread from her kettle . . . impaled on the tines of an iron fork!

Quietly, Roman Nose began to keen as his eyes fell to the ground. He turned slowly, then clambered aboard his pony like a man touched by the moon. Drunk with grief.

"What is this?" Tall Bull demanded, pulling his pony alongside the great war leader's. "Why are you crying as if a relative had been killed?"

"Yes!" agreed White Horse. "It will be the whiteman and his soldiers who will this day be killed!"

Yet, they both stopped their chiding, reading on the face of the tall warrior between them the unmistakable truth.

"My medicine-helper long ago instructed me not to eat food that had been touched with the whiteman's iron."

"Yes . . . all Cheyenne know of The Nose's powerful medicine calling," Tall Bull asserted. "But, what does——"

"I can use the whiteman's weapons," he went on. "Touch anything with my hands—but not take the food into my body that has been touched by the whiteman's own medicine!"

"What is this you are saying?" White Horse demanded, his own eyes flaring with the first tinge of fear.

"Behold," Roman Nose announced, pointing to the awning where the old Sioux woman dipped her fry-bread from the spitting kettle with a crude iron fork. He turned away without another word, knowing the power of his medicine was gone.

And that his life was now on his fingernails.

For the last few days Forsyth's scouts had been following an Indian trail so wide and deep, to young Jack Stillwell it resembled the scars of a wagon road. From time to time, they had come across a broken lodgepole. Old Trudeau told his young partner the squaws carried extras, replacing a bad travois pole with a new pole. Or they might run across dried strips of discarded buffalo meat, a torn legging, a worn-out moccasin. And always the dry, brittle horse-droppings that stretched at times a full quarter-mile wide across the prairie.

Only today, the sixteenth of September, those pony-droppings did not readily crumble in Sharp Grover's palm, or when rubbed between the immense paws of Liam O'Roarke. More trouble still, no man among them had spotted any game for the past two days along their march. Game hunted away, and driven off. A man didn't have to be a superstitious cuss to know that was a bad sign.

Jack scratched the fuzz on his smooth cheeks and swallowed his apprehension. Reminding himself that no one had yet seen an Indian. Consoling himself that his face showed no more fear than the faces of the older, more proven veterans in the major's command.

Each day young Stillwell grew more proud to be a member of Forsyth's fifty. True, he had to admit, they were a shaggy, ragged, Falstaffian lot, but most remained intent on the task to come. He was like them. Yet, he was not. These farmers burned off their homesteads. These hide hunters hungering for quick, easy money. These Indian-haters eager for a way to even a score. And always, like the ranks of the army itself, Forsyth's ranks were filled with the restless veterans become drifters with no home to return to after the war.

Still, Jack felt more a part of them every day, this company of scouts who talked crudely and spared no graces. They were no different from the men he had known at home, wearing their wide-brimmed, floppy hats that drooped after many soakings, decked in a rag-tag of greasy Indian buckskin or tattered army britches, perhaps a homespun cotton shirt or frayed army tunic.

Stillwell knew in the days to come, he would become a man among these plainsmen. A man among these men.

At noon break, Forsyth halted along a dry creekbed to rest the weary horses. Most of the men stayed near their mounts, fearing an attack. Others sat in the shade of the horse as it ate its fill of the stunted, brittle forage. In small knots, men argued the wisdom of following the swelling Indian road.

"Shit!" hollered Sergeant McCall as he stomped up on one group. "Sooner or later these red bastards will come out and fight us!"

"More'n likely, they'll break camp and skeedaddle fast," offered John Donovan. "Like they done time and again to Hancock and Custer last summer."

"Donovan's right," old Trudeau piped up. "They running from us. Leaving behind what they don't carry."

"Major's gonna be damned angry," McCall whispered, bending over the heads of the group as if sharing a secret with them. "He don't get a crack at this bunch—he's gonna be one mad whelp."

"Major may get his chance yet," Liam O'Roarke offered as he strolled over with his nephew at his side.

"Don't say?" McCall inquired, straightening.

"These Cheyenne don't look all that concerned with our little bunch, Sergeant. Ain't in too much the hurry."

"Liam's got a point," Grover joined in, knocking dust from his boots with blows from a hatbrim. "They ain't acting all that concerned. Like they know a small bunch like us can't do 'em much harm."

"Well, boys—that's just what Forsyth wants that bunch of red buggers to believe, I tell you!" McCall cheered. "Maybeso then they'll stop running and turn around."

"Then what, Sergeant?" Stillwell asked as the group fell quiet.

"Then . . . then we can get down to what we come out to this blazing-hot hell-hole to do . . . once't and for all."

"What's that, McCall?" Trudeau asked the question.

"Kill Injuns, old man. Kill some bloody Indians for Forsyth and Beecher."

"What happens we run out of food?" asked the young Sigmund Shlesinger, stepping forward.

McCall eyed him quickly. "You're the Jew, ain't you?"

"Y-yessir."

The sergeant considered his answer, flicking a look at the piece of shade nearby where Forsyth and Beecher sat in their own discussion. "True, we're sore on supplies, fellas. But we got us salt and coffee. And, all that ammunition as well."

"Sergeant's right," Seamus Donegan said, surprising his uncle as well as others. "Never did take a liking to army salt-pork during the war, I didn't. Better for us to hunt our own game."

"Providing there's game to be had, Nephew," Liam reminded everyone.

Some of the men rose and moved off. Those few who stayed on were as quiet as the shadows sprawled beneath their mounts with the high sun hung in mid-sky.

"Shit, fellas," Sharp Grover cheered, standing and dusting his britches, "we're bound to find game before too long. Not too far up yonder lies the Dry Fork of the Republican."

"That'un called the Arickaree?" John Donovan asked as he stood, working kinks out of his back.

"One the same," Grover replied.

"Major and Beecher both figure the next stream we cross will be Delaware Creek," McCall said to those still listening.

"I know they figure it for the Delaware," Sharp growled, winking at young Jack Stillwell. "But if those two'd listen to their chief of scouts—they'd realize that's the valley of the Arickaree up yonder."

"Arickaree?" Stillwell marched off alongside Grover as the group busted back to their hobbled mounts.

Grover grinned at him. "Arickaree, Jack. Just another small chunk of God-forgot country 'bout as dry as these boots of mine."

"Why we going there, Sharp?"

Grover shook his head. "Damned if I know, Jack. Except that Forsyth knows it's medicine ground to the Cheyenne."

Chapter 13

Seamus watched Forsyth signal a halt, the major's neck craning as he scanned the narrow valley. He pulled the fob from his pocket, cracking open his watch.

"Just past four, Sergeant," the major advised in the hearing of those at the head of the column. "The horses are pretty well done in. Let's make camp down opposite that island in the riverbed."

"Splendid idea," Fred Beecher piped up, slapping a hand across his thigh, knocking free some trail-dust. "This animal under me is turning to paunch-water, Major."

Forsyth said to his sergeant, "Keep the column closed up until we're down by the stream."

"To camp!" McCall hollered, then brought his weary mount around once more, waving an arm and pointing down into the beckoning valley where cottonwoods offered shade and that creekbed might offer a trickle of cool water born of the mountains on the far, far horizon.

Minutes later, as the scouts made camp on the north bank of the Arickaree, Liam O'Roarke and Sharp Grover rode in. After reporting to Forsyth, Liam joined his nephew in digging a firepit where the young Irishman had chosen to bivouac in a grassy swale, just north of the sandy island at the middle of the stream.

"I'll sup with you, then must be gone until after dark. The Indian trail we've followed goes upriver a good many leagues, then turns south by west."

"Sounds like the major's got you doing more riding."

"That's the cut of it, Seamus. Grover, we two. Make no mistake about it"—and he paused, gazing directly into the younger man's eyes—"Sharp senses well as I we're practically hammering up the backsides of the red buggers."

Seamus licked his sunburned lips, sensing an unfamiliar apprehension in his uncle's voice. For a moment he regarded the low, red-rimmed bluffs just to the south, accented now with the sinking sun. "I been too damned close to red backsides afore . . . and too many times to tell."

"You've told me of the Crazy Woman, Seamus," Liam said, scooping sand out of their firepit. "And the time you rode into that ambush trying to save that foolish lieutenant's life."

Seamus snorted. "Bored you already?"

Liam roared with laughter, quick and ready. "No, Nephew. Sweet saints of us all! But when you told me of that red bastard's arrow pinning your leg to a saddle . . . and finding yourself pinned down in that hayfield corral while the soldier boys twiddled their thumbs—them's the stories worth the stuff of legends, Seamus."

"When will you be sharing your stories with me, Uncle?"

O'Roarke quit scooping, but his eyes did not leave the widening hole. "The time has come, young Seamus. Yes."

Liam raised his eyes, gazing into Donegan's. "Time tonight to tell you of lost loves and a brother's hate. Of the discovery of gold that trickled so many, many times through me fingers that I lost count. Time to tell you of hiring on as a paid gun for a man who calls himself a god out here in all of this splendor." O'Roarke wagged his knife in the air, his lips for the moment pressed in remembrance.

"You speak of leaving Deseret, Liam?"

"That . . . and my coming to Wallace to find you, Seamus!" His voice suddenly had a happier ring to it as he slapped a big hand on his nephew's shoulder, smiling.

Donegan was struck with the bleak feeling that O'Roarke considered his time among the Saints in Salt Lake City too fresh and raw a wound to discuss.

"Tonight, Uncle?"

"You've me word on it, Seamus."

"We can talk at last of you going home to your sister?"

O'Roarke sighed, his eyes gone misty, a wistful look there.

"Erin. Sweet, green, cool land of our birth, Seamus Donegan. Yes, lad—let's talk of home. And talk of why you let a woman get away from you."

Liam rose from the sandy ground, taking up the reins to his horse as he stepped wearily into the saddle. "Let's you and me talk of affairs of the heart, Seamus. How foolish or crazy can be a man in love . . . yet fool or crazed—I tell you this, Nephew. Do what your soul tells you. Go where your heart leads."

Seamus stood, silently watching O'Roarke's back until his uncle disappeared upstream.

Then he whispered, "It will be good . . . good to talk of these things . . . after waiting so many, many years, Uncle."

By and large, most of the riverbank was grassy, providing some of the best grazing in many days for the horses and pack-mules. Donegan stripped The General of the Grimsley, finding some brush to lay the thick saddle-blanket upon so that it would dry, never a problem on these high, arid plains. After gathering kindling and driftwood, and getting a small fire started, Seamus curried both horses with handfuls of the fragrant grass.

Here and there a few men moved out from camp in several directions as McCall dispatched his first watch for the coming evening. He read his assignments from a small ledger he kept inside his shirt, next to the itchy long-handles that kept a man warm come sundown on these high plains. Despite their fatigue and hunger, most of the scouts appeared in high spirits, gratified to make camp earlier than had been Forsyth's practice on this long march.

Seamus stepped to the swamp-willows and plum thicket. He unbuttoned the fly on his cavalry britches, listening to the dry leaves rustle on the cottonwoods abounding on the creekbank. As he watered the dry ground, he gazed over the umber and orange light brushing the gentle slopes of a ridge almost due west of the sandy island in the middle of the stream.

Some one hundred seventy feet wide, the island had been recently formed owing to a gravel rift upstream at its head where the stream parted itself. Along either side of the island approximately fifteen feet of cool water flowed no more than half a foot deep, gently gurgling for two hundred fifty feet before rejoining at the far end. Sage grass and bunch-weed grew at the west extreme, while a thicket of swamp-willow, alder, and some plum dotted the center, all of it almost as tall as a man.

Then something cold grabbed him as his eyes snagged on the lone cottonwood at the far east end of the island.

Almost like a man it stood. The cottonwood facing the onslaught of spring run-off like a man rising to face the charge of Cheyenne horsemen.

Seamus blinked the vision clear. He shuddered, remembering another hot summer day on the plains of Montana Territory when the lathered-up warriors flung themselves at the hay-cutters' tiny corral.

As he turned back to his fire from the plum-thicket at the riverbank, Donegan gazed a moment to the north, studying the low hill beyond the bluffs rising some forty to fifty feet in height. And made mental note that from there someone could see a good piece of the country roundabout. If nothing else, after dinner it would make a good climb. From there, a man could look down on this part of the valley, and see everything.

Forsyth had led them to this place through a narrow gorge that opened itself into a valley some two miles in length, not nearly as wide. While the country to the south of the stream sloped away gently without much of any obstruction to view, the bluffs and hills rising behind the scouts' camp gave Seamus a feeling of walls and cantonments.

"Major figures we'll be up to our assholes in Injuns by midday tomorrow," Bob Smith announced with a dry drawl as Donegan marched back into camp. The Confederate trotted alongside to get in step.

Seamus nodded and kept on walking. Something about the Confederate's eyes, like blue chips lit with a strange fire. "O'Roarke says the same."

For a moment more the rebel soldier glared at Donegan's back before he grumbled, "You sure ain't sociable this evenin', are you?"

"Hungry," Donegan muttered.

"Damn you, anyway," Smith mumbled and moved off,

hurling his oaths in all directions. "Gawddamned Irish mick anyway . . ."

As Seamus settled by his fire, John Donovan marched up, delivering supper rations.

"You're commissary tonight, Donovan?"

" 'At's right, my friend!" he cheered, dropping off a small hunk of salt-pork, four pieces of crusty hard-bread, and four hand-scoops of dried beans he poured in Donegan's up-turned hat.

"That's not all you owe me," Seamus growled without malice. "There'll be two for dinner. Leave me his share as well."

"I just did, you idiot!"

He stared at the portions in his hat. "This? To feed two grown men?"

"All we got," Donovan explained as he continued on his rounds. "Major says we empty all the haversacks tonight. Tomorrow we scare up our own forage and game."

Seamus wagged his head, sensing his empty stomach growl. "And me . . . I could be supping on Jennie Wheatley's fluffy biscuits and juicy kidney pie, a big hunk of her flaky crust floating in a sea of cobbler. Instead, I have to eat this . . . and look at me uncle's ugly face!"

Donovan disappeared chuckling beyond the swamp-willow and alder, off on his rounds. A cold prickling at the saber scar caused Seamus to whirl about. Nothing but the sinking of the sun, and that lone cottonwood, like a sentinel on that island.

His heart beat faster with the unexplained dump of dread into his blood, worrying him as well.

If nothing else, this bunch can make a stand of it there, Seamus thought, almost mumbling the words to himself. Perhaps to hear the sound of something more than the dry rustle of the breeze through the brush and the anvil-pounding of his own pulse at his ears.

Nothing on that island to stop a bullet, though, he brooded. Brush . . . about like the hayfield corral last summer.

That fight had convinced some of the experienced plainsmen that Indian warfare was changing. No longer did the Sioux and Cheyenne practice war as they had in the past: individual sniping runs jabbing away at their enemy once they had the white man pinned down. Now it seemed, at both the hayfield and wagon-box fights that the warriors on the northern plains had learned to fight en masse. No longer did individual warriors hurl themselves suicidally at white defenders.

Now the Sioux and Cheyenne had seen the wisdom in massed charges that would attempt to overwhelm the enemy quickly.

As Seamus watched his strong coffee brew, he gnawed on the raw salt-pork and hard-bread, washing it down with gulps from his canteen. From time to time he heard guards hollering to one another near the herd where the horses grazed, hobbled for the evening. Come full dark, however, Forsyth had ordered the animals into camp, the long pin driven deep into the sandy soil and the picket-rope double-knotted for security.

Jumpy and not knowing why, the Irishman strode off to check on The General while his coffee cooled off the flames. He brought the big gray back to his lonely bivouac early. He would pick grass for the horse nearby if he had to. Something about this camp; that island had given him the spooks.

A smart man always kept his horse near in country like this. A land the Cheyenne and Sioux hunted, from where they would never retreat. A land where the white man found himself not welcome in the least.

Out of the night-sounds Donegan listened to the quiet footsteps of a man inching along the sand and grass, hugging close to the swamp-willow and alder that prospered beside the creek. As they neared his bivouac, the steps halted, waiting, then resumed their stealthy work.

Seamus rose slowly from his lonely fire, intent on finding out who kept to the brush in the deepening darkness.

At that moment instead, a familiar voice harkened from across the camp, opposite the willows.

"Like some company this evening, Mr. Donegan?"

Jack Stillwell strode into the light, tugging on the reins to his mount.

The Irishman sighed, more at ease, yet glanced once over his shoulder at the nearby alders. "Love to have you spend the night, friend. Picket your horse over there where there's still some good grass. Then join me in this hearty kettle-brew the army calls coffee."

Stillwell grinned like it would crack his young face. "McCall's got old Pete out standing watch. I got . . . well——"

"Was lonesome meself, Jack. Sit there."

"You see the lights on the hills, Mr. Donegan?"

Seamus tensed. "What lights?"

"Lookee yonder." Jack pointed toward the ridges in the west. "Like torch-lights."

"I don't see a thing now," Donegan admitted.

Jack shook his head. "Half dozen of us saw 'em while back. Culver hisself was first to spot 'em. Major figures it's lights from the Injun camp everybody says we'll run onto tomorrow."

He poured a tin of the steaming coffee for Stillwell. "Major's run out of time, Jack."

"And us," Stillwell added, "we've run out of trail to follow."

Time passed as they talked quietly, watching the bright stars slowly wheel overhead until moonrise. When Seamus finally realized his uncle would not be returning anytime soon, he pushed forward the kettle he had left warming near the fire.

"You hungry, Jack?"

"Ain't your uncle gotta eat?"

"Major's got him and Grover out sniffing round for h'athens. If you're hungry, it's yours."

Jack swallowed hard, licked his lips. "Ain't been eating well, Mr. Donegan. Old Trudeau somehow manages to get hisself the best cut of the sowbelly and a extra tack or two. Always got more to eat than me, it seems."

"Eat up, Jack. No telling when the lot of us will eat this good again."

As he let the fire grow low, sinking to coals, Seamus watched Stillwell scoop up boiled beans with his fingers, gnawing at half-cooked pork and crumbling hard-bread. Without much further said between them, the Irishman laid out his bedroll, then patted the ground beside him. The youngster was there to share the warmth of their bodies without delay. On these high plains at this time of the year, the days could fry a man's brains for him beneath the crown of his hat. Yet the nights might freeze him every bit as quickly. The prairie rendered itself quickly to the cold cloak of night. Beneath their communal blankets, Donegan and Stillwell fell quickly to sleep, listening to the horses cropping the dry grass, the snores of the others, and the faint gurgling of the nearby stream.

Sleep came a lot harder to their leader that dark night beneath a skimpy, thumbnail moon. Time and again the thirty-one-year-old Forsyth tossed his blanket aside and prowled through camp, speaking in a whisper here, then there, visiting his sentries throughout the night and into the small hours of morning. Almost obsessed with a goading sensation that he stood within striking distance of his goal. In reach, his chance to prove himself to Sheridan.

Knowing that if he did not achieve his objective of stinging the Cheyenne this time out, Custer would very likely become the general's favorite come the winter campaign that Sheridan was in the process of planning for the whole of Indian Territory.

Forsyth ached to have a crack at the Cheyenne. If only a small war-party.

More important, he had to get them to stop running, turn and fight. Sheridan would have a victory. And Forsyth would enjoy Sheridan's favor once more, a favor in the wain for some time now as Custer grew more and more flamboyant in his dress and his campaigns.

He shuddered with the morning cold as he paced one end of the camp to the other, oft-times gazing at the sandy island bathed in starlight. In the hills and craggy ridges behind their bivouac, a coyote set up a serenade. A second took up the chorus.

From the sound of things, he believed he was the only two-legged thing moving about on the prairie. Little could he know how wrong he was.

Although, Maj. George A. Forsyth was entirely correct in his hopeful estimation of the enemy.

The Sioux and Cheyenne were no longer running.

Chapter 14

By the time Roman Nose, Tall Bull, and White Horse had led the stirred-up Sioux warriors south to the Dog Soldier camp, overhead the sun was racing fast for its western sleep.

As the war-chiefs gazed over the combined forces of Cheyenne, Sioux, and Arapaho warriors, numbering more than a thousand horsemen, they reluctantly gave in to the falling sun. No man in fear of his own soul would consider fighting at night. For if a warrior were himself killed during a battle after the sun had disappeared from the sky, his spirit would forever roam this earth, unable to spend his forever days in *Seyan.*

"Our warriors ride before the sun climbs out of its bed, Nibsi," the tall war-leader declared as he slid from the back of his pony.

"Not now, Roman Nose?" Jack O'Neill asked, feeling the disappointment.

The Nose shook his head. "Come," he directed.

Jack obeyed, following the warrior into the small lodge of Roman Nose. He had no need of anything larger. With no wife, his furnishings were spartan to the point of poverty. Yet, the great war-leader had everything he desired: the respect of his people. That, and the fear he elicited in his enemies.

"I . . . I have never been asked to your lodge," Jack explained as he sat where Roman Nose indicated.

"In my youth, the water-spirits instructed me to remain

alone . . . never taking a wife. Instead, all *Shahiyena* are
my family. I must do everything for their good, Nibsi. Live
only for their protection."

Jack watched him remove a bandoleer of brass cartridges
from his shoulder, marveling at the flexing, tensing, rippling
musculature of the man.

"Start a fire, Nibsi. We will eat."

As they waited for the kettle to come to a boil, both men
stared into the swaying flames. Outside, the village took on a
festive atmosphere. With news of the white men coming,
every man older than sixteen summers had prepared for battle, bringing out his weapons. Most of the firearms possessed
by the warriors had been spoils of the Fetterman Massacre—
single-shot muzzle-loading Springfield muskets. Only a
handful owned repeaters, captured in recent raids on the
white man's roads.

In this village of Dog Soldiers the Cheyenne hosted visiting Sioux as all warriors reveled this night before resuming
their march to wipe out the half-a-hundred. Word had it this
evening that the fighting force following the villages had
camped no more than ten miles away. Within easy reach
before the sun rose on the ground they would splatter with
white blood.

On every lip this night was talk of the cold-time fight when
Crazy Horse had lured the soldiers out of their fort far north
in Red Cloud's country. On this occasion, however, there
would be no need to seduce the soldiers into the ambush. To
surround and attack the half-a-hundred would be more than
easy, everyone cheered. Like squashing a tick grown plump
and lazy between one's fingers. Watching the blood trickle
and ooze over one's hand.

"I have sworn to stop the smoke-belching medicine horse
that rides on the iron tracks," Roman Nose finally declared,
his face beaded with diamonds of sweat from the fire's heat.
"Together with the Dog Soldier chiefs, we Cheyenne had
planned to join Pawnee Killer's Sioux in a great raid against
the whiteman's settlements this summer-going. Since the
greening of the first grass, we have planned for this sweep
through the whiteman's villages—the coming of the first full
moon after the first frosts have licked the prairie ponds with
ice."

"I can go as well?" Jack asked, grown excited.

He nodded, smiling sadly. The strong, white teeth gleaming in the firelight. "Of course, Nibsi. Unless . . . unless you choose to take another path of vengeance."

"Another path?"

"I will explain soon enough," Roman Nose cheered, easing Jack's sudden apprehension. "In these great raids the *Shahiyena* will ride to the east in bands of fifty to a hundred warriors at most. Scattering out to do our killing. Leaving no whiteman alive, carrying his women and children away with us. Burning the whiteman's lodges. Taking all his horses and slow-buffalo for our own."

Jack felt the tingle of real excitement race down his spine like January icewater in the pumphouse back in Georgia. "We will be strong once more, and drive the whiteman back, will we not, Roman Nose?"

"For but a short time will our two-times-a-hundred raid and kill and burn, Nibsi. While that full moon shrinks to half its size. Then all warrior bands will turn from their destruction and journey north, to the land where Red Cloud himself defends our ancient hunting grounds, kept free of the whiteman. No more will the soldiers bother us there."

"Because of the snow and cold of *Winter Man?*"

"No," he answered, then smiled sadly again. "Though the whiteman knows not how to fight in the snow. Instead, the soldiers have learned their lesson. Instead, word comes from the northern country that Red Cloud has won. The soldiers are leaving the forts along his road leading into the land of the Sparrowhawk people where the crazed whitemen dig for the yellow rocks."

"The army is giving up the Bozeman Road, Roman Nose?" Jack asked, astonished.

"It is true. From the dirt fort on the Bighorn . . . to the Piney Woods fort, clear down to the dirt-walled fort on the Powder River. Our prayers to the Earth-Maker have been answered at last! Red Cloud has won!"

"Then the *Shahiyena* has won as well!"

"If the whiteman had continued his attacks on our hunting ground," The Nose explained, his voice gone grave, "the *Shahiyena* would become as few as the leaves of the trembling aspen in the cold moons . . . leaves clinging desperately to the shivering trees."

"The whiteman is a powerful devil, Roman Nose." Jack spoke every bit as gravely. "He and his soldiers are as many as the grasshoppers in this *Drying Grass Moon* now on this land."

Roman Nose laid his Winchester repeater across his thighs, stroking the stock, the barrel, the receiver. "These whitemen who hunt us now will soil their pants when they stare into the barrels of our guns."

Jack chuckled at the thought of that sight. Watching the white scouts soiling their pants like frightened children. Then he grew attentive as Roman Nose set the rifle aside. The Cheyenne's face hardened as he spoke.

"Last summer my medicine helper told me I would find a place of power on a river dried like a rawhide strip beneath the sun. Another winter came and went, and with the shortgrass time, I discovered myself consumed with finding that scorched river."

"What did your vision tell you?" Jack inquired, his brain carefully searching for the words.

"That I would charge down on a island of sand and grass in the middle of that river, leading our warriors in that charge."

"Leading them to victory. How will you know this place?"

Roman Nose did not answer at first. The firelight held his eyes captive. "At the far end of the island I would see standing a lone tree, not yet at full growth. And at the end nearest to my charge, I watched a lone whiteman rise, aim his rifle unafraid of the hundreds of pounding hooves hammering his way."

"Yes?" Jack asked, for the first time sensing his own anxiety, alone here with Roman Nose as the great war-leader unburdened his soul. "This whiteman fell beneath all those hooves as you passed over him . . . wiping out them all."

Only then did the Cheyenne gaze sadly into the eyes of the mulatto. "I do not know if the tall whiteman with the eyes of gray survived the hooves of all our ponies or not, Nibsi."

"Surely, he could not last——"

"For in my vision I myself could not make it to that lone cottonwood on the far end of the island."

When Jack opened his mouth to protest, Roman Nose raised his hand for silence.

"Nibsi, my pony obediently carried me away to the creekbank, away from the battle. There I saw myself fall from that wounded animal, bleeding myself from a terrible wound opened in my side."

"In your vision, we rescued you. Did we not, Roman Nose?"

He nodded gravely. "Yes. My body did not fall into the hands of the whitemen on that sandy island."

Jack swallowed. He felt momentarily better. "That is good, powerful one. That you should survive and the *Shahiyena* go on to rub the whitemen——"

"I died at sundown that day, Nibsi," Roman Nose said in a hoarse whisper. "It was not an easy journey. But I traveled that road as bravely as any man."

For the longest time, Jack stared at the Cheyenne's face, while Roman Nose watched the kettle roll into a boil. As he dragged it off the flames, the water slowed its tumble.

Once again Jack found that frightening, sad countenance directed at him.

"Nibsi must pay careful attention to what I now ask of him, for no one else will be capable of doing what Roman Nose asks."

Jack bobbed his head, frightened.

"I leave it to you to find the tall, gray-eyed one who killed me. You must follow him to the ends of the rivers, beyond the tall peaks, down to the big waters if need be. Follow him —and kill him for me. For our people, kill him."

O'Neill swallowed hard, like trying to force down a handful of cockleburrs, the kind that clung to his woolen trousers back in Georgia. "Your medicine tells you that I will do this for Roman Nose?"

"At the sundance, the water-spirits came to me again. I would die by the water, they told me. Flowing water. Telling me this tall man with the deadly gray eyes must die by still water."

"It is done, Roman Nose. I will follow the gray-eyed one, until my own medicine tells me the time has come. Until I have found the still water where the whiteman will meet his death."

"You are welcome to stay in my lodge this night . . . and all the nights to come. It is yours now that I am going far away, leaving this prairie of my birth. I will not sleep this last night, Nibsi. You may lay your head on my blankets here. They and everything else I own—all but the clothes I wear and this rifle I carry—are yours. Bury me only with my weapons of war."

"I will not sleep. Instead, I will see the morning come with Roman Nose," Jack O'Neill said finally, his voice cracking with the frightening sentiment about to overwhelm him. So many years since he had felt this way about anyone. His father, torn from him by other white men. Emmy, butchered by a white thief who escaped into the night. And now Roman Nose, his new friend. Who had seen his own death coming, staring into the face of the gray-eyed killer.

White men all.

Jack sensed his stomach tumble, not from hunger, but from revulsion. This would be an errand he would gladly undertake. The tracking of this tall, gray-eyed killer.

"It is good. We will see the morning come together, Nibsi," Roman Nose replied, handing the mulatto a hunk of the buffalo-fleece and some dripping ribs from the kettle.

"Yes, Roman Nose," Jack replied slowly, picking his words. "I will ride beside you, great warrior—and see for myself the face of this one who will kill you."

"I am cold, Starving Elk," complained the young warrior to his Cheyenne friend riding beside him.

"Soon enough, Little Hawk—you won't have time to think about the cold of this night."

The two young Cheyennes had never gone on a pony raid, much less attacked a camp of white men. Yet both had eagerly accepted the invitation of a half-dozen older Sioux boys to sneak out under the blackness of night in search of the soldier camp that Sioux scouts had announced lay somewhere nearby. They crept on foot into the herd to catch up their ponies without a sound, for had any of the eight been caught, the punishment would be severe. The old ones wanted no foolish coup-hunters alerting the soldiers before the dawn attack was ready.

But we are not fools, Starving Elk had told himself repeatedly as the eight had inched over hill after hill after hill, searching for the white man's camp. *We are due this look at the soldiers, before the rest of our brothers slaughter them the way surrounded buffalo are brought down, hamstrung by the wolf pack.*

One of the Sioux, the oldest of them all, had been among that group bringing the startling news of the soldiers' approach the previous day. Appointing himself leader, Bad Tongue had led the other seven into this darkness of the rolling plains the Northern Cheyenne and Brule claimed together as hunting ground. At the top of each hill sixteen eyes strained into the murky darkness. Some placed ears on the ground while the others held their ponies quiet. No sight of the white man here. No sound to hint they were drawing close.

Hill after hill after——

"Starving Elk!" Bad Tongue whispered sharply in his crude, unpracticed Cheyenne. Once the older Cheyenne boy drew alongside at the crest of the hill and knelt with the others, Bad Tongue began his hands-dancing, talking in sign.

"Yes, I can see!" Starving Elk answered with his hands, glancing at Little Hawk, his young head bobbing eagerly.

Far off, across the starlit prairie, twinkled the faint dots of light. Perhaps a handful of fires, a dim glowing beneath the dark skies. White-man fires.

"Let's go close enough to see these soldiers?" Little Hawk asked of the group leader.

Bad Tongue sneered. "Yes, my little friend. We go close enough for you to see all the soldiers."

"Then we ride back to wait for the others to attack at dawn," Starving Elk added, feeling an apprehensive nibble at the inside of his belly with the look he saw on Bad Tongue's face.

The Sioux youngsters stood, all six as one.

"We Lakota did not come to *see* the whiteman, my little friends. We came to take his horses."

Starving Elk swallowed hard. He had never been on a pony raid before. Not against an enemy tribe. Much less white soldiers heavily armed. Worst of all, he had not taken time to make his medicine for a pony raid. The others were looking at him now, daring him as boys will.

Starving Elk felt his knees turning to water. "I . . . I go to steal the horses. My friend Little Hawk can choose if he wishes to return to camp before the attack."

"No! I will ride with Starving Elk. He is my cousin and I will follow him."

Without another word, the half-dozen Sioux were atop their barebacked ponies, unfurling blankets, some unrolling stiff pieces of rawhide brought with them. One even pulled a large hand-drum from a coyote-skin cover hung over his shoulder.

"What is this you are doing with these things, Bad Tongue?"

The Sioux youngster glared at his Cheyenne companions. "Make ready, little ones. *Shahiyena* and Lakota go now to make war-music for the whiteman!"

Chapter 15

"Seamus!"

Uncle Liam's harsh whisper shattered the warmth of his dreaming, down where he swam swathed in sleep. Donegan came up from the depths quickly, kicking at his blankets. O'Roarke knelt over him, shushing.

"Be quiet, lad," he warned. "Want you come with me."

Seamus ground knuckles into his gritty eyes, ran a tongue round the inside of his scummy mouth. Already he was hungry. With regret he remembered Forsyth's fifty had eaten the last of their rations last night. Only salt and coffee now, until someone brought down some game.

His eyes quickly grew accustomed to the darkness. The fire at his feet had gone to coals. Nearby Jack Stillwell lay rolled up on an elbow, watching.

"Come with you?"

O'Roarke yanked on his nephew's arm.

"Why?"

"Just feel something in me gut, boy."

"Feel something——" Seamus started to say, then sensed his uncle stiffen as they both heard a single, distant bird whistle. A heartbeat parted a moment in time, then a second out-of-place chirp.

"Come . . . or stay here." Liam's tone was suddenly gruff. "No matter to me now."

Donegan clambered to his feet, grumbling and grabbing up the heavy Spencer. Finding it damp in his hand, here beside the river barely audible, just beyond the swamp-willow and plum-bushes. Standing, he thought he heard something foreign, and looked to the east, where the first thin ribbon of gray had strung itself across the horizon.

" 'At's right, Seamus," O'Roarke said at his nephew's ear. "But they won't be coming from there, out of the east."

"Why not?"

"Injuns come out of the light?" he snorted. "Thought you knew better. They'll come from this way."

"Damn you, Liam O'Roarke," Seamus snarled as he followed, skirting the fringe of camp, hurrying past black mounds against the gray sand, slipping by most of the stock scattered through Forsyth's bivouac.

On the far side of camp they found the major himself, just then reaching John Wilson, the picket stationed about a hundred yards to the west of their mounts grazing at the edge of camp.

"Surprised to see you awake, Liam," Forsyth whispered as the trio came to a halt in the darkness. "Figured you'd be sleeping in, as late as you were out last night."

"Didn't sleep a wink, Major," O'Roarke grumbled.

"Worrying about that village you were hunting for in the dark?"

Liam smiled. His teeth gleaming in the starlight. "Women, whiskey, or warriors—them's the only things worth losing sleep over. Looks you been up all night yourself."

"How would you know that?" Forsyth demanded.

"I'm the best damned scout you got along, Major. You'd expect me to know what was going on around me in camp."

Forsyth grinned. "It's good having you along on this one, Liam."

"My sentiments as well, Maj——"

"Shh! Dammit!" Wilson, the sentry, rasped, waving one arm as he knelt, his eyes straining at the horizon.

O'Roarke yanked Donegan down beside Forsyth, all holding their breath.

"There it is again, sir," Wilson whispered.

"I hear it too," Forsyth answered.

"Pony hooves," Liam replied. "You see anything out there, boys?"

"Not yet I don't," Seamus answered.

"There's one of the sonsabitches!" Wilson hollered suddenly, bolting to his feet as he threw his rifle to his shoulder.

"Don't shoot!" Sharp Grover hollered, sprinting for Wilson.

By putting his chin on the ground, Donegan could just then make out the shadowy form slipping up on horseback, feathers in a spray round the warrior's head as he emerged atop the far knoll. The sky just beginning to drain some of its black. The valley of the Arickaree drenched in bloody gray light.

"Don't look straight at it, Seamus," Liam instructed. "Look to the side of something you want to see at night. You can pick out the red bastard better that way."

"Here come the rest of 'em!" Sharp Grover shouted as he hurried up.

Grover and Wilson were moving like grapeshot from a cannon. Footsteps pounding the hard ground, grass and sage rustling. Then the hammering of unshod pony hooves could be heard on the chill morning breeze.

"They're after the horses, men!" Forsyth shouted, turning to hurl his voice back into the camp. "Turn out! The bastards are after our horses. Turn out!"

His last few words were drowned under the onrush of the warriors. The handful of horsemen shouted and shrieked, flapping blankets and rattling dried buffalo hides, beating on a drum and blowing on eagle wingbone whistles, making noise enough for twice their number.

"Indians!" Grover bawled, trotting straight for the enemy. "Get your asses up, boys! Indians!"

"Turn out, men!" Beecher ordered, in their midst a heartbeat later, his boots scuffing over the sandy ground.

"Dropped that bastard, I did!" O'Roarke shouted as he pulled his Spencer from his cheek.

Donegan watched one shadow weave, then topple from his pony as the rest, less than ten in all, reached the far western edge of camp itself, spooking horses and mules. With the screeching warriors, the whinnying horses, and the gunshots from the pickets, the whole camp was in instant pandemonium. Every man on his feet, furiously pulling at reins, many of the scouts having tied their horses to their belts through the night rather than trusting to picket-pins. Some began stomping out the coals of their fires to kill any back-light. All of them sweeping up their Spencers laid close at hand. Hollering questions and orders and curses. Animals yanked and prodded, bucking and rearing with the sudden noise and the gunfire and the hide-rattling of the warriors, who swept off the western horizon between the river and some low, inky bluffs north of camp in a whirl of noise and the clatter of hooves.

Heading for the middle of Forsyth's camp.

As they thundered into the midst of the confused scouts, the army mounts fought their handlers, dragging some of the men through the camp as they struggled to regain control. Like an oak tree, Martin Burke gripped two of the brutes, each horse fighting to tear off in different directions.

The Confederate came hurling by, vainly trying to hold on to his horse, and was dragged through the coals of a fire for his trouble. Smith yelped, releasing his mount as he slapped at his smoldering clothing, cussing a blue streak.

The warriors were gone as swiftly as had come the morning breeze. Their stampede a failure.

"McCall!" Forsyth bellowed, dashing back into camp.

The sky to the east grayed of a sudden.

"Over here, Major!"

"What'd they get?"

"Two of the damn mules," the sergeant reported breathlessly.

"Ammunition?"

"No, sir. Medical supplies. Some of our coffee, all our salt."

"No ammunition lost?"

He shook his head, watching Beecher trot up.

"Every man accounted for . . . but two of the fellas lost their mounts," declared the lieutenant.

Donegan watched Forsyth grind his teeth on that. "Damn those two! I gave orders to securely picket their mounts——"

"Both headed out now on foot to fetch 'em," Grover announced, pointing at the two.

"You men!" Forsyth screamed, his voice inflamed with anger. "You're fools to follow those animals!"

"The hostiles will have your hair inside of five minutes!"

Liam O'Roarke added as the two scouts shuffled back to the group like scolded schoolboys.

"Eutsler . . . and what's your name again?" Forsyth demanded.

"Smith," Bob North drawled.

"By damn—I gave orders to picket your animals."

"Major, I think we better give the order to saddle now, sir," Grover said, growing edgy.

"Sharp's right," O'Roarke agreed as he stepped up. "You'll want to move this bunch out bloody quick."

"Best hump it to the island, Major," Grover suggested.

"Yes, Sharp. The island seems our best bet," Forsyth echoed, turning to gaze at the sandbar in the center of the Arickaree Fork of the Republican River, for but a moment studying the lone cottonwood on the far end as the sky paled all the more.

"They'll come now that it's light," Liam urged quietly, his eyes glancing at his young nephew.

"Saddle up, men!" the major shouted above the clamor of man and animal. "Sergeant, have them stand to horse!"

McCall was gone into the half-light. Seamus watched after him, then slapped the thick blanket on The General, trying to calm the big gray with one hand. Then the McClellan saddle. Cinch down, up and in, yanked once, then a hard nudge against The General's belly. The horse blew, with Seamus there yanking up to secure the cinch. Down and buckled. Stirrup dropped, Spencer flung into one boot.

The Henry kept in hand now as he turned, conscious at last of the rumbling clatter about him as the others saddled, cursing, hollering at one another, every set of eyes locked on the western horizon.

They would not come out of the sun, but from the west. And if a man strained his ears hard enough, shut out enough of their noisy camp——

"By God, you were right, Liam!" Forsyth loomed out of the gray light.

"Told you when I come in last night. I never found it—but I'll be damned if I didn't have the feeling . . . my bones told me there was a village nearby."

"Lookee here, Major," old Pierre Trudeau announced as

he trotted out of the darkness, his reins in one hand, a long, dark object hanging from the other.

"Damn you, Trudeau. No one gave you the right to scalp that——"

"No one tell Pierre not to take scalp!" He shook it at arm's length. "Sioux, it is——"

"Get out of here with the damned thing!" Forsyth bawled. He whirled on Grover and Beecher. "We can be proud of our bunch, boys. Came out of that in good shape."

"They haven't even begun with us, Major," Liam grumbled sourly.

"Leave it to you damned Irish to find the fun in everything!" Grover said, pounding O'Roarke on the back as Seamus laughed with them.

"Stand to horse!" McCall shouted again.

"You hear that?" Liam asked.

"I do. Goddamn!" Grover answered.

"Major! Best be moving your boys now!" Liam was pulling up his nephew's and his own mount at the same time.

"Sweet Mither of Christ, I ain't heard anything like that since——"

Then Donegan made out the rumble like distant thunder out of the west. As he looked back to the east, the far end of the sandy island grew pale in the coming light.

"They're coming now!" Beecher was shouting. *"To the island!"*

"Cross to the island!" rose the chorus from the soldiers.

Echoed by the civilians in tatters of voices and the hammering of butts landing on saddles.

"Make the island!"

Seamus was sure of it now. No mistaking that sound. Any soldier who had lived through four years of that hell back east knew the sound of thousands of hooves, this time hammering the sun-baked prairie. Coming out of the dark like some ghostly thing you can't see—but you sense its coming before you ever lay eyes on your enemy.

Having heard enough, he was up on the saddle. Feeling the ground tremble with the quake of their coming.

The others were breaking out of camp, swirling around him, horses driven into the streambed, splashing across the shallow creek. In their midst stood McCall and Beecher and

Grover, still on the ground, reins in one hand. Their pistols in the other. Ordering everyone across before they would close the file.

A scattering of gunfire rattled round them.

Seamus felt one hiss by his head as The General came around, fighting the bit. The last men left in camp were shouting. Wanting to know where the gunfire was coming from. A second bullet came whining in.

And with it, Seamus recognized that unmistakable slap of lead against flesh.

The General staggered sideways, thrashing his head. Fighting the bit. Rearing and bucking. A third slapped the big gray low on the neck, grazing Donegan's arm where he gripped tightly to control the animal.

For an instant as the horse settled to all fours and shuddered; Donegan saw him. And blinked. Not believing.

A hundred yards downstream in the swamp-willow of the north bank stood the Confederate Smith, coolly aiming his Spencer at . . . at Donegan.

Not one enemy warrior firing into the wild retreat to the island. Instead, for some murderous reason, the Confederate was flinging lead.

"There they are! They're on us now!"

He heard Beecher's high voice shouting down by the water. Then raked his heels into The General's flanks as he watched the Confederate dive into the willows downstream, and splash across to the far end of the island on foot.

"C'mon, Seamus!"

O'Roarke was at the water with the three soldiers and Grover, all waving him on. Donegan was the last. Fighting The General around in a crazed circle. Blood drenched his left arm. Some his own, but mostly the big gray's. It brightened the horse's left flank like a dark patch, slick and shiny in the growing light of this new day. And Seamus recognized the lung-wheeze that told him the animal was going down.

Not this horse! his mind cried out, the utter stupidity of it burning through him in angry draughts.

He laid along the big gray's neck, stroking, murmuring to have the animal make this one last run for it as he saw the soldiers and his uncle splash across to the island, spraying sand and water in rooster tails. The General pranced round, and as he came full about, Seamus saw them for the first time. He had seen Indians before. On that hot July day at the Crazy Woman Crossing.

At the bottom of a crude jut of land on the far side of Lodge Trail Ridge.

And during their nonstop charges on the hayfield corral.

But none of that had prepared him for what materialized out of the west. Coming round the far bend of the river. Like disciplined cavalry. Row upon row upon row of the naked, gleaming chests heaving behind the bobbing, snorting heads of their ponies.

And Seamus was the last left to cross.

Suddenly the big gray settled, and shuddered, still on his legs. The General turned his head, snapping at the reins. Donegan fed the horse more, loosening his grip. Then he was off without having to nudge another heel into the bloody flanks.

More lead sang overhead as he flung himself alongside the horse's neck, hooves tearing into the sandy riverbed toward the shallow, beckoning water. More bullets from the Confederate, hidden now in the willows at the far end of the island.

Mixed with more and more rifle-fire from some snipers who ran and shot, ran some more and fired again as they tore down the near bank.

The horse stumbled, almost going down in the riverbed as it hit the soft sand. Spray and grit kicked up by the slashing hooves as it carried Donegan to the island. Closer and closer he could see Grover's face. Uncle Liam's in the growing light of new day. They were standing now, rifles at their shoulders. Covering his run for it. Shouting too, though he could not hear them. Many more of the scouts waving him on.

He held tight to that horse. Feeling the life pouring from the animal as he strained for the island. Then suddenly sensed the sky scooping him out of the saddle as his hands ripped loose of the bloody mane.

Helpless, he realized the gray had gone down and he was spinning through the air. The ground above and the sky beneath him as he hit the sand, tumbling into the brush.

More lead sang into swamp-willow where he lay. From the far end of the island.

Seamus painfully parted some of the brush and peered out.

Seeing the Confederate's dirty face and the stained-tooth smile disappearing behind some far willows a hundred yards away.

Might as well be a mile now.

Then he sighed, knowing for better or worse he had reached the island with the others. For the first time recognizing the pain shouting from every part of his body.

Yet pain nowhere near what he felt in his heart as he stared thirty feet away, watching The General roll agonizingly on his side, legs thrashing, still galloping his way into death.

Having carried his master this last, mad, throat-hollering charge into the face of the enemy. One last, bloody charge into the maw of death itself.

Chapter 16

Sergeant William McCall had to admit, it was one fine sight this new day, watching the sunrise play light off the lances and scalplocks and colorful streamers, feathers tied to rifle-barrels brandished by the warriors as they came on, circling the north side of the island, dropping to the far side of their ponies, hanging by a heel and a wrist tied in the mane, firing, yelling, lobbing hissing arrows among the frightened, milling horses.

If he hadn't seen it with his own eyes, the veteran wouldn't have believed it. During the war McCall had reached the rank of colonel among his native Pennsylvania unit, breveted brigadier-general for gallantry in action during the siege of Petersburg. It was now as Forsyth's first sergeant that Billy McCall was about to get a taste of just how bloody war on the frontier could get.

Almost like the ground itself sprouted the hostiles. Appearing out of nowhere. Growing out of the thickets, from the streambed itself. Atop every hill, in every direction. Every mouth screeching their death-songs.

Nothing but the echo of hammering hooves there one minute. The next, a riverbed filled with screeching, painted horsemen sweeping by the island. McCall thought he could actually feel the earth trembling beneath his feet, and wondered if it was the thousands of hooves. Or the rattle of his own knees.

"Make every cartridge worth it, boys!" he hollered. "Make every one worth one of these screaming bastards!"

Like the cool veterans they were, McCall and Grover and O'Roarke had covered the retreat to the island, carbines cracking on the still dawn air amid the noise of man and animal suddenly finding no place left to run.

Near the upstream end of the sandbar, four of the scouts hung back, hugging the shadows beneath an overhanging riverbank. Harrington. Gantt. Burke. And old man Farley. They had chosen to remain hidden at the bank when the charge came.

One by one as the men had reached the island, the scouts tied off their horses to the willow and yanked saddles from their backs as the first wave of brown horsemen barreled round the far bend of the river. Then hurled themselves down in the tall grass and swamp-willow.

The wave split at the west end of the island, at a disadvantage as they had to veer north sharply to drop off the bank into the dry riverbed. In this first, circling charge, the trio of marksmen under the eroded bank did their worst damage, spilling half a dozen to the sand in the first explosion of rifle-fire. More in the second wave of horsemen. Brown-skinned warriors crawling, wounded and bleeding up the dry wash, into the willow and plum.

Then as quickly as they had come in a united front, the chargers pulled off, followed by riderless ponies still caught up in the chase. The scouts had broken the hostiles' concerted charge. Dead and wounded warriors lay less than the length of two arms from the white men. The fifty had forced the horsemen back to their old way of fighting, the circle. Each warrior alone with his medicine against the white men hunkered down on the grassy island.

"Dig in! Dig in, dammit!" Forsyth was hollering, as the bravest riders came round for a second trip along the north bank of the island.

Beecher and Billy himself took up the call.

"Two feet down! Two feet . . . keep digging!"

Behind each horse and mule the men scraped at the sand, grabbing up chunks of grass and knotted roots to claw their way down.

"Two foot deep!" McCall shouted at a group of riflemen. "Long enough for you to get down in!"

Round and round the first wave circled the island: yipping

like coyotes on a spree, waving blankets, firing their bows and rifles, the whole parade a blur of wild color.

Down they tore into the riverbed, racing past the north shore of the island, across the riverbed to leap their ponies onto the south bank. Up the south bank and into the riverbed once again. Firing from beneath their snorting ponies' necks. Arrows, but mostly rifle and pistol-fire. Each one hanging from the far side of his little pony.

While the scouts' repeaters kept up a steady racket, hooves pounded the dry riverbed in a thunder of terror and noise, screeching matched only by the cries of the wounded horses as the animals reared and fought their handlers with each new bullet wound. Amid it all the mad curses muddied with grunts of angry, scared men, scrambling and scratching at the sand.

"Dig in while we still can!" Forsyth continued to instruct.

"Drop the horses!" Beecher was coolly hollering. "Drop the damned horses!"

Squeals of the frightened animals blocked out most sound now as the horses struggled, bolted, tearing back, kicking up sand as they went down.

All along the length of the island cracked the sharp blasts of the Colt pistols. Eerie, humanlike screaming of horses as their riders shot bullets into their heads, bringing the big animals down in a gritty spray of sand. One by one the men fought alone. Leading more of the fighting horses up to the selected place, each animal bolting against the smell of blood, eyes rolling, nostrils flaring. Biting, flinging phlegm and piss as they went down in the sand. All legs still fighting as a second bullet crashed into their brains.

"Watch the legs! Outta the way of the legs!" McCall ordered, watching as two of the scouts were sent sailing into the shallow river by kicking legs.

"Better hurt by them horses than them red niggers!" another scout growled at McCall as he danced his way between the struggling legs of a mule and hunkered down behind his Spencer.

McCall scampered away through the tall grass, reaching Sharp Grover's side. He collapsed behind a dying horse, plainly hearing the slashing quirts slapping pony rumps as the horsemen tore past. More sound now. Frightened voices filling the air above the island. Profane, desperate prayers. The cries of men hit and bleeding.

Billy figured the odds were damned good there were some of these good men dying, if not already dead.

"They got us outnumbered ten to one," McCall growled as he watched the young Irishman come tumbling to rest in the brush, the gray stallion half in the stream, thrashing at the sand and trying to rise as its blood seeped from half a dozen holes into the shallow water.

Beyond Donegan, others continued to struggle to bring their rearing, plunging animals down to form breastworks. These cries of wounded horses, the old cavalryman again marveled, so much like a child's cry of terror.

Sharp Grover snorted and tore loose a big cud of tobacco from a dark-leafed plug. "More'n likely, Sergeant—we're on the downside of twenty-to-one odds."

"Damn!" McCall whispered as he turned away, watching more of the scouts plopping down behind their dying horses, laying their hot-barreled Spencers over the quivering bodies of their weary, lathered mounts. Powdersmoke and clouds of spurting, yellow dust, punctuated by jabs of muzzle-flash obscured his vision for a moment.

Another group at the end of the island shouted.

"Hold your fire!" Forsyth was up and yelling.

His voice was all but drowned out by the growing shouts of the Indians.

Then McCall stood, hurrying among the men, joining Lieutenant Beecher, ordering the men to hold for the command.

"Volley-fire when ordered, boys!" Billy was shouting, thinking back on how time and again he had watched disciplined infantry hold against bloody Confederate cavalry charges. "Reload! Full magazines, goddammit!" Knowing in the pit of him they could hold their own. Knowing they had to. Sensing that they would find out within a matter of seconds. "When the major hollers, fire by volley!"

Liam brushed past McCall as the sergeant scanned the far shore and the brown bodies dotting the ground of the first skirmish.

"You don't keep down, they'll have to fit you for a new hat-size, O'Roarke!"

The big Irishman snorted as he skidded to a stop beside his young nephew, lying dazed in the willow and high grass at the side of the island. Craning about, he flung his bull-bellow at the sergeant.

"Jest like Roderick Dhu's whistle raised his army of Highlanders from the ground itself, Sergeant McCall!" Liam announced. "These red bastards spring from nowhere like Dhu's fighting Scots!"

McCall whirled, hearing Forsyth arguing with a handful of those hunkered close by. They pressed the major to look at his options. But one way remained open—the narrow gorge through which they had entered the valley. Make a run for it now. When Forsyth had him enough of their whimpering, he calmly shouted them down as the circling horsemen tightened their noose.

"Damned evident that our enemy wanted us to head that way, isn't it?"

McCall watched a lot of the faces turn sheepish.

"They left us that way to escape, can't you see? Good chance of a deadly ambush in that damned gorge."

More of them grumbled, some turning back to their breastworks.

"We'll stay here, Major!" Fred Beecher shouted.

"Damn right we will——" Forsyth whirled about with the rest of them when the faint bugle call sounded upstream.

"Must be soldiers in the——"

"——stupid horse's ass!"

"Ain't n'other white men 'cept'n us!"

"——white renegades, 'swhat it is!"

"We may be cornered, boys—but we aren't beaten . . . not by a long chalk. Besides, we've got plenty of water here."

"Don't waste your time arguing—use it to dig in, men. Pair up, covering one another—and finish digging in while you can!"

Then McCall understood why Forsyth had suggested digging in. The ground trembled beneath McCall, causing him to look upstream to the west. Another charge was coming.

"Shit!"

"Look at them fancy red bastards, will ye?"

"Holy . . . holy Keee-rist!"

Downstream floated the clear, brassy notes of a cavalry charge. No mistaking it.

"Some white bastard's gone over to the blanket!" Grover hissed angrily. "Heard them Arapahos had a renegade with 'em, Billy."

"Knows his bugle calls, don't he?"

"Let's hope I get a chance to stare that bastard in the eye!" Sharp growled, the warriors less than three hundred yards away. "I'm going over with those boys in the riverbank yonder. Over there the bastards will ride close enough to shake hands."

"You'll get your shot at that bugler."

"Damn right I will," Grover spat as he crabbed off across the grass and sand, splashing water at the edge of the river.

Savage war-cries hit the island first. Then McCall watched the Indians open fire as Grover reached the riverbank. A concerted, sustained rifle-fire as disciplined as any infantry unit could boast.

On the upstream end of the island, the bullets began falling among the last few horses and pack-mules tied within the willow. Some of the brown-skinned horsemen had abandoned their ponies, preferring to dive among the reeds and willow along both sides of the sandy riverbed. Stamping and snorting, crying out and fighting their restraints, one by one the horses thrashed on the bloody grass in the soft new light of coming day.

Yet the scouts had exacted their pound of horseflesh as well. Out on the sandy streambed and in the river itself lay the dying, squealing war-ponies. From time to time a scout brought down an unhorsed warrior as the Indian attempted to scamper to cover.

"Culver's dead!" a voice called out. "Bullet in the head."

From here and there on the island, men shouted that others nearby had been hit. Or a wounded man himself cried out in his private pain above the noise of the rifle-fire and orders and warrior chants and screams of the dying animals.

"I ain't gonna stay here and be shot down like a dog!"

McCall wheeled, finding Nichols shouting at Beecher as the lead from creekbank snipers flew overhead.

"C'mon . . . any of you! Try for the bank with me!"

Nichols implored, flecks of spittle dried at the corners of his fleshy lips.

"I'll go!" shouted one.

"Me too!"

"I'm goin'—we stay here, we'll get burned alive for sure by these bastards!"

"Let's git!" hollered another.

And just as there was a dozen of them rising from the grass and swamp-willow, Forsyth rose amid the hail.

"Stay where you are!" he hollered above the tumult, waving his pistol. "It's our only chance."

"We're going!" Nichols screamed, turning to leave.

"I'll shoot any man who attempts to leave the island!"

Nichols wheeled, his carbine 'volving up at his hip. Quaking dangerously.

"I'll shoot any deserters the major misses!" McCall hollered as he scrambled up on the other side of the group. "You try for the bank—you will be roasted on those bastards' fires!"

Nichols eyed the two soldiers. Then his eyes filled with genuine fear as he watched the warriors bearing down on them.

"Addle-headed fools!" Beecher dashed over, dodging lead from the riverbank snipers. "Have you men no sense?"

"Get back to the breastworks!" Forsyth ordered, waving the muzzle of his pistol at the wavering deserters.

"They're about on top of us!"

"Fire low . . . dammit! Fire low!" McCall shouted, sensing a sudden river of flame along his neck. He put his hand up to touch it. The fingers came away wet. Hot and wet.

"Don't waste a shot, boys!" Beecher shouted, sprinting to the far end of the island, firing his Spencer as he dodged horse carcasses.

Just as Beecher and McCall hit the grass behind a thrashing mule, the charge broke like water parting for a boulder in the middle of wild, foaming white-water. All the warriors reined away but one. While the rest swept over their dead and wounded to drag them away, the lone horseman rode directly over the island, leaping his pony over the dead-horse breastworks and the white men who shrank from the slashing hooves as he hurtled over them.

Astonishingly, this solitary warrior reached the cotton-wood at the far end of the island without a bullet touching him. His snorting pony splashed across the stream to the north bank, then carried its rider atop a low hill where he reined up, stopped, and surveyed the white men imprisoned on the sandy island.

"How you figure none of us hit him?" someone asked.

"Nobody was shooting at him till he was past 'em, you idjit!" another scout replied.

"Damn straight—I was hunkered outta the way of that bastard's war-club!"

"Billy!"

McCall turned, finding Beecher and Forsyth waving him over. He crawled to his feet and made a dash toward the end of the island, diving in behind a dead mule as Indian bullets smacked into the carcass with a soapy slap.

"You're wounded, Sergeant!" Beecher exclaimed.

McCall touched his neck. "Flesh-wound, Lieutenant."

Forsyth smiled warmly, admiration written on his face. "You ever see anything like this, Billy?"

"No, I ain't," he answered, slamming home another Blakeslee loading tube into the stock of his Spencer.

All three whirled to find Liam O'Roarke tumbling into their midst. He crawled through the sand and collapsed against the bloody mule, catching his breath.

"That's their women and children up there, ain't it, Irishman?" McCall asked, pointing with the muzzle of his Spencer.

Their eyes surveyed the surrounding hills. On the crests of many appeared spectators from the Cheyenne and Sioux villages. Besides the women and little ones, come to watch were the old ones and the boys too young to fight.

Liam smiled. "The bastards planning to make a grand show of rubbing us out now. Bringing their kin to watch the fight."

McCall watched Forsyth rise. "We best stay down now," McCall suggested. "You can't move around standing up, Major."

"I must see that the men are digging in," Forsyth argued as he clambered to crawl over the mule carcass, one leg at a time.

"I'll help, Major," Beecher said as he rose.

Forsyth grunted in pain as he tumbled back against Beecher, biting his lip from the bullet-wound in his right thigh. McCall and O'Roarke helped drag Forsyth behind the breastworks once again.

"The major hit?" a scout hollered close by.

"You say Forsyth's dead?" Another echoed the frightened call.

"He ain't dead!" McCall countered, gazing down into Forsyth's face as O'Roarke and Beecher ripped open the hole in the major's britches to inspect the bloody wound. Billy could tell Forsyth was in far too much pain to answer for himself.

"If the major's dead, then we——"

"He got hit in the leg is all!" McCall hollered back at the wild talk.

"Major"—Beecher leaned over Forsyth—"sounds like the boys still at the riverbank are doing their share of damage. Every time one of the snipers creeps up to get a good shot at the far end of the island, he gets his head blown off for his trouble."

Billy watched Forsyth nod, wordlessly, teeth gritted in pain.

"Lieutenant?" John Mooers shouted from nearby.

"Major's been hit, Doctor!" Beecher replied.

"If you fellas help me enlarge my rifle-pit, I'll have room for Forsyth in here."

"Capital idea!" Beecher cheered.

Work began immediately to enlarge Mooers's pit while others kept up some cover fire, including the doctor. With his dark beard flowing to mid-chest, the young physician who had eagerly signed on with Forsyth at Fort Hays was making good use of every shot from his Spencer. One of the few along on this ride who had retained his sense of humor, Mooers was known as an incurable practical joker. For now, he seemed intent on making the snipers the victims of his pointed jokes.

"Billy, that man . . . he's firing too quickly for good shooting," the major muttered, pointing out one of the scouts.

Forsyth hitched himself up, painfully dragging the wounded right leg when another Indian bullet crashed into his left leg halfway between knee and ankle, shattering the bone.

"Dammit—get the major down in here now!" Mooers shouted, crouching over to reach Forsyth. "He'll be dead if we don't!"

More bullets whined and slapped through the willows as the doctor and McCall scrambled to Forsyth, then dragged him into the enlarged pit.

"Chances are that's army lead, Major," McCall grunted as they plopped him against the side of the pit scooped out of the wet sand.

Forsyth appeared unable to catch his breath, finally opening his eyes, filling with tears of silent pain. "How well I know, Billy. Guns and bullets captured at Fort Phil Kearny almost two years ago."

"No fort there no more, Major. Army gave the country back to Red Cloud already."

"Suppose these same warriors who butchered Fetterman's men want us to give up as well, eh, Billy?"

McCall grinned. "Not a damned chance of that, Major." He watched the major turn his head aside, not knowing if it was the pain that misted Forsyth's eyes.

Billy looked away as well, not wanting to embarrass his commanding officer. Just beyond the fringe of willow and brush out of range from the island rode a milling horde of warriors, brandishing a variety of weapons, each one shouting his angry disappointment that they had not cut off the soldiers' retreat to the island.

"Get Grover for me, Billy."

Minutes later, Sharp Grover slid into Dr. Mooers's rifle-pit beside Forsyth.

"See the big one up there on the hill, Sharp?" the major inquired.

"The one with the long headdress?" He gazed at the major.

Forsyth nodded. "Is that Roman Nose?"

"Most likely," Grover replied quietly. "Not another Indian like him on the plains."

"That's sure a dark sonuvabitch riding beside him," Mooers commented dryly. "If I didn't know better, I'd say that's a darkie renegade."

Forsyth appeared to let some pain wash over him, then caught his breath. "If that's Roman Nose, then we've found the Northern Cheyenne."

"That's right, Major," Grover replied. "Plus Oglalla and Brule Sioux. Outcasts from other bands as well—outlaws and criminals among their own people."

"How many you make of it, Sharp?"

He was a moment in answering. Not that he was calculating, just that it wasn't good news to tell any man, much less your commanding officer lying beside you, his blood soaking into the sand from two bullet wounds.

"I make at least a thousand of 'em, Major," Grover grunted.

"I . . . can't seriously believe there's a thousand there."

"Major, Roman Nose leads at least half that himself."

"Nonsense!" Forsyth shouted, his eyes darting.

McCall understood that the major had no desire for that discouraging news to become general knowledge on their little island.

"Surely, Grover—you must be counting the women and children, the old men on the hillsides as well," Forsyth continued, imploring the learned scout with his eyes.

"I understand, goddammit!" Grover muttered almost under his breath. "You asked, Major. All I done was answer your question. If you want to keep it a secret from the rest, that's your business and I'll respect your wishes. But, as sure as the sun is rising in the east right at this moment—there are a thousand of the baddest red outlaws surrounding us."

"At least I've found Roman Nose."

"Major, you may've found Roman Nose—but I don't think that big red bastard is gonna work up a sweat worrying about us slipping away on him."

Chapter 17

*T*his band of war veterans and iron-hardened men forged on plains warfare had sprayed a cool and deadly fire into the front ranks of the horsemen bearing down on them, parting that first sunrise charge, turning it into a sweeping surround while the taunting grew louder from those warriors sniping in the creekbank brush.

For the next hour, things quieted over the island, although the Cheyenne and Sioux snipers kept up a steady rattle of rifle-fire from their brushy shelters. Men silently scratched at the sandy earth with their hands, knives, tin cups . . . anything they could use to claw holes in the ground and scoop up walls of the damp sand. The scouts were ordered to fire back at the banks only when there was a chance of hitting something.

From the downstream end of the island, Major Sandy Forsyth heard a mule's brass-lunged *scree-haws* as it collapsed, thrashing in its messy death. He was sighing, gritting with pain in the two leg wounds when the voice called out loudly from the far creekbank.

"There goes the last damned horse, anyhow!"

Forsyth couldn't believe his ears.

"You hear that, Major?" Fred Beecher inched over on his belly to the lip of Forsyth's rifle-pit.

"They've got a white renegade with 'em," Mooers growled.

"That, Doctor—or they've got one of old man Bent's half-breed sons riding with 'em this time out."

"Major's right," Beecher replied. "This is the country the Bent boys grew up in. Word has it on this part of the plains that Charlie Bent's become a bad seed, gotten worse for taking up with them Dog Soldiers."

"The voice came from that direction," Forsyth said, swallowing down the pain as he twisted himself against the side of the pit. "I'd like that bastard who speaks English to give a listen to what I've got to say——"

"Be careful, dammit!" Mooers said.

"I will, Doctor," the major replied.

"I wouldn't stick my head up like that," Beecher said, wagging his own.

"Just want to tell that bastard a thing or——"

A bullet caught Forsyth's regulation felt hat at the top of the crown where it sat creased on his head, knocking the major backward across the rifle-pit.

Mooers and Beecher were on him, sheltering the major with their bodies while McCall hurled himself to the edge of the pit and fired his carbine at the puff of smoke drifting above the creekbank. An instant thrashing and groaning from brush beside the Arickaree told the sergeant he had shot center.

"You're a lucky man, Major," Mooers declared as he inspected the furrowed row of bloody scalp across the top of Forsyth's head. "You lay here with two wounds already, and sustain a third that had it been a half-inch lower would have blown out the back of your skull."

"My lucky hat," Forsyth said, blinking till the temporary blindness caused by the wound faded. He groped about, his head pounding like nothing he had ever experienced. He retrieved the wide-brimmed felt hat, and poked a finger through the four holes in the crown that showed the bullet's path.

"Damned lucky," Beecher repeated, bellying up from the next rifle-pit. "Let's get us some Cheyenne while we can, Major."

Forsyth heard them as well as the rest of the men. Hooves hammering the sandy riverbed. "Got us a chance soon, Lieutenant."

About a dozen mounted horsemen dashed from the nearby

trees along the creekbank, riding into rifle range as they darted past the north side of the island.

"I'll get me one of those bastards myself," Mooers vowed, rising on one knee and slapping the Spencer's stock against his cheek.

"Watch yourself, Doctor."

Mooers waited, watching the horsemen over the front blade of his sights while one of the group swooped ever closer to the near side of the island. Then pulled his trigger, dropping the warrior into the shallow creek.

"That rascally red bastard won't trouble us again, Major," he said, turning with a grin that slashed his bearded face.

In the next moment that grin became something akin to astonishment, as Forsyth recognized the familiar crack of a bullet shattering human bone. Mooers sank slowly into the rifle-pit, both hands to his head, bright crimson spilling down his cheek, onto his shoulder.

"I . . . my God—I'm hit, M-Major——"

Mooers fell face forward, across Forsyth's wounded legs. Painfully dragging himself out from beneath the doctor, Forsyth muscled the man over. Mooers gurgled, still alive, his breathing gone shallow and rapid. The purple hole over the right eye told the major that Mooers had a mortal wound.

Forsyth found the doctor's dark eyes staring dimly at him, faint with a recognition that it was all but over. No words fell from Mooers's lips.

"My brave . . . and damned fool friend," Forsyth whispered, cradling the doctor across his wounded legs, nestling the bleeding head against his damp tunic. "Come all the way here to the plains from your beautiful Vermont. Just to die in this hole scooped out of hot sand in the middle of this hell."

He sensed a sob rising, threatening to choke him, but swallowed it down along with the pain gripping his legs.

"Come here for adventure and excitement . . . see what it got you, Doctor. See what it got the lot of us."

He gently laid his friend against the sandy slope of the pit, beneath the shadow of overhanging swamp-willow and tall grass, shading Mooers's face with the doctor's hat. Then inched back to his side of the pit. Digging in with his hands and elbows, Forsyth painfully crawled to the edge and peered over. He and the rest intently watched the swirling horsemen sweep by, then gather upstream. Sweep by again——

Another bugle's blare sounded up the Arickaree Fork. Obeying the call, the circling horsemen turned off and slowly made their way beyond the first bend of the shallow river. Others appeared on both banks, hundreds upon hundreds of them, all leading their ponies toward the mouth of a gorge hidden beyond the trees, just past that first bend.

It's Roman Nose, the murdering bastard. Forming his legions for their charge . . . out of sight and rifle range.

Forsyth sank below the lip of the rifle-pit as he turned away, exhausted already. For the moment no longer concerned with his wounds. Nothing any of them could do about the pain of the wounded. One of those two mules run off before dawn was packing Dr. Mooers's medical supplies.

He looked at his useless legs. All the major could do now was to try stopping the flow of blood before he grew too weak while the sun sizzled the rest of his juices out of him in this frying pan of a rifle-pit.

He knew he had to get his mind off his legs, and the pounding headache that drove shards of pain behind his eyes like splinters of broken glass.

"Beecher?"

"Over here, Major," came the voice from the adjoining rifle-pit.

"It's my belief the Indians are about to rush us, Lieutenant."

"Was thinking the same thing," Beecher answered.

"They're coming, Major." Sharp Grover's voice rose from the lieutenant's pit. "Soon enough."

"Fred . . ." And he swallowed down some pain. "Fred, get McCall . . . and you both quickly spread the word to all the men—that they're preparing a charge. Get the men ready . . . get us set up to turn their attack—and quickly . . ."

Beecher's head appeared over the edge of Forsyth's pit. "We'll turn 'em," he cheered. "I'm on my way." Then disappeared.

Forsyth listened to the soldiers go. Heard the scraping of boots on sand, the muttering voices in rifle-pits farther and farther away still.

Sandy Forsyth closed his eyes to the climbing sun, hung halfway now to mid-sky. He judged it was the middle of the morning, not having the inclination to pull his watch from his pocket again. So damned hot, and they weren't in the heat of it yet.

He only hoped Beecher would order every gun charged with a full loading tube: one in the breech and six in the Blakeslee for each Spencer. And he knew without asking that a plains-savvy lieutenant like Beecher would load the weapons of the dead and wounded as well, stationing them close to those who could still use them against the coming charge.

Slowly twisting to the side, his legs crying out in torment, he pulled up the mule-ear on his belt-holster and inched the pistol free. He caught his breath from the wave of pain that made him want to throw up what little lay in his nearly empty belly. Then breathed easier. Knowing when the island was overrun with the coming charge, he would have a few bullets waiting for those red sonsabitches who would come leaping over the side of his rifle-pit.

And one last bullet saved for himself.

"You gonna be all right, Irishman?" Sergeant McCall whispered.

Donegan nodded his head. "I will."

Liam gently slapped his nephew's shoulders in their rifle-pit as he nodded to Billy McCall. "He just took him a bad tumble from that wee horse of his. Shame of it," he tsked. "A bloody good animal he was, Seamus."

"I can't wait to get the bastard who killed him," Donegan growled, peering round his uncle at the far end of the island.

"Seamus is still a bit daft, Billy," Liam O'Roarke grumbled. "Keeps saying one of the scouts shot his horse out from under him."

"He did, the bleeming bastard!" Seamus cried.

His loud voice brought immediate rifle-fire from the bank, bullets kicking up the sand and slamming into the still, bloating horse carcasses the men huddled behind in the rising heat.

"Keep yer goddamned voice down, Nephew!" Liam hissed.

McCall crawled over their legs, heading away. "You'll get

plenty enough chance to kill some Indians in a few minutes, Donegan."

"Not Injins I want my hands on right now," Seamus spat, one eye trained on the far end of the island. "It's the Confederate I want to pay——"

"Some of you just won't let that war be over, will you!" McCall joked, smiling. "Just you both remember—Major's orders. No more firing at the creekbanks or the brush. Save your ammunition and keep your eyes skinned up yonder. Grover thinks the big charge is coming from upstream."

"We'll keep our weapons loaded, Sergeant. Won't we, Seamus, me boy?"

"Just 'cause I want to have a bullet or two ready for that damned Rebel what tried to kill me coming over."

"You was late getting saddled and taking off," Liam soothed. "Nothing more than getting caught in the redskins' cross-fire."

"Cross-fire, hell!" Donegan snapped, realizing that the sniping from the creekbanks was slacking off. He dabbed some fingers on the left forearm that oozed along the messy flesh-wound. "The Johnnie wanted me dead for some reason . . . and he smiled doing it, Liam."

"Listen!" O'Roarke ordered. "You hear it getting quiet?"

"I've heard that sort of thing afore meself," Donegan growled, still sour, his mind more on sorting out the means to work his way down the island and confront the Confederate named Smith.

"The snipers quitting . . . and them riders gone off to form for their charge. C'mon, Seamus—we're needed on upstream end of the island."

He shrugged off his uncle's hand, staring downstream, refusing to budge. "Staying right here till I get him in my sights."

A loud grunt brought them both around. Frank Harrington tumbled back against them, hands at his head, the front of his shirt covered with blood.

"Is he alive?" Liam asked as they pulled Harrington down.

"I am, you dumb Irishman," Harrington growled. "Took me an arrow for my trouble." For only a moment he pulled a bright red hand away from his right eye, showing the iron arrowpoint embedded in his skull.

"You're bleeding like a lamb in slaughter," Donegan said.

Harrington inched up against O'Roarke. "I'd swear . . . the arrow . . . it come from that end of the island." He pointed downstream as O'Roarke picked the arrowshaft from the sand.

That pricked Donegan's interest. "Down toward the tree?"

He nodded, then winced in pain. "I figger so."

Seamus gazed at his uncle. "Makes sense, doesn't it, Liam? Some of those horsemen dismounted down there . . . just so they could work their way up behind us."

"Wilson's hit!" someone shouted close by.

"Bill?"

"That's right," the voice answered. "It don't look good."

"Get the doc."

"Doc ain't no good to nobody now hisself."

Liam's eyes narrowed on Seamus. "All right. I'm throwing in with you, Nephew. Let's go sweep the far end clean of the red naggers."

Seamus smiled. "And find the bastird Confederate as well."

"Where you going?" The voice bellowed behind them as they clambered over the mule carcass.

Both turned. Donegan answered Beecher first. "We both make out that some of the horsemen dropped off at the end of the island."

Liam grinned widely. "We're off to clean out the vipers, Lieutenant."

"Don't expose yourselves needlessly," Beecher advised. "What with the number of wounded and dead . . . I can't chance losing any more riflemen."

"You watch upstream, Lieutenant. The boy and me will scrub the far end of the island clean."

Fifty yards of sweaty crawl through the tall grass brought them to a stand of plum-bushes. As they began to circle either side of the brush, bullets whined overhead, knocking Donegan's hat into the tumble of trampled grass.

"I smell 'em, boy," Liam whispered, wagging his pistol to give directions.

They would both crawl toward the solitary cottonwood——

A raucous war-cry split the air when five warriors rose as
one barely twenty yards away, sprinting for the white men.
Their mouths open and their weapons a blaze of smoke and
fire. Only one sent hissing arrows into the grass at the
younger Irishman.

Seamus fired his pistol once. Rolled to his right and fired
again, dropping the bowman. Rolled back to his left as
quickly to fire, bringing another warrior skidding onto his
knees. The painted Cheyenne slowly toppled forward, his
face gone in a spray of crimson.

Nearby, O'Roarke's pistol cracked four times. Then all
was quiet. Upstream, the sporadic rifle-fire from the creekbanks continued. Down at this end of the battle, everything
fell too quiet.

Seamus sensed his pulse slowing, some of the loud roar
disappearing from his ears. He crawled on his belly to the
first warrior. Then the second. Neither body what he wanted
most of all.

Slowly, Donegan parted the grass foot by foot, bellying it
toward the last sounds heard from Liam's side of the island.
Too quiet, it was. A knot of fear rose within him. Fearing his
uncle dead and the warriors lying in wait for him to show up.

He heard the hammer click about the same time the muzzle appeared out of the grass. Then a sigh of relief from the
big man holding the Colt pistol.

"Good thing you make more noise than a Cheyenne, little
nephew," O'Roarke whispered.

"They all dead?"

"On their way to Perdition as we speak, lad."

Something tensed within his belly again. "You seen the
Confederate down here?"

Liam's eyes narrowed as his face lost its smile. "No,
Seamus. He's gone."

"Gone?"

"Not a sign of him."

He felt the wings of sheer anxiety batter within the pit of
him. "But—I saw him down here . . . he crossed to the
island, fired the last few rounds at me from here as I was
crossing . . . by that tree." He pointed to the cottonwood.

Liam wagged his head. "Not here now. Likely these warriors killed 'im . . . mayhaps they captured the poor bastard and dragged him off. Save you the trouble of shooting him yourself . . . likely the savages will have their sport with him tonight after the sun goes down."

Seamus struggled to make some sense of it. The half-dozen or more they had seen scampering off the end of the island minutes ago. The five who had stayed to fight and lay dead in the grass for their trouble. And the mysterious disappearance of the Confederate. Perhaps Uncle Liam was right after all. Seeing how he knew the Indians in this country.

Yet something didn't cipher out right in Donegan's less-than-blissful ignorance.

"I don't think so, Liam." And he shook his head, the sun scorching the back of his neck. "Not captured. That bastird's laying off out there . . . somewhere. I don't know why—but I'll wager he'll be back—to finish what he didn't get done this morning."

Chapter 18

Seamus stared down at the bloody bandanna wrapping Forsyth's muscular leg. A strip of shirt-tail, an improvised bandage stained with a rusty brown patch on his shattered left calf. Another dirty patch drying on the bandage tied at the major's scalp.

"You looking at something funny, Irishman?"

Donegan glanced at Liam.

"I believe my nephew's thinking the same as me, Major," O'Roarke replied as he slid down into the rifle-pit. "You're lucky to be breathing, Forsyth."

"Bad thing about it, O'Roarke, I'm not the only one lucky to still be breathing." He struggled into his pants pocket, pulling free a tarnished watch. Snapping open the cover, he looked up at the sky a moment. "Like I thought. Not yet ten."

"We've had us four good hours of hell already, Major," Fred Beecher said.

Forsyth appeared to have to catch his breath after a new assault of pain. "How many wounded . . . Fred?" he whispered.

"Maybe a dozen."

"Including me?"

"Probably more," McCall advised.

Beecher nodded. "Didn't want to tell you, Major."

"Bad it is, Lieutenant." He smiled bravely. Looking around the group. "I'm sure we can all remember tougher scrapes we've . . . we've all been in—during the war, fellas."

Donegan watched Forsyth grind his teeth, fighting the mist in his eyes by blinking the tears away.

"Major," Seamus began.

"O'Roarke . . . you and your nephew get the hell out of here, will you? Go find someplace where you two can do some damage when the charge comes, by God."

"Yessir, Major," Liam replied, tugging Donegan along as he clambered out of the damp, sandy pit. "Be a good lad and obey the man, Seamus."

They crawled on hands and knees, skirting rifle-pits and horse carcasses, wounded scouts who moaned and called out for them to help, quietly whimpering for laudanum or a taste of tepid water from the canteens. Under the heat of a relentless sun, the stench of carcasses and blood, horse droppings, and dead men's bowels were enough to turn any stomach.

They passed through most pits without a word. Men sat grimly, studying the overgrown banks in solitude. From his position on the south side of the island, A. J. Pliley turned and nodded as the two Irishmen crawled past, then went back to scratching at the bottom of his pit. Patiently working his way down to murky, brackish water. Chauncey Whitney and Howard Morton dug in tandem to deepen their pit before the expected rush roared downstream.

"Up here!" Grover hollered when he turned to find the two Irishmen crawling his way. "Make yourselves to home, boys. Long as we can, that is. I figger these Cheyenne are about to let the wolf loose on us."

From this end of things, Donegan could gaze at the umber ridges, sun-burnt bluffs, and grass-cured hills. With an ache they reminded him of the warm corduroy of his boyhood britches back in County Kilkenny. He blinked his eyes, smarting at the tears in remembrance of her face as she stood on the dock at his sailing to Amerikay. Donegan hoped no man noticed his tears as he ground his knuckles into both eyes.

Looking about quickly to see if anyone had noticed, Seamus saw how the elder Farley and the Southern boy Dick Gantt among others had piled up the sand scooped from their pits on the upstream lip of the holes. Then both had

sawed the barrels of the carbines down through the lip of
damp sand to form narrow vees in which to rest their Spencers. Now they would command a wide field of fire when the
charge materialized.

Every one of them, in his own way, knew the riders were
coming.

Here the upstream end of the island was more blunt.
Down at the other end where he had gone hunting for the
Confederate near the crooked tree the island tapered off
more sharply.

Fifteen yards of shallow water separated the long, narrow
island from the north bank. Twenty yards, perhaps a little
more, of slow-moving water trickled past the south side of
the island.

Less than five yards away lay a half-dozen naked warriors.
Some of them crumpled as they had hit the riverbed. One lay
crushed beneath a dead war-pony.

Seamus swore that if he tried, he could reach out and
touch one of the copper-skins with his hand. The painted
Cheyenne wore a magpie tied to his greased hair. Tiny
crow's-feet scored the corners of the warrior's eyes as they
stared blankly at the sky.

Donegan looked away, remembering other battles. Other
screaming warriors. And knew once again, try as he had to
escape it, he had been pulled like a fleck of iron to a lode-
stone, drawn into the life of a soldier. These civilian mercenaries wore little he could call a uniform. Pieces, britches,
tunics, blouses. Yet beneath the hodgepodge of this rag-tag
bunch Forsyth proudly called his frontiersmen, Seamus
knew this fifty were of a kind.

A grateful Republic would move west in their wake.

"Looks like you boys seen the most of it up here," Liam
whispered.

Jack Stillwell turned at the brogue. His eyes caught Donegan's. They smiled at each other till Jack went back to
watching the bend upstream.

"That's right, you dumb Irishman," Grover said quietly.
"Up here we stare 'em in the eye. You know well as me when
you turn your back on a Injun—you're his meat."

Beside young Stillwell lay the oldest of them all, still frantically digging at his half of the rifle-pit. Scratching savagely

first with his huge knife, then jamming the blade into the dirt breastwork while his hands scooped out the cool, wet sand to fortify his position. Lou McLaughlin lay in a nearby pit. A dark, wet stain blotting his chest. Flecks of pink foam bubbled at his lips as he sucked in the hot air that hung like an ache over the island. Seamus could see he was in terrible pain. McLaughlin had dug at the grass while he was conscious, pulling up huge tufts with both hands. In McLaughlin's slack lips lay a short willow branch he bit into to keep from screaming until he passed out from the pain. That, and the blood seeping into the hot sand.

In the same pit lay old man Farley, and his boy, Hutch. Young Farley tied a knot again and again in the bloody bandanna around his father's arm, slowly twisting and untwisting the tourniquet to slow the loss of blood while his father fought down the pain.

Others continued to kick with their boot-heels, shoveling dirt up all round them as they gradually scraped themselves deeper and deeper into the sand. Certain the charge would come. It grew too damned quiet once the horsemen stopped circling and disappeared upstream. The snipers on both banks had eventually ended their withering fire.

The charge would come soon. And no man wanted to talk about their chances if five hundred or more horsemen rode down on . . . well, maybe there were thirty left who could hold a rifle.

He turned round, looking back down the island. In a rough ellipse of some twenty yards by forty yards, the remnants of Forsyth's fifty huddled in their pits. Like burrowing sowbugs hiding from swooping jays, the few still breathing waited. . . .

Thirty against——

Donegan stopped thinking about it. Shaming himself. A sane man never thought about the odds when he was down in it like this.

Beecher figured this was the Delaware Fork. Grover was every bit as certain this was the Arickaree. No matter the name, he figured. A shallow flow of yellowish water, seeping slowly down the middle of a wider channel between rows of cottonwoods and cutbanks of grassy sand.

Except for the stream itself, the riverbed lay as dry as

uncured rawhide at this late season of the year. The broad, cornsilk-yellow sky overhead and the sand of the Arickaree conspired with the undulating, heat-struck hills to form a bowl shimmering like a mirror down on the island, baking the top of Donegan's head until he wondered if his brain were simmering like the blood soup his mother loved to cook.

He cursed himself again for thinking about home, remembering that he had always thought about home before every battle.

Then he remembered there might no longer be a home for him back in County Kilkenny.

Before him, inches from his face, out where the barrel of the Henry lay, the breezes nudged the dry, brittle grasses left untrampled by the first waves of proud, brave warriors riding down the white men on the island. The way the wind snapped the brittle stalks, it reminded him at first of the horses and mules eating last night as he fell to sleep in the cool of darkness.

Yet, the snap made Seamus remember how at the first battle of Bull Run, he had come under fire for the first time in his life. How after four unsuccessful charges against the Confederate lines, riding back to regroup with fewer and fewer men each time—men cursing to the heavens that the Rebels were holding . . . Donegan remembered how the young regimental flag-boy, pimple-faced and peach-fuzzed, had taken his folding knife and begun slashing at their unit's flag.

With tears in his eyes, the boy explained to the young Irishman that with the next charge he knew he was going to fall, knew it as certain as he stood there cutting that flag into ribbons. So that was why he was cutting—to keep that flag from falling into the hands of those Johnnies . . . when it came time for him to die.

Donegan recalled turning away as the order was hollered, passed down the line for the next charge, sabers drawn and presented once more, watching that young, pimple-faced boy stuffing his flag down his shirt, holding the flagpole out like a lance as they broke into a gallop. And in the smoke and black cannon soot of that battlefield, he lost track of the boy. Not seeing him again, until Seamus found the youngster, pinned to the ground amid the carnage with a short chunk of that flagpole he had so proudly protected with his life.

The smells here reminded him of that day, and so many come later. Odors of men sweating fear, waiting to die alone in some unnamed place that existed on no map yet drawn. Knowing their bodies would know no grave, marked or otherwise.

He recognized the smell of sun warming the oiled wood of their rifles. The heat-stench of hot gun-oil sizzling in the breeches of the Spencers. Horse piss and the butchered mules' fetid organs drying on the grass. Blood seeping slowly, slowly into the sand of this unnamed little riverbed in the middle of . . .

Donegan felt himself start to cry inside. He didn't even know the name of the place he was asked to die for.

"Likely it's coming, boys!" someone shouted from behind. It sounded like Forsyth.

"One in the chamber and a full tube!" McCall this time.

"You heard the major," Grover growled. "If you ain't loaded, do it quick. The ball's about ready to open, girls!"

"Aye!" Liam roared, lusty. "And we'll dance every tune, you and me, Sharp Grover!"

As they laughed like men gone crazy, Seamus jammed hands into his dirty pants, each pocket filled with .44-caliber brass. He dug out a handful, then a second. He shoved what he could into the receiver. The rest he slipped between the fingers of both hands, leaving the trigger finger free. That gave him five shells he wouldn't have to dig for when it came time to reload.

He rolled to his side, inching an elbow down into the sandy lip of Grover's rifle-pit. And watched his uncle quietly sliding a Blakeslee loading tube from the wooden ammunition box that lay open at the rear of their pit. O'Roarke rammed it home, locking it up the butt of his Spencer.

"Best you make yourself as small as you can, young Seamus," Liam whispered. "See that fella what just rode atop that hill?"

"I do, Uncle."

"Looks like the ball is set to open now, O'Roarke!" Grover hissed.

Liam nodded, never taking his eyes off his nephew. "That

big one—horns on his head and the feathers falling down his back and off the side of the pretty war-pony of his—he's the one gonna get things started to make things hard on us."

"Hard on us?" Seamus squeaked. "What the divil can that one h'athen do to us them others already ain't?"

Liam grinned. Then hid his teeth behind a determined grimace and gazed at the top of the hill, where the big warrior had disappeared as quickly as he had come to appraise the island.

"Likely, Nephew—that was Roman Nose. Better that it were the divil hisself."

For those early hours of that morning, the great war-chief had remained behind in his lonely lodge in the Cheyenne village while the others went out to attack the white man's camp. Now with most everyone deserting the village to watch the show, old ones and the women as well as young boys, Roman Nose sensed a long silence settle over the great circle of buffalo-hide lodges.

He had sent the warriors on to the battle at dawn, telling them he would come after he had made peace with his medicine. So he had spent much of the morning here, desperate to find some way of propitiating his spirit-helpers, to repair the cracks in his theology.

In the background he listened to the faint staccato of gun-fire rattling many miles away down the creek.

Closer still, the war-chief heard the snuffling of camp-dogs raiding abandoned kettles left simmering over fires gone cold hours ago. Snarling, angry dogs, fighting over the spoils in this abandoned camp. Outside his lodge, the dog fight tumbled against the buffalo-hides. Then he listened as the mongrels suddenly darted away across the hard earth.

Two horses coming, he decided. Their pounding hooves skidded to a stop before his dark, stifling lodge, growing hot beneath the climbing of the sun toward mid-sky. He heard the ponies blow from their hard ride, come here from the fight to this deserted village.

"Does the great Roman Nose cower in the dark when there are whitemen to butcher like captured calves?"

It was White Contrary's voice. Once a friend. His voice now cut with a cruel edge.

"Roman Nose!"

A second voice. Two Crows. Arguing quietly with Two Crows.

"Roman Nose—come to the fight with us now. Our warriors need you to lead us!" Two Crows pleaded to the lodge.

"I don't know why they need a coward like you, Roman Nose!" White Contrary shouted. "Better that the men of the *Shahiyena* slaughter these whitemen without a leader . . . than be shamed by a war-chief who hides in the darkness of his lodge."

For the great Cheyenne war-chief, that warrior instinct running hot in his blood proved too strong.

One foot he planted outside the doorway, sensing the hot breeze that snarled his long breechclout reaching past his knees. Then he rose to full height outside his lodge, breathing deep and swelling his chest. He could see it in their eyes as he had moved into the light of mid-morning, saw them recognize the cruel determination in his own eyes on either side of that sharp, angular nose.

"You come here to shame an old friend?" he said quietly to the mounted warrior before him.

White Contrary had painted his face, the upper half black and the lower half striped in yellow. Two Crows wore his medicine-paint: the lower half of red ocher beneath four spreading wings to represent the two crows of his medicine dreams. Roman Nose wore no face-paint.

"I come here to bring you to the fight," White Contrary explained arrogantly. "Whatever it may take."

Two Crows's pony pranced as its rider studied both proud warriors, not certain of what blood might be spilled here in the silence of this abandoned village.

"Come, Roman Nose. The fight does not go well."

"The whitemen escaped?"

Two Crows shook his head. He saw White Contrary draw himself up in anger, his thin lips made thinner by the way he pressed them together.

"No, they have not run away. We have them circled on a long strip of sand in the river."

"I have heard much firing this morning."

"And surely you have heard many brave warriors dying as well!" White Contrary spat on the ground.

"If I go, old friends—it will be my own blood that dries on the sand of that riverbed."

"You trust too much to an old woman's medicine!"

He turned full on White Contrary, startling Two Crows with its suddenness. "For many winters I have trusted my medicine! And many were the times I raised the hair of the whiteman for trusting in it."

"An old woman cannot ruin the medicine of a powerful war-chief," White Contrary snorted, his head falling backward in loud laughter.

"Perhaps you are right, White Contrary," he finally said after a painful silence, his low voice very quiet now. "But there is no time to properly heal my medicine in the proscribed ceremony."

"If not healing your medicine, Roman Nose—what is it you have been doing all morning in the darkness of your smokeless lodge?"

"Praying, Two Crows."

He stepped behind his lodge, where he took up the rawhide tether for his war-pony where it stood picketed on some good grass. Returning immediately to the others, the warchief removed the famous buffalo-horned bonnet from the tripod in front of his lodge. Nudging it down upon his huge head, he swept himself atop his pony, allowing the long, double-tail of golden eagle feathers to sweep across the pony's flanks, just brushing the ground. His feet hung loose as he stared back at Two Crows.

"Praying that before I must die as commanded by the Powers Above . . . praying that I will have a chance to kill the tall, gray-eyed whiteman I am destined to meet on that strip of sand in the middle of that river."

Chapter 19

John Donovan watched the stocky, square-jawed Major Sandy Forsyth prop himself up against the side of his narrow rifle-pit, painfully swallowing down the torment of his wounds.

One of the lucky ones, Donovan thought to himself. *Figured I was lucky to get this chance to ride with the major. Lots more like me . . . farmers or hunters . . . all wanted to come have a go to even the score against these red bastards.*

But, I figured I was lucky the major picked me to ride with him.

Donovan didn't believe a bit of it now as they all waited for the charge. The men on the island could hear them beyond the first bend in the river. Up there, the warriors shouted, sang, and chanted. Noisy. Working themselves up for it.

Another crazy blast on that army bugle raised the hair on the back of his neck.

Upstream it echoed. Beyond the far bend where a man couldn't tell what was going on. Just that the horsemen, hundreds and hundreds of them, had disappeared there minutes ago. Then a handful of feathered bastards had crowned a nearby hill, gazing down as if studying the defenders on the island. A moment ago they too slipped out of sight.

Likely to join up with the rest now that they've given us a looking over . . . seeing how many of us can still hold a rifle.

Donovan looked the island over himself. Already close to half were dead or wounded from the first skirmishes. Still, some of the wounded were holding weapons now—what with talk of the charge coming.

Nearby a few of the men muttered among themselves. Old man Trudeau was even cursing at his Spencer in French, again and again jamming a loading tube into his Spencer. In a far pit, young Hutch Farley hovered over his badly wounded father, quietly reciting by rote those foreign words his mother had taught him long ago and far away when he was but a knee-hugger.

"Our Father, which art in heaven . . ."

Donovan felt the bile scorch the back of his throat. *Better that it comes now,* he figured. *The waiting will be the death of me if it don't.*

"Hold your fire when they come, boys!" Forsyth hollered.

He had raised himself on his elbows at the side of his pit to give the command, his voice weak, yet clear as the bright sky overhead. "I'll give the command to fire by volley."

"Aim low, fellas," Sergeant McCall added. "That way—you don't get a redskin, least you knock a horse down for good measure."

Donovan scraped up John Wilson's revolver and carbine, dragging them near. He discovered a pair of young eyes staring at him in wonder.

"What you looking at, Jew-boy?"

Sigmund Shlesinger swallowed, found out. "I . . . I——"

"It don't matter." Donovan came close to an apology, sorry already for his words. "Wilson don't need 'em anyway, not now."

"I suppose he don't," answered the youngster. Shlesinger turned away sheepishly.

"And us still alive," Donovan said, trying out a weak smile. "Up to us to make every shot worth at least one Injun."

"Have you not seen enough, Roman Nose?" White Contrary goaded the war-chief once more.

Down below, the fighting had all but stopped.

Instead of reacting immediately to White Contrary's prodding, the huge, bronzed war-chief stayed on his haunches, huddled in the grass of the hilltop as he looked down on the island.

On either side of the river, the banks stood slightly higher than the sandy island itself, giving the Sioux and Cheyenne snipers a good field of fire. They forced the white men to stay hidden for the most part, down in their pits and behind the bodies of their dead animals. Roman Nose could tell the warriors were milling about on the creekbanks now, having heard he had arrived. Now the anxious hundreds waited to learn what the war-chief would do to break the stalemate.

"That place where the whitemen gather will soon smell of rotting horses, Two Crows," he said quietly, holding out his hand. "Hand me my pouch, old friend."

White Contrary snorted. "You smoke here? Hah! While your warriors are spilling their blood below your feet, you prepare your pipe? Perhaps the great Roman Nose figures that by the time he finishes his pipe, the brave ones fighting below will win the fight for him . . . and he will not have to ride into battle."

Tangle Hair glared at the loudmouthed White Contrary. "Yesterday, the Sioux woman who cooked a meal for us destroyed the powerful war medicine of——"

"We have all heard the story, old man!" White Contrary snarled, his eyes never leaving Roman Nose.

How he hungers to have my place among our people, Roman Nose brooded to himself as his eyes followed Two Crows from his pony.

Two Crows handed his old friend the small pouch, watching Roman Nose open and pull forth the vial of bear grease and the ground-earth paints. The old man said, "Roman Nose has never let others do his fighting for him, White Contrary. Not even those with tongues like the magpies."

White Contrary started to lunge for the old warrior, but Roman Nose bolted to his feet, all six-foot-three of him, barring the way.

"White Contrary would do well to argue with the whitemen who are killing so many of us this day . . . and not pick a fight he cannot win," The Nose said, settling once more on his haunches, pulling a small hand mirror from the pouch.

"Here sits the powerful Roman Nose, the man that we

depend on, sitting behind this hill. He is the man that makes it easy for his men in any battle, leaving his warriors without his medicine."

"Even a Cheyenne without medicine is stronger than a Sioux with the strongest magic."

Slowly, carefully, as prescribed by his spirit helpers in his visions, Roman Nose applied the great streaks of ox-blood across his eyes, yellow ocher across his cheeks. A black smear down his chin. The colors he had worn into so many battles. In winter near the white soldiers' fort at the Piney Woods when he had captured himself a Springfield rifle. In summer heat, when he and others attacked the tiny corral of white men at the edge of the meadow where they cut the hay for the soldier fort on the Bighorn River.

"Do you listen, Roman Nose?" White Contrary went on. "Do you not see your men falling down there? Two fell just as I came up this hill to see what kept you from our fight. All those young ones fighting down there feel that they belong to the great Roman Nose. They will do anything that you tell them, throwing their bodies away if you command it. But here you sit, behind this hill!"

Now come another summer fight, brooded Roman Nose in silence. His sweat beading on his face beneath the high sun. Dampness mixing readily with the gummy bear grease and dry pigment in the palm of his hand as he finished painting his face, then circled that summer's fresh, pale pucker-scars on his chest from the sundance on the banks of the Beaver.

The day he realized his vision was come at last. Roman Nose stood, his eyes finding the big mulatto among the group.

"Nibsi!"

"Uncle!" Jack O'Neill drew close. "It is you these warriors need now!"

"Our medicine man will ride on one side of me, leading the charge. You will ride on the other side . . . so that you will see the face of the man you are to find."

"The one I am to kill for you, Roman Nose."

He smiled, those big, white teeth gleaming in the sun of this bloody day. "No, Nibsi. The face of the one you must kill for *you!*"

"*Aiyeee-yi-yi-yi!*" Jack O'Neill hollered, thumping his

bare chest, his cry answered by the rest of those war-chiefs who clustered round Roman Nose when he first arrived at the hilltop.

"Come, my brothers." The big one took up the reins to his chestnut and leaped aboard. O'Neill tossed him the old soldier Springfield from the fight of the Hundred-in-the-Hand.

Roman Nose tightened the horsehair surcingle twice round his legs, lashing himself to his pony. Then smoothed the brilliant scarlet silk sash he tied at his waist. A gift from the white treaty-talkers at the Fort Ellsworth peace conference summers ago.

One last time he shook out the long trail of war-eagle feathers and herons' plumes.

"You chiefs will watch Roman Nose die this day—as a warrior. See to it our people win a great victory to ease the long journey of my shattered body to the other side. May this be a victory washed in my blood!"

"Sweet Mither of God!"

He had seen the two thousand massed in the valley of the Peno after Fetterman had marched eighty men to the slaughter behind Lodge Trail Ridge.

A summer later he had watched the hundreds charge and circle, charge and circle the little corral at the edge of the hayfield near the Bighorn River.

Yet nothing had prepared Seamus Donegan for the sight of Roman Nose leading his horsemen round the far bend upstream, charging into view only seconds after the scouts heard the thunder of the two thousand hooves.

From bank to bank the front row stretched some sixty warriors strong. Behind them, row upon galloping row. Feathers fluttering on the breeze and they came on. Scalplocks tied to rifle-barrels catching the wind. Loose hair and braids and roached hair plastered with grease, standing as a challenge to any scalp-taker.

Ponies painted with magic symbols, scalp-locks pendant from lower jaws, every tail bound up for war in red ribbon and trade-cloth. Bows and repeaters and old Springfield muzzle-loaders, brandished aloft as they came on in a colorful show, held in check by the presence of the greatest war-chief on the Central Plains.

"Just look at him, will you?" Fred Beecher whispered, his voice rife with unconcealed admiration.

"Roman Nose makes a pretty impressive sight, lad," O'Roarke whispered at Donegan's ear.

"Think I've seen that bastird somewhere before," Seamus replied, the long, wide scar at his back burning. He glanced over his shoulder, sure he would find the Confederate. Instead, only the wide, disbelieving eyes of every scout still able to hold a rifle.

"Don't fire till the major gives the order, boys!" McCall shouted. "Like taking on cavalry, it is."

The rifle-fire from the creekbanks increased in fiery intensity. It was plain the snipers intended to force the scouts to keep their heads down under the deadly barrage of lead hail. Yet, Seamus knew their only chance lay in being able to keep their heads up and meet the charge.

"Wait!" Forsyth hollered behind them. "Get down, Curry!"

There was a rustling behind him, then silence once more. Seamus was certain he heard someone praying quietly off to his left. Then the voice was washed over with the growing crescendo of pounding hooves bearing down on this little unprotected heap of sand and spring-washed gravel in a riverbed called the Arickaree.

Suddenly the rattle of all rifle-fire from the banks withered away. And in its place was the first of the wild cries from the women and old ones on the surrounding hills. Instantly, the eerie blood-song rose in volume, a swelling chorus enough to chill any man still conscious on that island. Black smoke from the silenced Indian rifles drifted lazily across the hot riverbed as more rows of horsemen followed Roman Nose downstream.

"Get down, Major!" Lieutenant Beecher yelled.

"They can pick you off from the bank, sir!"

That time it was McCall hollering from somewhere behind Donegan. He did not turn around to see. Seamus kept his eyes on the advancing phalanx of brown-skinned cavalry.

"Aim and *hold!*"

Forsyth's order heeded, each man rested the Spencer's front blade on a warrior in the front line. And Donegan wondered when the major would give the order. He was used to riding with the cavalry, charging down on the fortified positions. Not like this. *Infantry work,* he thought now. *Burrowed like moles in this sand, waiting for them to ride over us.*

"Hold it! Hold it!" Beecher was hollering as well, moving now, his voice inching closer, the sound of his boots scraping sand coming closer as well.

Seamus felt himself ready to scream . . . this waiting. But suddenly took hope in the thought that these men were not green, pants-wetting youngsters in for their first fight. Most had faced guns before, if not Indians. His breathing grew shallow as he realized most of these already bore scars, as did he, from other long, long days.

He whispered to Liam, "When will he order——"

"When he's ready, Donegan!" Beecher snapped.

Liam glanced over and smiled at his nephew. "Easy, lad."

"I don't take to a man riding me down like this, Uncle."

"You're seeing history made, Donegan," Fred Beecher said, smiling. "Not a man's seen Indians charge like cavalry before!"

"Major knows what he's doing, lad," Liam replied. "Besides, us dug in here like we are . . . can't take the chance of wasting bullets—they're still too far out there."

"Far!" Seamus snorted. "I'll be shaking hands with the bastirds in but another breath——"

"Now!"

Forty guns exploded around him, their muzzles jetting brilliant tongues of fire.

"Now!" Beecher echoed Forsyth's command.

"Give it to 'em, boys!" hollered Billy McCall right behind Donegan.

That first volley unhorsed but two.

"Shoot low, dammit!" O'Roarke was yelling now. "Hold your breath and shoot for the ponies!"

"Spill 'em, fellas!" Sharp Grover added his voice.

On galloped the warriors, kicking their ponies into a full run without slowing for their fallen. Roman Nose answered the rifle-fire with an unearthly war-cry, popping his hand against his mouth as his head arched back, sending his curse of death to the heavens.

In a heartbeat that bloody cry was taken up by the five

hundred. On the hilltops a renewed chant thundered from the throats of the women and old ones.

"Again!"

A second volley roared from the island. The smoke from so many weapons hung in the stillness above the riflemen, turning the sky a murky, dirty gray.

"Fire, by damned!" Beecher was up on his knees, hollering behind them, urging.

More horsemen spilled this time, their ponies coming on with the rest. Charging without slowing, heeding neither the rifles nor their fallen. Their throaty cries for blood redoubled now as holes ripped open in their ranks. Then as quickly those holes filled anew with warriors lurching up from behind. The phalanx made solid once more.

Ponies wavering. A few going down as sand flew from their slashing hooves. Glittering like fine gold-dust in the high sun of this summer day.

Seventeenth day of September, he reminded himself. And waited with his finger on the trigger of his Henry for the next command.

Like a good soldier you are . . .

"Now!"

Forsyth's command was barely out of his mouth this time before the island ignited again for the third volley into the face of the five hundred. Closer now. He judged less than a hundred yards. Killing range. With every bullet, forty men had to kill more than sixty men on the front row.

From what Seamus could tell through the murky haze of yellow sunlight slanting through the powdersmoke, the warriors were falling over one another with that third volley. And ponies too. Going down in bloody, tumbling, spinning heaps. Shrieks from the hillsides as the women and old ones watched the slaughter of their chosen.

He slammed back the action on the Henry, ramming home another cartridge, then fed three into the receiver from his fingers. Hurried, his hands sweating, sticking to the brass cases. Hard to yank free from between his fingers. As much damage as they had done to the phalanx of horsemen, still they came on, riding faster. Hoofbeats pounding harder.

Odds told him that forty men volley-firing against a charge of hundreds would not work for long. Then he prayed good infantry soldiers like Forsyth and Beecher and Billy McCall knew how to fight this way against cavalry. Because this damned well was something new to Seamus Donegan. And damned scary as well.

"Fire!"

"Hit 'em with every shot, men!" Beecher reinforced Forsyth's order.

"Knock one of those godless fornicators straight to hell, Seamus," Liam said grimly, then winked as his face eased. "We don't, likely be us two dancing with the divil this night."

With that fourth volley the warriors ceased their mighty screeching. Most not already hollering in pain and frustration rode on grim-lipped into the mouth of the fire-spitting riflemen. Following their chosen leader at the center of the first line, every man weaving back and forth, making it hard to take a bead on him. Recklessly coming on, Roman Nose raised his arm, exhorting the hundreds behind him in the riverbed, splattering water and grit and gravel as they come on.

"By God, boys! We're whittling 'em down!" McCall shouted.

"Now!"

And a fifth volley split the air.

Through the gray smoke hung like dirty gauze above his rifle-pit, something shouted inside him now, telling Seamus to aim for the one Liam called Roman Nose.

Chapter 20

Roman Nose sensed the pony beneath him begin to falter. Nothing close to a stumble. Something so faint only a man raised from infancy with a powerful animal like this beneath him could sense.

As much as he himself had bobbed and weaved each time the soldier guns were trained on him, Roman Nose had not foreseen that the straining ponies would take the brunt of the white man's rifles. In all the battles past, the great war-chief had ridden out alone. But now, riding in this full-fronted charge, there was no way he could rein his pony from side to side, dipping his body from left and right.

One choice only—he and the others must ride the white men down, crushing them into the sand of the riverbed.

In barbaric splendor Roman Nose drew himself up when a second shock-wave exploded through the ranks, causing more of those about him to pitch from their ponies.

For an instant, The Nose glanced at the women and children and old ones too weak to fight, on the hilltops to watch the might of all the gathered bands sweep across the island in victory. One last time he raised his arm in the grandest of royal sweeps to his people of these plains.

They answered this war-prince with renewed cries of encouragement, screeching for Roman Nose himself to bring about the defeat of the half-a-hundred.

With their voices ringing in his ears, the breeze tugging at the horned bonnet tied beneath his bronze chin, Roman Nose once more glared into the muzzles of those rifles spitting fire at his charging followers. He tightened his hold on the chestnut pony, again sensing that failing in the lungs, a gasping, a straining for continued strength. His knees tightened about the pony's ribs, held tight beneath the horsehair surcingle. Then for an instant he let go of the short rawhide bridle, shaking his fist at his white-skinned enemies, burrowed like mice in their sandy holes.

At his right knee, a warrior fell with the third volley, blown backward off his pony in a spray of blood and brain.

Nearer and nearer they pounded toward the island, every man at a full gallop. The fallen warrior was replaced with the old medicine man, White Bull. The warrior-cries thundered about his ears as river spray and sandy grit flew in all directions.

He swallowed it down, and rejoiced in taking into his body the water and earth of this place where his medicine had brought him.

The fourth volley took the old medicine man from his side. He glanced at the cloudless blue overhead, cursing the white murderers. Shamans like White Bull were not supposed to fight, but this one had come to ride alongside Roman Nose, if only to assure the young Cheyenne warchief that his powerful medicine suffered no taint.

To have White Bull the medicine man riding at his right knee had been a good omen. When the old man spilled from his pony, dead before he hit the sand to be trampled beneath hundreds of hooves, Roman Nose knew the course of the day had been decided.

Still, he rode on.

Up ahead, the white men loomed closer. Heads only, peering over the lip of their rifle-pits. Down in the grass.

Only minutes ago he had knelt on the hilltop, gazing down at the island. It had reminded Roman Nose of a squat, oblong anthill, this place where the white men hid. Dead horses had been dragged into a ragged oval like the shape a Cheyenne lodge makes upon the camping ground.

What seemed like only heartbeats ago, it was in the gorge beyond the first bend of the river that Roman Nose had told the hundreds of his plan.

"The Brule and Oglalla and Arapaho will join us, my brothers. No more do we need to shoot at the island, because the whiteman burrows himself like the barking dogs of the prairie."

"H'gun—h'gun!" the Sioux warriors shouted, declaring their respect for Roman Nose in using the Lakota courage word.

"Send runners swiftly to both sides of the riverbank. Tell them to keep the whitemen down by shooting at them until our ponies are almost on top of them."

"H'gun!"

"Like mice forced into their holes by the bullets from our brothers on the riverbanks . . . the whiteman will soil their pants to watch us ride down on them. Crushing the life from their bodies."

"Hoka HEY!"

"The Arapaho's white brother, the one called Kansas, will blow his horn again during our charge. Blow, Kansas! Blow the death-song for these whitemen soon to give up their spirits to us!"

Out of the gorge, into the narrow valley itself he led his hundreds at a walk, Nibsi at his side. To his right, the wrinkled face of the medicine man smiled like cracking walnuts beneath the old shaman's owl-feather cap.

Turning a moment and seeing the last of the horsemen had cleared the gorge, Roman Nose had kicked his strong chestnut into a lope, the long trail of war-eagle feathers and herons' plumes bannered out on the hot wind.

The young white man and former bugler of the 7th U.S. Cavalry, Jack Clybor held the tin horn to his lips and blew for all he was worth. Abandoned the year before by his fellow soldiers, Clybor had been found and cared for by a small band of nomadic Arapaho. Ever since becoming "Kansas" to his adopted people, the renegade had become a bloodthirsty adversary as well, torturing cruelly, mercilessly killing white men, women, and children on the Central Plains.

"Come, my brothers! Let us turn their hearts to water!" Roman Nose shouted as Clybor's bugle call faded from the riverbanks.

Once he and the first row had come round the far bend of the river upstream from the island, a wild cry leaped from his throat as he beat his hand against his mouth with the Cheyenne call for death.

Behind him, the hundreds cried out their death-songs in response, until their haunting voices reverberated from river-bank to riverbank.

Though he heard the many behind him as they neared the island, Roman Nose nonetheless felt alone.

More alone than he had in all his life, a life spent without a woman, without children to exalt in his name after this glorious day. None of his blood carried on in his name. Instead, his juices would soak into this sandy riverbed. The sand of this place the only memorial to his passing.

He could pick out a few of the white faces now, some taut with fear. Others gone pale at the sight of what he led down on them.

Would none of these whites dare fight him like a man? Would they all lay in hiding? When would the gray-eyed one of his vision show himself?

The fifth volley ripped through his ranks, shredding the warriors and the ponies into bloody ribbons as they closed on seventy yards.

He recognized two in blue shirts, then a third behind the first row of riflemen. These must be the leaders, he decided. Three who knelt behind the protection of those guns, yelling their orders. When they spoke, the guns spat fire. He decided to ride directly over the top of the defenders, killing those leaders as he rode them down.

At twenty yards, Roman Nose ceased weaving, clamping his legs round the faltering pony, feeling the animal's warm blood on his own bare legs. He tensed his muscles for the coming leap out of the riverbed and onto the island itself, where the white men waited for him.

As it was in the sundance dream, he watched the hatless one in the blue shirt rise on his elbows, waving his arm wildly, his mouth silently giving voice to a wordless command. The one with a bloody bandage wrapped at his head.

Roman Nose tightened the hand he gripped in the pony's mane, yanking upward as he brought the muzzle of his rifle down, aiming at the soldier in the blue shirt and bandage. Then out of the smoke rising from those rifle-pits saw one stand.

A single white man stand.

In that sundance dream—rising. Solitary. Looming tall from the dense, yellow-gray powdersmoke.

The tall one of his medicine vision. Come to pass, here on the sandy riverbed of his prayer-dream.

He watched the tall one calmly throw his rifle against his shoulder, aiming.

The Cheyenne war-chief no longer aimed his captured rifle at the wounded soldier in blue. Aimed now at the tall, dark-haired one with the whiskers blackening his chin.

Roman Nose pulled the trigger on his Lodge Trail rifle at the exact moment he watched fire belch from the tall one's weapon.

Unable to reload, Roman Nose swung the rifle backward, preparing to use it as a club when his pony clawed from the riverbed onto the lip of the sandy island. The animal stumbled, down for a moment on its forelegs, then fought back up, leaping into a ragged gallop toward the first rifle-pits.

Those first rifle-pits where the tall one had cocked his rifle and slammed it against his shoulder once more. Standing above the others who remained huddled in their holes.

A brave one, this man, Roman Nose thought, the sounds of it inside his head like a prayer.

If I am to die, let it be this gray-eyed one who takes the breath from my body, oh—All-Spirit! Hear me!

Were it not for the surcingle lashing his legs to the weakening pony at that instant, Roman Nose would have tumbled into the rifle-pits himself. Instead, he swallowed down the sudden fire burning low in his back as his pony leaped, and leaped again over the scattered, struggling for the far riverbank.

Wearily, he laid his head alongside the pony's neck, feeling at last the warm, frothy blood and lather blowing against his cheeks from the countless wounds in the animal's chest.

And for the first time sensed that he was sitting in his own juices, warm and sticky as the chestnut shuddered to a halt on the riverbank opposite the island. Stopping so suddenly in the swamp-willow and plum-brush that its rider nearly slipped off. The pony trembled as it would to shed water, trying to stand beneath the growing weight of its rider.

Roman Nose himself could no longer stay on. The sunlight was disappearing from his mind, as if the bullet holes in his body had allowed the prayer-light to seep from his body in huge rivulets with his warm blood.

He sank to the grass, choking up clots of the sticky fluid collecting at the back of his throat. Sensing his eyes rolling back in his head. He fought it, like nothing else he had fought in his life. And began crawling, clawing with his hands, pulling with the waning strength left to his arms.

His legs useless now, his back shattered with the bullet from the gray-eyed one's rifle.

The darkness swept over him, remembering it felt much like this in the sundance.

When your body was no longer yours to control. And you gave yourself up to the Everywhere Spirit at last . . .

"Down, goddammit!" Billy McCall shrieked at the young Irishman, watching O'Roarke trying to pull Donegan back into the pit after that first shot.

As he said it the attacking warriors closed on twenty yards. With a parting swirl of the powdersmoke, McCall could see ponies' nostrils swell, their eyes widening like saucers of sour buttermilk back home in Pennsylvania. Time and again as a leader of infantry in the Civil War he had witnessed the charge of Confederate cavalry. Yet nothing this eerie: the wails and chants of the women, the screams of the ponies going down, the shrieks of the warriors' bone whistles.

Not that a man like Billy McCall was afraid of facing the charge standing. Any man who knew that Forsyth's sergeant had been breveted a brigadier-general for his heroism in taking Fort Steadman during the siege of Petersburg could hardly call Billy a coward.

He saw the huge warrior's pony suddenly, surging ahead as the Indian aimed his rifle at Donegan.

The bastard is using one of the Fetterman Springfields!

In a swirl of sand, grit, smoke, and yellow haze, the ponies leaped from the river, snorting in a hell of noisy terror onto the end of the island. As quickly some of the animals spilled with the seventh and final volley tearing into their ranks. Spilling warriors, turning the row upon row of naked horsemen to the side, like a wave crashing upon the rocky coast.

Brown bodies tumbled into the sand, lapping on the shallow, churning waters beaten to a froth by the thousand thundering hooves.

Cries of the wounded from both sides reverberated as the wave collided with the rocks, parting the waters in a violent explosion.

Donegan had to get that bastard!

Billy saw the bloody hole open up on the huge warrior's side as he leaped by the young Irishman, like a huge turkey-buzzard, so big it momentarily blotted out the sky above them.

Donegan stood his ground, pumping and firing, pumping and firing again and again. His muzzle swinging in a slow, controlled arch, following the single horseman that leaped and leaped again through the maze of rifle-pits.

Until the wounded, bloody rider reined his dying pony off the island, kicking up spray across the shallow branch of the creek, and into the swamp-willow. To disappear.

"Down, men!" Forsyth was shrieking, up on one elbow, as Billy's eyes found him through the murky haze.

A scattered cheer erupted. O'Roarke and Grover, hollering like bellowing bulls in contest. Leaping to their feet as the charge melted to either side of the island. Scouts clambering up out of their pits, pistols barking in their hands at the retreating warriors. Killing all the ones who fell close enough to finish off.

"Get down!" Beecher was shouting.

Joined by McCall: "Down for your lives, boys!"

But none of the scouts paid them any mind until the instant those snipers hidden on the banks saw the charge had been bested and opened fire on the island, furious at their failure.

Billy lunged for O'Roarke, who was clawing at Donegan, vainly trying to drag his nephew down into Grover's pit.

In a spray of blood he saw Liam arch his back, his huge body flung backward like a sack of damp oats hurled from the bed of a freight-wagon.

Donegan had watched it happen, surely must have felt his uncle's hands ripped from him while he continued to fire into the willows on the bank where the wounded Cheyenne horseman had disappeared on his dying pony.

Diving into the pit, kicking at the sand below him with

both legs, Billy reached O'Roarke as Donegan was collapsing into the pit as well, his own body suddenly sheltering his uncle. Together they rolled Liam gently over as sniper bullets whined and whistled overhead, smacking into wounded Cheyenne ponies, legs akimbo and thrashing as they jumbled with the white man's horses long dead now.

"Ain't no use, Irishman. The side of his damned head's gone," McCall whispered, swallowing hard and looking away at anything, even Donegan's face. As long as he did not have to look at O'Roarke's riven skull.

Grit and sand clung to the bright, sticky crimson that oozed itself down the side of O'Roarke's face and neck. Seamus swiped again and again at the sand, then ripped at the tail of his damp shirt. He pressed it against the awful wound.

McCall knew there was no chance. Too much skull gone. The brain turned to sausage-meat by a big-caliber lead ball fired from an old muzzle-loader.

He gripped Donegan's shoulder, snagging one hand with his. Seamus ripped his hand away. Went back to swiping the grit from the gaping head-wound the size of his clenched fist.

"Donegan . . . ain't nothing you can do for 'im now," Sharp Grover said quietly as he slid to the Irishman's far side, glancing at McCall for a desperate moment.

"*Liam!*" Seamus shouted. "Oh, sweet Mither of God . . . I have heartily offended thee——"

"C'mon, lemme wrap his head." Grover tried soothing, tried pulling Donegan's hands away from his uncle's head.

"Don't go on me, Liam! I promised," Donegan whimpered, the front of his shirt smeared dark and moist.

"I have to cover him, Seamus," Grover said strongly now. "Or he'll bleed to death before nightfall."

Suddenly Donegan stopped cradling his uncle's head against him, and for a moment there came a lull in the shooting. A thick gurgle rattled at the back of O'Roarke's throat as Seamus took his hands off the terrible wound. Grover was there as quickly with the rolled tail of his shirt. McCall's hands worked with the scout's, looping a dirty red bandanna around the bandage. Together they wiped blood and sand from Liam's cheeks and eyes, vainly wiping their hands off on their britches before wiping more wet grit off the Irishman.

McCall looked up at Seamus as he sank back against the side of the rifle-pit, staring still at his uncle's ashen face. In Donegan's eyes showed the first fear Sergeant McCall could admit to seeing.

"Oh, dear God," Seamus whispered, gnawing on his own bloody knuckle. "Looks now, Uncle—like you'll be going home afore me."

Chapter 21

"*K*ill that sonuvabitch!" one of the scouts shrieked. "God-damn red bastard fornicator!"

"I see'd him bleed," a second voice rose, not far from Donegan. "I see'd it!"

"You . . . you sure?" Donegan asked, inching up the back of a bloating mule.

Eli Ziegler turned. His eyes hard and as red as ten-hour coals. "I see'd it with my own eyes, Irishman. Gut-shot. 'Nother'n in the lights."

"I hit 'im twice?"

Ziegler nodded, tongue dabbing at his sun-chapped lips. "That blight on all the children of the Lord is done for this life. Cry, hallelujah!"

"Hurrah!" another scout called out. A few more cheered raggedly.

Seamus slid down from the bloated carcass.

Grover smiled grimly. "No matter how many of them goddammed bucks we killed in that charge . . . no one can say we didn't sure as hell put down a bunch of them ponies, Seamus." He pointed. "Look at 'em out there."

Seamus nodded. "Them h'athens ain't about to come dragging off their wounded now."

Sharp snorted, spitting tobacco-juice in a high arc, hitting the closest brown body with a dark splat. "Bastards can't drag off their dead ponies neither. That's what's gotta hurt. We killed us a bunch of horseflesh out there."

"Grover?"

It struck Seamus as he lay there in the rifle-pit, sensing his limbs finally tingling back to life after the flush of adrenaline from the charge had fired his veins, that Sandy Forsyth's voice sounded weakened, yet still filled with resolve.

All round him the scouts in their bloodied, trampled pits quickly yanked long Blakeslee tubes from their wooden ammunition boxes placed between each pair of men, ramming them home up the butts of their Spencers. His own weapon had never been so hot to the touch. The Henry scorched his palm as he laid it across his belly, letting his heart slow, staring at the bloodied form sprawled across his legs.

Sharp Grover rolled on his elbow, rising slightly to look down-island at the fatigue-taut, smoke-blackened face peering over the lip of a nearby pit. "Yes, Major?"

"C-can they do better than this, Sharp?"

The scout considered a moment, never taking his eyes off the commander of those men huddled on the island.

"Major, I been on my own, living on these here plains—as man and boy for more'n thirty years. I gotta tell you . . . all of you—I ain't never seen anything like what we just saw before. Far as my thinking, they done their level best to ride us into the ground, Major. The bastards can't do no better."

Seamus watched Forsyth and the two other soldiers relax almost imperceptibly, shoulders sagging.

Donegan had been in uniform and fought enough battles to recognize when a soldier knew he had his enemy beaten. And clearly, Forsyth considered what they had just done a victory. No matter that it was a costly one; surviving that massed charge was nothing short of a decisive victory.

"All right, men," Forsyth said clearly, his voice a bit stronger now as he swallowed down his pain. "We're good enough to beat 'em."

"Hear, hear!" Beecher shouted as the wails from the hilltops grew in volume and the creekbanks erupted with more sporadic gunfire.

Any man who dared stick his head over the sandy lip of his burrow could see the masses of warriors regathering round them once more. Not only those horsemen downstream, but those on foot, scampering helter-skelter like sow-beetles from an overturned buffalo-chip. Once more the hills throbbed five-thousand-fold with the noise of squaws and old

ones come to watch the great charge. Instead of cheering
their men onto victory, their passionate wails of anger and
rage and grief scraped against the summer-pale blue sky like
the jarring sound of someone dragging a fingernail across the
bottom of a rusty cast-iron kettle.

"Like Beecher said—you saw history made, boys!" Grover
hollered above their cheers. "No man I know of ever's seen
'em charge like these warriors done."

"Massed-front cavalry charge!" Beecher echoed. "And we
turned the bastards——"

As soon as the words fell from the lieutenant's lips, most
men in the surrounding pits heard bullets striking home. A
soft smacking thud like a wet hand slapping putty.

Seamus turned, watching Beecher claw his way out of his
pit, using a rifle as a crutch, one hand clutching his side,
blood shiny between his fingers, blotting a dark circle on his
sweat-stained shirt. He wobbled blindly, groping toward Forsyth's rifle-pit. Eyes glazed, inching forward in a fog, acting
under some instinct to survive.

Staggering, he stopped at the edge of the major's dugout,
weaving, then tumbled slowly below the line of fire.

Landing beside Forsyth, his face turned downward atop
an arm, Beecher moaned quietly, "I have my death-wound,
General."

"Oh, God . . . no!" Forsyth gritted the words as he
fought to get to Beecher.

"I'm shot in the side . . . and—dammit"—he swallowed
down his pain—"and . . . know I'm dying."

"No, no, no—Beecher!" Forsyth screamed in despair as he
rolled his lieutenant over, gazing down into the young,
bearded face, peering into those gentle, sad eyes. "Tell me,
please tell me—it can't be as bad as that!"

"Y-yes, General. G-good night."

Beecher's eyes rolled backward, the lids falling as the soldier slipped into unconsciousness.

"M-McCall," Forsyth said quietly to his fellow soldier.
"Take the lieutenant's boots off."

"Yessir. I'll make 'im comfortable as I can."

"Here, Sergeant," Grover said, handing McCall some torn
cloth for bandages. "For Beecher's wound."

As he bound up the two large holes in the lieutenant's

side, Beecher's eyes fluttered, opened halfway. He mumbled
something incoherent.

Forsyth struggled to turn on his wounded legs. He rolled
closer so he could put his ear over Beecher's lips. A few
moments later he sank back against the side of the rifle-pit.

"What'd he say, Major?" McCall asked.

"He said, '*M-my . . . p-poor mother,*'" Forsyth replied,
his eyes misting.

McCall turned back to his work, knotting the strips of
cloth torn and cut from their clothing. Bullets sailed overhead in a loud volley, some of them kicking up spouts of
drying sand from the bulwarks, others ricocheting, making a
sound akin to the screams of the horses as they lay thrashing
in the sand, crying out until they thrashed no more.

In his own pit, gazing back upstream past the dead warriors and downed ponies at the two dozen horsemen who
gathered by the trees near the far bend in the river, Donegan
fought beads of stinging sweat from his eyes. He figured the
bulk of the Cheyenne and Sioux had withdrawn to argue out
another angle of attack, fearing a repeat of their disastrous
charge that unhorsed at least thirty behind Roman Nose and
Medicine Man.

Until the hayfield last summer, he had never been forced
to fight like infantry. Dug in and holed up.

Always before he had been on the move, mobile, striking
—then retreating to strike another flank before the Confederate infantry could organize its counter.

But lying here, he was forcefully reminded of that steamy
August hayfield. The smells here were the same, here among
fighting men. The stench of hot gun-oil in the Spencers and
his own Henry. The gamey fragrance of blood baking as it
seeped into the sand or soured in the wounds of the men
forced to wait beneath a high, relentless sun. Stinking men
many long days in the saddle. And as before, the dead animals broiling, bloating, rotting in their own juices.

Grinding tears from his eyes with a knuckle, Seamus
glanced at his uncle. Although Liam's face had gone pale, his
chest still heaved. Donegan reached up. Using his knife, he
hacked off two willow branches as big around as his thumb.
He rammed both into the side of the pit, then stretched

O'Roarke's short-coat over them, making a little shade for his uncle.

The rattle of gunfire from both banks slowed again. Curious but cautious, he peered over the lip of the rifle-pit. Close enough to touch with the muzzle of his Henry lay three dead warriors. Within another ten feet of his pit lay a dozen or more. And stretching as far as the bend upstream where the charge had burst into view, lay ponies and warriors. Alone. Or piled in bunches.

Enough to show that the major's seven volleys had eaten into the warrior ranks with devastating effect.

Now he understood the reason twenty horsemen stood guard out of rifle-range upstream. Watching over the bodies of their tribesmen. Until they could work up the courage to gallop in to rescue their dead. Under the huge muzzles of the white man's repeaters.

Seamus knew all about the courage it took to recover your dead. He had been there on the far side of Lodge Trail Ridge minutes after the warriors of Crazy Horse and High Back-Bone had retreated from the Fetterman butchery.

"The bastards fear we'll mutilize their dead," Seamus whispered to himself.

"What's that, Donegan?" Grover asked, his boots kicking sand as he slid back into the front rifle-pit.

"You hear that?" Donegan himself asked.

"What?"

"Them bells?"

Grover listened to the hot, steamy stillness of the south bank. "Yeah. Hawks'-bells. Traders sell 'em to the bands all the time. Injuns like the tinkling noise they make. Tie 'em to pony manes and tails."

"Some bastard riding up and down that bank. You listen."

After a few moments, Grover nodded. "You're right. Sounds like one of 'em riding back and forth along the length of the island over yonder behind them willows."

"What say we give 'im a halloo, Sharp?"

Grover smiled grimly, licking his thumb, rubbing it over his front blade-sight. "You're a man after my own heart, Donegan."

Seamus rose with one knee jabbed into the sand at the side of the pit, levering the Henry. "I'll pull when you fire."

Donegan brought the brass-mounted repeater to his shoulder, finding the wounded right arm aching as he held on the invisible horseman beyond the wall of swamp-willow.

"Listen, me friend," he advised Grover, "and we'll tell which way he's moving."

"Lead him just a bit, Seamus. Lead him——"

Their guns roared almost simultaneously.

From beyond the far rim of willow came a startled grunt, a whicker of a pony, then the rapid jingling of the hawks'-bells.

"We hit something, Seamus."

"By the saints, we did at that." He slid down the side of the rifle-pit. Liam tossed his head, mumbling. A trickle of bright crimson cut the crease of his lips, dampening his beard.

"He say anything, Seamus?" Grover asked as Donegan brought his ear away from the bloody lips.

Donegan shook his head, frustrated. "Kiowa. It mean anything to you?"

"Injuns," Grover replied. "Mostly run with the Southern Cheyenne. Some of 'em been raising hell outta The Territories—raiding into Kansas past few months."

"Why you figure he told me?"

Now it was Grover's turn to study it, chewing on a chapped lip. "Haven't a notion, Seamus. Don't think Liam's ever been down in Kiowa country. Santanta's the big bull in that lick."

"Curse this outfit anyway!" Donegan growled. "You and Forsyth can both go to hell for getting me and the uncle roped up in this."

He nodded. "I only gave you a way to track your uncle down, Seamus. Don't recall pointing my pistol at your head to do it, neither."

Donegan snorted. "What good's it done me? Liam's all but gone. And look at us," he said, flinging an arm down the crude ellipse of rifle-pits. "Why, before that bleeming sun up there sets this day, the rest of us are good as dead."

"What time is it?" a voice back of Sharp Grover yelled.

"Three o'clock," another answered.

"Shit!" Grover hissed. "Time has a way of flying by, don't it."

Donegan nodded. "Had it figured no later than ten o'clock, meself."

"Sonsabitches," Chauncey Whitney cursed in his nearby pit. "We ever get outta this fix, boys—we gotta see to it the army does its share of some killing."

"What the hell you talking 'bout, Chance?" Thomas Ranahan asked.

"I'm saying it's 'bout time the army started killing more Injuns, by God!"

"Chance is right," Eli Ziegler joined in. "We kill enough of these frigging bastards . . . catch their sluts and mongrel offspring unawares in their villages—it'll teach the rest to keep their asses plopped down on the reservations."

"Lord Gawd Almighty!" Chance Whitney hurrahed. "Brother Ziegler knows what it's gonna take to win this land from these heathens. Put 'em on reservations where the mongrels can't do no harm to decent white folk—and them that don't wanna go, we kill and leave for the coyotes to fatten on."

"None us be here right now, hadn't been for that goddamned Carrington tucking his tail up north on the Bozeman!" Thomas O'Donnell added.

Seamus whirled on O'Donnell. "How the divil you figure Carrington's to blame?"

For a moment the older Irishman sat shocked into silence by the suddenness of Donegan's response. He collected his thoughts. "If his soldiers had done what they was sent to do on the Bozeman Road, none of these'r Injuns would be stirred up the way they are. Thinking they can get away with——"

"Tommy's right," Ziegler agreed. "Raiding and raping. If that yellow-backed coward Carrington and his bunch had busted down Red Cloud's bunch up there, 'stead of buckling under way they did—these Injuns wouldn't be acting so all-fired high and mighty."

"I was there meself," Donegan growled loudly. "None of you got room to talk."

"Ain't got room to talk?" George Oakes demanded. "I lost a brother, and my father as well, to these bastards. And this stupid mick tells me I ain't got room to talk?"

Seamus was crawling out of the rifle-pit before he even

realized that McCall and Grover were yanking him back down into the sand.

"That's enough of that talk, Oakes!" McCall shouted.

"Tell that mick bastard he don't belong with this bunch, Sarge!" C. B. Nichols chimed in.

"Right! Him and his kind, like Carrington, giving in to these red bastards—he's the kind to blame for Culver and Wilson."

"Beecher too, by God!"

"And the major. Him down with three wounds!"

"Any more of that"—Forsyth's voice finally rose above the heat-shimmering island—"and I'll see you forfeit pay for disobeying my orders."

"That Irishman's got him no room to talk!"

"Next man speaks out of line, he's my meat!" McCall roared.

Grover listened while the grumbling died, wiping sweat from his hands where they grew sticky holding the Spencer stock. He gazed at Seamus again.

"You got the right to talk, Donegan. Problem is—you always choose the wrong place to open your mouth."

"Carrington's a broken man."

"You really know him?" Forsyth's voice rose from the next pit.

"I was there, Major," Seamus answered. "From the beginning of it. Fought the skirmish at the Crazy Woman Fork."

"There at the time of the massacre?"

"Rode out with the relief party."

"When'd you come down this part of the country, Irishman?" McCall inquired.

"Last fall. After some of these same bastards pinned us down in a hayfield not far from C. F. Smith. They shot up a friend of mine pretty bad the next day down at Kearny."

"The wagon-box fight?"

"That's right, Major," Seamus replied. "I figure this republic broke its promise to Colonel Carrington."

"You're right, Irishman," Forsyth finally answered. "Because the republic had to punish someone, it chose Carrington. But the army will defend him."

Seamus snorted sourly as he gazed at his uncle, watching

the bloody shirt rise and fall, rise and fall beneath the steamy shadow of the improvised awning.

"Way I see it, Major Forsyth—your army won't even consider defending Carrington."

"I happen to believe in the honor of my fellow officers——"

"Major," Donegan interrupted with his deep colic, "your gawddamned army will side with that bastard Fetterman."

"Why do you say that, Irishman?"

"It's your army, Major—and on any day, your army will always choose dead heroes over a living symbol of a national defeat."

Chapter 22

$\mathcal{H}$is blood went cold.

Watching his pony rear back, thrashing its front legs, tearing its rawhide halter from the willow where he was about to tie it before kneeling there on the riverbank overlooking the island. The animal ripped itself from his grasp as the two bullets thudded home, whining past his cheeks like angry, red buffalo-gnats.

Round and round the pony pranced, its side pumping bright, liquid ooze as it danced its life away. The hawks'-bells he had tied for medicine in its mane tinkling with every dusty step into death.

Jack O'Neill watched the animal crumple to its side twenty yards out on the prairie. It had been a gift presented to him by Roman Nose. Now leg-running its way to a last breath.

As the four painted legs slowed to a stop, Jack sensed the hair standing on the back of his neck. His eyes muled, turning back to gaze at the island through the leafy willow-branches. Realizing but for seconds and inches, he would have been the creature breathing his last on the sandy prairie at this moment.

He found himself giving thanks to the Cheyenne's Everywhere Spirit, and for the first time was not ashamed to raise his face to the summer sky overhead in real prayer. Not the dancing, hand-waving, all-consuming trance both the black Bible-thumping preachers and sorcerers alike preferred to work up among their sweating congregations.

Jack felt the first tingle of real deliverance. For some reason he had been allowed to escape the white man's bullets fired from that hole on the end of the island.

As the battle had dragged on earlier in the day, before the first charge that had taken the life of Roman Nose, the mulatto had joined Two Crows and other warriors in crawling through the swamp-willow near the riverbank, searching for the bodies of Weasel Bear and White Thunder. Among the plum-brush they came across Cloud Chief, Black Moon, and Bear Feathers, three who had gone into the willow as well to rescue bodies of their fallen friends.

Black Moon whispered, his eyes wide and expressive, "Be careful how you creep through the grass. The whitemen watch the grass. And when they see it move, they shoot at us. Three times they came close to hitting us."

"I have a wound to show how close they come," Bear Feathers said, pointing to a flesh wound across his right shoulder.

"You should go back," Jack replied.

"No, Nibsi. We all come to fight the whitemen this day, eh?"

Jack nodded, smiling. "Yes. We have much blood to spill yet." He sank to his belly once more, and led the rest into the grass, slowly parting the tall stalks, then inching forward, causing as little disturbance as possible.

He came to a stop, old Two Crows bumping against his leg.

"What is it, Nibsi? You stop."

He smiled. "I see the bodies. Weasel Bear. White Thunder. They are ten feet from me."

Jack rolled carefully onto his side when his eyes caught the grass moving directly behind them. The faces of two warriors poked through the dried stalks of grass. Spotted Wolf and Star.

The two had not been careful crawling. A volley of shots erupted from the island, splitting the air inches above the ground.

"Uuunnhhh!"

"Cloud Chief!" Two Crows growled in a harsh whisper. "See?" he rolled, whirling on Star. "You cause this with your stupidity!"

"It is only my arm," Cloud Chief explained, his fingers moist with red. "I go on."

"They are right over there. Only a little way," Jack instructed.

Cautiously parting the grass, he showed Two Crows where the two bodies lay, a third close by on the bank. Having struggled that far to safety after reaching the island in their courageous first charge.

Very few had held their ponies behind Roman Nose. Most had veered off before reaching the island. But these three brave ones had given up their life-breath in the heroic charge into the muzzles of all those rifles.

As the rest inched up close, two more bullets whined overhead. But neither struck a warrior. Jack thought on the pony that had carried him into the charge, onto the end of the island, then into the willow on the riverbank at Roman Nose's side, until the chief could ride no more. The pony dead.

Jack knew the war-chief lay dying at this moment. While the sun began its quick journey from mid-sky into its western bed for the night.

Peeking through the grass, he could see the bodies of Weasel Bear and White Thunder, lying so close to each other they might be sleeping with their feet to a fire. Just in front of White Thunder lay Ermine Bear.

"Can you get him, Nibsi?"

Jack nodded. He reached out, his bare, coffee-colored arm, blending well with the summer-stunted grass and willow. By twisting the dead warrior's leg, he turned White Thunder onto his back, revealing the huge, blackened hole in his chest.

Jack found the body stiff already. "He is dead, Two Crows."

"Can you reach the others?"

"If I show myself," Jack replied.

"Do not, Nibsi. We come after dark has settled on the land," Two Crows advised. "Bring White Thunder with you."

As O'Neill pulled on the ankle, dragging the stiffened body into the tall grass, Cloud Chief took his hand from his bloody wound and pointed. He whispered loudly.

"Look! See Weasel Bear! He is not dead!"

"Yes!" Star added, excited. "I too saw him move."

Two Crows bellied up beside O'Neill, peering at the strip of sand where the bodies lay. "Weasel Bear? Are you alive?"

They waited, all watching the body. It moved slightly.

"Yes," came Weasel Bear's weakened reply.

"Wait for us," Two Crows went on, his voice louder now in his excitement. "We are trying to get your nephew, White Thunder, away from here. When we have him away, we will return for you."

"Is that my brother-in-law who speaks to me from the grass?" Weasel Bear asked, a little hope in his voice.

"Yes," Two Crows answered.

"Good," came the reply. "I have a bullet through my hips and cannot move my legs. But I will live. Come back for me when you can."

"Two Crows," Jack interrupted, "have one of the young ones return to their pony for a rope."

Star signaled, passing the word down the line. Minutes crawled by until one by one the warriors passed the end of the rope back to Nibsi. He lashed it round White Thunder's ankle.

Turning to Two Crows, he said, "Pull now, slowly . . . slowly."

Although they pulled the body through the grass slowly, the tall, dry stalks rustled, giving them away. Volley after volley sailed into the brush around them as they yanked the body to safety. One bullet slapped against the thick, rawhide shield Spotted Wolf had lashed to his back. Made from the glued and heated thick neck-hide of a bull buffalo, it was enough to turn the white man's lead.

Two young warriors dragged the body from the willow, and, draping it over a pony, hurried the dead man out of range, over the hill to the place many squaws and medicine dancers were nursing the wounded. Others prepared the dead for burial.

Two Crows bellied up beside O'Neill once more to whisper to Weasel Bear. "My brother-in-law. We have returned for you."

"That is good." Weasel Bear's voice grew weaker from

blood-loss. "I am glad you come, Two Crows. Help me, for my legs do not move when I command them."

"Tie this to my brother-in-law, Nibsi," the Cheyenne chief instructed. "As you did the last one."

As his eyes darted about, inching slowly toward Weasel Bear's foot, Jack O'Neill spotted the three white riflemen not hiding on the island. Instead, they hid beneath the riverbank. He pointed them out.

"They are the whitemen who have killed Dry Throat and Prairie Bear this morning at dawn, Two Crows."

The old chief nodded, his wrinkled face drawn taut in anger. "We did not know they had those rifles hidden under the riverbank."

The mulatto gazed into the sky. He smiled, thinking it was good to see the dark, tumbling thunderheads gathering above, reaching far, far into the sky. It would rain tonight. Perhaps sooner. And with a cloudy sky, there would be less chance of moonlight.

"I will bring others back with us this night, old one," Jack promised. "We will clean out this nest of scorpions for you."

Jack could smell the old man's sweat. The others repeatedly said old Trudeau always had some whiskey in his saddlebags. True enough, Stillwell figured—there was a good measure of whiskey in the saddlebags crushed beneath the dead horses now.

So it was no wonder that this afternoon, half a day gone since that first dawn rush on their camp, the old man was still sweating sour whiskey from every pore.

Stillwell sniffed. His own sweat gone old, grown cold. His gut no longer churning after that big charge some four hours back when the men cheered and called Roman Nose a godless fornicator. That was a word Jack had grown accustomed to, often hearing it back home when his mother and maiden aunt would discuss someone in town, speaking in their holy voices he had grown to despise.

To be a fornicator, Jack had decided, must have some element of fun. And too, fornicating must be the way a nineteen-year-old boy got himself turned into a man.

Jack prayed he would live long enough to survive this

attack. Live to get off the island. Live long enough to find out how much fun fornicating could be.

"You wanna drink?" C. B. Piatt bellied up with a big, blanket-wrapped canteen in his hand.

Jack took it, sniffed. Held it against his tongue. Then handed it back. "Thanks."

"No more?"

"No." He shook his head, sensing his stomach rumbling at the tepid, gritty water he had already swallowed in an attempt to slake his thirst.

Strange, but the smell of that canteen filled with harsh water spiked his nose with more of the growing stench of this place. The blood going bad. The horses and men both collecting the insects. Hardbacks that came crawling, the buzzing ones droning in black clouds overhead. Searching out the blood that sizzled beneath this mid-afternoon sun.

And the sour odor he recognized like an evil memory of that night in Wallace when he had himself too much bad whiskey and spent the night out at the edge of the prairie, passed out in his own vomit.

From the smell of it, someone nearby had spilled his belly. Maybe more than one. No matter that they called him *boy* from day one of this ride.

Jack Stillwell ain't bleeding, he thought proudly. *And he sure as hell hasn't spilled his sour belly on the sand.*

It lurched, and just about got away from him. What with all the brown grit and murky water he'd had to drink. Didn't have no food now. A few of the older ones had been chewing on coffee beans. Sweat and coffee and mule to eat. He sighed. Time enough to try some of that damned mule.

Looking at the animal, stiff-legged and gas-bloating, Jack watched the big-bellied September flies busy on the mule. Clustered on eyes and around the lips. Nostrils and anus. Encircling every moist arrow-wound and bullet hole.

Anywhere those sonsabitches can lay their eggs.

Flies fat and sassy and summer-sleek, feasting on all the gore and muck and blood the tiny critters could lap up. Flies and spiders and beetles getting drunk on the juices of the island's dead and dying.

Not far away he listened to Lieutenant Beecher mumbling. Earlier when the sun had hit mid-sky, Dr. Mooers had been shrieking incoherently. The men said the doctor was thrashing his way into St. Peter's Gates. Jack wanted it to come clean when it was time. He didn't want it to take so long as it was for Beecher and Mooers and Farley.

Quick. Like it had been for Culver and Bill Wilson in that first action of the morning, every man alone on his own hook, racing here to this sandy patch of hell in the middle of God knows where.

His mama would be angry for his taking the Lord's name like that, he decided. But, for the first time Jack didn't care. She wasn't here. She didn't know how afraid he was. How afraid any of the rest were as well, listening to the chants rocking off the hillsides, the shrieks of those squaws, the throbbing cadence of the incessant drums beyond the river-bend and over the brow of the low hills. Every ridgetop resounding with drums. And always the hammering of hoofbeats. On all sides of them. In an ever-tightening noose that felt like a starch-stiffened, strangling church-meeting collar his mother ironed and buttoned on him as a boy every Sunday.

He choked. And closed his eyes a minute. Remembering some of the words the preacher used in praying over the dying. Words used over the sick ones in their town. Maybe words he could use over the wounded here on this island now. After all, they had no medicine. Mooers had brought along enough to fill a whole pannier loading down one side of a mule when they left Hays behind last month.

Last month . . .

He forced that out of his mind. Because the mule with the bandages and the sulphur and the laudanum was gone. The Indians had it now. That peace-giving narcotic laudanum. That tincture of opium such a blessing for a wounded man anywhere on this frontier. None of that now to make the lot of the wounded more bearable. The surgeon's bag and all his plunder gone to the hostiles now. Jack figured the Indians were having themselves a time with those bottles of medicines now as they cracked open the supplies and other truck found on the captured mules. Maybe the red bastards would drink the laudanum and get drunk, the way old Pete got stiff from his rot-whiskey.

This morning when they were first digging, old Trudeau

cursed most the fact that Mooers let his surgeon's kit get away because the good doctor had carried an ample supply of stout brandy along.

Jack licked his chapped lips, tasting once more the brackish, harsh water. Making his sun and wind-raw lips burn.

With the brassy cry of the bugle, Stillwell jerked up, his bowels instantly tightening as they had before.

"Goddamnsonsabitches coming at us again!" Lane was hollering as he plopped on his belly at the edge of his pit beside Jack's.

"If you ain't reloaded, boys . . . now's your last chance to think about it!" Sergeant McCall was up and shouting as the rifle-fire from the riverbanks began again in earnest.

Sniper bullets kicked up sprays of dry sand, thudding into the stiff, juicy horse carcasses, spraying the flies into the air with a loud, buzzing protest before they resettled amid the singing, ricocheting lead balls.

In and out again, McCall dove from one pit to another, issuing orders gruffly as he checked weapons, helped others recover the wounded with coats and blankets retrieved from behind saddles on the dead horses. Time and again the Indians in the willows tried to find him with their bullets.

Jack figured McCall hollered so loud and stern just so the men would obey him without hesitation in the face of the coming charge they each could hear pounding the riverbottom. Upstream. Out of the mouth of the same gorge they had used that morning.

Then Jack realized that McCall talked gruff because he was probably just as scared as the rest, and if he didn't talk loudly right now with the sun staring down on their little island, he just might mess his pants like some of the others had done already.

"Tighten up your guts, son," A. J. Eutsler growled, turning to Lane and Stillwell. "They riding down on us again."

"We done it before, men!"

It was Forsyth's voice now, raised above the hubbub of moaning wounded, men crying out for water. And others telling them to shut up. The rumble of horsemen, and the rattle of rifle-fire. And filling every pause was the constant drone of wailing women and throbbing drums that caused Jack's head to ache. He'd have to find a bandanna to tie around his head when the charge was over since he had lost his hat in the race to the island at dawn. A bandanna—something to keep the sun from boiling his brain in a skull-kettle.

"Whiskey is the life of man!"

He looked up and to his left, finding where the familiar, loud voice originated. A voice thick with a peaty brogue. And saw the tall, young Irishman leaning on the front lip of his rifle-pit, the brass-mounted Henry in his hands, two Spencers atop the sand beside him. Next to Donegan sat Sharp Grover. The old scout was laughing at his young partner. Jack figured Grover laughed because Seamus was crazy. No one was supposed to sing when the goddamned Indians was riding you down.

> "Whiskey is the life of man!
> Whiskey, Abner—Abner, me friend!
> I'll drink whiskey whenever I can,
> Whiskey for me friend, Abner!"

"I hope you shoot better'n you sing, Irishman!" someone shouted, back a ways.

And they all had a laugh at that. The Irishman too. Seemed they were all a little more ready to laugh this time.

Now they knew they could turn this one back. The red bastards might take a man or two, but if they kept reloading and firing from the very first sight of the horsemen, they'd beat this charge back as well.

Just knowing you wasn't beat into the sand by the red bastards was enough to make you a little looser.

And then Jack couldn't hear the laughter anymore, the song momentarily drowned out. Just the hammering of a thousand hooves.

This time the horsemen rounded the bend and broke past the cottonwoods without a leader. Just a solid phalanx of riders coming like thick clouds of prairie dust boiling between the riverbanks. A roiling, throbbing mass of blazing colors bearing down on them once more. Row after god-damned row of naked, brown, screaming terror.

Bank to bank, working themselves and their ponies into a wild lather, throwing sand into a silvery grit caught in the afternoon light. Then, suddenly, above it all rose that peaty brogue again, singing, shouting in a lusty roar . . . giving them all the cheer they needed as the hoary, copper countenance of death bore down upon them.

> "Up from the South, at break o' day,
> Bringing to Winchester fresh dismay . . .
> Hurrah! Hurrah for Phil Sheridan!
> Hurrah! Hurrah for horse and man!"

Chapter 23

$\mathcal{T}$he taut skin across Billy McCall's cheeks felt less of the heat now. He glanced over his left shoulder, finding the sun sinking toward the far rim of the prairie. Soon enough it would disappear behind the cottonwood and swamp-willow and plum-brush. He grew remorseful that he would not be able to see the sun actually sink beyond the far rim of the earth this night.

A lull had settled over the island following that second massed charge the scouts had beaten back around two o'clock.

With things so quiet now, one heard the wounded moaning, begging, some screaming for the gritty water they were dredging out of Martin Burke's pit. Burke had dug down, persistently between every skirmish, so that he now had a sizable pool of brackish, cloudy water collecting at the bottom.

Beecher had never uttered another word after taking his wound that first mid-morning charge. But Mooers moaned and whimpered like a castrated calf from time to time. Shame of it was, McCall brooded, the surgeon and Forsyth were stuck in the same rifle-pit together now. Seemed the doctor's foot occasionally kicked out, striking one of the major's wounded legs, causing him immense pain. Yet Forsyth appeared to understand that in some mysterious way, the blinded Mooers was tapping out with his leg to assure himself that Forsyth, someone, was still in the pit with him.

"Strange as it seems, Billy," he recalled the major explaining an hour or so before, "this is Mooers's way of keeping touch with his surroundings as he descends into death."

McCall had moved his eyes to Beecher. "Lieutenant ain't gonna last much longer, sir."

"Fred's lost too much blood. Internal bleeding . . . I can't do anything more for him."

"None of us, Major."

"I want to rest now, Billy," Forsyth had said. "Just close my eyes for a little while."

"I'll be close—you need me, sir."

From a nearby pit the sergeant kept an eye on Forsyth. Though he didn't have to. Wasn't an able-bodied man there on that sundown island who wouldn't do anything to help the major. Billy liked the man. More than respected Forsyth. Now himself at thirty, a year younger than the major, Billy figured Forsyth was the sort of officer he wanted to be one day.

Ever since leaving Fort Hays behind, the major had never asked a man to do those sorts of things officers always had done for them in the army. Instead, Forsyth always stripped his own saddle each night and built his own fire and made his own bivouac like the rest of them.

And while he never stood watch himself as assigned in rotation by Sergeant McCall, Sandy Forsyth was nonetheless up and down throughout the cool summer nights, always restless and moving about from picket to picket on each watch. Talking quietly, reassuring his men. Letting them know he was no better than they. Only their leader on this trip out to catch them some Indians.

And catch them they had.

Just like Forsyth and Beecher wanted, McCall brooded. *And look what it's got the two of 'em. God help me—I pray I've got what it will take to get these men back to Wallace. If we get back to——*

"Sergeant!"

McCall turned at the young Irishman's call. "You want me?"

"You'll wanna see this, McCall!" Sharp Grover added his voice.

Billy slipped into their rifle-pit at the front of the island, gingerly crawling round the wounded, delirious O'Roarke.

"Have a look, Sergeant." Grover pointed upstream.

From bank to bank near the far bend of the river the horsemen were gathering once more, milling off the sandy slopes into the riverbed itself, huddling and swelling in numbers. Here and there among them, war-chiefs shouted and waved arms and weapons, exhorting their warriors into formation.

"What you make of it, Grover?"

He frowned. "One more run at us for the day."

"For the day?"

Grover nodded. "They won't fight after sundown." He pointed to the pink-orange underbellies of the thick, gray clouds scudding out of the northwest, quickly across the sky.

"This is it, eh?"

"Yeah," Grover added, with no smile. "Darkness or the rain coming will put an end to the fighting for this day."

"They'll be back tomorrow?" McCall asked, already knowing the answer.

"No doubt. But for today, this is their last hurrah, Sergeant."

"I'll bet they make this charge a bloody good one as well," Seamus Donegan remarked as he slipped the big, brass .44-caliber cartridges into the openings between his fingers, then pressed five more between his lips. He worked his left elbow into the dry sand at the lip of his rifle-pit.

The breeze shifted slowly, out of the northwest, as the warriors disappeared upstream. That breeze carried on it the thick, humid smell of prairie rain. Billy had been out here long enough since the end of the war in the regular army to recognize the smell of prairie rain. Not like back home in Pennsylvania.

He squeezed the thought of home out of his mind the way a man wrung his dirty socks out each night, leaving them to dry over the end of his bunk in barracks.

Whispers from the others nearby hung round him like ghosts, like a filmy cotton gauze dress . . .

The thought brought his mind around to her. Back home, waiting for him. Her, and their two-year-old daughter. He sensed his eyes moistening with the thought of his two, waiting for him. Billy swiped his eyes. Then a second time angrily, to be sure he could see. He could hear them now, and he needed to see. McCall clamped his lids shut, forcing his wife's face from his mind so that he could focus on the riverbed, three, four, five hundred yards off.

The riders were coming . . .

They came as they had before, massed shoulder to shoulder, knee to knee, flank to flank, spread from riverbank to riverbank. Shouting, drumming, screeching their blood-oaths as the willows on both sides of the island suddenly erupted with puffs of burnt powder and the cry of bullets singing into wood and sand-pits and the stiffening bodies of the gassy, bloating horses.

The scouts kept their heads down, as McCall had ordered. Telling them he would give the volley call in place of the major this time. Sensing they all knew what was expected of them anyway. Wasn't a one of them he could figure was going to do anything foolish now. Their only chance was to stay here, and stay alive. If only . . . they could just stay alive——

"Now!"

The island exploded with the roar of the Spencers as the forty-odd rifles cut a swath through the brown-skinned phalanx at two hundred yards in a full gallop. White-hot acid smoke spewed with jets of bright flame igniting rifle-muzzles from the plum-brush. Ponies reared, screaming in pain, throwing their riders into others. And still they came.

"Fire, goddammit!"

The horsemen came on, swaying side to side, their pistols and rifles at ready, riding low along the necks of their ponies. Some few crazy ones sitting full-up, their glistening chests an inviting target.

Between each rattle of rifle-fire from the riverbanks that was meant to keep the scouts' heads down while the horsemen rode the island down, Billy McCall heard that incessant pulsing of the drumbeat echoing off the surrounding knolls. From the top of every ridge rumbled the chants, wails of rage and cries for revenge from the squaws ministering to their dead and dying.

"Fire!"

He jerked around after yelling out his order, hearing Forsyth cry out. "You hit, Major?"

"N-no, Billy," Forsyth answered in a strong voice above

the rattle of gunfire. "The firing set Mooers off again . . . kicked me with his foot . . . like before—my leg——"

"You need help, sir?"

"No-no! Stay where you are, Sergeant. I need you . . . we all need you right there. Issue the fire order now, Sergeant!"

"Fire!"

And the rifles erupted, spitting orange flame in the fading light of early evening. That last volley wasn't really needed, he figured. They were already splitting at a hundred yards. Breaking off their charge. Heading for the riverbanks in a spray of gritty, silvery sand. Getting nowhere near the island as they had twice before. Only then did Billy realize the warriors knew how suicidal these charges had become. The riverbed still littered with the bodies of fallen warriors, some dead, others dying and unable to move out of the way of the slashing pony hooves.

Always, in the wake of each assault lay the wounded, butchered ponies, crying with that eerie, humanlike screeching whistle of theirs that had never failed to raise the hairs on his neck since the first battle at Bull Run, the first time he went to fight for Lincoln and Pennsylvania.

Watching the ponies clawing at the sand until they all fell silent with the sinking of the far sun.

"Hurrah!"

Several of the scouts were up and dancing about as the firing from the riverbanks fell off in despair of making a successful ride over the island. A few of the men pounded one another on the back again, as they had done twice before, congratulating themselves on making it through another charge alive and unscratched. And above it all rose the stench of more gases spewing from the punctured horse carcasses. Each time a bullet hit, the bloating gases hissed, reminding Billy of the stench around a trench latrine.

"Sergeant McCall?"

He turned at Forsyth's voice fifteen yards down the island. "Major?"

"Report, Sergeant."

Billy drew himself up amid the pounding he was taking on his back from both Grover and Donegan, looking down at

Stillwell in the nearby pit, seeing the tears in the boy's eyes. Realizing he had a mist in his own.

"By God, boys—we been delivered of this day!" he shouted, shaking a clenched fist at the far riverbank. Daring them to shoot him as he ran in a crouch to the major's pit.

"Here." And Forsyth handed McCall a blanket-wrapped canteen, its wool soaked with water and coated with sand. "See if Mooers wants some."

Billy tried, turning back to Forsyth with the sound of Beecher's frothy, labored breathing in his ears. "Sorry, Major. He's still gone. Him and the lieutenant both."

Forsyth sighed. "I'm surprised Fred's lasted this long, Billy. He's . . . a strong, determined man to hang on way he has."

McCall swallowed hard, sipping at the murky water himself. "You wanted a report as well, Major?"

"Yes, Sergeant," Forsyth answered, pushing some of his wavy hair from his eyes, and inching himself up on an elbow.

"Only the two dead. Culver and Wilson."

"What of the wounded?"

"Sixteen now, sir."

"Seventeen, Sergeant," the major replied, pointing to McCall's neck-wound.

He nodded, a grin cutting his face. "Yessir. Seventeen. Just a scratch . . . but, by damn, we turned those red bastards, Major."

He couldn't help it now, try as he might. Billy McCall felt the first of the hot tears spill down his cheeks.

"By God, Major—this rag-tag bunch of misfits turned 'em!"

The hands turning him were gentle. Not like the big, hard hands that had pulled him from the willows where he had dragged himself after falling from the chestnut pony. These hands were soft. A woman's.

How he missed never taking a woman now. Never coupling. Much less marrying. Roman Nose denied himself for his people. The *Shahiyena*.

He tried to say something, not even sure if he got the words out to thank her for bathing him with the cool water from this last river he would ever see. Accepting the death-

coming here as the sun sank. Even though his eyes had
glazed, clouded in pain, Roman Nose nonetheless knew the
sun was setting. Throughout the day he had tracked its heat
across his face. From the heat on his forehead in the plum-
brush and swamp-willow. To the waning warmth on his
cheek. Even that was fading with night-coming.

Like his own life, falling away into the cool nothingness of
his medicine vision.

One more time he remembered again the thrilling leap into
the jaws of those spitting guns, as the sun sank from his face.
Remembered smiling as he sang his death-song and aimed
his rifle at the tall, bearded one who rose to his feet in meeting the charge of Roman Nose. Exciting too was the ride
across the island, over all those gopher-holes the white men
had dug with their bare hands, until the pony could carry
him no more. So severe were its many wounds.

No matter, he had thought as he had sailed into the
swamp-willow in a jumble of pony and falling men. No matter, for he could no longer hold onto the pony himself anyway.

The lead from those white-man guns had kicked up the
grass and sand around him as he tumbled to a stop within
the brush. And found himself feeling no pain at first, only a
sense of remorse. Looking down and ashamed to see that he
had soiled himself.

Then understanding why he had disgraced himself when
he failed to move his legs. No power left in them.

As his breathing slowed, and the throbbing in his neck-
cords became regular once more, Roman Nose had suffered
the first shards of icy pain. Like cold slivers radiating from
the core of him. And he realized he had been shot in the side
at least once. Perhaps once in the front as well. Most certainly many times in the back for he could feel the sting of
the many pucker-holes growing icy-hot in the great muscles
like twisted rope beneath the damp, copper skin.

No more would he ride a pony. Perhaps the cruelest fate
he could imagine a warrior made to suffer. That, and missing
the gentle touch of a woman here with the falling of the sun.
Yearning for her, yet he laughed to himself. If he could not
move anything from his lower back down, Roman Nose was

certain his manhood part would not rise strong and swollen for the mating.

Too late for so many things now as he let the woman bathe him, listening to the chants of the medicine men nearby, their hand drums throbbing, a scrotum rattle filled with stream-pebbles shaking. More drums and singing and women wailing not far away. He figured there must be many dead and dying nearby.

It had been a charge the *Shahiyena* would talk about for robe seasons to come as the old ones passed down their winter-counts and battle-stories. A charge when Roman Nose knew he was destined to die, yet led his warriors into the face of those hot-mouthed white-man guns spitting fire into their ranks. To be proud as you rode to your death. To be a man was enough.

To die having carried the struggle onto the island itself when so many others had turned away seemed to Roman Nose as if his prayer had been answered by the Everywhere Spirit.

He recalled the joy on the faces of the many as he had ridden into their midst atop the great chestnut, hearing them sing his praises that now, at last, they would take the island, wiping the white man out. Sending a message to soldiers up and down the Central Plains that the Dog Soldiers were a force to be reckoned with.

The mud-colored face swam before him, milky, like a rain-filled pocket on the prairie coming clear after you had stirred the bottom looking for the little swimming ones.

"Nibsi." He choked the mulatto's name, able to speak for the first time in hours.

"I am here, my chief."

He tried to raise his hand to touch the friend's face. "Tell me . . . did you see him?"

O'Neill nodded, sweeping up the chief's hand in both of his. "I saw, Roman Nose. I saw the one who killed you."

"He was tall, was he not?"

"Tall as a cottonwood. As tall as you, my chief."

"The hair on his face?"

"I saw. With the words from your sundance vision, you described him to me. When I rode at your side to the island, with my own eyes I saw him. Now I am certain, while the others aimed at you, my heart is sure his bullets found you."

His eyes fluttered. "The way I was told it would be, Nibsi." He felt the mulatto squeeze his hand, wrapping it with great strength.

"You must not go," O'Neill pleaded.

"Do not be afraid, Nibsi. My people are your people now."

Through the fog he gazed into the mulatto's face, watching the tears course down the coffee-colored cheeks. Falling on his bare chest where the woman's hands had bathed him in cool water moments ago.

"I will miss you, Roman Nose."

"No, do not miss me. For my spirit rides with you. Nibsi will not stalk the tall, gray-eyed one alone."

"Yes." O'Neill drew back, with fingers of one hand angrily slapping the hot tears from his dark cheeks. "I will follow that one—your killer—into the bowels of the Earth-Mother if I must. Until I hold his life in my hands."

The great Cheyenne war-chief's eyelids fluttered, then fell slowly with his last, painful breath.

O'Neill felt the hand sag within his two. He laid it on the brown chest and rose, intent on finding Two Crows.

Then gazed one last time upon the face of Roman Nose.

Finding there the smile of blood's work, the smile of revenge.

Chapter 24

$\mathcal{L}$ate-summer nights on the high plains had a way of coming slowly down, like a red-hued damask curtain being drawn on a too-long day.

Like the sun, so the heat eased out of the day, bringing little relief to the seventeen wounded after that final charge.

Only twenty-eight of those fifty-one who had marched out of Fort Wallace were not suffering some description of painful wound in the day-long sniping and massed attacks.

Though severely wounded himself, Maj. George Forsyth gave the orders for work to continue connecting the rifle-pits, having a handful carry on with work to widen a central pit where the severely wounded would be watched. Then he sent McCall after the marksmen in the farthest rifle-pit. One of them, for many years a trusted scout for the army, this day having proved himself once more invaluable to Major Forsyth.

The other, a late-comer and troublemaker who had only signed on to reach Fort Wallace in safety, there to run down his uncle. An uncle who lay close to death at this twilight hour, yet clung to life with a tenacity of a street-brawler in olde County Tyrone.

"Sergeant said you wanted to see us," Grover announced as he and Donegan sank into Forsyth's pit.

The major nodded, with both hands lifting the leg shattered by a Cheyenne bullet. He swallowed down the pain. "My chain of command's been whittled down a bit today, boys. You're it."

Seamus glanced at the other two, astounded. "I ain't no sojur. Why me, Major?"

"McCall here, he's army. An impressive record in the war. Sharp there, he's about the best there is in this part of the country. And you . . . well, you, Mr. Donegan, are somewhere in between, I suppose."

"I figure you can take that as a compliment, Seamus," Grover said, smiling.

"About as close to one as I'll hand you," Forsyth added. "I called you three here to talk of night defense of the island."

"These Indians ain't gonna attack at night, Major," Sharp said.

"Far as everything I've learned from the likes of Jim Bridger himself, Grover's right," Donegan added.

"They fear for their souls if they're killed at night."

"All right." Forsyth sighed. "Let's assume we have no fear until dawn."

"That's when it will come," Grover said.

"I've been thinking ever since things calmed down after that last charge." Forsyth plunged ahead with his agenda. "Besides some housekeeping chores with food and water, the most important matter is getting word out that we're here. Pinned down. And in need of relief."

"Getting word out, Major?" Grover asked, his voice rising.

"I'll volunteer, sir." McCall inched forward, saluting.

"Thank you, Billy—but you're not going."

"You're sending these two?" McCall asked.

He finally wagged his head. "That's the damned thing of it. I need all three of you here. Nine of us are so critically wounded that I can't spare any of you. So, Billy—it's time you gathered the able-bodied men. Call them all here now for a short meeting."

Minutes later Donegan watched the first of the weary, red-eyed scouts limp up to the edge of the major's pit in the deepening dusk of the plains. Without a word, the twenty-eight crouched in the lengthening shadows of the swamp-willow and brush and tall grass, huddled near the protective ring of the bloating horse carcasses.

"Fellas, I think it's time we took inventory of our situation," Forsyth began.

Donegan heard some man grumble from the growing darkness.

"What was that?" the major demanded. "Who spoke?"

"I did, Major."

"Sounds like that was you, Lane."

"Aye, Major."

"What you got to say?"

"Just that we all damned well know what our frigging situation is."

Forsyth let a few others spew out the venom they had dammed up all day long, hunkered down in their bloody gopher-holes.

"You boys aren't in such bad shape, are you now?"

No one replied to Forsyth's prodding.

"Perhaps you're right. Wilson and Culver. Beecher and Mooers may have it best of all, don't they?"

Suddenly McCall wheeled on the group. Donegan could see the sergeant's sunburned face glow all the redder.

"You sonsabitches! Here the major lays, bleeding in three places—and you chugwater rats think you got room to flap your jaws. Damn you!"

"Sergeant McCall." Forsyth reached out, tugging on the non-com's pants-leg to get him seated once more. "I'll conduct the business at hand."

"I . . . I'm sorry, Major," Lane spoke up, crumpling his hat in his bloody hands. "I figure I speak for the rest, sir—maybe we wouldn't made it through the day without you stopping us going for the riverbank."

"Hear! Hear!" shouted a few more.

"Huzzahs for the major!"

"That's more like it," Grover added as they simmered down. "I ain't any more army than the rest of you, by God. But I'll tell you what. I figure the major here's gonna get the rest of us off this goddamned island . . . and I'll be one to let him give the orders. Besides"—and he let them see his smile—"any of you figure you're going to try things on your own and not play it Forsyth's way—you'll have me and my friend here to reckon with."

Donegan watched most of the twenty-six faces turn his

way, then found Grover pointing him out. He nodded reluctantly.

"Time now for us to have but one commander," Seamus said. "Not a one of us will see the sun set on another day if we don't stand behind the major now."

Donegan felt something wet hit his cheek. He gazed into the sky, finding the dark underbellies of pewter clouds boiling in prairie torment.

"That rain I feel?" McCall asked, swiping at his own forehead.

"Be a blessing for us all," replied John Donovan.

"Long as none of us gets chilled to the bone," Forsyth added. "Gets cold enough out here on the prairie without the rain to soak a man."

"Only a drizzle, Major," Sharp Grover cheered. "Won't none of us get a soaking. Just enough to take the heat off us and the guns."

A few of the scouts chuckled, then waited for Forsyth to get on with it.

"Like Sergeant McCall was telling me after that last charge, fellas: We turned 'em today. And by God—I know in my guts we can turn 'em again tomorrow if we have to."

"Major," Grover jumped in, "we've taken some starch out of 'em already."

"That's right," Forsyth said, smiling weakly. "Now, you boys crawl in here a bit closer. I'm a little weak now, so I can't holler too loud."

He waited while the twenty-eight crowded in, the stench of their stale, cold sweat and dried blood along with what fear they had shared as brothers-in-arms all washed anew with the cool, summer drizzle softly splattering against their bearded faces, gently soaking their damp wool and linsey-cotton shirts.

"Sergeant McCall's in charge of work details tonight."

"Work details?" whined more than one voice from the darkness.

"We'll work at what's got to be done. Then we'll rest." The major went ahead, undaunted. "I want Burke to widen his water supply some. He's down to a good source at the bottom of his pit."

"Aye, Major," Martin Burke replied. "Consider it done."

"McCall will get about a dozen of you connecting the rifle-pits. That way when the attack comes at sunrise tomorrow, we can get from one pit to another without exposing ourselves needlessly."

"Good thinking, Major," Grover commented, scratching a week's worth of stubby whiskers on the side of his chin.

"We have water, ammunition, and a place to hunker down when they start bombarding us again. All we need now is food."

"Ah, for milk and honey!" Pliley cheered, drawing a few laughs.

"Sorry, A. J. We'll have to settle for horse," Forsyth said with a grin.

"Just as long as it ain't mule!" a voice called out, eliciting more chuckles.

"McCall, see that you get about a half-dozen put to work skinning back the horses and cutting meat from them. We can salvage a lot if we get the meat cooled down quick enough."

"Come tomorrow, that sun up there's gonna turn the rest to soup, Major," Donegan added sourly.

"You're right, Irishman. That's why I want as much cut and cooked tonight as possible. We'll wrap what we don't eat tonight in a rubber poncho and bury it in a pit next to the central one where we're bringing the wounded."

"What do you want the rest of the men doing, sir?"

"Sergeant," he said, gazing up at McCall, "you'll assign men to bring the wounded into the central pit. The rest are to start fires. But don't light them till you've dug yourself a deep fire-hole. And those of you the sergeant has cooking meat—stay out of the light as much as possible. I don't want any more casualties tonight."

"What about the rest of us?" Donegan asked.

He turned to face the big civilian. "Once you've seen Liam O'Roarke made comfortable here in the pit with the rest of the wounded, I want you standing guard over the others. You and Grover. Hutch Farley?"

"Yes, Major?" the youngster answered quietly.

"Once your pa is resting here with me, you get out there and stand watch with Grover."

"Stillwell's a good shot too, sir," Sharp commented.

"I know, but I've got plans for him," Forsyth hinted. "Once we've strengthened our pits by ringing them with the saddles taken off all the dead horses, I turn to the next immediate problem."

"Getting outta here?" someone snorted from the dark. A few of the scouts laughed self-consciously.

"Damn right, fellas," Forsyth answered softly. "All we've got to eat is horsemeat that's started to go bad. And we haven't got a blessed drop of medicine for our wounded, no bandages except for rags torn from our own shirts and dipped in this muddy water seeping into the bottom of our rifle-pits. Our only chance, boys—is getting word to Wallace."

"A damned fool's errand that is, Major!" Pete Trudeau snarled sourly.

Forsyth turned to the oldest of the plainsmen gathered in that pit as the drizzle slacked off. Off in the distance some green phosphorescent lightning brightened the western prairie for an instant. Then Forsyth dropped the canister of shot on them.

"I'm asking for volunteers, Trudeau. No one ordering a man to go."

"I offered, Major."

"You're staying, Irishman." He turned, his eyes piercing the dark.

"How far you figure it is, Major?"

"Over a hundred miles."

"I'll go."

"That sounded like Jack Stillwell's voice."

"It were, Major. Said I'd go."

Donegan thought he heard the breath catch in Forsyth's throat before he spoke. "Y-you're just a . . . a youngster . . . lot younger that the rest of these——"

"I'm volunteering, Major. I'm every bit as good as——"

"Dammit! I know that, Jack," he snapped, the aggravation, the indecision, edging his voice. "All right. All right, you'll go, Stillwell."

"And if I'm going, Major—I'm requesting permission to pick my partner."

Forsyth was silent for a few moments. They could all hear

the rise and fall of Mooers's ragged breath in the same pit. Then the major spoke.

"Who you want to try with you, Jack?"

"Old Pete."

"You'll go with Jack, Trudeau?"

He cleared his throat. "I go with the boy, Major."

Forsyth snorted back some dribble from the end of his nose, then gave his orders. "All right. You men know what we need doing. McCall, get these fellas to work. I want a lot of meat cooked—for the wounded, and for the two who leave at full-dark."

Forsyth waited while McCall assigned duty, calling names out of memory rather than referring to the small notebook he had carried out of Fort Hays nearly three weeks ago, pages filled with his scrawl detailing duty rosters.

Once the twenty-six spread out along the rifle-pits, cutting meat, building fires, connecting rifle-pits, Forsyth whispered to McCall, Grover, and Donegan to draw close.

"Fellas, the pain's getting pretty bad in my leg."

"That bullet's got to come out, Major," Grover said.

"No." He said it a little too strongly. "Not . . . just yet, Sharp."

"What I'm worried about is come a time I lose consciousness." And Forsyth gazed down at Dr. Mooers. "Get like our surgeon . . . or worse, like Beecher in his final hours. I . . . I just want you three to understand where things stand if I can't command here."

"I'll take over, sir," McCall spoke up.

"This is hard, Billy, but I want you to understand me. You and me—we aren't fighting Rebels anymore. This is a whole new game out here. Don't take offense at what orders I'm laying down. You're a damned good soldier . . . but to keep these men pulled together . . . to hold out until we get word to Wallace and a relief column gets back, I need Grover in charge."

"Major, for the better part of a week we'll be holed up here, waiting for them two to make it to Wallace and back with help."

"That's why you're in charge if I can't command, Sharp."

"Yes, Major."

"I . . . I understand, sir," McCall said, his voice cracking a bit. "I'll help Sharp every way I can."

"I know you will, Billy. That's why I asked to have you along. You're the best damned sergeant I could get my hands on. And I know you won't let me down now."

"No, sir."

"We all understand one another?"

"I do, Major."

"You, Donegan?"

"Aye, Major. I'm here to follow orders—like the rest."

"By God, Irishman—you damned well better let Grover know what you're thinking as well. You come up with an idea how to defend this hell-hole, you tell him."

"Blessed saints, I've never been one to keep my mouth shut, Major. And with every Dog Soldier in the territory camped on our doorstep out there—I sure as hell ain't gonna worry about speaking my mind if it gets these men off this island in one piece."

"Thank you, boys." Forsyth sighed in the dark, turning to watch a handful of fires beginning to twinkle brightly, glowing red on the faces of those who had started them down in fire-pits.

"We'll pull through, Major," McCall cheered.

"That's right, Billy," Forsyth replied. "If hunger and thirst and infected wounds don't do to us what the Cheyenne couldn't."

Chapter 25

*I*n that day this far eastern rim of Colorado Territory was a veritable paradise for the nomadic tribes who followed the great Republican herds in their seasonal migrations. Not much of any settlement east of Denver or west of Fort Wallace marred the landscape. In 1868 this land was a hunter's paradise, whether he sought turkey, quail, or blue-grouse whirring into the sky. Deer, elk and antelope hid in the thick cover along water-courses and immediately bounded out of range at man's approach. Ducks and geese annually made two passes over this rolling prairie grassland, staying only a short time amongst the lush reeds and tall, protective brush beside each river, stream and creek, water-fowl going and coming with their own seasonal imperatives.

Just like that country of the Big Horns, Seamus thought as he felt his way back toward his rifle pit and Uncle Liam. *Places as good as these the Injins hold on to with a mighty fierce grip.*

He stopped suddenly, crouching. His ears strained as he held his breath, eyes widening to catch any movement on the bank as the sky grayed with dusk. Movement along the north bank. He figured they were pickets ordered posted by the war-chiefs, to assure themselves none of the white men crept off the island and sneaked away in the dark.

Injuns don't attack at night, he recalled Jim Bridger telling him across their five-day journey to Crow country, where they would visit the aging mulatto mountain man, Jim

Beckwourth. Bridger echoed Sharp Grover's words to Major Forsyth.

Brownskins don't never fight at night, neither. Bad medicine to their kind—when a warrior is killed after sundown, his soul wanders for all time. Never finding rest because it wanders between earth and sky.

His stomach growled, reminding him of the wild plums he had picked that last evening they made camp below the bluffs on the north bank. He had wrapped them in some oilcloth, then strapped them in his saddlebags. That made him remember The General.

It was a painful walk, groping his way among the men and the dark pits to reach the north slope of the sandy island. Painful, too, finding the big animal already stinking, bloating after some fourteen hours beneath a summer sun. Its lips drawn back, teeth bared in a grotesque, mournful grin. Ribcage dotted with huge, dark holes, each one puffy at the end of a dried streamer of blood.

Here beside the carcass, amid the faint noises of the others digging in the wet sand behind him, Seamus listened to the night-sounds of the insects at work on the gore and blood. Glad he didn't have to see it.

Making quick work of the McClellan saddle, he yanked it, his bedroll, and saddlebags from the big animal, then splashed out of the shallow stream onto the sandy island once more. He tossed his wet tack onto the grass, turned, and knelt by The General's eyes, open and glazed from those last frantic seconds of the hardest ride of its life.

He stroked the animal's neck, ran his fingers through the mane. Patted the strong jawline, saying good-bye in his own way. And when he had it all cried out, Seamus ran a damp sleeve across his face, gathered his saddle-tack, and moved off through the plum thicket.

"Seamus."

"Sharp," he replied as he approached the front of the island. "Liam . . . is he still——"

"Still breathing," Grover replied. "Don't figure it, how a man like him can hold on like this, what with losing so much . . ."

"I know," he answered as Grover's voice dropped off self-

consciously. Seamus stepped into the pit, sand-sliding his
way to O'Roarke's side.

As he moved close, a vapor of mosquitoes rose with an
angry whir from Liam's face. During the day, the bloody
head wound had been crusted with flies, laying their eggs in
the gore. Now with the cool of evening, the mosquitoes had
risen from the slow water along the river, and came to torment the wounded as well. Seamus swatted them away angrily, repeatedly killing them on his own bare cheeks as well.

Then, taking a plum from the oil-cloth wrapper, he placed
it between his uncle's lips and squeezed some juice into the
slack mouth.

He tried to drive the stench of this place from his mind.
Not only the decaying horse carcasses and dead men. But the
awful stench from the wounded as well.

"Liam," he said softly. "We ain't got any bacon or hard-
bread left now. Found these plums in me saddle-sack. I don't
know if you can hear me or not . . . but suck on it till
you're down to the pit. I'll put you 'nother between your
lips."

He watched for some sign of recognition. Then as he was
about to turn away, Seamus saw the eyes flutter half open.
The plum tumbled from the lips as O'Roarke began to
whisper in a harsh rasp, half his mouth immobile.

"Don't want no plums, Seamus."

"Don't try to talk. You haven't eaten since yesterday. The
plums will give you——"

"No idea how long I've got left on this earthly veil,
Nephew. We must talk before I pass out again. The pain—
sweet God, this pain is almost exquisite . . . you're still
there, Seamus?"

"I am, Uncle," he replied, sliding closer and squatting beside O'Roarke, lifting a hand in his.

"Good . . ." Liam sighed, eyes closing slightly. "Your
mother, bless her—tell her it weren't none of your fault you
didn't bring me home."

He squeezed his uncle's hand. "We're both going home,
Liam."

"Aye, in the end—we all go home, don't we, lad?" He
sputtered softly, licking his dry lips. "Put some water on me
mouth, will you?"

After Seamus had bathed his uncle's mouth with drops of water, Liam spoke again.

"I have to tell you, before I go home . . . go home afore you, Seamus. Me and brother Ian would never done anything to hurt your mother, or her seed. Never had us a notion you was coming."

"We talked of this already, Liam," he said. "Save your strength now."

"It's night?"

He glanced about, into the darkness. It made him uneasy that O'Roarke could not tell. "Yes, Uncle. Well past sundown now."

He seemed to smile. "Last I remember of the day was the sun's light going down behind the far mountains, me boy. A pretty, pretty sight i' t'were. I've scratched for gold in the mountains, you see."

Seamus gazed to the west. As far as he remembered, there were no mountains he had seen. No mountains Liam could have seen. "You wrote Mother of it. California."

"That, and not far from here as well in the Colorado high country. Scratched up enough to buy meself a trip to Bannack City up in Alder Gulch."

"Was headed there meself two years ago now," Seamus murmured. "Did Ian go with you?"

He sighed, eyes slipping down. "No, lad. Me brither and me had us a falling out in Cripple Creek."

"Falling out?"

"I'm tired now, Nephew. Growing cold."

Seamus drew a second smelly saddle-blanket over his uncle, then unlashed his own bedroll and laid it out. Glancing at the sky, he noticed the heavy, scudding clouds beginning to break apart, a few sparkles of starshine showing through the cracks. Less chance of any more rain now.

"You'll be warm and dry now, Uncle. Tell me before you go to sleep . . . about you fighting with Ian. You went north. He went where?"

Seamus listened as the breathing became more regular. Figuring Liam asleep, he drew the thick horse-blanket under his uncle's chin.

"I to Bannack," said the weary voice within the whiskers. "And Ian . . . he took the woman west . . ."

"West?" He waited, listening to the breathing. Seamus grabbed his uncle's hand again, clutching it beneath the blanket. "California?"

"No, lad. West. Not . . . California."

"Where, Uncle?"

No reply came from the bloodied lips.

Donegan eased back, finding Grover standing at the lip of the rifle-pit. "I don't make any sense of it."

"What's west, if not California, Seamus?"

He shook his head in exasperation, tucking the blanket securely round his uncle. I'll have to wait to find out, when he's in a talking mood again."

"You're damned lucky Liam talked much as he did."

He finally nodded. "Lucky me uncle's still alive, ain't I?"

"Someone's said their prayers over him, no doubt."

"I know who, Sharp," Seamus replied as he clambered out of the pit to stand beside the army scout.

"Who?"

"His sister."

"Sister, eh?"

"Me own mither. She prays over us all."

He had heard most of what he wanted to hear. From his spot far down the south bank where he had hidden himself throughout the day-long battle, Bob North moved out at slap-dark and crept into the swamp-willow directly opposite the place where Major Forsyth gathered his twenty-eight able-bodied men. North heard most of it, connecting the rifle-pits, cutting meat off the horses and roasting it, making the wounded comfortable. And assigning guards to watch over the others. He thought he had seen the big, tall Irishman standing beside Grover at the sunset meeting.

And figured his chance to gut the Irish bastard would come sometime just before midnight when the sky had finally drained to black.

Creep on the island, hugging the shadows of the overhanging willow. Slow, across the shallow river and into the tall grass.

North felt for his knife in its rawhide sheath. As much as he wanted to put a lead ball into the tall bastard's brain—to pay him for the ball he had suffered in his gut—the knife would do his work this night.

Someone on the island began singing. North had to smile. It sounded good. Like those nights in camp with his fellow Confederate soldiers, singing round their fires and working themselves up for the next day's fight. But he was captured and left to rot in a prison called Rock Island before getting "galvanized" to become a Yankee soldier sent west to fight Indians during the war back east. As long as he didn't have to fight any of his fellow Southerners, North had figured. And shipped west.

It had been his ticket out. Soon finding the chance to escape from Camp Connor on the Powder River. And getting himself taken in by an outlaw bunch of Arapaho.

All day long North had worked it over in his mind, figuring the chances were good there might be some Araps with Roman Nose's bunch upstream.

Was some Araps with Roman Nose last summer, wasn't there, boy?

He amused himself, remembering the day-long attack on the hayfield workers.

Inching forward, he cautiously pushed the tall grass aside and peered at the island, sniffing the cool breeze that carried the strong, heady fragrance of horseflesh roasting over an open fire. He realized he hadn't eaten all day either.

North sniffed again, listening with a surge of strange joy as the Yankee scout continued his song over the dull, red glow of his cooking-pit.

> "Give ear unto my story,
> And the truth to you I'll tell
> Concerning many a soldier,
> Who for his country fell."

Damn, if that wasn't some fine singing to his way of thinking. Even if it was a blue-belly song . . . and about the war too.

But, fine singing nonetheless, and a most welcome change from the drumming, chanting, shrieking racket going on upstream. He figured the squaws and old medicine shakers were busy tonight, what with all the bucks he had seen knocked from their ponies.

North smiled. Only one more white man did he want to go down this night.

Chapter 26

"Y̶ou value it, you'll take your hand off me, Grover!" Seamus growled, whirling on the scout who gripped his arm.

Sharp slowly released the lock he had on the Irishman. "You're on a fool's errand, Donegan."

"Am I, now?" He turned in the darkness, the cool breeze left in the thunderstorm's wake brushing his cheeks dappled with week-old whiskers now. His last shave at Wallace. Too many miles away now to be anything more than a faint ripple in his memory.

"The Cheyennes got him by now anyway."

"Damn sure of that, aren't you?"

Grover pursed his lips, and his eyes gave him away. "No telling, Seamus," he finally said quietly. "What would you say a white man's chances were off this island? Much as the bastards were swarming over us . . . around us all day." His arm swept in a wide arc as his eyes narrowed on his friend. Above them the dim starlight peeked through cracks in the clouds. "You play a lotta poker, Seamus. So, tell me, what's that bastard's chances of still being alive?"

He sighed, sinking in a dejected heap to the sand. He rubbed the bandage wrapped round his left arm. Its brown stain no more than a dark afterthought on the dirty tail of his shirt he had used to bind up the holes from Bob North's bullet.

"Five hundred to one. That's his chances," Donegan admitted.

"Be yours too, dammit." Grover slid to the sand beside him. Five feet away, both could hear the shallow, labored breathing of Liam O'Roarke, motionless beneath his blankets as the night turned cold. "Here you wanna go off and do something foolish, Seamus—when the high, low, and the jack are all against you."

"Don't understand it, I don't," Seamus grumped, his shoulders sagging. "Who the divil he is, and what he wants with me dead."

"Likely it don't matter now at all," Grover consoled his friend. "Likely, Seamus—them Cheyenne turned him to dogmeat already."

Donegan stared into the darkness. "The horse—why'd he go and have to kill the horse?"

Grover wagged his head a moment. "Suppose it's no different from what we tried to do with that charge of warriors we stared in the eye all day. If the Confederate could drop your horse and put you afoot out in the open, he'd better his chances of killing you as you ran to the island."

"That big, beautiful brute carried me here . . . across the river," Seamus said, sensing the sting at his eyes, recalling just some of what the horse had carried him through since capturing the animal in 1863.

"And by damned, it might come down to it that we all might have to walk that hundred miles back to Wallace," Grover said, "but you try sneaking off this island tonight— or anytime with those Injuns thick as bears round a honey-tree—mark my words, Seamus Donegan won't be alive to walk outta here."

For the longest time he sat staring at the lone cottonwood silhouetted in the starlight at the far end of the island, forced to listen to the death-rattle of his uncle's breathing.

"All right," he finally whispered. "By the saints, Sharp— I'll allow that Seamus Donegan lets his heart do his thinking for him most oft . . . but comes a time when I've got to swallow down what's gnawing at me, and back off."

"C'mon, Seamus. Time enough for us finding out why he was trying to kill you. Right now, the major needs us standing watch over the rest of the boys."

Cautiously, the two prowled the length of the island for the first time through that long night, assuring themselves and Forsyth that the hostiles were not skulking across the shallow river under the cover of darkness. Quietly the pair returned to the dim glow of the fires buried down in holes at the bottom of a few of the rifle-pits.

Already some of the scouts had skinned back the hide from the meaty rumps of the army mounts. On their chapped lips glistened the moist juices as they chewed or sucked on the raw flesh while slicing more they laid on willow frames over the low flames. Stacks of the firewood collected by others sat in the shadows of the pits, driftwood found on the island, smooth as elk antlers after a seasonal rubbing. Those men at the fires understood only this night to cook as much of the stringy horsemeat as possible. By the time the sun would crawl to mid-sky tomorrow, the flesh of the dead animals would simmer into a putrid gruel no man could stomach.

What the men could not choke down before sunup they would bury in the sand, wrapped in canvas haversacks and gum ponchos, to stay sweet for two, maybe three days at the most. The trip here from Wallace for a relief column would take longer than that in itself.

The crackle of fat dripping into the fires and the heady aroma of broiling meat hovered close around the rifle-pits while the summer air turned sharper with each renewed gust of night-breeze.

A season of change arrived here on the high plains. Days hot enough to bake a man in his britches and nights cold enough to remind him winter could not be far off.

Seamus squatted by a fire overseen by John Donovan and Chance Whitney. Donovan handed his fellow Irishman a charred strip of flesh.

"Thankee," Seamus replied, then chewed at the tough, raw meat encased in a charred coating.

"Sorry, Seamus," Donovan apologized. "It's pretty bad at that."

"This?" Donegan choked it down, smiling within his Vandyke whiskers. "I remember the war, boys. That was bad food, now i' t'was. Our grub back then was enough to make a army mule desert. And all the while them generals ate seven-course meals . . . from the lentil soup to the pecans after dinner."

Some of the others squatted in close, chuckling. Donegan sensed that it felt good to them to laugh a bit, what with all they had shared that long day come to an end and no man wanting to think about what sunrise would bring. Least of all Seamus himself, forcing from his mind the thought of Liam O'Roarke lying in the far rifle-pit, his life oozing from that gaping hole in his head.

But only a matter of time . . .

"Most of you boys served like me . . . so you know bloody well what I'm talking about, don't you?" he asked them as they gathered round, some of them pulling knives to help with the roasting.

"Goddamn officers—begging the major's pardon . . ." John Donovan cursed, turning to Forsyth in apology. "There's good officers and there's bad'uns."

The major smiled warmly in the firelight, his brow beaded with sweat though the night had turned cool. "No offense taken, Donovan."

"Not many of the good ones, hows'ever, Major Forsyth," Seamus added. "Not many like you, sir."

Forsyth's eyes softened as he gazed quickly at the young Irishman. "You've a lot of your Uncle Liam in you, Donegan. Of that you can be proud."

"Every hour he hangs on, I find meself more proud, I do," he replied, then sensed the talk made the group go sour and morose on him. So, despite the cold rock he felt in his belly, Donegan chuckled as warm as a summer morn.

"Hope you make it to your general's stars, Major Forsyth. Best job in the world . . . from what I seen during the war."

"Damned right," John Donovan replied. "Every general I served under was always warm and comfy in his tent: popping corks on their decanters and squeezing squealing wenches."

"Aye," Donegan agreed, "preferring them comely wenches to fighting 'longside us enlisted. But, the major here's a different breed, ain't he, fellas?"

Seamus listened to the grunts of approval.

"While he could be back at Hays or Larned with the rest of this army's officers having their time with a spare-rib, he's out here getting hell knocked outta him!"

"And what, pray tell, is a *spare-rib,* Donegan?" Forsyth asked.

"Know ye not your Bible stories, Major? Eve was created out of a rib took from poor Adam, bless his carnal soul!"

Forsyth chortled at that. "So a woman is my spare-rib, is it?"

"Aye. You've got that to look forward to, Major, we get you back to headquarters with Li'l Phil Sheridan. You'll find some *weed monkey* to do some sack duty with you."

" 'At's it!" John Donovan cheered, leaping to his feet and standing straight as a ramrod, saluting Forsyth. "Private Donovan reporting, sir! Found you a comely wench as ordered, sir! Wench safely ensconced in your quarters and ready for *horizontal drill,* sir!"

The battered, burned, and weary scouts rolled against one another in laughter as Donovan rubbed himself against Seamus in a most suggestive, and feminine, manner. Tossing his imaginary head of long curls back and eyeing the supposed bulge in Donegan's pants.

"Say, soldier," Donovan wheezed in a high voice, "are you carrying a concealed pistol in your britches . . . or are you just overjoyed to see me!"

Donegan playfully shrugged Donovan off. "Be off from me, you field-hussy!" He knelt by the fire once more while the group laughed easily. Perhaps the best part of the day this, keeping at bay the thoughts of tomorrow and all the rest of the tomorrows yet to come.

"Let's have me 'nother slice of that Jenny steak," he asked.

"Another it is." Chance Whitney passed a charred, dripping strip of fragrant mule-haunch.

"Time again for another stroll downstream, Seamus," Grover reminded.

"Aye," he replied, rising, still chewing on his stringy mule. "Just when the enlisted are being fed, body and soul—the officers come 'long and yank a man off for guard-duty!"

With the easy laughter he heard coming from the island, and able to see the shadows of many men moving about in the central rifle-pits, Capt. Bob North figured it was time to make his move on the Irishman who had shot him on the far side of Lodge Trail Ridge almost two years ago.

No better time than now, what with the voices of men consumed by their cooking, eating, and digging. Best part of it was that from what he had seen earlier in the evening at twilight, the Irishman shared a rifle-pit with Sharp Grover on the far upstream end of the island. But for a dismal spray of starlight, the rifle-pit lay in the dark. Nothing could be better.

With a fingertip, North tested the six nipples of the pistol. Each held a percussion cap. He stuffed it in his belt, then felt once more for the Arapaho knife. Over his hip.

Silently the Confederate crawled on his belly to the edge of the slow-moving river. At this time of the year, it presented no problem in fording on his belly as well. It flowed less than two feet deep, so he decided he would crawl across the sandy bottom, keeping his head and the pistol just above waterline. In the dim light, no man on the island would see him inching across the dark water.

At the island bank, only some twenty feet from the rifle-pit, North stopped, breathing shallow, conscious of the noise it caused. Hearing some reassuring laughter from the central pits. His eyes widened in the growing darkness as a few clouds scudded past. A breeze drifting from upstream carried on it the muted noises of the Indians removing their dead from the streambed. Behind it all, the constant beat of drums rose beyond the hills, accented by the keening wails of the women and old men.

Then he heard the most reassuring sound of all. The raspy snores of a man asleep in the Irishman's rifle-pit.

Foot by foot he inched himself out of the stream, still on his belly, into the dry grass. He froze at the rustle it made. Then, hearing the heavy breathing continue, North slithered on. Each foot brought him closer and closer to the snoring Irishman. Closer to the man whose bullet had caused North's belly to burn with a pain that never left him.

At the lip of the rifle-pit, North held up, listening to the night-sounds. Then carefully peered over the edge, between some saddles, allowing his eyes to adjust to the shadows in the hole scooped from the sand. Straining his eyes for a few seconds, he located the dark form contrasting against the lighter sand.

North drew his knife, slipping one leg over the hard lip of the pit where damp sand had been piled as a bulwark. He waited three heartbeats for the sleeping man to move. When he did not, he slid on down into the pit.

Inching to his victim's side like a scorpion, knife raised like its deadly stinger, poised in the starlight and ready to fall, North held a moment, savoring this last taste of triumph. After so many months and so many miles, to be crouching here, ready to spring.

Still, more than anything he wanted in a long, long time, North wanted the Irishman to know who had killed him. Just as he had this morning during the dawn attack when he was suddenly overwhelmed with the idea of shooting the Irishman out of his saddle during the mad rush to the island. North jabbed the point of the thin-bladed weapon against his victim's throat, at the same time jamming his fingers into the thick hair, yanking the head back, chin jutting, exposing more of the bearded throat.

The man below North exploded into life, cursing in a garbled Irish brogue. And twisted his head aside, thrashing, pulling his neck from the knife-point as his arms vainly struggled to toss off the damp, heavy horse-blankets.

One fist came free, wildly swinging with the blows of a man dying, yet not ready. Once, then twice, a fist glanced off North's head as the Confederate sprawled atop his victim.

Grunting in effort, North fought the surprising strength of the Irishman cursing, babbling incoherently beneath him, until he got one arm pinned beneath his leg. And rose over his victim.

He brought the point of his knife to the throat again, his other hand yanking the bearded chin to the side so he would have a clean slash at the jugular.

The entire massive bulk of his victim convulsed beneath him like the power of horse ready to shed its rider. North held the beard, slashing back and forth with his knife at any flesh he could sink the knife into.

At last he felt the warm syrup splatter over his fingers. North's victim slowed his thrashing enough that the Confederate could bring the bloody knife-hand back for one last blow.

He shoved the long, thin blade between the ribs on the victim's left side, sensing the Irishman sag even more, a few last words mumbled from the lips.

As his dying curse fell silent, North wheeled.

Footsteps approaching from down-island.

Two, perhaps three, men. Boots dragging across both sand and summer-cured swamp-grass.

Frightened like a weasel discovered in the chicken-yard, he lunged for the side of the pit. The footsteps were joined by voices. At least two men drawing close.

If North was anything, he was a man who never fought against a stacked deck. One on one might be a flip of a coin for the renegade. Bob North wanted nothing to chance when he went for the kill. And, grinning like a wolf slipping into the darkness, Bob North had killed again.

The Confederate rolled over the lip of the pit, bellied into the tall grass, and slithered quickly to the water. There he let his eyes grow adjusted to the starshine once more, then slipped into the river again. This time heading for the north bank.

Behind him the voices grew louder. He reached midstream on his belly. Clambered to his hands and knees, his eyes searching the willows and plum-brush on the bank for Indians who might mistake him for a white man escaping the island.

Who you kidding, boy? he chided himself. *You are a white man. But, you got Arapaho friends out there in the night. And, much as you're 'fraid of that big bastard, the red devil Roman Nose hisself ought'n remember you from last summer . . . when you and he went riding down to burn up Fort C. F. Smith.*

Ol' Roman Nose hisself. Him looking to wipe the soldiers off the Big Horn River. And you, Capt. Robert North—you was looking to find a certain tall, dark-headed, brogue-spitting Irishman!

Chapter 27

"**B**y damned, you're a darkie!" exclaimed the thin man standing before Jack O'Neill with a battered bugle hung over one shoulder. His tobacco-stained smiled shined in the firelight. "I ain't seen a darkie since I left home in Ohio back to '66. A damned darkie . . . out here——"

"My mother was African," Jack replied, studying the sun-bronzed white man dressed in nothing but a breechclout, moccasins, and held a blanket round his shoulders to ward off the cool breezes of this summer night on the high plains. He was still somewhat in shock to find himself addressed in English here at the fires in the great Sioux and Cheyenne war-camps hidden behind the low ridge by the river, not far from the sandy island where the soldiers lay in their burrows this night. "I mean . . . her parents were——"

"Your mother was a slave 'swhat you mean," the stranger corrected. "My name's Clybor. Jack Clybor. Pawnee Killer's Brule Sioux gave me name of 'Comanche.' "

"A white man!" O'Neill exclaimed, holding forth his hand.

They shook, a gesture both suddenly realized to be very out of place in this war-camp still very much alive at this late hour, its inhabitants mourning for the dead with eerie chants for those wounded waiting to die.

"Year ago this summer, I was a young recruit to Custer's Seventh Cavalry. Out on patrol with Lieutenant Kidder. We was jumped, tried running for it." He shook his head, grinning. "Never had us a chance. I was wounded," he explained, pulling the blanket from his shoulder to expose the bullet wound pocked and strangely white in the copper firelight. "Pawnee Killer's band butchered the rest. Always figured it strange they didn't knock my brains in."

"They saved you, like the Cheyenne done me."

Clybor grinned all the bigger. "Looking at you, darkie—you could almost pass for Cheyenne, you could."

"Roman Nose watched over me more than most."

"That big buck's forked his last horse, darkie," Clybor replied.

"Call me Nibsi—something meaning *black* in their tongue," the mulatto explained.

"What's your slave name?"

"O'Neill. Jack O'Neill."

"Lordy, you got a Christian name too!"

"My daddy took a special shine to my mama. Raised me up right, down in Georgia. Had schooling with his other children."

Clybor grinned and clucked. "I can tell. You talk better'n any darkie I ever knowed back to home."

"How come you stayed on after your wounds healed?" O'Neill asked, noticing the women hurry about their errands, bathing wounds, boiling roots, preparing poultices for the medicine men.

"I figured if I went back, I'd have to go back into the army," Clybor explained. "Sonsabitches left me for dead. Don't want no part of 'em. Least with Pawnee Killer's bunch, I can get my fill of killing . . . and the squaws is good too. They like taking a roll with a whiteman."

Clybor leaned close to O'Neill. "Bet you like diddling them Cheyenne squaws, darkie."

O'Neill regarded Clybor a moment, then looked away. "You like killing, you say."

Clybor straightened, his eyes narrowing, as if confused that the mulatto had not risen to his bait. "Sure. What you ask——"

"I've just come from talking with Two Crows and some of the others . . . after Roman Nose died. We are going to search for the three whitemen who hid under the bank on the north side of the river during the first charge this morning. They might still be there."

"Them bastards did a handsome job on Roman Nose."

O'Neill glared down at the white man. "My chief was not killed by the three under the riverbank. He was killed by one who stood in his rifle-pit on the island."

Clybor bit his lip, struck with a feeling more than nervousness by this haughty, muscular Negro. "So . . . Nibsi. You gonna go do some killing tonight?"

O'Neill smiled. "Now you have it . . . Comanche. You come. You stay. Makes no difference to me."

"No, no. I'm coming," Clybor explained hurriedly. "Count me in, you got some blood work to do. I like it best when it's up close . . . close enough you can smell the fear in their mouths, see it in their eyes as you come for 'em."

"You have your weapons?"

Clybor nodded. "I have a pistol. Knife and a club."

"Then you are ready to go with me?"

"Lemme get my shirt over yonder by the rocks. If we're crawling out there in them bushes, I'm gonna leave my blanket here. 'Sides, one of these Sioux gals will wanna wrap herself up in it till I come back. I loan her my blanket, she'll diddle me when I bring her one of them white bastard's scalps. Something to sing over later."

O'Neill smiled. "It is good, Jack Clybor. Good that you come to do this killing with me tonight. We'll creep down the north bank . . . just this side of the near end of the island . . . where the first rifle-pit is."

Clybor started to turn away, then stopped, and turned as he scratched the back of his neck, coming away with a small, white louse. "Say, didn't you just tell me that's where the fella was who killed Roman Nose this morning?"

O'Neill, grinned. A sadistic, wolf-slash of an expression he drew no little pleasure in basking on young Clybor. Seeing its effect on the Ohio boy.

"Yes, Comanche . . . I'm hunting whitemen tonight."

"Major, I been thinking." John Donovan crouched at the edge of the pit, where Forsyth lay against the sand after Seamus Donegan and Billy McCall joined Sharp Grover in patrolling once more toward the far end of the island.

Jack Stillwell and Pierre Trudeau slid to the bottom of the trench.

"What you got on your mind, Donovan?" Forsyth asked.

"Trudeau's too old to make this race to Wallace with Stillwell. I'll go in his place, you let me."

"Am not, too old, Major," Trudeau growled.

"You heard Pete yourself, Donovan. Besides, Jack picked ol' Pierre." He turned to Stillwell. "Still want Trudeau?"

"If I'm going, sir—he's going with me."

"It's settled," Forsyth said, giving a wave of his hand that told everyone it had been finalized, turning back to the two couriers who were leaving the island. "You have an idea what direction you're going to start out, Jack?"

"Pete and I talked some while we was roasting meat, Major. Figure we'll go straight south by the north star. If the clouds don't blow off, we'll keep pushing south by feel."

"All right. Just want you to have this for tomorrow."

"What is it, Major?" Jack asked, accepting the thick folds of paper from Forsyth.

"My only map. I'm trusting you with it. I know you can read a bit, and ol' Pierre can't. So, it's yours to carry, Jack."

"Thank you, Major," Jack replied, already sensing an immense loneliness as he stuffed the map inside his damp shirt. He figured Forsyth considered him the more intelligent of the two. "I'll keep the map safe and give it back to you in a few days, sir."

"Explain our situation to Colonel Bankhead." Forsyth chewed at a lip. "Let us all pray you get through, Jack. We're going to be here awhile, and it'll take some doing for you two to get away. Have you fellas got a plan?"

Jack glanced at Trudeau. Then both looked back at Forsyth, and shrugged.

"Just getting off the island is the bone of it, Major," Jack replied sourly.

"We take our boots off, walk backward in stockings," Trudeau finally spoke up. "Old Injun trick. Our footprints will look like moccasin tracks, coming toward the island."

"Take two pistols apiece, fellas."

"Decided we're not carrying carbines, sir. Just get in the way," Stillwell added.

Forsyth nodded. "I understand. We can use your Spencers here come morning. Besides, where you two are headed, no amount of fire-power is going to help if they catch you."

"No, sir," Stillwell replied softly. "They catch us, we'll do what we can to take some with us. But . . . me and Pete here——"

"We talk 'bout it some, Major," Trudeau interrupted. "Them red bastards circle us, and start closing in—we'll kill ourselfs."

"Better than the torture them sonsabitches can do on a man," Sharp Grover added.

"They damned sure got enough firearms. Been slinging lead our way all day." Forsyth groaned, shifting his position from one tired buttock to another.

"Army guns and army bullets," Sergeant McCall growled sourly. "Taken off Caspar Collins's outfit at Platte River Bridge."

"Don't forget what they took from Fetterman's dead on Lodge Trail Ridge," Donegan echoed.

"Got enough meat?"

Stillwell tapped the canvas haversack he had filled with charred strips of half-raw flesh. "I got the horsemeat. Pete's carrying two canteens."

"Strapped 'em to me so they won't rattle and give them pesky brownskins news."

"From what I remember of the map, fellas—Wallace is about due south of here. A relief column will have to march almost due north to get to us, on the bearing Custer used marching south from the Republican last summer."

"We make it, Major," Pete replied, rising. "If I have to smell with my nose that terrible latrine in the walls of Fort Wallace."

Stillwell rose beside Trudeau, noticing how the short, silvery whiskers, aglow in the dim firelight, looked all the more ragged against the old man's browned, leathery face. "Avalanche will see us through, Major."

"Why do you call Trudeau *Avalanche?*"

"Marching up here, Pete told me 'bout a time couple years back when he was scouting for the army and got stoved-up by a mule-kick. They laid him in an ambulance . . . but Pete couldn't say it right. So, I call him *Avalanche.*"

Forsyth held his hand up to Trudeau. "Pete, you and young Jack here don't take any unnecessary chances. Get back here if you can't make it tonight. We'll figure something else out."

"Good-bye, Major," the old man almost whispered. "Been a honor serving you." He pulled his hand out of Forsyth's grip and dragged it under his bulbous, red nose, turning away.

Trudeau clambered out of the pit and squatted as he yanked his boots off, lashing them together with a strip of hide he looped over his neck. He unfurled two blankets as Jack finished shaking hands with Forsyth.

"You best be going," Forsyth explained. "It's nearly midnight."

"So long, Major." Stillwell felt the words catching in his thickening throat. He tried to smile. "Rest of you too."

Some of the others pounded him on the back as he got his boots off, slung around his neck, and took his blanket from Trudeau.

"C'mon, li'l one," Pete whispered, turning into the darkness.

Jack looked over his shoulder a last time, staring at the faces of those he was leaving behind, haggard faces red-lit with the dim glow of fiery coals.

He turned away, gliding noiselessly into the black of prairie night behind Trudeau.

Before any of the men he left behind saw his eyes moisten in the starlight from above.

"He ain't breathing, Sharp!"

Seamus's raspy whisper came quick as he slipped and skidded over the saddles and sand they had built up around the parapet of their rifle-pit. Grover was on his heels, kicking loose sand on his way down to Liam O'Roarke's side.

Donegan drew his uncle's head into his lap, cradling it in both arms as Sharp came to a stop and knelt on the other side of the body.

"Seamus," he began quietly, "we both knew he was gonna die. Just a matter of——"

"I know," Donegan whimpered, whispering, rocking his uncle back and forth in the darkness. "I needed to know, Sharp. Needed to know what's west . . . if California ain't."

"Liam's brother?"

He nodded, choking back the hot, sour ball clogging his throat. "We come all the way from Wallace . . . seemed like he was going to tell me so much last night."

"Major had me and him out, sniffing round——"

"By Jesus, I know that, Sharp!" Donegan snapped. "Look what good Liam did us, him being out. What good it done him as well."

As he ran the fingers of one hand along his uncle's face, Seamus felt the sticky, cool syrup. Coagulating blood.

"Wait a minute, Sharp!" he hissed, something instantly pricking his suspicions.

Donegan twisted his uncle's head gently. "He's shot on the right side of the head."

"Yeah, I remember."

"But here's some fresh blood just starting to dry on the left side of his face and neck," he explained, his fingers exploring. "By the Mither of God, Grover! Fresh wounds!"

His fingers inched down the bearded jawline. Into the slashed, cleaved neck wounds.

"Feel this, Sharp. Here on his neck."

Grover knelt forward in the murky darkness. Groping. Donegan heard the scout's breath catch as he discovered it.

Sharp sat back on his haunches. "Liam didn't die from his head-wound, Seamus."

" 'Sactly what I was thinking meself, Sharp," he snarled.

"It doesn't make sense," Grover whispered, his eyes piercing the darkness. "These Injuns wouldn't skulk on this island and go murdering Liam in his sleep. Just listen to 'em, Seamus." He flung an arm off to the north, pointing out the ridges back-lit with glowing fires. Drums and singing, wailing, and the high, eerie cries of squaws echoed down into the riverbed.

"Who the hell else gonna come up here to this pit and kill me uncle?" he demanded, his tone shoving Grover backward as much as Donegan's big fist would in cracking against the scout's jaw.

"It . . . it ain't like these Injuns . . . they're scairt of fighting . . . killing in the dark, Donegan," Grover tried, grappling for an explanation.

He slowly lowered the body from his lap as he said, "I got

more reason now than ever to kill me these Cheyenne. Bastards crawl in this hole and murder a man already dying. These red h'athens ain't got no soul——"

Grover sensed something strange in Donegan's voice as he broke off. "You hear something, Irishman? Somebody still around?"

"No," Donegan finally answered, his voice grown hard. "But, whoever was here left something behind. I just found it. Put your hand down here along Liam's chest . . . here on your side of his body."

Grover did as told. Reaching out with his hand until he felt the cool, thick moistness that told of much blood having oozed from O'Roarke's side before he died. Then he touched Donegan's hand. Held in the Irishman's hand, still sticky and protruding from the side of Liam's chest, was the hilt of a knife.

"Pull . . . pull it, Seamus," Grover instructed. "I want a look at it."

As Donegan slowly pulled the long-bladed knife from his uncle's chest, Sharp Grover dug round in his vest pockets and located a lucifer. He dragged the sulphur-headed wooden match across the butt of his pistol as it stuck out of his waistband like a goat's hoof. The rifle-pit flared into yellow brightness.

Grover moved the flickering light over the body. Seamus held the knife across both palms, moving it under the hissing match.

"It's Indian, all right. Damn!" Grover moaned. "Can't figure them bastards taking the chance creeping onto the——"

"Red bastirds didn't kill Liam," Seamus interrupted him sharply. "It's an Injin knife for certain. But, I've seen this one before."

Grover searched Seamus's eyes in the yellow light as the match burned down. "You . . . you're sure?"

"I'd never forget that knife," Donegan hissed. "Or the murdering bastird who I saw using it, cutting plums a few days back."

"What?" Grover asked, shaking his head as if were coming all too quickly. "What're you talking about . . . you saw the . . . not an Injun?"

"That's the Confederate's knife."

"Shit!" Grover growled. "None of it makes sense to me, him coming here to . . . why the hell'd he wanna kill Liam?"

"I figure he either killed Liam knowing it was a sure way to get me to come after him," Donegan said as he began wiping the blood from the knife across his thigh. "That, or . . ."

"Or what?"

"Or that rebel bastird figured he was murdering me."

Chapter 28

Jack crouched beside old Trudeau in the last rifle-pit on the far end of the island. From here by the lone cotton-wood, his eyes darted to the south bank, across the river.

Beneath the starshine, the streambed lay drenched in silver light.

He shivered beneath his army blanket. Both wore the blankets wrapped about them Indian-fashion. Time of night it was, these plains had grown more than chill. He was cold.

Yet Jack shivered from more than the cold.

Then the clouds shrank over the ragged patches of starry sky and it began to drizzle once more as they listened and looked from the end of the island. Their friends behind them. Nothing but scalp-hunters and a hundred miles of cactus between them and Fort Wallace now.

Pete nudged Jack, by signs showing the youngster it was time to walk backward from here. They rose together, quietly stepped into the riverbed and backed into the mist that Jack hoped would conceal them from watchful eyes on the shrouded banks.

Every few painstaking yards, Pete signaled they must drop to their hands and knees when the cover along the riverbank grew skimpy. Then they rose once more, walking backward in their stockings, boots slung round their necks, hidden beneath the thin blankets.

Jack worried of doing the right thing as his heart hovered in his throat those first long, dark minutes grinding past as they began their escape.

A thousand to one is what you got here, Jack, he cursed himself. *Things weren't bad enough during the light when the bastards was charging and shooting at us—I'll bet they've tightened their noose 'round us come nightfall. Figuring on someone sneaking off the island. Someone . . . like me . . .*

The mist was turning the brim of Jack's hat soft. Cold water began to spill down the neck of his shirt, slipping beneath the blanket. Each step they made quietly, one foot at a time, until they had crept close to a quarter-mile in the sandy bed. Inching over to the grassy bank, old Pete heaved himself into the willow and lay still, panting, waiting for Stillwell to join him near the mouth of a ravine that opened into the streambed.

Trudeau turned to whisper, something Jack just sensed the old man was about to do. He clamped his fingers over Pete's mouth.

Jack also sensed Indians nearby.

Pete understood. His hands talked for him as he explained they must lay buried in the tall grass. Pickets likely were out, riding in search of any white man intent upon escape from the island.

A scritch-scritching arrested Jack's ears. His heart sealed his throat shut as he laid an ear against the ground, hearing for certain the steps of a pony slowly moving through the damp grass along the riverbank.

The hoofbeats stopped. Then, more came. From what Stillwell could tell with that one ear on the damp earth, three more riders joined the first.

All four quietly continued in the same direction. Toward the mouth of the ravine dumping its run-off into the riverbed. The grassy mouth where Jack and Pete lay waiting in the mist.

A frightening vision of it came before his eyes there in the darkness, made real once more as he recalled the guttural words the old ones like Trudeau had used to describe what Cheyenne and Sioux warriors could do to torture a man. From that first day at Fort Hays, Stillwell had listened to tale after tale of mutilations and butchery. And every one of the seasoned plainsmen, from old man Farley to Pete Trudeau, said the tales shared the same moral.

Don't ever let the red bastards catch you alive.

Here in the tall grass, his mind echoed on that grisly warning.

Stillwell turned slightly, rolling onto his side, letting the blanket slide from his shoulders as he reached for his knife. Pete's hand was there in the next breathless heartbeat, clamping Jack's. Stillwell felt Pete shaking his head slowly in the drizzle.

Trudeau wagged a finger, pointing.

Jack nodded. Then followed the old frontiersman into the tall, damp grass that was their only hope for escape. Had the grass been day-time dry, discovery would have been immediate. But with the cold drizzle that continued to soak their blankets and britches, seeping down the collars of Stillwell's sweaty shirt, that same drizzle softened their escape, dampening the summer-cured grass so it would not tattle-tale the desperate crawl of the whitemen from the mouth of that ravine.

They're coming!

Jack dropped to his belly in the grass at the same instant Trudeau yanked him down.

With one ear against the sodden ground, Stillwell listened as the hooves clopped out of the darkness. Stopped. And waited.

One of the horsemen whispered orders. Two riders headed off upstream once more. While the other two moved into the tall grass along the riverbank.

As he waited there, eyes clenched as if to shut out discovery, Stillwell imagined he saw the ponies' legs slicing through the dewy grass, slowly, ever slowly inching toward the white men.

Ten yards. Eight . . . then four. And when the horsemen were no more than an arm's length away in the sodden, drizzling darkness, they clopped right on by.

He hugged the ground, his fingers clawing at the damp stalks of grass, feeling the water running down his cheeks and into the week's stubble of fuzz. When his ear told him the horsemen had gone off downstream, Jack realized that not all the droplets on his cheek were cold rain.

Some were warm.

He felt delivered as the old man nudged him, motioning

that they would strike out onto the prairie. The hot sting at his eyes reassured young Stillwell he was still alive.

But he balked, shaking his head, arguing in sign with Trudeau that they would stand a better chance staying with the riverbed.

Old Pete shook his head. Telling Jack that was just what the Injuns would figure as well.

Stillwell finally relented. He followed Trudeau onto the prairie, into the cold mist, his feet banging against the first of the spiny cactus that dotted the plain. Jack bit on the inside of his cheek, then his lip, to keep from crying out in frustration and pain. Needle after needle snapped off in the soles of his stocking feet as they crept onto the yawning expanse of the Central Plains.

When the drizzle left them behind agonized hours later, a stiff wind swirled out of the east, chilling Jack to the bone. As it came up, Trudeau turned them face-on into the wind.

The clouds scattered, breaking apart as they scudded across the endless dark canopy, forming huge cracks for a sprinkling of dim starshine. For what seemed like days the old man had them walking into that life-robbing wind, eventually turning south by southeast now that they could read the patches of stars overhead.

Without saying a word when he altered their course every so often in their walk beneath the swirling night-sky, the old man led the young map-bearer into the uncharted darkness of that rolling, desolate wilderness.

He hunched over the jumble of tracks, slowly inching the tiny, burning brand he held over the sand. The mist drew an angry hiss from the driftwood torch he carried.

Looking, hoping to find something.

Twice already Seamus Donegan had circled the rifle-pit where the Confederate had murdered his uncle. Trying to make some sense out of the crossed-over, stomped-on tracks of men and horses, moccasins and ponies.

"No telling where he went, Seamus."

Donegan squatted in disgust, and eventually nodded to Sharp Grover. "Likely he went from here to the riverbank."

"Trouble is knowing which one," the army scout added.

"Not a track in sight, I gotta figure what Bridger'd do."

"Jim Bridger?"

He looked up in the early-morning darkness at his friend. "Ol' Gabe himself, Sharp."

"You met him up the Montana Road?"

"More than met. He taught me a thing or two. So that's what I figure he'd do. You haven't a track of the bastard you're trailing to put you on his scent . . . Bridger would likely sit down and try to think like the man he's stalking."

"By damned, Irishman. It's a smart notion!"

"I sit here looking at it, figuring what the killer would do. South bank or north," he moped, minutes of head-scratching later. "Nothing to go on . . . but my gut tells me that from here at the pit, the north bank is closer by a few yards."

Donegan stood, bringing Grover up with him.

"You can't be figuring on creeping off this island again, are you? We already been through that——"

He whirled on the army scout. "You spoke your piece, Sharp. Be pleased you stand out of my way."

Sharp Grover did just that. Watching the Irishman check his holstered pistol. Then stuff Liam's Colt in his own belt. From O'Roarke's sheath, Seamus pulled a knife before replacing the damp blanket over his uncle's body.

"I'll see you afore breakfast in the morning," Seamus whispered, stepping into the heavy drizzle.

"Coffee for damn fools, is it?"

Donegan turned and grinned, giving his hand to Grover. They shook. "Don't expect me to eat no more of that horse's ass, do you?"

"Good luck, Irishman," Grover replied as he released Donegan's hand.

"If I don't see you again, Sharp," Donegan rasped, "see that Liam gets buried proper. With some of the right words said over him."

"I'll find a Catholic boy to say 'em, Seamus."

"Whoever you choose, probably end up knowing them words better'n me."

"Just you come back afore first light," Sharp ordered sternly. "Major'll have your hide he knows you're gone."

"Bloody right! It's Forsyth . . . or them red h'athens gonna have Seamus Donegan's hide by first light."

He turned and slipped into the night, inching off the gentle slope to the water.

Crossing on hands and knees, Seamus held up at the grassy north bank. Waiting and listening to the night-sounds. Feeling the icy cut of the wind dallying with his wet sleeves and britches. Thinking there under some overhang of willow about old Trudeau and the youngster who crept away some two hours back.

Downstream he was certain he heard the guttural, yet hushed voices of unseen warriors dragging bodies over the riverbed. Removing their dead. Laying here against the north bank, away from the noise on the island, the sounds of the Indian camps had new dimensions. Heartbeat drumming, hair-prickling wails, and high-pitched trilling of mourners. No doubt working themselves up to finish come dawn what they had only begun that first, long day.

As much as he hated the thought, Trudeau and Stillwell might have the better part of it. At least they were out there, doing something right now. And from the sounds of things, they had evidently made it some distance. At least, none of those who had remained behind on the island had heard any war-whoops or gunshots after the pair trudged off into the drizzle and darkness. Lucky so far.

Four grueling days or more getting back to Wallace on foot. Most likely, he brooded, *take Bankhead another day to organize and outfit his relief column. Then the better part of two more days galloping here to this stretch of sandy riverbed.*

A week more of holding out . . .

And every day, the brown riders would come roaring down on the island, whittling away at the twenty-eight who weren't wounded. Every hour increasing the stench of dead horses turning to a putrid soup, while the moans of the wounded men were becoming more desperate with every sunrise.

Any way he put his mind to adding and subtracting, Seamus couldn't come up with a figure that showed the scouts had a chance to last seven more days. With the way fifty-one men had been reduced to twenty-eight that first morning, his crude ciphering as he clung beneath that overhang of swamp-willow didn't spell success for Major Forsyth's little bunch.

But Seamus Donegan had been in tight spots with slim odds before.

In the mid-distance, among the ridges and hills, he could make out for the first time the yapping of coyotes. Brought in by the smell of blood in this place. Closer still, the yammering of Indian dogs answering back their feral cousins, claiming this feast as their own. Then in the midst of the night around him, faint sounds of horsemen prowling the riverbanks, scouting for any white man foolish enough to escape the island.

He asked himself how the Confederate could begin to hope of eluding the milling warriors in the drizzling rain. Then something bright came on in his cold thinking, like someone had reached inside his head and turned up the wick-roller on an oil-lamp. And Seamus Donegan cursed himself for not thinking of it sooner.

"The knife," he murmured to himself as he hunkered into the shadows beneath the willow's overhang. "That bleeming knife."

That was the key. Only explanation it could be. The reason now for all those odd things about the Confederate. The way he only ate with his hands instead of using the iron forks the rest of them carried in their mess-kits.

That pony of his wasn't a white man's horse at all, now that he thought of it. More a rangy cayuse. A war-pony if nothing else.

Especially the way the man slipped in and out of some guttural, nonsense gibberish he was forever apologizing for.

"Sonuvabitch talks Injin," Seamus hissed silently, as the hoofbeats inched up the riverbank.

He doesn't have to worry about escaping from these h'athens . . . he's a damned turn-coat renegade hisself!

Lying there hidden in the night-shadows, the cold drizzle plipping off the willow above him, Seamus realized he had made one big mistake trying to track the Confederate. He sensed that Liam O'Roarke's murderer already sat at some warm fire, eating his supper, while a dusky-skinned, comely wench snuggled at his side, waiting the bastard's bidding.

While the man who had minutes ago dreamed of stalking that murderer down lay in the darkness to see the night through, with a puddle of cold water gathering round him, he heard two . . . no, three horsemen slipping from their ponies not far away.

Donegan clenched his eyes shut for a moment, cursing himself like only the Irish in him could. Thinking strangely on the others he had left behind on the island. Forsyth and McCall. Grover and Donovan. And the rest of them as wasn't laid out with bullet-holes seeping red life into the sand.

Good men, he was proud to say.

Good men who this night have laughed for fear of the darty Reaper hisself.

And when good men are all laughed out . . . they cry in the dark.

Chapter 29

"*W*ho was the one said he thinks a whiteman passed him in the dark?" Jack O'Neill demanded in his throaty Cheyenne.

"Stands On The Prairie," another young warrior admitted, pushing forward a youth, no more than a boy.

Clybor laughed. "This young fool wouldn't know if one of those soldiers walked by and knocked him on the head."

O'Neill wasn't so sure. He stepped close to the youth, studying him beneath the starshine. Minutes ago the drizzle had withered off to the east. The mulatto had left the warcamp, leading the other renegade, Clybor, with half a dozen Cheyenne warriors curious on determining if Roman Nose's powerful medicine had indeed been passed down to this adopted black-whiteman.

They had begun by prowling down the north bank of the river, looking first for any signs of the soldiers escaping before they would determine a way onto the island where the big, black Nibsi would gut him a soldier or two before morning shed its early, summer light on the plains.

Nearly opposite the upstream end of the island where the bullets had struck Roman Nose, the mulatto had ordered a halt as the excited youngsters had galloped up from the darkness.

"Stands On The Prairie," the mulatto addressed the youngster, "you are sure one of the white ones passed you in the night?"

He turned sideways, flinging an arm across the river. "It

was far, over there. Far from the other end of the island. On the south bank, Nibsi."

"You saw him and did not want his scalp?"

The youth bit his lip. "I never saw him."

Clybor laughed again, loud with the sound of a heavy rasp drawn across rusty iron. O'Neill wheeled on him, saying nothing. Not needing to. Clybor shut up.

Turning back to the youth, the mulatto continued. "You did not see the man. How is it you know he passed you?"

"My nose, Nibsi."

"You smelled him?"

He nodded. "He stank of broiled meat. Cold sweat. Coffee."

"One of our own could be doing the same as you out there in the dark," O'Neill said reluctantly, because he wanted to believe the boy.

The youth ground a moccasin into the sand nervously. "Yes. But, the man I smelled stank of strong tobacco."

O'Neill clamped a hand on the youngster's shoulder, glaring over at Clybor as he spoke in English. "There you have it, my white friend. These bands have not traded with a whiteman in so long, there is no real tobacco left among any but the old men."

"And no old man is going to be out there in this dark and rain, damned fools like us——"

"Go on back to your squaws, Clybor," O'Neill hissed. "I'll find the whiteman who sneaked off the island. And alone I will kill the tall one who killed my chief."

"How you gonna find that soldier what sneaked off the island, eh? You ain't got a good Injun nose. Your damned darkie nose ain't no good smelling out——"

"You haven't anything better than to twist my tail, Clybor —best you get before I show these strong-nosed boys just how to kill a whiteman."

"A w-whiteman?"

O'Neill leaned close, almost in Clybor's face. He spat his words like blacksmith's nails into the drizzling rain. "I see only one *white* man here . . . don't you, Jack Clybor?"

The white man swallowed, forcefully, like choking down some dry meat. "I . . . I see, Nibsi. Keep my m-mouth shut from here on out. And stay on your tail like you told me."

O'Neill turned to the others who had ridden here with him. "You may choose to stay with me here on the north bank, or continue your search. But, if you want to hunt down the whiteman who smelled of strong tobacco escaping from the island . . . meet me on the south bank of the river come first light. Opposite the single, tall tree on that far end of the island."

"I will come," Stands On The Prairie said proudly. "Do not leave without me, Nibsi."

His big, wide teeth shined in the dim light. "I would not leave you behind, young one. Nibsi is going to show you how to find the rats who have run from their gopher-holes."

Sandy Forsyth couldn't call it sleep. Whatever it was he did each time he closed his eyes through that long night, it wasn't sleep. Something closer to passing out from pure, exquisite exhaustion. Closer still to passing out from the pain he had endured for so long already.

God, but for laudanum, this might almost be something I could put up with, Forsyth thought as he shifted position in the pit, inching weight off the broken leg, momentarily rolling weight onto the bullet-riven thigh. He caught his breath at the sudden wave of pain, letting the nausea roll over him, then ebbing like the retreat of breakers against the rocks.

"Billy?"

"I'm right here, Major," McCall answered, inching up.

"Do we have a fire going?"

"We let 'em go out overnight," the sergeant apologized.

"It'll be dawn soon, Billy. They'll be coming back."

McCall rose above the major. "I'll get a fire started."

"Boil some of the water for the men. Have them go through saddlebags looking for coffee. If nothing else, hot water might perk them up."

Grover watched McCall crouch off to start his fire. "One of these days, Major—I'm gonna quit scouting for the army."

"Why you go and do that?"

"Getting damned tired of army cooking. Hot, muddy water 'stead of coffee . . . and a thick, tasteless strip of half-broiled horse's ass for breakfast!"

Forsyth chuckled quietly in the chill pre-dawn air as the

prairie to the east of them stretched itself with a thin, gray line that quickly grew pink. He was letting his head sink back against the sandy edge of his pit when he saw a strange look pass over Grover's face.

Sharp slowly rolled to this knees, gazing intently upstream as he crawled over Forsyth. "We got us visitors, Major."

"Already."

"Yep. I figure they come for those three bodies they couldn't get last night."

"The three warriors that fell near the pit you share with O'Roarke and his nephew?"

Grover glanced down at Forsyth. "Figure I'm alone in that pit now. O'Roarke's dead."

"Bless his soul——"

"But he didn't die of his wound, Major. Someone come on the island last night and killed him—stabbed with a knife. Donegan figures it was the Confederate."

"Dick Gantt?"

"No, the older one. Strange fella."

"Smith?"

"That's what he called himself when he signed on," Grover answered. "And now I figure Seamus Donegan is done as well." He studied the pain etched on the major's face a moment. "He left the island last night to search for his uncle's killer."

Forsyth clenched both his eyes and pressed his lips shut to keep from screaming as his head fell back in exasperation. "Damn him!" his whispered hoarsely, his brain once more beginning to throb like last night's drums.

"I'll go look for him, you want me to."

He shook his head. "No, Sharp. No sense in me losing two marksmen."

"Donegan's a pain in the backside, Major—but he was about as good with a rifle as old man Farley——"

"Here I thought you was me friend, Sharp Grover!"

Both the scout and Forsyth whirled at the merry brogue. Donegan crabbed up, clambering over the wounded and skirting the wide water-pit Martin Burke had dug nearby.

"Damn you, Donegan!" Forsyth swore, his voice low.

Seamus halted, fingertips to his heart. "That any way to

welcome this long-lost prodigal son back to your fold, Major?"

"Where you been all night?" Grover demanded.

"Under a willow-bush," he explained, pointing to his damp clothing as he squatted down beside Forsyth. "Didn't get no farther. That north bank was nasty with the h'athens. Could hear 'em talking a'times. Even heard me a loud scuffle between a few of 'em. A beating like nothing I've heard in my tavern escapades. One fella sure got the worst of it."

"By damned if you were in my outfit, I'd have your stripes for desertion, Donegan."

"Custer got there ahead of you, Major," Donegan replied. Then as he smiled himself, Seamus watched a smile grow in Forsyth's weary, seamed face. "Besides, I didn't desert. I was only out . . . on a little forward reconnaissance."

"Glad you made it back," Grover said, tapping Donegan on the shoulder. He turned to Forsyth. "No time to chat, Major. Them visitors is moving down the riverbed toward us now."

Sandy Forsyth looked upstream through the inky light of false-dawn. He wasn't sure how Sharp Grover could tell, but —if he really didn't concentrate on the riverbed itself, he thought he could see some faint shadows bunching some distance away. Grover and Donegan slipped off wordlessly among the rifle-pits, headed toward the far end of the island.

"You see 'em, Major?"

He watched Billy McCall crabbing back close. "Think so. Not sure if I'm seeing warriors, or if it's this aching skull of mine playing tricks on me."

"Twenty or so of 'em," McCall whispered, jamming his pistol back into Forsyth's hand. "Keep this, in case they make a big rush on us, sir."

The major saw that scowl of concern in the sergeant's red-rimmed eyes. "You want me to keep the last bullet for myself."

McCall nodded. "No telling what this bunch coming means."

"Getting the day started early."

He wagged his head, eyes locked on the shadows inching closer and closer to the island. "More'n half of 'em dropped from their ponies now, sir."

"They're searching, Billy."

"More bodies?"

"No. Us. They aren't sure if we're still here."

The familiar yammer of a coyote floated in from a nearby hill.

A single gunshot suddenly tore through the growing, gray light of pre-dawn darkness.

"Dammit!"

Forsyth recognized the anger in Sharp Grover's voice somewhere on the upstream end of the island.

"Who fired that bleeming shot?"

That was Donegan, demanding.

There was a scuffle of boot-soles on the sand. A hurried pounding of moccasined feet beating a retreat back to their ponies accompanied by shrill warnings among the warriors. A hurried mounting.

Then the wild yelp of one brave Cheyenne intent on counting coup on the unsuspecting white men. His was quickly echoed by close to two dozen. The gray light erupted with the hammering of hoofbeats splashing up the shallow riverbed.

"Don't let them ride over us!" Sharp was hollering, loud as he could.

"They're coming!" Others took up the chorus.

All round Forsyth the island burst into a sudden flurry of motion, blurred by the lack of light, while behind them the horizon to the east grew from pink to a fiery orange, making strange shadows and stringing movement out behind the scurrying men.

Then Forsyth saw them. At least twenty. Dodging behind their ponies in their spontaneous charge on the island now that they had discovered the white men still burrowed in.

His chief of scouts was up, waving an arm.

"Fire!"

The sudden roar of the carbines in answer to Grover's order caught Forsyth by surprise. He watched the small charge split itself not far from the island, horsemen yelping into the willow and out of sight.

Grover was there behind Forsyth in the next moment, gazing over the lip of the rifle-pit. "Some sonuvabitch got a case of itchy finger, Major."

"I heard."

"Just some young bucks. Skulking toward the island on foot. I figure they was looking in the sand for footprints, see if we'd left or not."

Forsyth's stomach rumbled as his head swam, pain flushing his pale cheeks. "S-Sharp," he murmured, his eyelids falling. "Have one of the men . . . change my dressings."

Grover hunkered over him, protective as a sage hen over her young. "I'll do it myself, Major."

As the first, gray light spread itself across the prairie, the Indian guns along both banks took to rattling. Snipers put out to keep the white men in their burrows for another day.

"Sonsabitches figure to starve us out," Sharp whispered over the major as he went to work. He carefully untied the strips of cloth men had ripped from the long tails of their pull-over, four-button shirts for their commander's wounds.

Forsyth gritted his words between his clenched teeth, swallowing down the pain best he could. "They won't beat us, by damned."

The first bandage came off with a considerable amount of struggle and pain for the major.

"That's right," Sharp whispered, as cheerfully as he could muster, studying the festering white ooze in the thigh wound.

Forsyth's wound had already begun to smell. Almost as bad as the half-butchered horses.

"We got us enough prime U.S. Army steak on the hoof . . . and all the muddy water any man can drink."

Forsyth caught his breath, glanced at the oozy wound, then looked away again before he threw up. He tried out a weak smile. "That's right, Mr. Grover. We'll just hunker down here and make ourselves to home with all these wonderful comforts . . . until Bankhead's troops arrive."

Sandy Forsyth sensed that Grover's unknotting the bandage over his broken left calf was going to be a bit more than he could stand and turned his head just before his stomach revolted at the pain, throwing up the sour, brackish water they were drinking from the bottom of the pits.

He let his cheek rest against the side of the pit as he struggled to separate himself from the murderous pain in the leg Grover worked on. Rinsing out the bloodstained bandages.

Retying the newly soaked strips of cloth back on their original wounds. Nothing more a man could do for any of the wounded.

"Oh, God . . ." he muttered under his breath, squeezing his mind down on the warming, soothing thoughts of Chicago and home.

He had taken four bullets in his time . . . three of them while serving with Phil Sheridan down in the Shenandoah during the war.

Oh, sweet . . . sweet Jesus, his mind sang as his stomach threw up more of the thick, yellow bile and the brackish, milky water.

But for the want of laudanum . . . my sweet, sweet morphine . . .

Chapter 30

*A*lthough that early charge broke off before it got anywhere close to the island, it was nonetheless enough to
start hearts pumping among those men huddled in those
grimy, bloody holes filled with seep-water.

When the angry sniping from both riverbanks withered
into an annoying nuisance, Donegan slid down to the bottom
of his rifle-pit once more. He gazed at the long, thin-bladed
knife he had pulled from his uncle's heart a handful of hours
ago.

Before first light Seamus had unhooked the big, brass
buckle on O'Roarke's belt and pulled free the worn knife-
sheath his uncle had evidently carried for many years.
Trimmed with a center rosette of porcupine quills dyed
greasy yellow and oxblood, the outer rim of the sheath had a
narrow row of quillwork tracing its border.

He found the buckskin itself a pleasing tobacco color. And
a sniff was enough to tell the Irishman the hide had been
smoked by the squaw who made the sheath for trade. Perhaps even with her love for the old Irishman.

Seamus pulled Liam's crude iron knife from the sheath
and exchanged it with the dull knife he had carried at his
side since arriving in Kansas. The thought yanked him back,
there in the rising heat of that muggy rifle-pit. *Kansas.*

Seamus was helpless, made to think back on Sam Marr
and the start of their glorious journey to Alder Gulch and
the goldfields of Montana. The last he had seen of the cap-

tain was up the Montana Road, in the reeky infirmary at Fort Phil Kearny.

No such place now . . .

Just before Forsyth had ordered them out of Fort Wallace on their forced march a week or so back, rumor had it that the army was abandoning the Bozeman Trail posts. Signed a treaty with Red Cloud and was shutting down the Road.

Seamus brooded how could he ever hope to find Sam Marr again out here in the middle of the big, big land.

Hell, only thing you've got to worry about now, you bleeming idjit, is how you're getting off this island . . . finding that Confederate who killed your uncle—then you can think about Sam Marr and . . . and . . . Jennie——

"Goddammit!" Why did he have to go and think about her?

But he knew. Because they had some unfinished business between them. So many things left unsaid.

He thanked God for the moans of the wounded, the monotonous, troublesome buzz of the big, green-backed, September flies suspended like clouds over them all. Crawling in and out of the wounds. While they busily laid their eggs. At least their noisy drone kept Seamus from thinking too much.

Not good to think in this heat. Just wait it out. The old man and the boy will bring help.

Donegan knelt over Liam's body, holding his breath. Already O'Roarke smelled of decomposing in this heat of midday. Seamus tucked in the edges of the blankets around the body so that no flies could trouble the bloody holes or the missing scraps of skull. Depositing their eggs.

Torment that only hours later would begin as the wriggling maggots squirmed from the oozy wounds.

That night of stumbling across cactus through the dark with old Pete seemed as if it would never end. Yet before young Stillwell knew it, the first bloody tearing of the dawn sky ripped itself away from the east in an explosion of orange and red.

"Gotta find us place soon, Jack," Trudeau murmured at his side as they stopped, catching their breath.

As the light came up like a lamp-wick raised in a dark

room, Stillwell could see they were crossing a bare scut of land naked of any vegetation that could hide them.

"They'll be coming . . . won't they, Pete?"

Trudeau glanced behind him. His red-rimmed eyes frantic on the skyline to the north. "Sure as you and me standing here."

"We gotta move . . . find us something." Jack tugged the old man along beside him, his feet swollen and bleeding inside his boots from the hundreds of cactus thorns broken off during their escape from the island.

And find something they did. As the early lip of a brilliant orange globe slipped itself over the eastern rim of the earth, the two stumbled upon a dry washout. Each spring the coulee would fill with prairie run-off. But right now there was enough loose rock and scrub-brush to cover their tracks off the open plains and into this narrow, shadowy laceration on the rolling breast of this endless land.

As he helped the old man down into the shadows of the narrow gorge that reminded him of a grave, Jack Stillwell prayed it would not be his.

After sharing a few sips of murky water from a canteen, the two silently chewed on the burned strips of stringy horse-meat. Refreshed, and with the chill retreating as the sun climbed over the prairie, Jack inched himself to the edge of the coulee. Digging a place for his boot-toes and his elbows, he made himself comfortable.

"You take first watch, Jack?" Trudeau whispered, yanking his blanket around his shoulders.

"Yes, Pete. Take my blanket too. You come up later, when I get tired."

Almost immediately, the ebb and flow of heavy breathing rose quietly from beneath those two blankets. Jack inched himself onto a crumbling jut of outcrop at the side of the coulee and spread some of the dried weed-scrub apart. With the rising sun coming up over his right shoulder, Stillwell studied the northern prairie.

They'll come from that direction . . . once they find our tracks and figure out they weren't moccasins . . .

Stillwell was sure the Indians would find out. Last night his feet had started to bleed from the cactus thorns early enough. Likely the warriors would find the blood that had seeped from his stockings into his dusty footprints. Before he resigned himself to putting on his boots.

Old Pete had told him he had better put on the boots or his battered feet would swell up so bad Jack never would get them on.

Right now as his tired, gritty eyes scanned the horizon, Jack wagered he never would get those boots off his swollen, bleeding feet, not for the rest of his life.

Jack stood watch, gazing at the far northern horizon, hoping his boots would last a long . . . long time.

He tossed in his sleep. The distant firing of many guns like a nightmare. Jack grew frightened, sensing he was back on the island again . . . and the long, painful walk with the thorns in his feet was the real nightmare.

"Jack!" Trudeau whispered harshly again.

Stillwell bolted upright, instantly awake and shivering with a cold sweat in the dank shade of the coulee.

Then he recognized the distant rifle-fire. And realized it wasn't a dream. All morning long the rumble of gunfire had echoed from the north while he stood watch. Then turned in when Trudeau climbed up to the brush to take over.

For the first time since last night, his feet ached when he rocked his weight on them.

"I give you a hand," Pete said, stretching his arm out, helping Jack crawl slowly up the side of the coulee.

"The boys are having another hot day of it." Jack sighed as he settled beside the old man.

"All morning . . . no stop," Pete replied. "Sometimes more. Sometimes not. But the guns—they never stop."

"Was I talking in my sleep?"

"No matter. Good you awake. Want you see that."

Stillwell followed Trudeau's arm. "How long they been out there?"

Pete calculated on the position of the sun, then shook his head. "Some time, boy. Coming on slow. Looking at the ground."

"We left tracks for them?"

"Seems so."

"They'll be riding down on us soon," Jack whimpered, his

fingers brushing the butt of the big Colt pistol protruding from his belt like a lamb's hoof.

In silence, they watched the dozen to fifteen warriors ride a short distance, then halt briefly, while one or two dropped to the ground, sniffing, feeling, pointing, and arguing. Then ride on. Back and forth across the northern stretch of prairie the war-party came. First indistinct little dots on the buckskin-colored tableland, like black sow-bugs streaming from an overturned buffalo-chip.

Eventually they became well-defined horsemen, shimmering in the heat-waves boiling off the land.

"Lemme have a bite of that," Jack asked. He took the dark plug from Pete and ground off a corner with his teeth. "Thanks."

"Man always gets a last chew, boy."

Jack looked at the old man for a minute. "They come, I'm glad you're here to die with me."

Old Pete smiled. Usually a sour, taciturn man, Stillwell was instantly struck by the fact that old Pete had smiled.

"Me too, boy." His face wrinkled back, gap-toothed. "I always liked you, from first day, Jack."

"Thanks," he choked, pulling his pistol from his britches. "Y-you save a bullet for me . . . I'll keep the last one for you. We'll count off when it comes time."

The smile faded. "Awright, young'un. We count off together . . . when our time comes."

As much lead as was flung over the island that long, insufferably hot day, the eighteenth of September, every bit of it was wasted by the warriors. They drew white blood but once. And then because C. B. Piatt didn't keep his hindquarters down low enough when the sniping roared at its worst.

Sharp Grover and John Donovan dragged Piatt into Forsyth's pit, where they yanked down his britches and examined the ugly red furrow that had slashed across C. B.'s buttocks.

"Dammit . . . just shut up!" Grover snapped, then chuckled as he thought about it. "Flesh-wound." He crawled off to join Forsyth and McCall, turning to tell John Donovan, "Wrap Piatt's ass with a bandage. I hate to see a growed man whimper like that."

"Damn you, Grover! Like to see you get your ass shot up."

"Just pour some water on it, Donovan . . . and get him to shut his mouth. If the Cheyenne can't kill you, Piatt—I'll bet the smell of these goddamned horses will."

"Awright, damn you!" Piatt growled as John Donovan dribbled cool water into the open, oozy furrow of angry flesh. "I s'pose I won't be needing to sit a saddle for a few days anyhow."

"That's more like it, Piatt," Seamus Donegan cheered. "Just figure that you got time to get healed up in our beautiful, open-air infirmary the army's so thoughtfully provided you."

Several of them shared a laugh at Piatt's wound, and in time Piatt's whining faded.

The afternoon crawled on. As the sun rose, so did the big green flies and the growing stench that attracted them. The carcasses were decomposing even more rapidly this second day under a blazing sun.

During a brief lull in the sniping, Sergeant McCall assigned a handful to harvest some thick willow-branches along the length of the island. These they jammed into the sides of the rifle-pits to provide modest shade for the wounded suffering most with the steamy heat of late summer on the high plains.

A few of the men hovered round the critically wounded. Bathing their faces in the muddy, cool water that seeped into the bottom of Martin Burke's central pit. Dr. Mooers and Louis Farley were by far the worst off. Then there were Tucker and Clarke and O'Donnell. Morton and Haley and Gilbert. By now most of them quietly moaned in pain only as their dressings were changed with more of the water and filthy rags.

Young Hutch Farley slipped chunks of raw horsemeat between his father's lips, letting the elder Farley suck on the sun-warmed juices to keep up his strength. Others slowly chewed on the raw strips, eventually grinding the stringy flesh enough to swallow it. No matter that it took a long time to get a bite down that way. They had nowhere to go, and nothing better to do.

Dusk settled like a benevolent benediction on the island at

the end of that long day. For many, it seemed this second day, Friday, had been all the longer than their first. Yesterday, at least, the scouts had been more active. Fighting off the swirling, circling horsemen, turning back the three massed charges, digging their rifle-pits, stripping meat from the carcasses, enthused over the pair who would leave for Wallace at midnight.

But today, hope slipped a notch or two as they held out. Most men wondering what had become of Stillwell and Trudeau.

"They made it," Grover said.

"How you so sure?" grumped sour-mouthed Joe Lane.

He glared at Lane's eyes, recognizing the fear there behind all the bluster. Sharp had seen enough of Lane's kind in the army. "If they'd caught Jack and old Pete, believe me— they'd send 'em back in here strapped to a pair of old ponies."

"Strapped over . . . a pair——"

"Damn right," Grover went on as more of the scouts moved up to overhear the conversation. "Them Cheyenne . . . Pawnee Killer's Brule Sioux as well—they'd love to tell us if they caught our boys. Knowing damned well that it'd take the starch out of us to know Jack and Pete was caught."

Lane swallowed. "Hope them two . . . they make it."

Forsyth inched up on his elbow, his red eyes showing the extent of his edgy fatigue. "Best you pray on that, Lane."

"Never been much of a praying man," Lane apologized.

"Never too late to start," John Donovan added quietly, moving up beside Forsyth when a young voice came out of the twilight, approaching their pit.

"Who wants some plums?"

They all turned to find Sigmund Shlesinger, sliding down into their burrow, carrying a bloodstained, three-buttoned, canvas haversack. Lane had his hand out. Others as well when Sharp Grover was in the middle of them, shoving the beggars off the youngster.

"I think the wounded ought'n get first call on those plums," Grover snarled.

"I'm just as hungry as the next man!" Nichols growled.

"You heard Sharp." Seamus Donegan stood towering over them at the lip of the rifle-pit, the muzzle of his Henry repeater in a hand, as if he threatened to use it as a club. "The plums are for the wounded."

"Irishman's right. Rest of you can forage for yourselves," Billy McCall joined in.

"Horsemeat again?"

"That's right," McCall added. "Or you can eat them horseflies if you've a mind to."

"They're big enough!" John Donovan roared. Most of the others laughed, breaking up and moving away into the growing dusk. The tension eased.

"This is the biggest," Shlesinger said, showing it proudly to Forsyth. "Brought it for you, Major."

He looked at it, then at the young Jew's face. "Thanks, Slinger. I'd prefer you give it to the surgeon."

"Doc Mooers?"

"He's out right now. Comes and goes in fits . . . way he's been hanging on. Lay that plum on his lips and squeeze a little taste into his mouth. It'll be there when he comes to and can eat a bite."

"I'll thank you for the surgeon, who can't, Slinger." Seamus Donovan knelt at the lip of the rifle-pit, watching the youth place the plum in Mooers's lips.

"I oughta thank you, Irishman. You and most of the others, you're better shots."

Seamus smiled back, then turned away, watching the south riverbank, where the heaviest sniping had rattled all day.

"I think the Irishman's trying to say thank-you, Slinger . . . because each of us has been doing what we can to take care of the rest," Grover explained as the light faded in the pit.

The sky turned a deepening shade of blue, then purple, as the underbellies of a few clouds flamed over.

"Nowhere else in the world you see that, Seamus." Sharp squatted down beside Donegan.

"Other places I'd rather be right now."

"Wouldn't we all. But we're here."

He sighed. "Trouble is, Sharp—I don't know why I'm here now."

"Maybe you'll be like the rest of us, gonna find out why—sooner or later."

Chapter 31

"Sharp!"

McCall called across the island late that afternoon of the eighteenth as the shadows lengthened.

Seamus Donegan joined Grover in crabbing over to the sergeant's position.

"What you make of that?" the soldier asked.

To the north on the ridges and along the riverbanks, a large gathering of Indians was moving slowly upstream, leading some two dozen ponies pulling travois.

"I'll be damned." Grover sighed. "Travois, fellas. Dragging off their wounded. Or, their dead."

"That mean they're giving up?" In McCall's voice rose the hope of all.

He shook his head. "Sorry, don't think so, Billy. That bunch is just taking the travois back to their villages nearby. Chances were we would've bumped into their camps before noon yesterday . . . if they hadn't jumped us first."

"Following that big trail way we were," McCall replied.

"Forsyth found what he wanted, didn't he?" Donegan remarked. "Army sent him out here, looking for trouble . . . I'll be damned if the army don't always find it."

"C'mon, lemme buy you boys a drink."

Instantly Seamus grabbed hold of Grover's dirty sleeve, yanking the scout around. "You got whiskey? Been holding out on me all this time?"

Sharp snorted. "Leggo of me, you crazed Irishman. I ain't got any whiskey for you. Only talking about the boot-water."

Slowly Donegan's fingers released Grover's arm. He felt silly, springing on the man like that. "No whiskey, eh? Go raising a fella's hopes too. Sorry . . . I suppose it's the sun getting to me——"

"Sharp Grover!"

"Over here, Major."

"Bring McCall with you," Forsyth said. "Rest of you, gather round."

As Seamus hunkered down on the lip of the pit, cradling the Henry across his legs, a low blat of thunder rolled off the prairie.

"More blasted rain tonight," one of the men grumbled as they all made themselves a place surrounding the wounded.

"I'll damn well take the rain each night," answered one of the wounded across the pit.

"Better it than boiling in my own juices."

"We won't be long, men," Forsyth broke in. "I'm calling for two more volunteers."

"I'll go, Major," Chauncey Whitney chimed in.

"All right, Chance."

"Two more, Major?"

Forsyth gazed at his questioner. "Two more. Call it . . . a safety measure, fellas. To assure someone gets to Wallace."

"To be sure a relief column gets back here," Seamus Donegan added. "Count me in, Major. I'll volunteer."

"You can't go, Donegan. I've made that clear."

"If Seamus can't, by God, then Irish blood better go in his place," A. J. Pliley stood and saluted smartly.

Forsyth chuckled. "You'll do nicely, Irishman."

"It's settled?" Pliley asked, presenting his hand to Whitney. "We're going?"

"You two can leave about midnight . . . same as Stillwell and Trudeau."

"Damn right," Whitney echoed. "It'll be a foot-race. We'll just see if that boy and the old man get there before us."

As some of the scouts clapped their approval, Forsyth went ahead with his meeting.

"I want McCall to assign four of you to dig up the horse-meat we cooked and buried last night . . . to keep it sweet. Get yourselves two canteens and a haversack apiece for the

meat. I'll write another dispatch for Bankhead at Wallace for
you to carry."

"Pistols for two, Major?" Pliley joked.

"Aye, A. J. And let's pray you don't need them."

"We'll make it, sir. The dirty brownskins ain't caught up
with Trudeau and the boy yet. Me and Chance will get
through."

"Let's all pray . . . in your own way . . . that Trudeau
and young Jack did make it so far. Take a moment after dark
comes down, each of you—and pray they make it through
another night."

*Funny, ain't it, how things come along and just sweep a
fella up?*

Jack O'Neill considered it as he inched his pony along
behind the two young warriors who plodded on foot, crouching over the prairie, testing the ground with their fingertips,
sometimes the flats of their palms. Studying the sun-burnt
grass. Resting an ear on the earth itself. Eyes scanning the
far line of the prairie, where the umber land reached out and
gripped the far sky.

The two were the best trackers Two Crows's band of Dog
Soldiers had to offer. And since sunup, the mulatto had been
leading about ten others who were strung out behind him, all
of them like his daddy's dogs on the scent of coon, behind
this pair of trackers.

Following what turned out to be a faint set of tracks leading south from the island.

"They know some of our tricks, Nibsi," one of the young
warriors had whispered as they set out from the river at
sunrise. "One walks with blanket strips wrapped round his
feet. The other . . . he is not barefoot . . . but, he does
not walk in boots either."

As the morning hours wore on, Jack grew restive. He had
come on this hunt for the sake of capture, perhaps some
torture, then the killing of the escapees.

Hoping for something like last night's capture on the
north bank of the river. The struggle with their prisoner, and
the beating O'Neill was more than happy to give his new
captive. He liked the Cheyenne idea about prisoners. A captive belonged to the man who had captured that prisoner.

But this journey this morning had become . . . work.

Boring, tedious, hot work. Plodding slowly, ever slowly across the baked, iron-hard ground the two white men had chosen to use for their journey south. And behind him all the while, he heard the faint cracks of the Indian rifles. The occasional booms of the big-bore soldier guns.

At times O'Neill caught himself looking over his shoulder at the far northern rim of the prairie. Beyond it lay the river where the others fought and killed the white men.

But he was here on this broad, never-ending expanse of tableland, under a sun threatening to boil his brains, with these young warriors who smiled grimly, and said nothing as they kept at their stalk.

The gnats had come first, not long after the rising of the sun. Little red ones, buzzing round his hot face, intent on getting to his eyes, swimming in the beads of moisture that poked through every pore of his body. The earth-paint the warriors wore had long ago turned to a runny sap as their hot sweat melted the bear-grease and the colors ran like a rainbow caught upside down in a prairieland puddle after a summer shower.

Last winter while he was still with the white man, Jack O'Neill had started to let his hair grow, since it remained under his old hat most of the time. And after he had been captured and taken in by Two Crows's band, O'Neill had amused himself in realizing there was no longer any need to trim his nappy hair, just because that was the way of the white man and expected of the black man too.

Even though his daddy had been a white man, some of those things white men did no longer made any sense to him.

So Jack had let his hair grow. Not that it was all that long now. Just that it had become wild as it grew. Scattering at all directions in wild, black sprigs reminding him of frost-burnt sunflower stalks. Yet, the way the Cheyenne women admired his head of hair had caused him some pride, even though his daddy had time and again warned him against pride.

O'Neill enjoyed the way the women liked to run their fingers through the coarse, thick sprigs of his wild, nappy hair after he had rutted with them like a randy stud down on spring-grass.

He watched the two trackers ahead of him whispering to

each other, pointing out on the prairie, then back north. Arguing, he figured. Though he had no notion what they could be arguing about. Jack ran a pink palm over his damp face, once more marveling at the smoothness of his skin.

One young squaw had exercised an insatiable hunger for O'Neill. And it had been she who had talked him into plucking his facial hair, like all powerful Cheyenne warriors. Like Roman Nose himself.

No beard, no mustache, no whiskers at all. Not even eyebrows. Every hair plucked by the young one with her healthy appetite for the mulatto, plucked one at a time between bone tweezers until Jack's face was as soft as . . . well as soft as the squaw's bare breasts as she arched her back up to him every time he drove his coffee-colored flesh into her moistness——

It was a pleasant thought, a diverting one, but a thought he was forced to forget as the two trackers motioned him and the others forward. And as he urged the pony across the hard ground, Jack sensed something strange and out of place. He could not put his finger on it.

Wondering on the odd feeling, O'Neill gazed over the pale, summer sky the color of cream skimmed from the milk back at his daddy's home.

His eyes quickly roamed the flat tableland, from east to south to west. Nothing raised itself from the horizon to indicate the two white men heading south. Yet he was drawn to a rough stand of some tall weeds several hundred yards ahead.

Something troubled him as he drew up by the two trackers.

"We must go on!" one of them argued, his face flushed with anger. "We have the trail——"

"We are going on," O'Neill agreed, gazing at the far copse of weed and growing peeved himself with this silly delay, with these young warriors.

"Nibsi, listen!" demanded the other tracker, flinging his arm behind them all. Pointing to the north.

O'Neill turned, bareback on his pony. It took but a moment for the mulatto to realize what it had been the very world around him had been trying to say in the last few minutes. Telling him something was wrong.

They no longer heard the gunfire from the river. Now he

realized it had been many, many minutes since he had heard any of the Indian rifles crack. Or the soldier guns boom.

"They have killed all the soldiers!" one yelled.

"No, not until we find these two and kill them . . . then all will be killed!" argued the other.

"Be quiet, my friends!" Jack shouted in his loudest Cheyenne, his eyes straining south across the prairie for some sign of the white men. Eyes drawn to that stand of tall weed. His ears nonetheless strained to hear something from the north.

"Nibsi," said one older warrior as he edged his pony beside the mulatto, "the soldiers have not been killed. The firing died off slowly, the way a beaver dams a stream. The whitemen are not dead . . . what I fear most is that the old chiefs are giving up the fight."

O'Neill's eyes narrowed, sweat beading and burning them. "Give up the fight?"

"Perhaps they ride away!" another warrior cursed. "Like cowards."

"Why do you say this?" O'Neill demanded, suddenly afraid of losing his own private battle, of denying Roman Nose his victory over the tall, gray-eyed white man.

"The chiefs, they talked long last night while we were out searching the river with you," the older warrior explained. "My woman told me their hearts were turning sour on the fight."

"They cannot give up this fight!" Jack roared, yanking the rein harshly, bringing his pony around. "We go!"

"*Aiyee-yi-yiiii!*" some of the young warriors hollered, anxious to be done with this hot, dusty work of tracking.

Jack knew they wanted to be back at the fighting, with the chance to count coup and steal guns, galloping over the white men in glory.

He too had grown tired of this stalking. Let someone else come chase the two who had escaped the island. He too wanted to take charge of the fight now if the old ones were giving up.

"The Dog Soldiers will never ride away from this fight!" The older warrior laughed, throwing his head back.

"Yes!" cried another. "Lead us, Nibsi. Show us the power

and medicine that Roman Nose passed on to you when he crossed over!"

"Nibsi! NIBSI! *NIBSI!*"

It had been one thing to face that warrior charge roaring down the riverbed from beneath the overhanging, grassy bank when you had fifty other men with you. But to Jack Stillwell, it had been a horse of a completely different color when he found himself waiting from their frost-blacked stand of weed-brush for the big, nappy-haired warrior to lead his bunch along their trail.

"I'd swear that's one's a darkie," Jack had whispered as he squinted at the leader.

"Hang on, young Jack. You can find out for yourself shortly."

Jack chewed and spat. "Likely you're right. Seems I'll be shaking hands with the black bastard here shortly."

Then as suddenly as the horsemen had appeared on the prairie, the band of stalkers stopped, then turned away, making a slow loop to the east, and back to the north, where they disappeared over the shimmering horizon.

Stillwell had slid back down to the bottom of the dark, airless hollow to roll himself atop the blankets. No more did he need warmth. Now he needed only to keep that sun hung at mid-sky from basting him in his own juices as he tried to sleep. He was fretful through his nap. Then stood watch while the old frontiersman slept some more.

In the middle of the afternoon, Stillwell heard a spate of gunfire rattle, then slacken, from the north. He brooded sourly that he and old Pete had not really made it that far in their first night. Too much cornering, back and forth, covering their tracks, trying to locate hard ground where their tracks would not show as readily.

He climbed down into the coulee again as the sun slid into the western quadrant, to try some more shut-eye in the lengthening shadows. But try as he might, the echo of some renewed rifle-fire in the late afternoon kept him from sleeping.

"Means the rest is still holding on," Stillwell whispered as he crawled to edge of the coulee to join Trudeau.

"They all strong," Pierre said in his troubled accent. "They hold on."

"And every one of 'em counting on us, Pete."

"Look there."

Jack gazed at the western horizon, watching the jumble of roiling thunderheads boiling off the far mountains, rolling onto the plains.

"We'll have rain again tonight," Stillwell said.

"Is good," Pete said. "We go when it gets dark."

"I'm ready."

"You walk all right?"

"Yes," Jack lied. "I'll be all right, Pete."

"Your feet, they——"

"Forget about my feet." He cut the old man off. "We . . . we'll go when it gets dark."

Chapter 32

"Major?"

Forsyth blinked his eyes open in the inky gray light of pre-dawn. He dragged a tongue across his chapped lips. "Who is it?"

"Me, sir. A. J. Pliley," he answered, feeling as if he ought to apologize. "Sorry I woke you, Major."

Forsyth inched up a bit, then grimaced with the pain in his legs. "What the hell are you doing here, Pliley?" he snapped.

"They had the island pretty well——"

"For the past two nights you were so damned anxious to get off the island, I figured you'd stay off."

Pliley felt chastised, pursing his lips to keep from snapping back at the soldier. But he knew it was the major's pain talking. The way with some men the whiskey does all their talking for them. With Sandy Forsyth being one of the most straight-ahead army commanders ever sat a saddle, A. J. figured the major wasn't really chewing him out. Only the pain of the major's wounds.

"Me and Pliley tried, Major," Chauncey Whitney explained. "We left here 'bout eleven last night and laid out there, trying this direction, then that."

"What time is it now?" Forsyth asked, watching Sergeant McCall creep up to join their circle.

McCall pulled his watch from its pocket, quickly to his ear, then held it near the dull, red glow of the coals in the firepit.

"Little after three, Major."

"Four hours we tried," Whitney apologized.

Forsyth sank back against the side of his pit, pulling the blanket under his chin once more as he shivered without control.

Pliley tried to explain again. "I figure after the old man and the boy got off, and them red bastards found their tracks —they got bound and determined not to let any of the rest of us get off this island."

"Way I figure too, Major," Whitney replied.

"All right," Forsyth said weakly. "You two get some shut-eye now. It'll be too light to sneak off the island in a few minutes. You'll have to try again tonight. Sergeant, get these men something to eat before they turn in."

"G'night, Major."

"You and Chance did well enough to get back here with your hair, A. J."

Pliley snorted quietly, chuckling in the darkness as Forsyth's eyes closed in pain. "I knew you really needed me here, Major. Just to keep your spirits up for another hot day of it."

"Sharp said you wanted to see me, Major?"

"Sit a moment, Donegan," Forsyth offered, patting the sand beside him. The morning sun had yet to heat the rifle-pits into steamy bowls where the men simmered in their own juices. Ever since dawn, the sun had crawled into a partly cloudy sky, which made not as hot as the two previous days.

At first light this nineteenth day of September, the Indians had once more opened up on the island, but this time many fired from their own trenches and rifle-pits. The Cheyenne and Sioux appeared to be digging in for a long haul of it.

There came but one concerted attack, and that a half-hearted one the scouts quickly repulsed. Following the brief flurry of excitement, things settled back down into the routine of Indian sniping: constant gunfire rattling overhead while the scouts stayed burrowed in their pits. Listening to the drums and shrieks and chants.

Along with the cursing moans of the wounded. Some tossed and cursed in fitful sleep. Others murmured quietly in their private delirium. With no laudanum, each man struggled alone and lonely with his pain.

A bullet sang overhead. A few more rattled from the opposite bank.

"They aren't trying very hard this morning, sir," Sergeant McCall said as he rose to his knees. "If you two will excuse me, I'm going to see about killing me some more Indians."

"Always did dread sitting with an officer," Seamus declared, grinning as he plopped beside Forsyth, watching McCall crab off so the two of them could have privacy. Something else that made him a bit uneasy. "Seemed they always had something in mind for me—only time they wanted to talk."

"You're wrong about me, Donegan. Because this time, I only want to talk. Care for some of McCall's rib-eye?"

"Horsemeat? I'll pass on it for now," Seamus answered. "What have you on your mind, Major?"

"Grover told me you went through Liam's belongings yesterday."

Instantly he felt guarded. "He's me uncle. Them were his private effects. And, being his next of kin . . . they belong to me as well."

"Sit back down, Mr. Donegan. I'm not questioning your right to Liam's effects at all. Dammit, sit down."

Donegan finally crouched again beside Forsyth.

"I only want to know if he carried any papers on him. Letters, dispatches . . . the sort of thing that might be——"

"Official . . . army business?"

"No," Forsyth answered. "Something that might give some insight into what Liam did, or was witness to, in Deseret City."

Donegan's brow knitted. "No," he answered quietly. "Didn't find a thing like that in his bags."

"You check his pockets?"

"Made me feel like a sham undertaker, it did, Major. Stuffing me hands down his pockets, digging round in his vest and all," Seamus explained. "But, no papers."

"You're sure?"

"Only thing like that I found in his bags was a book."

"Book?"

He nodded. "A novel, Major. Englishman. *Oliver Twist* by Charles Dickens."

"You read, Donegan?"

"Aye. And that's a story in itself. A woman in Boston taught me."

"Your mother?"

He laughed easily. "By the saints, no. The woman taught me to read . . . she entertained gentlemen callers, Major. In one of the finest establishments in Boston Town."

"That's all you found in Liam's things?"

"Besides two shirts, some stockings, and the rest——"

"I understand," Forsyth replied, turning slightly as he brushed at the maggots squirming in his thigh wound. His eyes apologized to the Irishman. "Sorry, Donegan. I keep the flies out much as I can. But still some manage to sneak through to lay their eggs. This broken leg's the worst."

He pulled back the blanket he had over the leg, revealing the two oozing wounds. Besides a faint odor of decay that rose from the angry, purplish holes, they both appeared alive with small, crawling white slivers, wriggling like fresh-cooked rice.

"Can't reach it," Forsyth began. "If I could, I'd——"

"No reason to apologize, Major. I'll get them for you, you'd like."

"If . . . if you don't mind, Donegan. I'd be in your debt."

"I didn't keep Liam alive," he said with a grim smile, gazing at the soldier's pain-etched face as he set to work picking the slippery maggots from each of the major's three wounds. "Let's see what we can do to keep you in command of this outfit."

His head fell back as a wave of pain slapped Forsyth hard. "Last night . . . I think it was last night . . . I swear I heard some geese going overhead. Honking."

"I heard 'em too, Major," Donegan replied.

"Good," he replied, gritting his teeth. "Afraid I was beginning to . . . to see or even hear things."

"Damned early for the season, i' t'was."

Forsyth chewed on his thoughts as the Irishman continued his work on the wounds. "Seamus, I figure it bodes an early winter . . . a cold winter . . . those geese do." He fell silent, keeping his head turned to the overcast sky, his eyes averted from the infected wounds. "W-we've been whipped on . . . pretty bad, haven't we, Irishman?"

"But we ain't been whipped, Major."

"T-trouble is . . ." Forsyth gasped as the pain washed over him. "I'm beginning to have some fear."

"You, Major?"

"Don't tell the others, Donegan . . . but I'm afraid what the Cheyenne and Sioux weren't able to do . . . that thirst and hunger and . . . hopelessness will finish us off."

Later that morning Grover turned his nose up at McCall's offer of a charred strip of horsemeat. "No, thanks, Sergeant."

"We buried it the first night, Sharp," Major Forsyth explained. "Hoping it would stay sweet a bit longer than it has."

"Care for some yourself, Major?" McCall asked.

"I'll pass as well, Sergeant."

"Afraid it's all gone bad, sir. I'm sure it's these horses making the wolves howl all round us at night."

Grover nodded. "The stench has brought in every wolf and coyote in this part of the country. They get bold enough, hungry enough—they'll come on the island for the high-meat."

"We have coffee," Forsyth said. "But for the want of salt. What we could do with this rotting horsemeat——"

"What'd you say?" Grover interrupted.

"The rotting horsemeat——"

"No." Grover stopped him. "About salt?" He got up on his knees excitedly.

"Yes," Forsyth said apprehensively. "If we had some salt. You have some cached away in your bags, Sharp?"

"No, sir. But something just jumped through my mind that might be about as good." He looked at McCall. "Billy, what'd you do with that keg of extra powder we had along? It get to the island?"

"With the rest of the ammunition boxes on the two mules," McCall answered, finding Grover's enthusiasm contagious. "Why?"

He turned to Forsyth. "Major, at the rate our men are

firing, we won't come close to running out of cartridges for at least six, maybe eight, days."

"Yes . . . tell us what you got on your mind."

"Major, the gunpowder's made with saltpeter." Grover watched it strike the major's imagination, brightening Forsyth's pain-pale face.

"And the saltpeter is a damned good substitute for . . ." The Major turned to McCall, suddenly excited. "Billy, get that keg and bust it open. Call the men in. Get them sprinkling the gunpowder on the best meat we can cut off the carcasses now. Sprinkle the meat we already cooked and buried in the gum-ponchos."

"Yes, sir," McCall replied as he turned to go.

"Tell the others what we're doing too," Forsyth advised. "A little good news like this will go a long way to brightening the flagging spirits of them all."

"Yes, sir!"

"Slinger! Front and center, boy!"

Sigmund Shlesinger had long ago gotten used to his nickname. Last winter in Hays he was proud that some of the other mule-whackers and teamsters had given him that handle. It was a sign they had finally accepted him into their world, despite the fact that he was a Jew from New York City.

"Yessir, Sergeant?" He crawled over, dragging his Spencer behind him.

"Major wants me to pick three of our best shots to give a try at something. I'm rounding the marksmen up. Go report and I'll be along shortly."

Shlesinger found Sharp Grover and the young Irishman already with Forsyth at the edge of the major's pit, discussing the absence of warriors there at midday with the sun hung almost directly overhead. Only the nearby hills showed any sign of life. A few horsemen, sitting, unmoving. Waiting on something.

Most startling of all was the movement of ponies beneath a growing cloud of dust from the ridges and knolls.

"Women and children, Major," Sharp Grover was explaining as Shlesinger came up.

"They're retreating?"

"I don't think they're giving up yet," Grover replied. "The warriors are going to stay."

"Just sending the squaws and children back to the villages," Donegan said. "Probably in case the army comes up . . . they'll have time to hold them off here while the camps tear down and scoot away."

"I'd like to see for myself," Forsyth brooded. "But first, I want you boys to take care of that annoying bastard over there."

For the first time, young Shlesinger got a look at the reason he had been called there.

"He's been there for a few minutes, Slinger," Forsyth explained, pointing out the lone, fat, and very fleshy Indian who danced and cavorted about on the far bank.

Completely naked. No breechclout to cover his manhood. The naked warrior wheeled and shook his flesh, letting his ample belly wiggle, bent over repeatedly patting his buttocks and making obscene taunts at the white men.

Young Shlesinger turned, grinning widely, ready to say something, when he found Forsyth far from smiling. Sigmund realized with the major's condition, no man would be in a happy frame of mind.

"Give Slinger that Springfield, Grover," Forsyth ordered. "Maybe some of the Jew's shooting will wipe that smug smile off that red bastard's face. I want you to try as well, Donegan."

Grover passed to each man one of the three heavy, metal-banded Long-Tom infantry Springfield rifles the command had transported with them from Fort Hays. Sharp crouched with the third, flipping up the long-range leaf-sights.

"That's better'n twelve hundred yards," Grover advised his fellow shooters.

Like the army scout, Donegan chose to shoot from a sitting position, locking his elbows inside his knees. The third young rifleman plopped on his belly and spread his legs at an angle.

"Hold high on him," Forsyth hissed. "I want one of you to hit that fat, red bastard dancing out there like a trained monkey. Tell me when you're ready . . . I'll give the command to fire in volley."

Each of the three slammed their cartridge home in the breech.

"Last notch, Seamus," Grover suggested.

He winked. "Won't be your bullet hits him, Sharp. Me, or the boy will."

"You so damned sure?"

"Your eyes just getting too old, Grover——"

"I suppose your chatter means you're ready."

"Anytime, Major," Sharp said.

"Fire!"

Almost as one, the three rifles boomed their throaty roar. Immediately the three marksmen scrambled to their feet to peer over the muzzle-smoke. On the far riverbank, the fleshy, naked Indian leaped into the air, arms and legs thrashing in surprise.

The fleshy, copper-skinned dancer landed in a heap, a small cloud of dust puffing round his naked body.

"Hurrah!" a few of the spectators shouted.

"Three cheers for Slinger!" someone else hollered.

Donegan and Grover turned on the exuberant scouts, seeing Forsyth shaking his fist at the dead Indian's retreating friends.

Seamus looked at Grover, laughing. "How the hell they so sure Slinger hit him, 'stead of us?"

"Remember me? I'm the one with bad eyes, you said!"

Seamus nodded. "But I'm one divil of a good shot!"

"I know . . . but I figure your hands only get steady when you've got a strong dose of some saddle-varnish under your belt!"

All three had just begun to slap the others on the back when the willows on both sides of the stream erupted with the rattle of rifle-fire.

The marksmen dived into the pits as the bullets whined overhead.

Grover sat smiling at Donegan, like a cat with feathers in its whiskers.

"What's so funny, Grover?"

"Just thinking myself how good would be a long draw on a tall-necked bottle of saddle-varnish right about now, my friend."

Chapter 33

The brassy blare of a trumpet broke the hot stillness of that afternoon of the nineteenth, shattering Donegan's painful, bittersweet memories of the auburn-haired Jennifer Wheatley.

As the ragged notes of the tin horn floated over the hot valley, Seamus cursed himself once more for being a fool ever to fall for a woman. It had always been much safer to dance out of their lives, before chancing the woman would dance out of his. A broken piece of something deep inside of Seamus grew thankful for that shabby trumpet call as Grover came leaping into the pit, scurrying to the front lip with the Irishman.

"That bloody renegade bugler," Sharp growled.

"One thing we know, Sharp—can't be the Confederate," Donegan added.

"Whoever the sonuvabitch is . . . he's my meat." Grover inched over the lip and peered up the long stretch of riverbed bordering the narrow run of water.

"He's yours, Sharp—unless that bugler turns out to be the Confederate."

Grover smiled cruelly. "He ain't, because the first bugle call we heard the first morning. But, I'd still give the bastard to you with pleasure, Irishman."

"What the devil's going on up there, Grover?" called Forsyth from his pit. "They fixing to charge again?"

"No, Major," Sharp flung his voice over his shoulder. "By God, it's a white flag!"

"Where?" the major yelled.

"Yonder . . . to the northeast." Grover pointed. Heads turned.

Making their appearance from a gap between some low bluffs to the northeast of the island came a half-dozen or so young warriors. One, wearing a good-sized bonnet of war-eagle feathers tipped with plumes and horse-hair tassels, rode out from the center of the bunch some twenty yards and stopped. The rest spread out behind the leader.

"Don't trust them bastards!" Sergeant McCall shouted.

Forsyth inched himself up as much as he could. "Tell us how to play it, Grover. You want to honor that truce flag?"

Sharp chewed on his lip, gazing into Donegan's eyes.

"You tell me what you need, Sharp," Seamus whispered, patting the brass receiver on the Henry. "Both of us ready to help you."

Sharp looked back at the expectant faces of the scouts peering over the edges of their sandy burrows. "No, Major. No reason to trust this bunch."

"But, if they want to parley?"

"They didn't come to parley, Major," Grover replied, snappish.

"Is it Two Crows? He's the leader of this bunch, ain't——"

"None of these bucks are old enough to be Two Crows, Major Forsyth. This bunch is fighters."

"Maybe Two Crows sent them to talk for him——"

"The bastards only wanna get on the island and see how bad we're chewed up, Major," Donegan interrupted loudly.

"You've had some firsthand experience in this, have you?" Forsyth sounded acerbic.

"No me. But Bridger did, the day Black Horse's Cheyenne come to visit Carrington at Fort Phil Kearny. To feel out the soldier fort's defenses."

Grover nodded once, a grin come of certainty crossing his seamed face. "That's the truth of it, Major. They're wanting to see how bad off we are."

The entire delegation of warriors put their decorated ponies in slow motion, walking toward the island under the white flag tied to the end of a long lance. The traditional Cheyenne war weapon. And this one was decorated like all the rest—with brown and blond and red-haired scalps, fluttering on the hot, steamy breeze.

"You best get them to stop before they get any closer, Major!" Grover hollered.

"What the hell am I . . . Sergeant, order those Indians to halt where they are!"

Scrambling over the lip of his rifle-pit, McCall hurried to the north side of the island, waving his arms and shouting, attempting to stop the horsemen.

"Them young bucks must take us for fools," a voice behind Donegan said.

Seamus turned to find C. B. Piatt crawling up on his hands and knees, wincing with the pain of yesterday's wound. Dragging his Spencer at Piatt's heels crawled Sigmund Shlesinger.

"They'll get away with what they can, Piatt."

"If the major lets 'em get away with it," Piatt hissed.

"Damned fools!" Grover snapped, lumbering to his feet, kicking sand in three directions as he stomped from the pit to McCall's side.

He shouted his warning in throaty Cheyenne, for emphasis waving his own Spencer at the end of his arm.

Whether they heard or not, whether they understood or not, the half-dozen kept on walking toward the riverbank and the sandy island. Waving their white flag on the end of that scalp-adorned lance. Grover grabbed McCall's arm.

"You best be looking for a hole to dive into, Sergeant. We're their meat out here."

"Major wants 'em stopped——"

"But they ain't stopping for the major!" Plain as paint the strain sounded in Grover's voice as he whirled on Forsyth's pit. "You ready to do things my way, Major?"

"Do it!"

"Donegan!"

"Over here, Sharp!"

"Lay a round out there . . . right over the head of that one in the fancy bonnet." Grover snagged McCall's arm and both went scrambling arm in arm for a rifle-pit in the next breath.

Seamus nestled his cheek along the stock of the Henry, peered down the blued steel of the barrel and fired.

With the whine of the bullet splitting the air overhead, the horsemen stopped immediately, arguing excitedly among themselves and gesturing wildly. The bonneted one pulled out from the group and stopped again. He shouted.

Grover hollered back in Cheyenne, then turned to Forsyth. "He wants to palaver with the soldier-chief, Major."

"Who is that?"

"Sounds like Charlie Bent."

"Old man Bent's son?" Forsyth muttered.

"Owl Woman's boy . . . the one what went back to the blanket."

"The one who went bad, what you mean," McCall snarled.

"He wants to palaver with you," Grover advised. "I think the chiefs are trying to figure out if we're in so bad shape they could ride over us . . . or maybe they should just fold their tents and get the hell out of here while they can lick their wounds."

"They're still coming!" Donegan shouted.

Grover and the rest watched the bonneted warrior leading the rest, the horsemen nearing the flat, sandy riverbed. Less than a hundred yards from the island now.

"Some of you," Grover shouted, "put a few rounds in the ground at their feet!"

An abrupt, ragged volley roared, kicking up plumes of sand and dirt among the ponies' hooves. A few reared, their riders gripping halters and manes to calm the frightened animals.

The bonneted man ordered the others to stand their ground. Three wheeled and loped back to the gap in the bluffs. Two stayed with the leader, who put a hand to his mouth, hollering at the island.

"Indian-talker! I speak some English."

"Speak your English from there, Charlie!"

"You know who I am?"

"We have met, Charlie Bent."

"Maybe I should have killed you when I had the chance . . . back then, no?"

"You couldn't do it back then—at Fort Lyon . . . and I'll be damned if your bunch is gonna wipe us out now."

"Ha, Indian-talker! You have no chance. Today you die.

Let us come on the island to talk . . . we may let you go.
We talk, or Two Crows will send his warriors to crush you
under their ponies."

"The joke's on you, Charlie. We'll fight you for a month of
Sundays."

"Whiteman talks big. But his words are like pony-dung.
No good to shoot in my guns . . . and sure no good to eat."

"If you and Two Crows want to try charging us again,
Charlie Bent—then get ready to die. We have more bullets
here than all your ponies could shit in a year!"

"You will be begging me to eat my pony's shit before this
day . . ."

Meanwhile, Grover had turned aside, not intending to
hear any more of the young half-breed's angry banter.
"Donegan! Show that sonuvabitch what I think of his white
flag!"

"Kill 'im?"

"Yes, goddammit!"

"No!" Forsyth's voice rose shrill, in command.

Seamus watched the major and his chief of scouts glare at
one another, neither budging. Realizing what toll the days of
siege were taking on the relationships between these men.

Sharp thought on it, eyes narrowing. "It's up to the major,
Seamus," Grover stated with a flat sound to it. "One less
Injun ain't gonna hurt none——"

"Donegan!"

"Yeah, Major?"

"Just run him off," Forsyth ordered, a bit more quietly
this time. "Like Sharp, I'm sick of hearing his greasy-
mouthed bragging."

Donegan walked a series of four rounds in on the half-
breed's pony, causing the animal to rear. Bent brought the
animal down, twice around in a tight circle, cursing the
white men as his lance fluttered in the breeze. His two companions had long since scampered when Charlie Bent finally
reined his pony about and slowly, deliberately, turned his
backside on the island.

He rose slightly, pulled his breechclout aside and patted
the bared seam of his brown buttocks. Defiantly he inched
his way toward the protective bluffs, showing that he was far
from afraid of the white men.

"He makes an inviting target, Major," Seamus sputtered.

"As much as any of us would like to see you blow that brown ass off, let him go," Forsyth chuckled.

"I'll run up against him again someday," Grover grumbled as he slid back into the steamy pit with Donegan.

Overhead the sun had climbed halfway to mid-sky, along with the temperature of another hot day.

"I'd like to be there when you do," Seamus replied quietly. "You get your hands on Charlie Bent . . . and me, I'll have these hands on the Confederate."

The boy and the old man had reached a stream of sorts at the first blush of dawn that morning. Discovering at the same time that in the darkness they had walked within a few hundred yards of one of the hostile villages.

With the sun's bloody appearance out of the east, the pair was forced to hide themselves in the tall grasses bordering the stream at the edge of a small salt marsh. With hurried hand signals, Trudeau told Stillwell to make himself even smaller than they had their first day in the coulee. Being so close to the village, Pete whispered as they stretched out among the tall stalks in the boggy marsh, chances for discovery might prove even greater than before.

No time to backtrack. No time to push on. They had run out of time, and darkness. And luck.

Both dozed until full light, when voices awoke them. Old women and girls, headed their way, looking for squaw-wood for their morning cook-fires. Dogs barked in the nearby village, and old men shouted, gathering up their ponies. Still the white men stretched their luck a few more hours. And one went back to sleeping while the other kept a fitful watch on the village through that day.

In the afternoon a handful of old men rode by at an unhurried pace, moseying north to the fighting. As they passed, Trudeau strained to overhear their conversation. When the old men were long over the horizon to the north, Pete whispered to his wide-eyed young partner.

"Didn't catch much talk. But . . . their village lost many."

Jack nodded. Knowing what a coup it would be for that

grieving village to capture two of the island's white men alive.

Immediately he grew conscious of the big pistol gouging a hole in his gut. And realized that he would not let the Indians take him alive. He closed his eyes to sleep once more.

Later as Jack lay on the soggy ground, at times pushing the tall stalks aside to peer at a part of the village, he listened to the old man's soft snores. He glanced over his shoulder, finding Trudeau curled up like a child. So small. Pete's deeply wrinkled face tranquil. He reminded Jack of his little brother for a moment in time.

Then realized once more how close they both were to the precipice of terror.

First one squaw in the village, then more, and finally it seemed the whole world was trilling. Keening. Chanting their shrill mourning until the eerie screech filled the summer blue overhead.

Pete came awake suddenly, troubled with the singing. Hurrying with a rustle to Jack's side.

From the village poured a procession of the women, leading travois ponies and children and old men. All screaming their grief. For the rest of the afternoon into the falling of the sun, a noisy funeral was conducted on the prairie. Constructing the scaffolds from broken lodgepoles. Raising the dead warriors they had cleaned and painted and bound tightly in buffalo robes, then placed upon those rickety platforms.

At sundown the last of the mourners left their dead for the village. And supper. And nightfall.

Once the last vestige of blue had drained from the western sky, Pete signaled that they should leave. Up from the tall grasses of the marsh, into the shocking cold of the wide, shallow stream that would separate them from the village.

"Republican," Pete whispered as they hunkered down in the grass, gazing one last time at the fire-lit village behind them. "South Fork."

Jack tried to make sense of it. It felt as if they had been walking across this tableland in the dark forever. At least for two nights already. So here they were, at the start of their third night's journey. And no closer to Fort Wallace than the south fork?

Pete tried to smile, sensing in the growing darkness the

youngster's gloom. "We can hurry now, like the antelope. Come, Jack. It's cold."

With the deepening twilight they left the river behind, scurrying north. At times they trotted. Other times they walked until they regained their strength to trot again. Pointing their noses south by southeast.

And with each gust of cruel wind shifting out of the north that hinted of snow and freezing rain, the pair watched their breath-smoke puff in huge tissues from their gaping mouths.

The cold, cold air stung Stillwell's lungs as he ran into the darkness for his life.

And every time he began to tire, young Jack forced himself onward behind the old man, forced himself to recall the keening cries of the squaws over their dead.

Chapter 34

"Where's Whitney?" Forsyth demanded of John Donovan as he eyed Allison J. Pliley suspiciously.

Donovan shrugged his shoulders as he and Pliley slid down into the major's pit. "Said he didn't wanna come tonight."

"Second thoughts?" The major's eyes came back to Donovan.

John felt the accusation in Forsyth's glare, then relaxed when he realized he did not stand accused. "Maybe so, Major. Said he's better off staying to fight here with the rest of you."

"And you?" Forsyth's mouth curved up in a wry grin. "You figure you'll take your chances out there again?"

"Them two have had two nights and two whole days, Major." John sought a way of explaining. "The old man and Stillwell ain't been brought back dead yet. I figure I could go alone and beat 'em to Wallace by myself."

"That's out of the question," Forsyth replied, quickly eyeing Pliley again. "I want pairs sent out. Two men can watch each other's backsides. No, you'll have to choose someone to go with you, A. J."

Donovan glanced sheepishly at Pliley. Both shrugged.

Pliley admitted, "I told Donovan he could go with me, sir."

"You sure he didn't sweet-talk you into taking him, A. J.?"

Pliley grinned. "No, sir. Donovan, he's a talker, for sure

. . . but, if Chance don't go . . . I suppose Donovan wants a try."

"We'll make it, sir," Donovan replied, patting the haversack. "Got our meat . . . what there is of the foul-tasting stuff. And canteens."

"Pistols?"

His head bobbed quickly, anxious to get started. After sundown the western sky had filled with angry gray clouds scudding across the high land. Pushed along in their path by a harsh, wintry wind. "We're set."

"Not quite," Forsyth said. He shoved a cold hand beneath his blanket, inside his coat and shirt, from where he pulled his small, leather-covered memoranda book. "I wrote this to Colonel Bankhead earlier today." Forsyth tore free two sheets of the loose paper on which he had penciled his scrawl:

> *To Colonel Bankhead, or Commanding Officer*
> *Fort Wallace:*
>
> *I sent you two messengers on the night of the 17th instant, informing you of my critical situation. If the others have not arrived, then hasten at once to my assistance. I have eight badly wounded and ten slightly wounded men to take in, and every animal I had was killed, save seven, which the Indians stampeded. Lieutenant Beecher is dead, and Acting-Assistant-Surgeon Mooers probably cannot live the night out. He was hit in the head Thursday, and has spoken but one rational word since. I am wounded in two places—in the right thigh and my left leg broken below the knee. The Cheyennes alone number four hundred and fifty or more. Mr. Grover says they never fought so before. They were splendidly armed with Spencer and Henry rifles. We killed at least thirty-five of them, and wounded many more, besides killing and wounding a quantity of their stock. I am on a little island, and have plenty of ammunition left. We are living on mule and horse meat, and are entirely out of rations. If it was not for so many wounded, I would come in, and take the chances of whipping them if attacked. They are evidently sick of the bargain.*

I had two of the members of my company killed on the 17th—namely William Wilson and George W. Culver. You had better start with no less than seventy-five men, and bring all the wagons and ambulances you can spare. Bring a six-pound howitzer with you. I can hold out here for six days longer if absolutely necessary, but please lose no time.

> *Very respectfully, your obedient servant,*
> *GEORGE A. FORSYTH*
> *U.S. Army,*
> *Commanding Company Scouts*

P.S.—My surgeon having been mortally wounded, none of my wounded have had their wounds dressed yet, so please bring a surgeon with you.

"Like you wrote for Jack?"

Forsyth nodded. "For the most part. One of you two will make it to Wallace."

Donovan held his hand out. "Major, I'll see you soon."

Forsyth smiled warmly as he shuddered with the flush of fever despite the chilling breeze. "We'll count on that, Donovan."

Both messengers shook hands round with most of the others, then squatted to remove their boots like the pair gone two nights before. With their blankets wrapped about them to ward off the growing cold, Donovan and Pliley hurried to the far end of the island, where they disappeared into the misty darkness.

Overhead the snow-filled clouds bled over the sliver of moon, nearly blotting out all the starshine. From the sky oozed a cold drizzle, quickly turning to a freezing rain as Forsyth's messengers disappeared into the murky wall of chilling darkness.

McCall awoke with a start, sensing the damp blankets grown heavy for some reason. The quiet that greeted his ears proved almost suffocating after the roar and rattle of the rifles for the past three days.

Days . . .

His mind quickly calculated them.

*Seventeenth . . . we came here to the island. Eighteenth
. . . Trudeau and the boy left. Nineteenth . . . Donovan es-
capes, his second try . . .*

He sat up, shaking the wet one-inch layer of snow off his
blanket. A cold wind cut over the island in the night-black
just relinquishing itself to the gray of pre-dawn. All was still,
and cold. Like the beginning of time. Then he remembered.

It's the twentieth . . . our fourth goddamned day.

Billy McCall rolled out of his blanket, kicked the kinks
out of his cold bones, rubbing his hands, blowing into them
as he gazed over the other wet and snowy humps in the pit.

*Trudeau ought to have the boy at Wallace by sometime
early today. Donovan and Pliley right behind——*

McCall dropped to his knees, listening to the coming of
dawn. Not really the bird that called far downstream. Nor
the gentle, almost unheard ripple of the river over its sandy
bed. Something was different. Then he knew. That something drawing him across the rifle-pit, near Forsyth's sleeping form.

When he knew, he gently shook the major, the cold snow a
shock to his bare hands. Forsyth roused himself quickly,
coming up from his deep sleep with eyes moving and lips
pressed in a granite line of pain when both legs reminded
him of their wounds.

"What is it, Mc——"

"The surgeon, Major."

Forsyth jerked, startled. Gazing at the blanketed form beside him while McCall pulled the snowy shroud back. The
sergeant held an ear over Mooers's face, listening.

After a long time at it he raised his head, shook it. "He's
dead, sir."

"God have mercy on his soul," Forsyth whispered. "The
pain he was . . . I'm glad it's a Sunday that the Lord takes
him——"

"Don't worry about this one getting in the Gates of
Heaven, sir," McCall said as he lifted the uneaten plum from
John Mooers's lips. "The doc was a saint."

Forsyth wagged his head. "Why is it so many times the
good men are the first to go?"

"Like Beecher."

"Now Mooers. Give me the plum, Billy. The little Jew laid it there sometime back."

"Slinger?"

"Yeah. Hoping Mooers would eat it."

He nodded once. "Good lad. It's been tough on the young ones like him, seeing this kind of sudden death . . . this slow death as well."

"Young Hutch Farley's holding up, keeping his pa together body and soul."

"And Morton—dear God. With a bullet gone in one eye and out the side of his head. Hanging on and talking all the time."

"Most of the men been talking, Major."

Forsyth's eyes narrowed. "What about, Billy?"

"You, sir. That's why all of 'em are standing tall. They decided that first night to stand tall for you."

"For me?"

"Yes, sir. You . . . what with your three wounds and all . . . still in command here—putting up a fight of it against these red devils. Making a damned fight of it against the pain you're in."

He drew in a long breath, reminded. "Well, Billy. That makes me damned proud to know that the men look up to me——"

"They admire you the way you've hung on, sir." As he said it, McCall gazed up, hearing the big-winged honkers overhead. Somewhere high above the clouds that squatted like pewter toadstools over the land.

Forsyth listened to that beautiful sound as well in the darkness.

"Heading south, Billy."

"Yessir. Like Donovan and Pliley. God bless 'em."

"Amen, Sergeant McCall. God bless 'em—like that old man and the boy."

In what gray light was shed from the stingy sky, Jack Stillwell and the old man huddled over Forsyth's map, forming a windbreak of their bodies as it rattled in their shivering hands.

"I can't make out where we'd be," Stillwell groaned, wanting to cry with the cold, gazing up from the map and looking across the rolling tableland. To keep from looking at the old man.

Pierre Trudeau stabbed at the map with a gnarled finger. "Damn things anyway, Jack. Forget it and come on. We'll make the Denver Road soon enough this day."

"How can you be sure?" Jack wanted to whimper. "We could be miles off."

"Time now to lemme take you on in," Pete said quietly. "You get us here this far. Look. See that over there?"

Stillwell did look. But saw nothing spectacular. Much less a landmark.

"We get close to Goose Creek, boy." He helped Jack fold the map quickly. "C'mon now. We keep walking."

"Yes," he agreed. One thing certain about it, moving would keep them warmer. "No sign of Injuns now. Don't have to hide."

"Sun comes up under the clouds, we both feel warmer. Walk now, Jack."

Stillwell set off again, renewed by Trudeau's enthusiasm. Yet he knew it was nothing more than a patina hiding the old man's flagging strength. Step by step they hurried, south by southeast, with the smell of something close to home in old Pete's nostrils bringing him on while the sun rose red, then orange, beneath the dark clouds roiling across the snowswept land.

From time to time, one or the other of the messengers turned, looking back over their shoulders like escaping prisoners. Knowing they were followed. Not knowing when they would be caught.

After the sun disappeared into the clouds, the drizzle returned, softening the dusting of snow. Tiny pockets of snow-melt hugged every stand of bunch-grass and outcrop of silver sage. Soaking their boots, making Jack's swollen, bleeding feet even more miserable. And in trying to put his mind on something other than the pain of every step, Stillwell noticed the horizon behind him.

He stopped, not sure. Then rubbed his eyes again, thinking he could be fooled as the overcast light reflected off the pools and snow-pockets dotting the prairie. Trudeau stopped as well, wondering what had caused Jack to turn.

"Indians, Pete," he whispered, choking the words out as the old man hurried to his side.

Four, perhaps five. Now they could count six. A half-dozen horsemen breaking the northern horizon on the rolling grassland. Close enough to recognize the long hair tossed in the cold wind. Their blankets and robes troubled as they came on. Steadily . . . ever on.

"Get down!" Trudeau hissed.

Jack did not delay. Knowing that the warriors might be following their tracks. But that if he and Pete stood contrasted against the rolling prairie's skyline, even a one-eyed, rheumy old Indian would have no trouble spotting the white men.

"There!" Jack ordered, eyeing a clump of tall sunflower stalks and weeds some forty feet away.

They crawled, raking hands and legs against the prickly pear cactus. With every yard, Jack winced, needles driven deep into his hide. As they crabbed into the tall weeds that might provide a little shelter, the pair stumbled on a soggy buffalo-wallow. Here in the late summer, with little rain come the last three months, the wallow was for the most part parched. Yet in the last day some snow-melt and rain had been captured in its muddy center.

Still, what captured Stillwell's attention lay across the wallow in a stand of weeds well fertilized with the decomposing carcass of an old bull buffalo.

He tapped Trudeau. And there was no further need to explain.

Both men crawled directly across the muddy alkali-wallow to the dried carcass. From the looks of it, the bull had died there more than a year past. Four seasons on these high plains had already taken their toll, along with the predators. Enough hide clung to the bleaching rib-cage to provide some concealment. What was even better was that the carnivorous cousins of this prairie, both wolf and coyote, had feasted on the bull, fairly scouring out the dried, rotted carcass.

Trudeau stopped short, his eyes swimming, his face gone pale.

Stillwell hissed. "C'mon, old man. Get in here with me. It don't smell too bad."

"Not the buffalo, not bad smell . . ." Pete explained,

barely getting his words out just before his stomach tried to
lurch. Nothing came up but some bile.

Jack reached out of the ribby shadows and grabbed Trudeau, dragging the old man into the sanctuary of the decaying beast with him.

Minutes passed. And still more came and went. Then,
Jack heard them talking, their voices carried on the wind,
then other words forced away in a powerful, brutally cold
gust. It was not the same tongue he had heard near the Sioux
village. Stillwell figured these must be Cheyenne Dog
Soldiers.

The sort who never gave up.

He glanced at Trudeau in the shadows, back out of the
wind. Eyes closed, swallowing hard to keep his stomach
down.

And just as Jack was congratulating himself for finding
this carcass, he had something a little more immediate to
worry about than those Cheyenne warriors slowly approaching the wallow.

His mind raced, wanting to turn immediately and look for
himself. But instead, something inside him told him to do it
slowly. The old man's ragged breathing sounded too loud.
Gagging on his own bile. And the hammering of Jack's
heart, pounding in his ears like the pony hooves drawing
closer and closer. The mournful, keening wind slicing
through the old hide and bleaching ribs of the carcass . . .

Yet none of it so loud that he could not hear that unmistakable sound that brought fear to every plainsman's heart,
and turned some to water. It was a warning that made many
a lesser man soil his pants.

Turning slowly, biting his lip to keep from cursing his
damned luck, Jack spotted first the whirring buttons at the
tip of the tail. Rattler buds.

The high weeds gave the snake the perfect protection for
hunting, and the mid-morning light on the dried-up wallow
had made for a welcome place where the rattler warmed
himself, waiting for the sun. Instead this day, in had crawled
two men to interrupt its lazy slumber. Yet, to the cold-
blooded rattler, the bodies of those two humans would prove
far warmer than lying in this wallow, waiting for the clouds
to part.

He swallowed, listening behind him now as the grasses rustled and the pieces of voices came over the prairie again. The ponies were coming on.

Ever so slowly he put his hand in his pocket, taking out the last of the black plug of Virginia burley Trudeau had purchased weeks ago at Hays. Jack stuffed what there was onto his tongue and chewed as he had never chewed before, watching the rattler flick its tongue, baring fangs with a hiss. Coil and uncoil slightly as it inched forward for a strike. Inching forward a bit more, then recoiling with a noisy rattle . . . set to spring——

Jack let fly a long stream of brown juice, hitting the rattler as it sank back onto its coils to leap.

The tobacco splattered into the snake's eyes and mouth, stinging. Immediately the rattler fell from its coil and retreated into the weeds less than six feet away.

Jack sent another spray into the grass. Then grinned when he heard the angry hiss tell him he had struck pay-dirt once more, speeding the rattler on its way.

"Good trick, boy. Saw you was good shooting your gun at the island."

He turned quickly, surprised to see Trudeau watching the whole thing.

"Yeah," he whispered, pulling himself back in the carcass with the old man and making himself small once more. "I missed that snake . . . he'd have me for dinner."

"Snake . . . or Dog Soldiers. Take your pick."

"I'll take the Dog Soldiers any day," Jack replied, putting a finger to his lips as the ponies drew closer, then stopped. He judged them to be no farther than a hundred feet away.

The moments dragged by as they listened to the warriors arguing. Then the grass rustled again beneath the wind. But no voices as the sounds faded.

"They go," Pete whispered after a few minutes, his breath rank with stomach acid.

"We'll wait," Jack said, weary to the bone. "Get a little rest. Then we go on."

Stillwell closed his eyes too, welcoming the sleep and the mournful hiss of the wind through the buffalo's ribs. Then Trudeau whispered at his ear.

"You shoot good with 'baccy juice too, boy."

Chapter 35

"*B*iggest goddamned mistake I made was giving up my boots," John Donovan grumbled as he rubbed the soles of his feet, fingertips searching for broken cactus spines. He hawked up great balls of night-spit, hurling them into the muddy wallow they lay beside.

"We talked each other into it," A. J. Pliley replied. "Come too far to do a thing about it. We're going on."

"Your feet must be made of rawhide, Pliley," Donovan cursed, rustling some of the dried weeds. "These damned moccasins we stole off dead Injuns ain't no better'n wearing holey stockings."

"Moccasins the Injuns couldn't track. But I didn't count on the rain and snow. Didn't figure on the moccasins getting soaked. Made it easy for the cactus to push through."

"Here, A. J.," Donovan said, smiling as he watched Pliley gaze off into the distance, wounded. "I'm just belly-aching, don't you see? Have some jerky."

They laid at the edge of their muddy buffalo-wallow for the better part of the day, spelling each other at sleep. Watching the skyline in all directions, but especially to the north. Nursing sips of muddy water from their canteens, for the next water might be ten, as much as thirty, miles off. And eating rotten horsemeat. Watching the sun track the mapless sky.

"Still say we're heading too much due south," Donovan said after the sun had begun to fall from mid-sky. "If I didn't know better, you're heading us southwest, A. J."

"I am," he admitted. "Aim for us to find the Federal Road."

"And walk it into Wallace?"

He shook his head, eyes watering under the bright sun that shimmered things distant. "No. If the goddamned stage is still running, by God, we'll ride."

John felt something leap inside him, like hope. "Damn, A. J. Now that's one fine notion you have there. Say, how you know so much about this country out here?"

"Done some duty as a scout with the Eighteenth Kansas Cavalry."

"Was you in the war?"

"Second Lieutenant in the Fifteenth Kansas Volunteer Cavalry."

"You a Kansas boy?"

Pliley shook his head, still watching the distance. "No. New York. Happened I was out here when the war broke out. After mustering out, I went to Topeka, for the study of law." He chuckled quietly. "Worst thing for a man like me to do."

"How's that?"

"Law keeps a man out of the sun, don't you see. Work like this, on the other hand—a man gets to see one big piece of country. A job more to my liking."

Donovan wagged his head, pulling his face out of the sun. "You are a crazy one, A. J. Liking this sort of thing to being in a fancy law office in Topeka."

He smiled. "It is crazy. Maybe being raised in New York is why. But, I like how different I feel being out here. In the wind and the sun. Even the rain and the——"

It took a moment for Donovan to realize that Pliley had stopped talking. John opened his eyes, seeing his fellow scout tense, then freeze, as he peered off to the north. He looked for himself.

"How you make it, A. J.?"

"Twenty. Maybe twenty-five."

"They coming this way?"

He nodded. "They see the tall grass growing round this waller. They coming, for sure."

"Ten minutes?"

"No longer'n that, Donovan."

Without a word the men went about checking their guns, preparing to sell their lives as dearly as possible.

"I figure we can get us about half afore they get in too close."

"Then the crazy ones," Pliley hissed, "they come in to finish us off up close and dirty."

The minutes crawled by while the sun broke through the scattered clouds once again. That painted war-party steadfast on its course. Until at less than a quarter-mile a warrior in the center of the line threw up his arm, stopping the rest while he studied the landscape ahead.

After some wild gesturing, the leader led his group off to the right, heading into the bright sunlight to the northwest.

Once the war-party had disappeared beyond the rolling swales of grassland, Donovan sank to his belly and let out a long sigh.

"Lucky for us," Pliley said, "that big buck didn't figure there'd be any water here for 'em."

Donovan began to laugh. And it felt good. "Lucky for them and us both, A. J.! Them red bastards come here— they'd go away thirsty . . . and us—we'd be on our way to hell right now!"

A bloody fourth sun raised itself on the island. Sunday. 20 September. The green-bottle flies returned early with the promise of more scorching heat.

Seamus Donegan wondered how long he could take the despair of waiting, listening to the moans of the wounded, delirious in their sleep. Then he cursed himself, ashamed for blaming them. Their blessed sleep. God-sent deliriums that had somehow dulled their pain for more than three days now.

Had the renegade Confederate who called himself Smith joined up with the hostiles and pulled out?

He tried to think on that as the new light of morn crept up behind him like the drawing of a damask window-shade. Maybe he ought to go in search of Smith himself, now that he could not see a single warrior in evidence along the river-banks. But as he began to crawl over the saddles at the edge of his rifle-pit, Donegan finally spotted the few horsemen dotting the surrounding hilltops. With the new, rose light coming up from the east, the mounted warriors stood out against the pale, dawn sky. No more than a couple dozen vedettes, blanket-wrapped, feathers stirring in the cool breeze. As weak and feverish as he was, Seamus wanted no truck with them.

He sank back into the pit next to the stench of Liam's decomposing body.

"I want to see things for myself!"

Seamus heard Forsyth's voice, suddenly loud and strident. Then other voices, quieter, trying to make sense with the major.

"I've given you and Grover an order, Sergeant. Now, lift me."

Donegan hurried through the connecting pits, skirting the slumbering men who slept in until the sun's rising heated the land like a sheet-iron oven.

"I'll help, Major."

Forsyth turned on Donegan. He smiled weakly. Instantly Seamus felt sorry for the soldier, knowing by all rights that Forsyth was dying. If not from blood-poisoning from that bullet still in his leg, then surely from hunger like the rest of them. Knowing it was nothing more than a matter of time.

"Get a few more, McCall." Forsyth turned away, his red eyes bagged with liver-colored fatigue.

Six each grabbed an edge of the blanket, gently, carefully raising Forsyth from the floor of his rifle-pit so that he could have a look at things for himself.

"It's one thing for you to tell your commanding officer the condition of affairs," Forsyth was jabbering, his dry lips tearing away from his teeth as he spoke. "I want to see that the hostiles have left for myse——"

Indian repeaters snapped and rattled like the sharp cracking of dry twigs. Lead whistled, keening through their ranks. White and gray puffs of powdersmoke erupted from the riverbank. The scouts in other rifle-pits dove for cover.

Lane, who had a grip on the lower blanket corner nearest Forsyth's broken left leg, panicked. Hurling himself down into the pit as the bullets zinged overhead, Lane released the blanket.

Forsyth slid as the others tried reaching out, grabbing for

him. The major struck the ground on that leg shattered by
an Indian ball the first day of fighting.

"Arrrggggh!" he cried in intense pain, swallowing down
the rest of it in a grunt.

The impact with the ground splintered the bone even
more, sending shards of purple-red bone ripping through the
skin.

He was cursing at his leg like an English sailor, swearing
louder at Lane and giving no thought to those records St.
Peter kept at the Gates of Heaven.

Continuing to ignore the bullets slapping the brush overhead, Grover, McCall, and Donegan dragged Forsyth
roughly to the bottom of the pit, where they gently pulled on
the leg to relieve the pain, holding the enraged soldier down
until he eventually calmed.

"Damn you, Lane!" Forsyth hissed.

"I-I'm sorry, Major." Lane twisted his hands, biting his
lip. "Got scared, sir."

"Get out of my sight for the rest of the day!"

Lane scampered down the island as Grover looked at
Donegan. The broken leg was one thing, bone-ends splintered through the bloody skin. Yet, from the looks of Forsyth's right leg, they both knew what had to be done.

"Major, it ain't that busted leg what's gonna trouble you
most."

He glared at his chief of scouts, finding many eyes studying the swollen right thigh.

"Sharp's right. That bullet's gotta come out."

"I can't," Forsyth whimpered, then caught himself. "If I
lose consciousness . . . one of you will have to command
when I pass out."

"Trouble is," McCall said softly, "the bullet's in there next
to that big artery. Without Doc Mooers . . . shit—maybe
we oughta wait till a real surgeon gets here."

"No," Forsyth answered, his brow beaded, eyes rimmed
with pain. He knew. "It'll take too long. I won't last. One of
you . . . get my razor. Saddlebag."

McCall dragged over the major's kit, pulling out the memoranda book, a faded chromo of Forsyth's parents, then
found the straight razor in the narrow saddle-wallet, en-

closed in a small, hard-leather case. The sergeant presented it to Grover.

Sharp held his hands up, refusing to take the razor. "I can't do it."

Forsyth gritted his words between his teeth. "You've skinned more game and buffalo than any of——"

"Lotta difference 'tween that and digging round in your leg for a bullet, Major."

"Donegan?"

Seamus swallowed, shaking his head, staring at the puffy white rim around the purple wound. "No, sir. I slip with that razor . . . I'd kill you for cer——"

"Gimme the goddamned razor, McCall!" Forsyth snapped. "The whole damned lot of you're cowards."

Seamus felt shamed, although Forsyth had spoken the truth. "When it comes to facing them Cheyenne, I'll do it to my last breath, Major. But . . . this could mean killing you. If I'm a coward 'cause I don't wanna kill a brave man . . . one of the best army officers I've ever known—then call me a coward. So be it."

Forsyth sighed. "All right . . . all right. Just help me do it. I can't rightly ask any of you men to chance killing me. But, by damned, you'll help me dig it out."

"What you want from us, Major?" McCall asked.

"Pull that gum-poncho over here," he said, pointing. "Stuff it under the leg . . . there, like that. It'll catch the blood. Good. Now"—and Forsyth took a long, deep breath—"Grover, you and Donegan hold the leg down. Flat. That's it. I don't want it flinching . . . not while this blade is down in the meat of the leg."

He took the razor from its case, pulling the blade from the handle in the morning sunlight where the polished steel glinted brightly. Seamus could already see the major's eyes welling with the expectation of coming pain.

"All right, McCall. You and Slinger are next. Both you push your fingers down around that bullet hole . . . *uuunn-nhhh!*" he exclaimed as they pressed. "Easy . . . No! Don't stop, pull the skin apart as I . . . as I cut."

He dragged the razor over the wound one time. Then caught his breath.

"Hang on, Major," Donegan whispered.

"You're doing fine," Grover echoed.

Forsyth let the pain wash over him, then blinked his eyes clear before he made a second pass with the blade, sundering more of the rotting, white flesh. Puss and blood oozed freely. Forsyth scraped the blood away as he choked back his stomach's attempt to vomit.

"Take 'er easy," Grover said. "We got all the time in the world."

Forsyth tried a brave smile, more diamonds of sweat dappling his powder-smudged brow. "I suppose so, boys. We haven't got anyplace to go."

While the rest started to chuckle, Forsyth dragged the blade against the parting, yielding flesh. Shlesinger and McCall gently pried back the bloody, infected muscle as the blade worked its way down.

The major rocked his head back, eyes closed, swallowing down the pain after that deep stroke. When he could talk: "I felt the blade catch . . . catch on something . . . It must be the ball."

"Careful now, Major," McCall whispered.

"You, Billy. Use your fingers now. Pinch up the muscle round the ball."

"Sir, I don't——"

"Just do it!" he snapped, his eyes red as six-hour coals. His eyes forcing his sergeant to dip his dirty fingers into the bloody meat, gingerly feeling for the bullet.

"I got it."

"Pinch it!" Forsyth hissed, clenching his jaw in excruciating pain. "Pull it up . . . away from the artery . . . I'll cut the last muscle out of the way . . ."

The bloodied, white muscle puffed up between McCall's fingers. With his lips compressed in a thin line of determination, Forsyth steadied his left hand across the thigh like a brace, laying the knife-hand atop the left. Then in one swift movement he dragged the thin-bladed razor across the knotted flesh.

"You're lucky, Major," Donegan whispered as the bullet puffed through the angry, purple muscle.

"We got it," Grover said, snagging the flattened lead bullet from the knot of flesh McCall had pinched. He held it before the major's eyes.

But Forsyth was already sagging backward, his face gone fish-gut gray, his eyes fluttering closed to blessed unconsciousness.

"Stop that bleeding with your hand, Sergeant," Donegan suggested, yanking at what he had left of his shirttail. "Slinger, tear off a piece of your shirt as well. We'll get it wrapped up afore he comes to."

"Damn, but Forsyth's got grit," McCall marveled as he pressed his fingers into the lacerated flesh to slow the trickle of bright red blood.

"That's for sure," Grover said. "Major's craw is plumb full of sand and fighting tallow."

"Don't know of another man would stand to cut on themselves like that," Donegan said finally as they finished wrapping the leg in a new bandage. He looked up at the eyes of those three men gathered with him, seeing more of the scouts now, those who lay near the rim of the rifle-pit, watching it all with admiration on their weary, blackened faces.

"Gentlemen," the tall man from County Kilkenny spoke softly, "with this man leading us . . . I don't think there's a one among you can doubt any longer that we'll get off this island."

"Hear! Hear!" McCall shouted, echoed by most of those who had watched the surgery.

"By God, Forsyth's seen us through this far." Donegan raised his voice, louder and stronger now. "It's time we see him through the rest of it!"

By dusk of that twentieth day of September spent back in the shadows of their buffalo carcass, Jack Stillwell found his partner sick, and getting no better. Sleeping fitfully, Pierre Trudeau complained of stomach cramps. He lay in the weeds, moaning, for most of the day after the boy had run the rattler off with a well-aimed stream of tobacco juice.

But Jack knew they could not stay. Hunting parties were out. Looking for them. And besides, chances were good that Major Forsyth had sent other messengers out as well. With evidence that at least two parties had escaped from the island, the warriors would be furious, scouring the prairie for them like owls after field-mice.

He eventually succeeded in getting Trudeau to his feet,

supporting the old man as they stumbled into the deepening darkness.

Jack glanced from time to time over his shoulder, checking the position of the north star. By the time they reached a small stream, both men were ready to refill their canteens. The water they found brackish, alkaline, not much better than what had seeped into the rifle-pits on the island. At least this water ran cool.

They both lay on the bank for the longest time, guzzling, their faces submerged in the creek, watching the sky darken. Ever since his childhood, this time of night had always made young Jack lonely. Even more so now that Trudeau's belly cramps had returned.

"Here." Stillwell held a strip of charred horsemeat to the old man's lips. "Eat this, Pete."

He turned his head aside. "Can't. Belly . . ." His voice fell off, moaning. "Belly come up . . ."

"Eat. If you throw it up, you'll stay here and . . . I'll go on."

His watery, red eyes blinked their gratitude for the youngster's kindness as he took the strip between his chapped lips. He chewed, choking from time to time, but he got it and another strip down. Then Pete drank some more of the alkali water. Minutes later he rose from his elbows, holding his hand up to Stillwell.

"Help me up, Jack."

"For a while there, I was scared I'd be going on alone."

Pete slung his haversack over his shoulder, still clutching Stillwell for support as they hobbled off into the darkness.

"For a time there, Jack—Pierre afraid you leave him."

"I'd do it—to save the rest . . . back there, Pete," Jack replied.

"Yes," old Trudeau whispered in reply. "We go together now. To save the rest back there."

Chapter 36

"Y ou got more lives than a six-toed cat," Grover congratulated Forsyth as the major came to later that Sunday, their fourth day on the island.

Seamus smiled at Forsyth. A faint brightness was returning to his eyes. Not recovered yet, but the major was on the way now with that bullet cut from his leg.

His improvement that cloudy, drizzly afternoon did much to cheer some of the other wounded. Though blinded in the right eye by an Indian bullet during the first charge on the seventeenth, Howard Morton had wrapped a crude bandage round his head and fought on through the last three days.

Young Hutch Farley had been struck in the shoulder by a bullet during the first charge, and later that morning his father had suffered his fearful wound. Yet both had quietly put their Spencers to the job at hand, while old man Farley grew worse with each passing day.

The iron-tipped point of a Sioux arrow had lodged in the front of Frank Harrington's skull that first day as well. Another scout had loosened the sinew binding the shaft to arrow-point so that the wound could be bandaged. Harrington went back to defending the island with the rest. Even after an Indian bullet grazed his forehead, knocking loose the embedded iron arrow-tip. A new bandage was all that was required to keep the blood from Harrington's eyes as he returned to fighting with the snipers hidden on the riverbanks.

Many of those imprisoned on that sandy island swallowed

down their own pain and squeezed the thoughts of their own misery out of their minds, alone. Brushing the maggots from the open wounds. Bathing the bullet holes with rags of murky water.

Life descended into nothing more than the essentials. Food. Water. And never thinking about home.

"Here, Major." McCall came up with a steaming tin mess-cup that hissed with the cold drops of drizzling rain. "Drink some of this."

Forsyth held it under his nose. "What is it?"

"Don't ask," Seamus suggested, grinning. "Try it first."

The major drank. "Not horse. What'd you fellas do? Boil down some Cheyenne moccasins?"

They shared a quiet laugh.

Grover spoke up. "Slinger bagged him a little coyote."

"Coyote?"

"One what got a little too curious, I'd say," Donegan added.

"Bless that little Jew," Forsyth replied, then sipped at his hot soup.

"I recall how most of the rest gave Slinger a hard time when we were riding out those first few days," Donegan said.

"Weren't too kind to him, were they?" McCall asked.

"Times were, I felt bad for talking him into joining," Forsyth admitted. "But he's acquitted himself courageously."

"He was hurt when you wouldn't let him go with Jack Stillwell that first night," McCall said.

Forsyth nodded, staring at the dregs of coyote stew in his tin cup. "I know. But he'd have no business out there. At least Stillwell grew up out in this country. Living outdoors. Slinger . . . the Jew would have no business on his own out there."

"A good shot," Donegan offered. "I don't think there's a man wouldn't be proud to fight alongside Slinger now."

Forsyth smiled. "And that Lyden fella, the one who gave Slinger such a time of it, right up to the morning we were attacked."

Grover snorted. "Ain't it always like that, Major? The bullies who blow hard like they're the biggest bulls in the lick."

McCall chuckled as well. "Soon as we made it to the island that first charge, Lyden throwed himself down . . . shaking like a willow in a windstorm."

"He hasn't fought since," Grover growled.

"I doubt he will," Forsyth added. "He's been sufficiently shamed by Slinger's quiet courage."

Donegan watched the sun creep out of the gray clouds to the west, firing the hillsides with orange and purple hues. "That boy's become a man this trip out, Major."

"For all but Lyden," Forsyth said, handing his cup to McCall, "I'm certain we've all found something new inside to be proud of. Billy, it's time I speak to the men. Call them together now."

As McCall stretched out of the pit to round up the rest, Grover looked back at Forsyth. "Major, none of the men can even stomach the horsemeat no more."

"That's a big part of why I'm calling the men here," he explained. "We're on the brink of starvation."

"I never had a particular touchy stomach, Major," Seamus said, "but even I can't keep the horsemeat down . . . even with gunpowder sprinkled on it."

"It's plums or coyote now," Grover added as the others came out of the first fading light of summer's early evening.

"Men, we've survived four days now. But the real test is yet to come."

He waited for some of the muttering to quiet itself. "Without horsemeat, we're in a mess of it now. Slinger here got us a coyote that's gone through three boilings to feed the wounded and the rest. That's what it's going to take now. From each of you. We're going to have to try a little harder, hunt a little longer, perhaps hunt a bit farther from the island."

The muttering from some grew louder.

"I know it's not the safest thing we can do is try to get off the island to hunt for game. But, if we don't—we'll all starve here together."

"Major Forsyth's right," Donegan spoke up. "If a man wants and volunteers, he can hunt off the island. That's the only way we're going to last."

"What about us as can walk, Major?"

Forsyth looked over at Lyden, his bushy brows narrowing. "What are you saying? Spit it out."

"If we can get off the island, Major . . . we can walk on out of here, can't we?"

Forsyth drew himself up against the side of the rifle-pit. "Some of you can walk, Lyden. Some of us . . . well—right now the best of chances for us all is to stay with the island until help arrives."

"But, Major——"

"That's all, Lyden!" he snapped, then watched the civilian slink back into the crowd. "I called you here for just a moment, to tell you about the hunting . . . and to thank you men. I fought with Phil Sheridan in the Shenandoah, and took some Confederate bullets down there . . . no offense meant, Dick Gantt!"

Most of the men laughed along with the Southerner.

"Damn, Major. I'd feel proud if man like you was wearin' my rebel lead!"

Forsyth chuckled, feeling better for the warm, pasty soup awash in his belly. "I fought with Sheridan . . . and I know the general will be proud of each one of you for what you've done here."

"We've made history, Major. Nothing short of it," McCall cheered.

"Hear! Hear!" some of the others shouted.

"To Major Forsyth!" Donegan raised his thick brogue. "He led us out . . . and by the saints—he'll lead us back again!"

Corporal Reuben Waller liked the smell of the air here on the high plains. Nothing like the air back in the South. Out here, nothing was like that life he had left far behind.

When the war ended, Waller had come to Kansas, hoping like so many others of both armies to start anew. But quickly found there was little opportunity for a Negro here on the plains. The army welcomed him with open arms the next year so that by the end of 1866, Rube Waller had been sworn in as a member of the new 10th Cavalry. He had been assigned to Company H, under the command of Capt. L. H. Carpenter. An honest, tee-totalling New Jersey man who brooked no disobedience from his brunettes, but neither did he sneer at his Negro soldiers behind their backs in the way of other white officers.

It was a proud moment one cold, crisp day early last fall when Carpenter had called Waller aside after arriving at Fort Wallace. The captain asked the tall, lean Negro to become his new orderly. Ever since that day, a warm surge of camaraderie for his commander had never diminished.

L. H. Carpenter, he thought again as the captain led his H Company west from the walls of Fort Wallace on routine patrol to keep the Denver Road open this dawn of 20 September, eighteen-and-sixty-eight. *Twice breveted for gallantry during the war. Once at Gettysburg . . . and again in the Shenandoah at Winchester. Riding for General Phil Sheridan his own goddamned self!*

Talk had it the last couple of days that the bunch of civilians Major Forsyth had rounded up to chase the Cheyenne were probably going to strike a match to the powder-keg in this part of the Central Plains. And that pleased Carpenter's H Company no measure. Like Waller, they had all been itching for a good scrap with the Indians.

Beneath the overcast sky, orderly Rube Waller brushed his gold chevrons, proud to be riding beside Captain Carpenter. And smiled as he gazed into the distance across the awakening plains. Carpenter had them pointing their noses west, for Sandy Creek, some forty-odd miles from Wallace.

The only thing that could make him more proud would be riding with the captain into a good fight of it with the Cheyenne.

As the sun fell over John Donovan and A. J. Pliley alone on this western rim of rolling tableland, the whole sky pinked up in a blaze before going purple. In no time were the heavens dark and dusted with stars, they came to the banks of a water-course a good deal wider than the streams and creeks they had been stumbling across so far.

"What night is it, Donovan?" Pliley asked after immersing his face in the cool water.

"Twenty-first. How far you think it is now?"

"Not far now, Jack." And he leaned back, reaching for his canteen. "I figure this is a fork of the Smoky Hill. Taste it."

"No shit?"

He nodded, dipping his canteen into the sweet water. "We

keep going west, we'll bump into the wagon-road going to Cheyenne Wells."

"West?" Donovan squeaked. "But Wallace gotta be east of here. Here I thought you'd done some scouting for the Kansas cavalry."

"I did. And you're right. Wallace is east of here."

"Then why the hell we going west?"

"Let's say I'd like to ride into Wallace, Jack. Your feet gotta be every bit as dogged as mine are by now."

"How far a piece is it?"

"Can't say . . . till we hit the Federal Road."

"And once we hit the road?"

Pliley came up, wringing back his long, greasy hair he had dipped in the cool water. "Thirty, maybe forty mile."

"That's all!" Donovan felt cheered. "We can do that walking on our hands, A. J."

He snorted a quick laugh. "If them Indians got the road shut down and we don't find a coach or wagon headed east to Wallace . . . we may just have to walk the rest of it on our hands."

"For now, I'll stick with these sore, bloody feet of mine." Muttering, Donovan turned southwest from the stream with Pliley. "Can't see how them red niggers stand to wear these moccasins when they should jump at the chance to wear a good pair of boots."

The cool dip at the river lasted Donovan for the next few hours as his shirt dried. Then the wind shifted out of the northwest as clouds scudded across the sky, blotting the quarter-moon.

"Hold up, A. J. How we gonna tell which way to go now?" Donovan stopped, catching his breath from their bruising pace.

Pliley sniffed.

"What you smelling for now?"

Pliley came closer. "Air always smelled different farther west I come. Suppose it's closer to the mountains."

"So?"

"So, from the smell of things, we might be in Colorady Territory."

"Colorady? Jesus, you got us off——"

"We ain't far now, Jack."

"You sure?"

"Road can't be that far."

"Let's go," Donovan said, his spirits renewed once more.

Four hours later as they blindly felt their way west by south under the heaving sky, the pair ran onto the Smoky Hill Road.

"It's wagon-ruts, by God!" Donovan hollered, dancing on his wounded, tired feet in the middle of the dusty trail.

"Told you," Pliley answered wearily, head turning east, then west, then east again.

"Which way now, A. J.?" Donovan asked, seeing for the first time the signs of strain coming over his partner.

"I . . . I think . . ."

"Yes?"

"West?"

"Still west?"

"Cheyenne Wells . . . it's gotta be west of here."

"Is that a guess—a hunch or what?" Donovan grew suspicious, grabbing Pliley, supporting his weary partner.

"Yeah." Pliley drew himself up again, shoulders back. "Cheyenne Wells gotta be over there."

Donovan followed his partner on into the darkness, hoping.

A. J. Pliley came through that black, cold morning of 22 September. A few miles' more brought them to the road-ranch situated three miles east of Cheyenne Wells in Colorado Territory. They hurried toward the dim lantern-lit structure that loomed out of the early morning gloom.

"Hold it right there!" a voice boomed out of the darkness.

They halted in their tracks.

"Howdy, friend!" John Donovan shouted back. "Me and my partner sure done in."

A figure approached. Even in the darkness Donovan could see the shotgun in his hands. "Who you?"

"We were with Major Forsyth. Out of Wallace. Got hit by the whole Cheyenne nation four days back. Five now."

"You fellas all that escaped?" the ranchman asked as he came close enough to look the two in the face.

"There's more alive . . . was," Pliley explained. "Back there. When's next stage east?"

"Be here six in the morning," the ranchman answered,

using the shotgun muzzle to signal the pair ahead to the low, adobe building surrounded on three sides with corrals. "C'mon in. You boys could do with something to eat."

"Eat?" Donovan asked, his voice rising in a squeaky rasp. "Why the hell would we wanna eat when you probably don't have anything to offer what's better'n mule jerky?"

By late that same morning of the twenty-second, Jack Stillwell dragged Trudeau over a low rise to find the sun shining dull on a narrow cut of dusty wagon-road.

"Sit, Pete. Rest. We'll go on in a minute."

For what would be the last time in his journey south, Jack reached inside his shirt, pulling out Forsyth's only map. Slowly he sounded out the words as his fingers traced the route from the X the major had showed him he figured for the island's position. South by east he ran a dirty fingernail, crossing rivers and streams he and the old man had forded in their dangerous journey.

He clenched his teeth at last, glancing into the hazy sun of an overcast sky. Fighting back the sting of tears and the knot at his throat.

"C'mon, Pete. We almost home now."

He was pulling Trudeau to his feet when he caught wind of hammering hoofbeats on the road. Out of the east. From the sounds of it, wasn't many of them. The tears poured onto his cheeks as he cursed himself. To come this far and get so close . . . only to have to sell his life here by this dusty road that would have taken him on to Wallace.

"We fight," Pete whispered, his strength almost gone.

Jack nodded. "Yes, old man. We made a good try of it, didn't we?"

Trudeau smiled, his eyes glistening, his stained teeth like pine shavings. "You got me this far, boy. I go the rest of the way myself."

They pulled their pistols, inching backward into a stand of weeds as the horsemen broke the hilltop.

Pete choked, rubbing his eyes. "S-sol . . ."

"Yes, by God!" Jack shouted as he recognized dusty blue tunics worn by the two riders.

"Buff . . . buffalo soldiers . . ." Pete cheered weakly, waving his pistol.

"Brunettes!" Jack shouted, dancing round the old man, letting the tears fall without shame.

"Hold up there!" One of the Negro soldiers flung up his arm. Bouncing beneath the arm he carried a leather satchel, strapped over his left shoulder. The pair skidded to a stop in the dust. "Who you fellas?"

"Come from up on the Republican," Jack answered, snorting back some of his tears. "Mighty glad to see you."

"From the Republican?"

"With Major Forsyth's scouts."

The soldier glanced at his companion, wide-eyed. "You with Forsyth?"

"That's right."

"Colonel Bankhead at Wallace starting to believe you all done in," the soldier explained.

"Wallace that way?" Jack asked, pointing east.

"Yessuh."

"Where you two going in such a hurry?" Stillwell prodded.

"Dispatches for Captain Carpenter, Tenth Cavalry." He patted his dispatch satchel.

"Carpenter?"

"On patrol northwest of here," the soldier explained.

"Where'bouts?" Jack asked, yanking his map out again.

"Up by Sandy Creek."

Stillwell found it on the map. "Listen close!" The excitement rose in his voice, drawing the soldiers close, until they sat directly over the young scout. "That horse you riding got some bottom left in it?"

"Why, I s'pose so. Why?"

"You take this map to Captain Carpenter. Make sure he sees this X Major Forsyth put on it. You see it?"

"I do."

"Carpenter can make it to the river before anyone else. So tell the captain this X shows where Forsyth and the rest of 'em are holding out against the Cheyenne."

"How many Cheyenne?"

Jack shook his head. "Damn lots. Sioux and Arapaho too. Can't figure——"

"We'll tell him," the soldier said, snatching up the map

and stuffing it in with his dispatches. "You go on into Wallace. Your friend there looks done in."

How dearly Jack wanted to ride on with the couriers, to be there when that Captain Carpenter and his brunettes rode into that distant river valley, just so he could see the looks on those faces of his new friends. Especially Slinger's. His good friend, Slinger.

But as Stillwell gazed back at old Pete, squatting in the dust alongside that wagon-road, he realized he most needed to see Trudeau to Fort Wallace.

"You need a canteen of water?" the second soldier asked, speaking for the first time.

Jack took it, handing it on to Pete. "We thank you, soldiers."

"No, we thank you!" the first courier said, his teeth gleaming in his shiny, ebony face. "We'uns in Captain Carpenter's unit been looking for some action for a long time now. And this is it. A chance to get a lick or two in for ourselves again' Roman Nose and his hellions!"

Chapter 37

"We will rejoin you before the new moon," Jack O'Neill told Two Crows.

He held an arm out to indicate the fifty warriors who were staying behind, both Cheyenne and Sioux, as the villages of Two Crows and Pawnee Killer struck their lodges in a hasty, noisy departure.

"How long will you stay, Nibsi?" Two Crows asked.

"As long as it takes. Until there are no more whitemen on the island. Or, until all these warriors are dead."

"Some say you have a blood-debt to avenge for Roman Nose," Two Crows spoke without raising his voice.

O'Neill felt the sting of the chief's words. Accusation in them. "Roman Nose asked me, in his final minutes, to take up his medicine quest."

"Because of it, some say you stalk one of the whitemen on the island."

"The one who killed Roman Nose," O'Neill replied proudly. "There is great power in this blood-debt I take on my shoulders."

Two Crows looked over the fifty horsemen, young men mostly, of both tribes, eager to hurl themselves at the island again, not content to run from the huge guns of the white men. The old chief turned back to the mulatto.

"How many of these will die before you give up your hunt?" he asked.

O'Neill glanced over the young, copper-skinned warriors. Licking his lips. "They do not matter to me, Two Crows.

Only two lives matter now. The whiteman I hunt. And mine . . . only so that I can live as long as it takes to kill the man who robbed Roman Nose of his life."

"In the short time you have been with us, Nibsi . . . you have become a dangerous man," Two Crows said as he clambered aboard his pony. He eyed the lodges coming down, the others loaded on travois and already on their way, spreading out as did the fingers of a hand across the trail they would take to the north. Away from the soldiers they knew would come.

The soldiers always came.

Jack swelled his chest. "I am proud to be a dangerous man, Two Crows. Perhaps the Dog Soldiers no more belong camping with your Cheyenne. Perhaps we are the last fighters on these plains, the ones who do not know how to live among people who will run from a fight."

"You come to this land from a faraway place. How do you know——"

"I know hate for the whiteman, Two Crows!" he spat.

The old chief fell silent for a minute, chastised by the mulatto's anger. "If you would be Cheyenne, then you must learn. Learn there are some fights you must leave . . . so that you are free to choose another place, another time to do battle."

"Perhaps. But time will tell the Cheyenne. Time will tell the Dog Soldiers. And Nibsi will know when it is time to kill again."

Two Crows tore his eyes from the mulatto, gazing for a moment at the small brush arbor some of the young warriors had constructed to shade Nibsi and the other war-leaders when they were in conference during the days of battle.

"Tell me one last thing, Nibsi. When is it time to kill the whiteman?"

"The one on the island?"

"No," he answered, turning. "The one you keep in there." Two Crows pointed to the brush arbor.

O'Neill smiled, turning, his face gleaming with sweat beneath the high-plains sun. "Clybor!" He shouted the English name of the Sioux renegade from Custer's 7th Cavalry.

Jack Clybor poked his head out of the arbor. "What d'you want, O'Neill?" he answered in English.

"Bring our guest out now. Two Crows wants to say farewell to him," he snarled.

Clybor's head disappeared into the shady arbor, then reappeared a moment later, tugging on a man's arm. A bloody, white arm. At the end of which was dragged a beaten, bruised, and bloody white prisoner. His shaggy, disheveled hair, hung clotted with blood. One eye puffed shut. The other watering, filled with fright as it darted anxiously over the crowd.

"Bring him here," Nibsi commanded.

Clybor dragged the white man over to the pony ridden by Two Crows. The shirt had been long ago ripped from the prisoner's back, and his leather britches hung in bloody shreds above his bruised and burned feet. O'Neill smiled. He had enjoyed watching the Cheyenne and Sioux women make sport of the prisoner, anything just short of death.

"The Arapaho village left a day ago because you did this to him, their old friend," Two Crows accused.

"The Arapaho are old women," Nibsi retorted. "They left because they are guilty."

The big mulatto stomped over to Clybor, grabbed the prisoner's hair and yanked it backward, coming close to snapping the man's neck.

"They call him North among his own people," O'Neill explained. "But he ran away to live for a time among the Arapaho."

"I know this," Two Crows replied acidly.

"Do you know he left me with these scars?"

O'Neill flung the prisoner's head down with a harsh snap, watching him crumple at the knees before he marched boldly to the old chief on the pony. The mulatto held up the backs of both wrists, showing the old chief the wide, puckered scars where North's knife had slashed in that whore's crib near Fort Lyon.

"Know this too, Two Crows—last winter this man was not with the Arapaho. He left them. Returned to the whiteman's towns."

"Is that not where you truly belong, Nibsi?"

He spat on the ground. "Old man, I am not like this prisoner, North. Nor am I like Comanche. They are white. While I . . . I do not belong among them. If there is a man out here in this land who is hated more than the Indian, it is a man like me. Yes, Two Crows. You are right. I am dangerous. But, dangerous only to whitemen like this man, North."

"What did he do among his own kind that brings his death at your hand?"

"Not what he did among his own kind . . . but what he did to me. And someone I loved." Jack watched the old man's eyebrow lift at that.

"A woman?"

"I loved her. Back near Fort Lyon. This one killed her," O'Neill explained.

"You need say no more," Two Crows replied. "The prisoner is yours to do with as you wish. Kill him if you want."

The chief tapped his heels against his pony's ribs and eased into the dust cloud rising above the many travois scratching the earth as thousands of ponies spread the villages across the prairie.

O'Neill stared after him a moment, then looked down on the unconscious, bloodied form of Capt. Robert North, Arapaho renegade captured on the banks of the river as he was seeking to escape the sandy island.

"The joke is on you, Two Crows," the mulatto sneered, his eyes half-closing. "North was mine to do with as I wish all along. And like North, the tall, gray-eyed one still on the island belongs to me."

Yesterday, their fifth on the island, none of the men worried of eating the mule and horsemeat any longer. The stench of the flesh turning to a putrid, gray soup was enough to cause any of them to lose his appetite.

Because his stomach still growled a little, Seamus Donegan pulled a small canvas satchel of roasted coffee beans from his saddlebags. Throughout that day and into slap-dark he sucked on the beans for their strong flavor, to keep himself awake beneath the cloudless sky and blazing light reflecting off the surrounding ridges and bluffs. And to give his dry mouth something to salivate on instead of the grim curses he wanted to hurl at the empty hills.

A few of them wandered some short distance from the island, returning with prickly pear fruit, sweet and chewy and sticky enough. But there was still not enough of it to give all of them more than a taste. Another hapless coyote wandered in too close, within the range of their Spencers. Four-legged soup was on the menu that fifth evening, the first boiling for the seriously wounded, the second boiling for the rest of those who had spilled some blood. A third and final thin, almost tasteless, broth was warmed for the rest.

That evening as the sun sank, allowing the furnace of this land to cool, they no longer noticed any warriors dippling the hilltops, keeping watch on the island. Near sunset a handful ventured upstream a few yards to inspect the three warriors abandoned by their comrades when the bodies could not be recovered.

"I'll go with you, Mr. Donegan," Sigmund Shlesinger said quietly as he came up beside Seamus.

He tried to smile, tired and weak from hunger and blood loss the way he was. "Let's see if we can get you something to show your grandchildren of this day years from now, Slinger."

At the bodies, several of the scouts stood back, waiting on others. Some took moccasins. Others claimed the guns. There were knives to distribute and a belt pouch or two.

"Who wants these scalps?" Joe Lane asked, blustering. He wheeled on Shlesinger. "Hey, boy . . . a scalp that this'un here would surely be some big medicine to show to your Jew-folk. You want it?"

Slinger glanced up at Donegan. Seamus nodded, saying, "Go 'head. If you want it."

The youngster knelt beside the body, lifting a braid crusted with blood from a massive head-wound. Donegan could see Slinger was going pale as he stuck his knife-blade behind the Indian's ear as Lane was instructing him. Suddenly the boy dropped the blood-crusted braid and struggled to his feet, working at keeping the vomit down.

Lane rared his head back, laughing as he knelt, yanking up the bloody braid. "Say, Jew-boy—this make you sick, eh? Well, watch this."

He inserted the point of his knife beneath the taut skin, quickly slashing round the entire head, then held the neck down with one hand while the other yanked the scalp off with a moist, sucking pop that reminded Donegan of freeing his boot from thick mud.

"All there is to it, Jew-boy!" Lane shook the scalp in front of Shlesinger's face.

"I don't want it——"

"Take it, Jew-boy! Said you wanted the goddamned thing!" Lane shoved it at the youngster's face, shaking the hair and gore.

Until he winced in pain, his neck caught in the vise of Donegan's big hand.

"Drop the scalp, Lane," Seamus hissed. "Or there'll be one more dead man for us to scalp."

"Didn't mean the boy no harm," Lane whined, attempting to turn within the vise. "Lemme go, goddammit."

"Any of the rest of you want to poke your fun at Slinger," McCall's voice boomed behind them all, "you'll take it up with Major Forsyth and me!"

"Just having ourselves a little fun, we was, Sergeant," Lane said, scampering away from the Irishman when Donegan released him.

"I've made myself clear," McCall said. "Major wants you all back in the pits. Now, listen. Eutsler and Curry come back without any game from their hunt. But they didn't come back empty-handed. They've filled their hats with plums."

"Plums!" another man shouted, bolting away.

The rest hurried as well, eager for the treat.

After each man had been given a plum to eat, the rest of the fruit was simmered over some low flames licking along a driftwood fire as the sky sank in a blazing sunset. A thick plum stew was spooned into the mouths of the seriously wounded.

Seamus sat next to Forsyth, watching the wounded eat their stew as he sucked the last juicy fibers off the plum pit, making at the back of his throat those same muted sounds migrating geese made on good feeding grounds.

"Better than the rotten meat," Forsyth said as he licked his fingers.

"I've myself eaten rotten meat of a time before," Sharp Grover commented. "Not all that bad when you don't worry 'bout the smell."

Forsyth laughed a little now this morning of the twenty-second, laughed pitifully. Remembering last night's grim supper as the men sucked on their plum pits and lapped at their coyote stew. Their sixth day on the Arickaree Fork of the Republican somewhere on the Central Plains.

By midday many of the wounded had become delirious with the fever caused of infection in their maggot-filled wounds. Try as they might, the able-bodied scouts were powerless to stop the big flies from continually reinfesting the bloody, oozy wounds with their eggs, which daily turned into squirming, writhing maggots.

Some of the wounded already suffered from advanced gangrene. Those who could see their own wounds knew it, watching the slow, painless creep of the angry, red welts running up limbs, toward the heart.

Seamus had about given up on keeping his own arm wound clean. From all he could remember, it had been at least two days now since he had last rinsed out the dirty bandage and bathed the wound, washing it free of the eggs flies continually laid in the moist bullet holes. He had all but given up on his wounds as closer he drew to abandoning the hope of ever making it off this sandy stretch of low-water island.

As the sun eased out of the day, Donegan stared at his arm, hypnotized by the monotonous whirring buzz of the green-backed September flies warming over the oozy track of the Confederate's bullet. He didn't brush them off any longer. Staring. Mesmerized as the flies reminded him of a black, writhing mass, something pulsating with life while his own was ebbing away.

The rustle of the wild plum nearby stirred him from his reverie, time and again squeezing painful images out of his mind: his mother and home. Jennie Wheatley and the home he wanted with her. He stared at the deepening sky for a long . . . long time.

Seamus did not know how long he had been asleep when Grover hunched over him, rousting him.

He blinked. Night was coming slowly down on them once more. "What day is it?"

Grover helped him to his feet. "Why, it's the sixth, Irishman."

"Good." He sighed. "Dreamed I was out for a long, long time."

"C'mon," Grover urged, lines of concern crossing his brow. "Major wants to see every man able to make it in his trench."

"Whyn't you leave me, Sharp? I'm sleepy."

"You're able, Donegan," he chided, helping Seamus along. "And as long as I'm able, you'll not get down so bad you can't get back up."

As the scouts came to a rest in and around Forsyth's rifle-pit, the flies descended on them once more like a noisy cloud.

"Men." Forsyth paused, drawing himself up. It reminded Seamus of the way the major had steeled himself to cut that bullet out of his own swollen leg. "Stillwell and Trudeau probably got through to Fort Wallace. I believe that with all my being because the Indians haven't sent their bodies back in to us. Very likely, Donovan and Pliley made it in as well. If any of the four arrived, we can count on having a relief column reach us in two . . . perhaps three more days."

He waited while some of the scouts murmured their agreement to his optimism.

"Yet, we must steel ourselves for the possibility that none of the four will make it. Maybe the Indians. Or, wandering off and getting lost in all that country out there . . ." And he waved an arm to the south, an arm that finally collapsed back into his lap. "So, if none of those four made it, we're in bad straights, boys. Help won't be coming like we've hoped."

"You sure know how to cheer a fella up, Major," William Reilly said during the quiet pause.

He looked at Reilly. "All of you who are still able-bodied, I want to give the chance to save yourselves. Decide now if you want to stay here with us . . . or go try for the settlements."

Forsyth's red eyes, rimmed with liver-colored bags, slewed round the group slowly. "If you fellas do go, leave us half the ammunition to defend ourselves."

"Ammunition?" McCall asked, shaking his head as if trying to make sense of what Forsyth was saying to them.

The major turned slowly on his sergeant. "Billy, you boys take half the cartridges and weapons. I don't think the Indians in this country will give you a try, since we've delivered them as sound a whipping as they'll ever get. But . . . if they catch you on the plains making good your escape, you can defend yourselves equitably."

"Escape?" asked the big bruiser James Curry.

Seamus listened to the mutterings of the men. Then a hollow pounding in his ears caused him to look away from the ring of scouts hunched at the lip of Forsyth's pit.

For the first time in all their days here, he noticed a pack of wolves slinking over the crest of the bluffs to the north. Ten. Twelve. Fifteen and more. Black and gray and brown. Lanky animals with their long snouts and lolling tongues bobbing as they came on, drawn by the smell of blood and carrion. Their sleek, lean legs rhythmically carrying them down into the valley of the Arickaree. Come for the meat.

Perhaps come for the men . . .

"——want you each to take some time now to decide if you want to leave tonight like the first four," Forsyth was saying in the background.

. . . Now the smaller coyotes started their evening yammer from the tops of the ridges. Perhaps angry that their wolf cousins had come in to boldly claim what the coyotes had been staking out as their feed for days now . . .

"——to move the wounded now would be to kill them . . . us."

. . . The four-leggeds circled, snarling quietly, nipping at one another in anticipation of the feast . . .

"——any event, the wounded would slow you boys down. And, well—honestly, we're all soldiers, no matter that you don't wear uniforms," Forsyth continued, as tough as it was. "And a soldier knows how to meet his fate. So, men—I leave it in your hands to decide."

Forsyth sank back against the side of his pit, exhausted from his speech, watching, waiting for the scouts to disperse as he had suggested. A dead silence fell over the island for a few moments while the men looked at one another, stunned speechless.

"Never, General!" a voice suddenly called out from the rear.

Eli Ziegler's.

"Damn right, Major Forsyth!" Another voice, Thomas Ranahan's, joined Eli's.

Seamus felt the sting of it in his throat, the surge of

strength returning as he discovered himself among these strong-hearted men. "By glory, Major . . . you damned well won't find any of us running off on the rest of you!"

"Hear! Hear!" the crowd raised its voice as one, strong. Proud. Resolved to fight on.

"We'll stand by you, General—to the end!" Issac Thayer vowed.

Billy McCall stood in the center of the pit now, his arm pointing round the men until his eyes locked on Forsyth's. "We've fought together, Major . . . and, by heaven, if need be . . . we'll die together!"

"Hurrah! Hurrah! Hurrah!" The island rocked with the courageous oath of those steadfast souls.

"D-dismissed," Forsyth issued his orders quietly, watching the men disperse into the deepening gloom of night. His eyes moist.

Awhile later, Donegan lay alone in his pit, thinking on Liam O'Roarke and the life his uncle had chosen to lead among these men. Seamus knew anyone could expect regular soldiers to stay and persevere under orders.

Yet, these men were not soldiers. Simply a company of civilian scouts. Bound together now like no company of bluecoats or pony-soldiers ever could be. Bound to one and the other by something stronger than army discipline. A special bond shared among these brothers-in-arms, something none of them dared the thought of breaking.

Seamus felt his stomach roll, empty but for the murky warm water from the bottom of the pits. Yet now, for the first time in a handful of days, he did not mind his belly being so empty as he listened to the night-sounds.

The soft voice of the river flowed past him on two sides. Drying leaves stirred on the plum and swamp-willow.

The first, mournful howls of the wolves and coyotes, drawing closer . . . closer still to that bloody island of death.

Chapter 38

"Lieutenant! Lieutenant Johnson!"

Acting post adjutant for Fort Wallace rolled off his rope bunk in the O.D.'s room, yanking a suspender over his shoulder with one hand, the other rubbing grit from an eye.

"What is it, Sergeant?" he demanded, blinking in the dim light as he stumbled to his desk, where he turned up the wick on a lamp.

"These fellas, sir."

Hugh Johnson watched two poor excuses for humanity shoulder their way past the sergeant of the guard and enter his tiny office. He was immediately struck with the smell, figuring the men in some need of a bath. Their shabby clothing showed the lieutenant the pair had been out on the prairie for some time. Torn, greasy, and bloody. And the way they limped in tender-footed in those cracked, dusty boots.

Still, Johnson's nose troubled him, picking up something more than the stench of sour sweat. A days'-old odor of cooked meat and alkali water seemed to seep from the civilians' every pore.

"You are?" Johnson asked, yanking up the second suspender.

"Jack Stillwell, sir. Forsyth's scouts. Me . . . and him."

Johnson looked over the old man. "He's about done in. Sergeant, get this man to the infirmary."

"Yessir. Come 'long with me, ol' timer."

"Name's Trudeau. Pierre Trudeau, by God. Me and boy, we been to hell and back . . ."

Johnson watched the old man and the sergeant fade into the light before he realized he had pulled his watch from his pocket. Holding it at the length of the fob under the pale, saffron lamplight, the lieutenant noted the time, muttering under his breath.

"Eleven—goddamned—o'clock." He turned, looking Stillwell over again. "Now, what's this about Forsyth's men?"

"I was with the major up on the Republican." Jack gushed it out. "Me and ol' Pete snuck off five days ago. Forsyth sent me for relief. Need to talk with the post commander, Colonel Bankhead."

"Relief?"

"Listen, goddammit. Forsyth and the rest of his outfit—we got ourselves pretty chewed up. There was two dead when I left the first night."

"Two dead," Johnson repeated, skirting his tiny desk for some paper and the stub of a pencil.

"There's likely more dead now," Stillwell kept on. "The way we was having the wounded pile up that first day. No telling how many the Cheyenne shot up since me and Pete escaped."

"You escaped?" Johnson asked, striding past Stillwell to the open door.

"Yessir. We escaped and been walking ever——"

"Guard!" Johnson was hollering at the door. Footsteps dashed up outside. "You'll find Colonel Bankhead at the sutler's store. Tell him word has arrived that Major Forsyth is in sore need of a relief expedition."

Johnson turned back to the young civilian as the guard trotted off into the black of night. "Yesterday morning Bankhead dispatched H Company under Carpenter to patrol west of here along the Denver Road."

"I run onto a couple darkies riding with dispatches to Carpenter's outfit," Stillwell disclosed. "Give 'em Major Forsyth's map."

"What the hell you give it to them boys for?"

"Carpenter's gonna need it," Jack explained, sinking in a ladder-backed chair that complained as he settled on it.

"We could've used that map," Johnson griped. "The colonel's gonna be mighty angry about you giving away Forsyth's map like——"

"What the hell am I going to be so angry about . . . besides you interrupting my game of dominoes, Mr. Johnson?" asked Colonel Bankhead in his loud but cheerful voice. He strode into the room grandly, bringing with him the odors of cheese and pungent cigar smoke, his eyes flicking from his adjutant to the young civilian in tattered clothing. "And just what's all this about Forsyth needing relief?" He looked from Stillwell to Johnson, back to Stillwell.

Jack told his story in a single gush, from the dawn attack, to the three big charges and the snipers on both banks and the horses all killed by Indians or the scouts using them for barricades and surgeon Mooers down with a head-wound, then Lieutenant Beecher shot in the side and died that sundown before they started cutting up the horses and digging for more water, then Forsyth gave him the map and sent him on his way into the night with word for the colonel but he ran onto the two brunettes riding for Carpenter's camp so he gave them the map and the message, then turned his nose east for Fort Wallace and the colonel.

Bankhead sighed, slowly settling in the horsehide chair behind Johnson's tiny desk. He tapped a finger against his lower lip. The size of the colonel made the desk look even smaller. Leaning over, he turned up the lamp so far that the wick smoked. By this time the whole post was on the alert. Voices were heard hollering to one another across the parade, announcing the arrival of the scouts, spreading what rumor they had of the siege on the island and talking one another up on the rescue they wagered was about to set forth.

At the doorway, listening through Stillwell's short story of the day-long fight, were two civilians: Richard Blake, a clerk with the fort commissary, and the post sutler, Homer Wheeler.

"Homer," the colonel said, "you're a good soldier but a damned poor domino player."

"That your way of telling me I can go along with you, Henry?"

"Damn right it is." Bankhead turned to his sergeant of the guard. "If they aren't up, inform all company captains there will be a meeting in my office in ten minutes. No, make that five minutes. And tell them to alert their units, we'll be selecting companies for light marching order in . . . in one hour. Now, go!"

"One hour, sir?"

"I gave you an order, Sergeant!"

"Yessir!"

"Lieutenant, take down a message to Captain Carpenter," Bankhead began, rising from the chair and patting it for the adjutant's attention.

Johnson sat, dipping his best quill in the inkwell, then began moving his shaking hand over the foolscap. There had been nothing this exciting for him since the battle of Vicksburg. His hand flew across the page, transcribing Bankhead's orders.

> *Headquarters, Fort Wallace, Kansas*
> *September 22, 1868, 11 P.M.*

Brevet Lieutenant-Colonel L. H. Carpenter,
On Scout.

Colonel:

The commanding officer directs you to proceed at once to a point on the Dry Fork of the Republican, about seventy-five or eighty miles north, northwest from this point, thirty or forty miles west by a little south from the forks of the Republican, with all possible despatch.

Two scouts from Colonel Forsyth's command arrived here this evening and bring word that he (Forsyth) was attacked on the morning of Thursday last by an overpowering force of Indians (700), who killed all the animals, broke Colonel Forsyth's leg with a rifle-ball, and severely wounded him in the groin, wounded Surgeon Mooers in the head and wounded Lieutenant Beecher in several places. His back is supposed to be broken. Two men of the command were killed and eighteen or twenty wounded.

Then men bringing word crawled on hands and knees two miles, and then traveled only by night on account of the Indians, whom they saw daily.

Forsyth's men were entrenched in the dry bed of the

creek with a well in the trench, but had only horse-flesh to eat and only sixty rounds of ammunition.

General Sheridan orders that the greatest despatch be used and every means employed to succor Forsyth at once.

Colonel Bankhead will leave here in one hour with one hundred men and two mountain howitzers.

Bring all your scouts with you.

Order Doctor Fitzgerald at once to this post, to replace Doctor Turner, who accompanies Colonel Bankhead for the purpose of dressing the wounded of Forsyth's party.

"Now sign it, Lieutenant. As my adjutant."

"Yessir," Johnson replied. Finishing the dispatch with a flourish of his pen.

I am, Colonel, very respectfully
your obedient servant,

Hugh Johnson,
First Lieutenant Fifth Infantry,
Acting Post Adjutant

"Did I get down everything right, Mr. Stillwell?" Bankhead said, turning on the young scout.

He swallowed. "Yessir, far as I knew when I left. But, I already told them two brunettes about it all too."

"I know," Bankhead replied. "But I'll trust this dispatch to explain things to Carpenter just the same."

"May I go with you, sir?"

Bankhead eyed the youngster. "You're in pretty bad shape, son. Probably wore out and in need of a decent meal and some sleep."

"I asked if I could go, Colonel," Stillwell repeated, standing straight in his shabby, bloody clothing.

Bankhead turned to Blake at the door. "Richard, I want to see just how much food you can stuff in this boy before we pull out."

"You got it, Colonel," Blake answered, waving Stillwell

out the door. "Let's get you some supper . . . on the colonel."

Bankhead turned back after watching Stillwell limp out of the room on his wounded feet. He impatiently patted Johnson on the shoulder. "Once you've got a courier on the way . . . immediately—get the telegraph operator out of his bunk and get word of this to General Sheridan. Now see that this message is started by courier . . . *immediately.*"

"They'd probably be somewhere near Sandy Creek, sir."

"Sandy Creek, Cheyenne Wells . . . I don't give a damn," Bankhead blustered, running a palm across his thinning hair and bald spot. "Just give the order to your courier that he's not to get out of the saddle until he locates Carpenter."

"Not out of the saddle . . . yes*sir!*"

"Reuben!"

Corporal Waller heard his name called, but nonetheless worked his black cheek down in the warmth of his saddle blanket. Dreaming of home back in Mississippi before the war, and the way his mama called out to him each long summer night to come in to bed with his brothers and sisters.

"Reuben Waller!"

And that voice sounded a damned lot like his owner's, the man he had followed on foot, trotting behind the owner's big thoroughbred into and out of battle after battle after defeat through the war. Until Reuben figured out he no longer had to return to the plantation behind his owner in the tattered butternuts and instead wandered west to Kansas looking for a start.

"Corporal!"

He sat up, blinking his eyes, realizing he was on the prairie, encamped near Sandy Creek with H Company. On patrol.

"What is it?" he asked, bleary-eyed and staring up in the dark at the three black men looking down at him in the light of some six-hour coals.

"These two couriers just come in from Wallace," one of the night pickets disclosed. "Say they gotta see the captain 'bout something."

He shook his head. "Don't you boys know better'n that? When the captain getting his sleep, goddammit——"

"We was give this map for the captain." One of the couriers shoved round the picket's carbine. "It's mighty important, Corp'ral. Major Forsyth got hisself in a bad way of things."

"Forsyth?" Waller bolted out of his blankets.

"Yessir," the courier answered. "His scouts got themse'ves shot up by Roman Nose."

"Why didn't you say that in the first place?" Waller burst as he leaped to his feet, his smile suddenly bright in the cloudy darkness. He yanked on the first courier as he turned and set off.

"Captain Carpenter won't mind me waking him up to hear this news!"

"Just gimme some coffee, biscuits, and some side-meat that don't whinny or bray," John Donovan requested of Lieutenant Johnson as they hurried across the Fort Wallace parade, headed for sutler Wheeler's store.

Minutes ago in the small hours of the morning of 23 September, Donovan and A. J. Pliley had scrambled off the eastbound coach coming in from Denver on the Federal Road. After reaching the road ranch outside of Cheyenne Wells, the station-master had treated Forsyth's messengers to a royal breakfast of bacon, fresh eggs, and sourdough flapjacks. With their bellies full for the first time in the better part of a week, both men dozed until the catch-up call awakened them. Outside the station-master and his hired hand harnessed a new team for the incoming coach.

Once the ragged, bleary-eyed scouts were on board and rocking their way toward Fort Wallace in the brick-red, yellow-wheeled Dearborn coach, they watched the stars whirl overhead as they regaled their fellow passengers with bloody tales of three days' fighting on Forsyth's island.

With a great deal of shouting and excitement, Fort Wallace sprang alive for the second time that short, summer night. Two more civilians showing up out of the prairie black of night, asking for Colonel Bankhead.

"He isn't here," Hugh Johnson explained, sleepy-eyed again, checking his watch beneath the lamp he refused to turn up this time. His red eyes came wide when he closely studied the two men standing before him in his tiny office. "You? You from Forsyth too?"

"How you know?" Donovan asked.

"Young fella and an old man came in late last night——"

"Jack Stillwell? He still here?"

"No, sir. Left as guide for Colonel Bankhead."

"When'd they pull out?"

"About an hour ago."

"The old man . . . Trudeau—he go with 'em?"

"He was used up, I'm afraid," Johnson replied, settling in his chair. "He's in bed, the infirmary. Not sure how he'll fare."

Donovan turned on his partner, collapsed in a hard chair. "A. J. That's where you need to be. In a bed like Pete."

"Where you going?" Pliley asked weakly, about done in.

"I'm riding out of here soon as the lieutenant gets me some rations." He turned on Johnson. "You got a surgeon here for Pliley? He's in a bad way."

The lieutenant shook his head. "Surgeon Theo Turner set out with Bankhead. Carpenter's been ordered to send surgeon Fitzgerald back before he sets out north."

"Make sure the surgeon sees to Pliley when he gets here."

"Him," Johnson replied, "and that Trudeau too."

"By the way, you'll want this," Donovan said, pulling the folded scrap of paper from his greasy shirt. He watched Johnson's eyes read Forsyth's pencil scratchings once, then twice.

The lieutenant looked up, with amazement, even admiration spreading across his face. "You had no surgeon——"

Donovan scratched his fuzzy cheek, cutting the soldier off. "How'd Bankhead figure on going?"

Johnson turned, consulting the map on his wall. He traced a line with his finger. "North by northwest, cross the Beaver, from there to——"

"That'll take him too damned long," Donovan snapped. "Likely Forsyth and the rest be dead by then." Suddenly, John's face lit up. "Where's this Carpenter's outfit you was talking about 'while back?"

Johnson held a fingertip on the map, west and north some

of Wallace. "Most likely be here tonight, on Sandy Creek. Heading over toward Cheyenne W——"

"That's where I'll go," Donovan said quietly, almost to himself as he held the lamp up, casting a murky, yellow light on the wall-map.

"You'll miss him now."

"No, I won't," Donovan replied. "I'll head out this way . . . most likely run onto him somewhere . . . somewhere out there." His fingertip circled a good-sized chunk of eastern Colorado Territory. He turned on the lieutenant. "You have a half-dozen soldiers what can ride with me?"

"No soldiers left I can spare, mister," Johnson apologized. "But, I did get a wire from General Sheridan little while ago, saying I had his authorization to pay a hundred dollars to any civilians who volunteered to go to Forsyth's relief."

"That count me?" Donovan asked, his voice rising.

"Yes, I suppose it does."

"What we waiting for, Lieutenant? Get your guards busy rounding up some hungry civilians who want to take old Phil Sheridan up on his hundred-dollar gamble . . . and find me that side-meat, by God. Side-meat that don't fight the bit, whinny, or bray! By God, I'm heading out to find this Captain Carpenter!"

Chapter 39

A late-summer sun came up on this, 23 September, their seventh day on the island. With the Indians apparently gone, those survivors still strong enough ventured out to hunt in the coming light. They found no game and were forced to return to Major Forsyth with their news.

Everyone notched their belts a little tighter. Said their prayers. And tried to stay out of the scorching sun as they kept constant watch toward the south and east, eyes yearning for some sign of troops coming to their rescue. Ears always on the alert for a distant bugle-call.

Besides the constant, heavy drone of the flies carpeting everything in black masses, the only sound that met their ears was the quiet rustle of the dry-leafed cottonwood and swamp-willow. As the afternoon sun slipped in its westward path, Seamus Donegan watched Sigmund Shlesinger pull a small, three-and-a-half-by-eight-inch notebook from his shirt.

"That your journal, Slinger?" Seamus asked as the young scout wet the nib of a stubby pencil.

He grinned self-consciously. "Try to write when no one's paying attention. Figured you was asleep, what with your eyes closed."

Seamus smiled. "It's sleep . . . or have to think about being hungry. Forced to think on things I don't want to think on, Slinger."

The youngster nodded, bending over his notebook he laid open on a knee.

"You mind reading to me?" Seamus asked.

A startled look crossed his face. "It ain't much, Mr. Donegan. I just write a few words what happens each day."

"A few words is all that counts. Go 'head. Read it to me."

Slinger cleared his throat, then began reading in a soft voice:

"Friday, August 28, 1868. I put my name down for scouting. Drawed horses.

"Saturday 29. Drawed arms and grubb. Started at 4 o'clock P.M. Struck the Salina River at 11 o'clock in the night. Heavy rain all night. I was detailed for guard.

"Sunday 30. Started at 8 o'clock. Raining all day. Stop for rest at 12 o'clock.

"Monday, August 31, 1868. Found a deserted Indian camp.

"Tuesday, September 1. Traveled as usual. No wood.

"Wednesday 2. Struck the Beaver Creek. Plenty plums and grapes.

"Thursday, September 3, 1868. Got out of grubb.

"Friday 4. Was purty hungry.

"Saturday 5. Got in a hay camp. Little to eat. Charged on haymakers supposed to be Indians on their return from Fort Wallace. One of our boys was thrown from the horse. Badly injured. Arrived in Fort Wallace at 12 to 2 o'clock in night.

"Sunday, September 6, 1868. Took it easy in Wallace.

"Monday 7. Stopped in Wallace.

"Tuesday 8. Slept with Franklin in Pond City.

"Wednesday, September 9, 1868. Prepared to leave in the morning of the 10th.

"Thursday 10. Left Wallace for Sheridan. Mexicans had a fight with Indians. Two of them were killed. We took up the Indians' trail leading north. Found two wagons and cattle, which the Indians drove from the Mexicans.

"Friday 11. Lost trail. Marched on." He looked up, grinning a bit. "I didn't write anything more down till the fifteenth."

"Go ahead, Slinger. I think it's good."

"Do you?"

"I really do."

He cleared his throat. "Tuesday, September 15, 1868. Our grubb is nearly out.

"Wednesday 16. Seen signal fire on a hill three miles off in evening late.

"Thursday 17," the youngster read, then paused. His Adam's apple bobbed as he choked down the galling remembrance of it. "About 12 Indians carched on us. Stampeded seven horses. Ten minutes after about 600 Indians attacked us. Killed Beecher, Culver and Wilson. Wounded nineteen men and killed all the horses. We was without grubb and water all day. Dug holes in the sand . . ." He paused again, his eyes moist. "Dug holes in the sand with our hands."

"You don't have to read more if you don't want, Slinger."

He smiled at the Irishman through the glistening eyes. "Thanks, but I ain't got much left to go. Friday, September 18, 1868. In the night I dug my hole deeper. Cut meat off the horses and hung it up on the bushes. Indians made a charge on us at daybreak, but retreated. Kept shooting nearly all day. They put up a white flag. Left us at 9 o'clock in the evening. Rained all night.

"Saturday 19. The Indians came back again. Kept sharpshooting all day. Two boys started for Fort Wallace. Rained all night.

"Sunday 20. Dr. Mooers died last night. Raining part of the day. Snow about one inch thick. Indians kept sharpshooting." Slinger looked up from his journal. "You remember Monday, don't you, Mr. Donegan?"

"Monday?" he replied, his mind squeezing on it, trying to remember. Some things so foggy, others as clear as rinsed crystal.

"Day we went to scalp the three Injuns."

"Yeah. I remember now."

"Some of the fellas give me hard time. And you . . . you helped me."

Seamus did remember then. He grinned, feeling a bit renewed. "The scalps. Yes."

"Monday, September 21, 1868. Scalped three Indians which were found about fifteen feet from my hole concealed in the grass.

"Tuesday 22. Killed a coyote and ate him all up." His eyes rose from that last journal entry. "Can't for the life of me figure out what to write for today."

Seamus smiled gently. "Why don't you wait till evening?"

Sigmund closed the journal slowly. "S'pose you're right . . . 'bout waiting."

"In the meantime, let me recite something I memorized. last night. You like poetry?"

"Never read much of it to know if I like it or not."

"I . . . I always liked poetry. Irish poets mostly," Seamus replied, his eyes wistful as they gazed upon the far horizon shimmering beneath the late afternoon sun.

"I'd . . . like to hear the poem, Mr. Donegan."

Seamus gazed at the youngster a moment, then away again. "Like I said, I read it last night. In the major's pit. Forsyth wrote it himself."

"The major's writing poetry?"

"I don't figure he'd want it to get out, Slinger . . . least not to everyone. But, he let me read what he'd been writing in his little book, 'cause he knows I can read."

Shlesinger leaned forward, his red-rimmed eyes showing fatigue like all the rest, yet an eager curiosity lit within them all the same.

Donegan began:

> "When the foe charged on the breastworks
>   With the madness of despair,
> And the bravest souls were tested,
>   The little Jew was there.

> "When the weary dozed on duty
>   Or the wounded needed care,
> When another shot was called for,
>   The little Jew was there.

> "With the festering dead around them,
>   Shedding poison in the air,
> When the crippled chieftain ordered,
>   The little Jew was there."*

The Irishman gazed now at the youngster, finding him wide-eyed. Eventually the stunned youth spoke.

"He . . . the major's talking 'bout me, ain't he?"

* Original poem written by Maj. George A. Forsyth—author.

"With words that would make any man proud, Slinger. That's why I'll cover your backside any time. You've proved yourself a man."

"You mean that . . . honest, Mr. Donegan?"

He nodded, grinning. "Every word of it. I'm proud to know you . . . fight alongside you, meself."

Slinger scrambled over, presenting his powder-smudged hand to Donegan, dragging his floppy hat from his head.

"I'm proud I fought alongside you . . . and your uncle, Irishman."

They shook. Then Seamus leaned back into his little patch of shade beneath the blanket he had spread over outstretched willow-limbs. Closing his eyes.

"Think I'll . . . sleep for a while, Slinger . . . you don't mind."

Wallace is more than a hundred miles away. Might as well be ten thousand for all you can do about. And Jennie's farther still . . .

Beneath both tired eyes sagged pouches as if Seamus had been stung by hornets.

Not a bleeming soul you can name would claim to give a blessed damn about this fight that's turned into a struggle to stay alive. On this island that'll likely be the grave of us all . . .

The big floppy-brimmed hat kept most of the troublesome flies from his face. Yet they and the hot-footed red gnats still found his ears and neck, and any bare skin he had overlooked.

Blessed goddamned river . . . in the middle of hell. Ain't leading nowhere. River like this just brings a man's thinking back on himself again . . .

The flies buzzed, the gnats droned. Every time he shifted the hat slightly, dozing off, the late sun's rays crept beneath the brim to slash at his face. That merciless light shimmered off the ridges and the sandy riverbed itself, dazzling, making his eyes water until he fell asleep.

In that pre-dawn darkness of the twenty-third, Captain Carpenter had roused his company in the bracing darkness, informing them they had no more than a half-hour for breakfast and to prepare themselves to stand to horse.

Here and there above that company of black faces a star peeked through the cloudy sky as a gusty, cold wind whipped the collars of their tunics when Lieutenant Orleman gave the command.

"Stand to horse! At ease, boys. The captain wants a word with you."

Carpenter stepped forward, wiping a hand across his mustache to free the last drops of that final cup of coffee Reuben Waller had poured for him. He didn't know how to begin, really. Not knowing where they were headed for sure. He had pored over the Forsyth map again and again, studying that big, black X Forsyth had planted there. Knowing the courier said the scouts were on a dry fork of the Republican. Hell, there were a lot of dry forks of that river.

And worst of all, Louis H. Carpenter wasn't sure what he was leading his men into.

"By now most of you've heard where we're heading this morning," he began, shuffling a boot. "Don't need to tell any of you how bad those white men probably been shot up by the Cheyenne and Sioux been running crazed round this country."

Louis watched his two lieutenants smile, shifting their belts. He figured they were ready. *But, what of these men who have never had themselves a real scrap of it before?*

"But I figure we're their best bet for staying alive, men. There's no veterans among you to know what we're heading into, but it's time H Company showed the army what it's made of. We're going to make a hard march of it . . . doing what horse soldiers do best."

The Negro troopers hollered and hooted, cheering their loudest, knowing they were at ease for this talk before climbing into the saddles. Their sudden, enthusiastic response caused their captain to choke on his next words.

He turned to Dr. Fitzgerald. "My standing orders from Bankhead are that if we run into trouble, I'm to send you and an escort back to Wallace."

"I don't really think——"

"But, I'm forgetting I ever heard that order, Surgeon. You'll ride with us."

"Now you're talking, Carpenter!"

"What of our supply train, Captain?" asked Lieutenant Banzhaf.

"Going with us as well." He turned back to his soldiers, who came suddenly straight. Every mouth of a sudden silent. Carpenter stepped forward two more steps, grinding one fist inside a palm.

"Men, I fought with Major George A. Forsyth at The Wilderness. I was there when he took three rebel minnie-balls in the Shenandoah. So . . . I think you all know how I personally feel about this march to rescue the major's command. And I'm sure all of you will remember it was soldiers like Major Forsyth who helped Bill Sherman and Phil Sheridan win the war for the North. None of you have to look back that far to remember life in the South for a black man before the war."

"Captain?"

He turned to his orderly. "Yes, Corporal Waller."

"I think I speak for all the men, sir. We want to be the ones find the major and his scouts. Wherever you lead us, by damned, sir—we gonna follow you."

Reuben turned toward the rows of eager black men restless beside their sleek horses. "That right, men?"

"Hurrah!"

"Hurrah for Forsyth!"

"Hurrah for Captain Carpenter!"

With their cheers ringing in his ears, Louis Carpenter turned and flung a hand to his chief of scouts, J. J. Peate, sending him and his contingent of white civilian trackers out as he climbed aboard his mount.

"Mount!" came the cry from First Lieutenant Orleman.

"Mount!" bawled the first sergeant.

There was a squeak of saddle leather and a rattle of bit-chains, a shuffle of hooves and a snort from the animals.

"Bring 'em around and point 'em north, Lieutenant," Carpenter ordered. "We're marching at a gallop!"

Chapter 40

$\mathcal{R}$euben watched Captain Carpenter take off his hat and wipe his brow as he climbed the knoll while the sun's light sank from the sky.

On the twenty-third they had put thirty-five grueling miles behind them, alternating between a walk and a trot, with pickets sent out wide on both flanks, before Carpenter finally ordered them into camp well after dark. On the twenty-fourth, they had been turned out before the moon sank from the sky for a cold breakfast, taking no time to boil coffee. Orders passed quietly to saddle and stand to horse, while they ate the hard-bread and a handful of the bacon come down from the supply wagons.

Few of the men ate. The majority of the buffalo soldiers took only a piece of bread for their bellies, knowing they would not have another chance to eat until a noon-rest. Most of them had no real appetite now anyway, thinking on those men on that island, somewhere off in the distance. With nothing to eat but horses killed by screaming Indians eight days gone now. If imagining the stench of decaying horse-flesh was not enough for a man to lose his appetite, then the thought of eating fat bacon while those white men had no food surely was.

Waller had been proud that almost all save for the most arrogant had turned down the bacon. Deciding to save the side-meat for the major's men.

Throughout that long, hot day, Corporal Reuben Waller

had ridden a succession of mounts, required to ride at least twice as many miles as the rest of the cavalry.

Under orders of his company commander, Reuben had provided the communication link between Carpenter's ground-eating cavalry and Lieutenant Banzhaf's wagon-train. The orderly was to stay on high ground when possible to keep Banzhaf's train in sight. And when it disappeared from the view of the rear of the cavalry columns, Waller was faced with riding back and forth between the two throughout the rest of the day, carrying word between the two commands.

Not long after nine o'clock, the lieutenant's teamsters finally threw their weight against their squealing brakes, halting in a camp chosen by J. J. Peate's white scouts near some shallow water holes. The wagons were quickly corraled, mules picketed, and men rolled into their blankets without argument.

Company H, 10th U.S. Negro Cavalry, grabbed what sleep they could before setting off across the trackless plains in search of a nameless sandy island on one of the many dry forks of the Republican River.

Eight.
With that last notch he carved just after sunrise, Seamus Donegan counted eight notches in the stock of the Spencer carbine they had issued him at Hays. September 24. The eighth dawning of the hot sun over this stinking island.

It had been a few days now, he could not be sure how many, that he had felt any hunger. Grown used to the gnawing pinch of it. Only thirst now. Even his appetite for whiskey gone. Knowing he would gamble most anything for a cup filled with clear, cold water. Not the half-warm, murky fluid that seeped into the bottom of their rifle-pits that reminded him of the black-bean soup served him in that little tavern in Boston Towne, even the alkaline water they took from the river itself.

The last two nights the hills had been dotted with their share of coyotes and wolves, lured into the valley from the surrounding prairie by the strong stench of rotting carrion. He remembered thinking that the Cheyenne must have run off. Else the four-legged predators would dare not come in to sit and wait on their haunches, just out of range of his Henry as if they sensed how far his rifle could shoot.

He had tried anyway, until Sharp Grover told him to stop wasting cartridges on the far-away wolves. But he was angry, he had told Grover. And the army scout had eventually walked away, saying Donegan wasn't angry. Saying Donegan was just going mad.

The sun and the wait. The sun and the hunger. The sun and the not-knowing had a way of doing that to a man. Watching the others, watching yourself die a little bit more each day.

Sometime before dawn, Seamus had awakened slowly, startled to hear the soft voice of one of the men singing low, cracking in emotion or hunger or loss of blood.

> "Shall we gather at the river
> The beautiful, the beautiful river.
> Shall we gather at the river,
> That flows by the throne of God."

Donegan had wept, easily there in the dark. Laying his hand on the blanket-covered sandy mound beside him. Where he had scooped sand over the body of Liam O'Roarke.

Soon enough more of these men would be dead as well. Men who should not have perished. But would for want of attention to their horrible wounds. Like Farley's arm. Morton's eye blown out. Others stinking with infection.

His own arm itched. He touched the oozy ribbon of flesh with his fingers, brushing maggots off without looking. No longer could he stand to look at the wound, nor the dull, red streaks marching farther and farther up the arm each day.

By afternoon the bright sun was tracking a little more to the south, it seemed. Then he remembered it was getting on in the month of September. Soon it would be autumn. Then another winter come behind it.

The sun would feel good on his skin come that time of the year. He shuddered, recalling having his fill of cold on that trip he made from Fort Phil Kearny to Fort C. F. Smith, enough cold to make his bones ache for a lifetime.

Good to feel the sun now as it eased down from mid-sky,

reflecting off the sandy, umber bluffs like light off a quicksilver mirror.

He dabbed sweat from his tortured eyes, feeling them swim with the intense radiance, then leaned back under his willow and blanket shelter. The red gnats with the hot, stinging feet were at him again.

Blessed Mother of Virgins . . .

The sun was going down at last on this eighth day. He could take his sweaty hat off his head. That little place between crown and his skull was like the tiny brick oven where his mother baked black beans back in County Kilkenny. Hot enough to melt his brain.

Like Grover said . . . perhaps you are going mad, Seamus . . .

He closed his eyes, too weak to hold them open now, laughing to himself as he imagined him slipping into insanity, like trying to hold onto a steep slope of mud. With no place to get a grip. No way to hang on.

Seamus laughed to himself, sensing his brain turning to that soft, thick, amber syrup that was his favorite hot-buttered rum back in that little tavern in Boston-Towne-by-the-Bay.

That twenty-fourth day of September, Captain Carpenter goaded his wagon-burdened command into another forty-five grueling miles. No man complained at the pace. Especially after coming across one of the hostiles' hastily abandoned campsites that morning.

"All orders will be given verbally here on out," Carpenter told his two lieutenants as he climbed back atop his damp McClellan. "If we're giving calls with our damned bugles, every Indian in a twenty-mile radius is going to know we're coming. Mr. Banzhaf, keep your men closed up on the wagons . . . and the wagons close on my tail. Mr. Orleman, you'll see the men stay together. We're in Cheyenne country now, if there ever was one. Ride to the guidon, gentlemen."

He flung his arm forward as lieutenants and sergeants alike bawled their commands to move out at a trot once more.

Reuben Waller posted to the guidon, a little right and to the rear, where he was supposed to be. And sensed the fatigue coming over his mount, the first creamy lather appearing along the animal's flanks. His mother had talked to God a lot when he was a boy before heading off to war. But Reuben never had.

He supposed it was about time to start. Asking God to give this old horse strength to keep going on until they found those men on the island.

And as the afternoon wore on, Reuben got better at prayer. Asking God that Captain Carpenter and H Troop would get to that dry fork of the Republican River while there were still men alive to rescue.

Close to sundown army scout J. J. Peate drew up at the top of a ridge that sloped in an easy grade to the north. Behind them was bunch-grass and cactus prairie. Ahead of them lay a stretch of country verdant in buffalo-grass. The grass told a story any one-eyed, dim-witted man could read. And J. J. Peate was far from being dim-witted.

"How many ponies came through here?" Carpenter asked his chief of scouts, some worry etched on his face.

"Two thousand . . . at least."

"How many fighting men that make it?"

"I can't tell you for sure, Captain," Peate replied, moving up to the group studying the trampled grass in a swath a good four hundred yards wide. "Five hundred warriors. Maybe as much as eight hundred."

Carpenter didn't like that, J. J. could tell.

"That many could eat us up, fellas," the captain conjectured. Carpenter squinted, looking over a nearby hill, then turned to Reuben Waller. "Orderly, I'm sorry I've got to order you to the saddle. Ride back to Lieutenant Banzhaf. With the sun going down, he's got to get his wagons in here at all costs."

They watched Waller ride off, spurring his weary mount.

Carpenter looked at Peate again. "If those hostiles are still in the neighborhood, we've got a lot to worry about."

J. J. nodded grimly. "It's certain Forsyth hurt 'em, Captain. But not near bad enough. Their scouts spot this little outfit of yours, they just might like to get some licks in on your brunettes."

The captain pointed to the nearby hill. "If need be, fellas, we can defend that high ground. Let's go have a look, J. J."

While they saw no sign of the fleeing villages from the high ground, they did see a number of burial scaffolds on top of a nearby hill.

"Lieutenant Orleman, post a picket here who will remain in view of us and the column. Then join us on that hill."

After the short ride, Peate dropped to the ground with the others, awe-struck at the feel this hilltop gave him.

"They haven't been here long, Captain," he told Carpenter.

"Let's . . . let's have a look," Carpenter replied.

A half-hour later, they had examined five of the scaffolds. In each case the blanket-wrapped body showed the warrior had died of gunshot wounds. Slain ponies lay alongside each scaffold.

"Like you said, J. J., Forsyth did some damage," Carpenter whispered quietly as the sun sank in the west, a chill wind whispering up the slope of this hallowed ground.

"Those boys gave the Cheyenne back what they came for, Captain," Peate replied.

"Captain?" Lieutenant Orleman said as he rode up, dismounting. "Take a look down there."

At the bottom of a sharp ravine that led down to the river stood an elaborate buffalo-hide tipi.

"This one isn't all that old," Peate explained at the bottom of the slope. "New lodge-skins. An important man."

"Someone inside?" the captain asked.

"That's why this ceremonial lodge was left here," the scout replied. "A proper lodge burial for a special man."

"Chief?"

"Most likely."

With the failing light, they hurriedly examined the body, stretched upon a low scaffold inside the lodge. A gaping hole over the heart had been bathed before the victim had been placed in his best buckskins.

"Is this Roman Nose?" Carpenter inquired quietly.

"I don't know," Peate replied, puzzled, and not feeling any good for standing in the medicine lodge.

"Would you know him, J. J?"

The civilian shook his head. "It could be. I don't know.

Don't think any white man would know Roman Nose on sight."

He whispered, almost reverently. "Chances are good this is him. So I don't want this body disturbed further. Lieutenant, you'll take this drum back to camp for me. We've got preparations to make for the night."

Riding back to camp, Peate brooded that it was taking far longer than he wanted to reach the island. With every hour, every day, every sunset, he grew more scared Carpenter's bunch would arrive at the island too late.

If they were not killed by the Cheyenne warriors, then J. J. Peate was certain Maj. George A. Forsyth's scouts would die of hunger, thirst, and . . . despair.

Chapter 41

$\mathcal{M}$ ost of the men were already awake as the coming light shed itself on the valley of Arickaree. Nonetheless, the majority of them did not stir from the shade. Only a handful shouldered their Spencers and walked off the island in search of something that would fend off starvation just one more day.

Seamus had carved a ninth notch in the butt of his rifle by the time Sharp Grover brought him a foul-smelling soup in a tin cup. "What's this?"

"Hold your nose and drink it," Sharp advised.

"Holding my nose ain't going to help a't'all," Seamus replied. "My stomach knows it's rotten horsemeat."

"I got some down Forsyth," Sharp said, collapsing against the side of the pit. The seams on his weathered face appeared deeper than normal. "Major's in a bad way. Comes and goes. Don't know if he's dreaming or not."

Seamus wagged his head, watching the sun inch off the horizon. "Do any of us know, Sharp. What's the dream in this, or no."

"Forsyth's ordered all the able-bodied to make their escape tomorrow. If no help arrives today."

He looked at Grover. "What are the chances of that?"

"Slim," he answered. "A relief column should have been here by now."

"You must be figuring Stillwell or the rest made it to Wallace."

He nodded, daring not look at Donegan. "I am, Seamus.

I've got to keep hope alive. If not for you and the major. For myself."

Seamus reached over and squeezed Grover's hand. "Thanks, friend. I want to help you keep hope's candle burning as well."

The Irishman crawled up to his feet, weak and wobbly at first, leaning on the Spencer carbine. "What say we go hunting this morning, Sharp? You and me. Together. Maybe coyote. Perhaps some prairie dog. Might even run across a tasty morsel, say a side-dish like cactus."

Sharp rose as well, clamping a hand on Donegan's shoulder, eyes fixed on the flies buzzing round the Irishman's smelly wound. "I figured you had a mind to give up. Not tending your wound . . . not coming out of this pit for the past couple days."

"What's to get out for?" Then Seamus shook his head. "No, you're right, Sharp. There's a lot of reason to keep that candle burning."

Together they clambered over the lip of the pit, pushing saddles and bulwark aside. No longer did any of them really fear a return of the hostiles. It had been too many days now since a shot had been fired. And the enemy feared most was a faceless thief, come to rob them of hope, leaving despair in its place.

Seamus looked at Grover, smiling weakly. It felt good to use his legs again. The carbine was heavy at the end of his arm. For moments he felt light-headed, woozy, and once almost went down in the soft sand. But he was determined he would not fall, knowing how hard it would be to get back up.

Donegan grinned again. "Glad you're with me, friend."

Grover smiled back.

They walked toward the rising sun.

"Captain!"

Carpenter reined away from the long column of dusty blue and black troopers just then preparing to mount in the first light of dawn this twenty-fifth day of September. Reuben Waller tore up on his mount.

"Our flankers report riders coming in on a gallop, sir."

"Indians?"

Reuben shook his head, still a little out of breath. "Don't look like it—what I can tell."

"How many?"

"I figure half a dozen, Captain. Size of the dust."

"Let's go have us a look," Carpenter said, swinging into the saddle. "Lieutenant Orleman, you and Mr. Banzhaf have command here. Stand the men to horse and prepare to move out at once. Without any delays, I'm hopeful we'll find Forsyth's island by sundown."

Waller watched his captain remove his hat from his head as they loped up a nearby knoll.

"Horsemen, sir," the picket on the hill said quietly, pointing, as Waller and Carpenter reached him.

Reuben shaded his eyes against the morning light stretching itself along the east. "Coming on fast, Captain."

"And out of the southeast as well," Carpenter said as he reached into a pocket on his McClellan, pulling from it a pair of field-glasses. "Your guess was a good one, Corporal," he said a moment later, bringing the glasses from his eyes. "Five of them."

"They aren't Injuns then, Captain."

"No, look more like civilians. I'll wait here. You go escort them in."

Reuben enjoyed the flush of pride that washed over him as he kicked his horse into motion, spurring into the cool morning air before the dust rose and the sun came up and the horses got tired and lathered.

Up and down the rolling swales of the inland grass-sea he galloped, bearing on a spot he figured he would meet the five horsemen. When the group came within hailing distance he waved his hat at the end of his arm, seeing the men were dressed as civilians. No blue among them.

"You with Carpenter?" the lead man hollered as he began to slow his snorting animal.

"H Company, Tenth Negro Cavalry. Captain Louis H. Carpenter, commanding," Reuben replied, grinning with a dusty smile, and a salute.

"John Donovan," the civilian replied, presenting his hand to Reuben.

That surprised the Negro soldier. Even more the four other civilians who glanced quickly at one another.

"By damn," Donovan said, turning to his companions. "We done it, men! Made it to Carpenter's troop." He whirled on Waller, his horse restive and prancing. "Take me to the captain, boy. We ain't got time to lose now."

By the time Reuben loped over the last rise with the five horsemen, Carpenter was ordering the mount. Banzhaf's teamsters had their wagons and the ungainly ambulance stretched out across the prairie, ready to depart in the gray light of this new day. The entire company rose as one to saddle.

The captain turned to greet the incoming riders. Introductions were made all around with the shaking of hands and the tipping of dusty hats. No man in that group much concerned with social amenities or military niceties.

Donovan slapped some dust from his britches. "Captain, you're taking the long way in to that dry fork where Forsyth is."

"Surely, mister—you're aware of the wagons I'm escorting."

The civilian nodded. "I am. But, you must remember I just walked out of this country, and come across it on foot myself these last few days. I can take you there, directly— you want me to, Captain."

"Thank you, but I have some scouts assigned——"

"Carpenter, if you're not coming on now, we're going by ourselves. The island ain't far."

"How far?"

"Twenty miles."

"Good Lord, man! Why didn't you tell me?" Carpenter wheeled his horse, prancing.

"Mr. Orleman, you're in charge of the troops. Select thirty of the best horsemen from their number. They'll ride with me."

Carpenter watched his first lieutenant trot off to break his troop. He turned then to Second Lieutenant Banzhaf. "Mr. Banzhaf, you'll take your escort cross-country with the wagon-train as we have planned. I'll leave half the scouts with you, taking Peate and the rest with me."

"What's going on, Captain?" Banzhaf asked, his lips pressed.

"We're making a gallop for the island where this man says Forsyth's men can be found."

"May I suggest you take the ambulance with you, Captain?" Dr. Jenkins Fitzgerald asked as he inched up.

Carpenter considered a moment. "Good idea, Surgeon. Banzhaf, get four men to quickly off-load some rations into the ambulance . . . bacon, hardtack, and some coffee."

"God bless you, Captain Carpenter!" Donovan cheered. "Those boys been without decent food for over a week."

Carpenter grinned as he saw his command undergo an instant excitement. The thirty galloped up and halted, ready to ride. "It's just army chow, Mr. Donovan. Too bad I don't have decent food to give those men," he said, smiling.

The civilians chuckled.

"I pray this army food will do in its place," Carpenter added wryly. "All right, Mr. Donovan. Take us to Major Forsyth."

Reuben posted to the guidon, though he wanted to be riding up ahead with J. J. Peate and his scouts.

Carpenter was spurring his horsemen on at a fast trot. Waller knew there would be no slowing his captain now.

From time to time, the civilian Donovan yelled out, pointing, on occasion waving his hat in the air. Reuben figured it meant the man had recognized something familiar in the dismal terrain they were racing across.

They followed the wide swath of trampled grass for the most part. Crossing a narrow, dry stream, continuing north. Led by Donovan and Peate. Hurried on by Captain Carpenter himself. The sun peeked over the horizon as they nosed into some broken country and Reuben thought with some worry on his friends escorting Lieutenant Banzhaf's wagons. The captain had ordered them to come on at all possible speed, but in this stretch of territory, scarred and rumpled like a tattered bedspread on an old tick mattress, it would be hard for those wagons to make good time, having to pick their way through and around the way the terrain demanded.

The sun had just cleared the eastern prairie when Reuben noticed Peate and Donovan had reined up in a dusty halt. The rest of the army scouts clattered to a halt around them, sending up sprays of yellow dust in the new light. Their horses turning round and round. The white men were waving Carpenter and his thirty black horsemen on.

Then from the top of that ridge, Reuben heard the shouting voices, excited by the men standing in their stirrups as Lieutenant Orleman ordered a halt for the column. Carpenter and Waller dashed the last ten yards up the slope to join the scouts at the crest.

Down below lay a wide swath of sandy streambed. Through it a narrow sliver of water ran.

Donovan was screaming like a man gone mad, so loud now Reuben could not make sense of it. Carpenter and Peate ordered the civilian to hold his water till they got the glasses out.

"That's it, goddammit! I know that's it!" Donovan shouted.

Carpenter handed the field-glasses to Peate.

The scout looked it over for himself, nodded. "Look to the far end of the valley . . . just this side of the bend." He passed the glasses on to Donovan.

Despite Donovan's enthusiasm, Reuben didn't like the feel of it. Whatever it was down there, it gave him an eerie feeling. Buzzards blacked the overcast sky. Swooping and circling. Circling slowly. A wolf loped by down below, disappearing into the cottonwoods at the bottom of the slope where the ridge itself bled into riverbed.

Buzzards gave him the willies.

"Told you, by God!" Donovan was shouting, pounding Peate on the back as he handed over the field-glasses. "They're alive!"

"Whoooeee!" Waller was shouting before he realized his mouth was open, waving his hat in the air. The rest of the shiny-faced horsemen downslope set up a wild cheer, nudging, jostling one another, slapping one another in congratulations.

"You saw some movement down there, Peate?" Carpenter asked amid the noise.

He nodded. "We got here in time, Captain."

"Praise God for his blessings," Carpenter replied quietly. Then he twisted in the saddle. "Lieutenant Orleman! Select your best rider on the strongest horse. Dispatch him back to

Mr. Banzhaf with word to come on at all possible speed now. We've located the major's position . . . and his men! By God—we've found Forsyth!"

Off the ridge, down a steep slope they followed Carpenter, driving their horses, spurring hell-bent. Suddenly there was such an electrifying tension shared among the columns. So much that Waller did not notice Carpenter signaling him forward at first. Reuben hammered his heels into the snorting mount. Dashing past the guidon.

"Want you ride with me, Corporal!" the captain shouted, a smile of victory cutting his face. "Let's share this together."

"Thank you, sir!" he flung his voice into the dry wind.

Along the beaten grass beside the sandy riverbed. Stringing out a bit more now, the stronger horses lunged ahead, their riders restraining them no longer. Whoops and hollers from the civilians. J. J. Peate tall in the stirrups. Donovan waving his hat, then whipping the flank of his horse with it.

Reuben sensed the hair stand at the back of his neck, his skin prickling. What seemed like so many years since he had been among fighting men celebrating such joy.

They still could not see anything like the island Donovan had described, far down the riverbed. Around two more bends in the stream they raced. Stands of cottonwood blocked their view. Horses' hooves pounded the hard ground. Yet from the looks of things, not the first hooves to hammer this riverbed.

As they rounded a wide bend in the river, they got their first good view of a sizable stretch of the streambed. And with that view came the overpowering stench of death. Buzzards loomed overhead now.

Suddenly he saw movement. To his left. A lone man darting for the trees, slow and ungainly, running for his life. He stumbled and fell. Got back up, hurrying before he fell again. Scrambling to pick up his rifle before disappearing into the trees.

"Spread out!" Peate was hollering.

"Spread out like he ordered!" Carpenter echoed.

"They figure we're Injuns!" J. J. explained, his words quickly sapped in a dry scut of wind.

"Don't shoot!" Donovan was hollering, waving to two

men off to the right, north of the streambed. "It's me, John Donovan, by God!"

Suddenly the figure they had seen off to the left emerged from the trees, tossing both carbine and hat into the air, jumping clumsily again and again. His mouth like a tiny black O as he sang out.

Careening through the thick brush, kicking up skiffs of sand, scrambled more of the gaunt, wolf-like survivors. Reuben sensed his heart rise into his throat. Burning like nothing he'd felt before.

To his right, he watched the pair Donovan had first sighted, stumbling down the slope, hugging each other, stopping to dance round and round, then running arm in arm again. Something tugged at Waller now, unexplained, though he felt he recognized one of the two. Not sure, their wolfish, sunburned faces streaked, shining with tears.

And of a sudden, Reuben tasted salt himself. Felt the sting of his own tears whipping from the corners of his eyes.

He could never remember feeling this good in his life. Nor so close to his God.

Chapter 42

"By the saints!"

Donegan was crying, hammering Sharp Grover on the back, while round and round they danced.

Then raced down the dusty slope toward the riverbed, arm in arm, shaking their carbines in the air. Cracking voices crying out in whoops of joy.

Then stopped again for a moment, clutching each other and dancing round and round before they would run a little farther, still heading for the island and Forsyth and the rescuers all at the same time.

"Ain't that Doc Fitzgerald's dog?" hollered one of the scouts across the stream, pointing.

"It is, goddammit! It's Doc's dog! I 'member it from Wallace!"

A slim, brown greyhound burst ahead of the horsemen, tongue lolling, weaving in and out of the plum and buffalo-grass, adding its crazed bark to this wild celebration of deliverance.

From every bush and stand of swamp-willow on the river-bank rose the reedy huzzahs and cheers from the weakened, desperate men as they realized the horsemen were not painted warriors returned to finish them off. Instead, their lonely prayers had been answered. Someone had made it through to Wallace.

They were like wild men, not only in appearance and ragged, bloody clothing, but in the way they gaped and danced, whirling nonstop, running about pounding comrades on the

backs, hugging others. And in the midst of them all stood a
few too stunned to grasp that they had been rescued. Cries of
joy and pain from the wounded as well, the ones who could
not rise from their bloody blankets to join in the celebration.
Weeping, tears seeping ever so slowly, softening their
wounds.

Young Slinger ran to east end of the island to greet them,
one of the few with any strength left. A soldier on a buckskin
horse splashed out of the river, coming on at full tilt. Hollering out of the big hole in his black face. His momentum
carried him past Shlesinger, but not before the young scout
lunged for a hold on the soldier's saddlebag.

"Damn, you're hungry, boy!" the soldier exclaimed, bringing his mount to a knee-jarring halt, spraying sand in a
rooster-tail.

"You got food? Gimme some of your food!" Slinger
begged.

Together they loosened the three straps on the bag, filling
both of Slinger's hands with the hard-bread. More scouts
stumbled up as the soldier tossed out more of the "tacks" to
the starving men. They cried and ate, filling their mouths
and letting the tears pour. Then laughed and ate some more,
and still the tears flowed.

"They've come, Major," Grover said to Forsyth as he and
Donegan skidded to a halt at the edge of the rifle-pit, watching the men scramble for the bread, eating voraciously.

Forsyth kept swallowing, as if the news were something
hard to get down, to understand, to actually believe. His eyes
misted, blinking again and again. His tongue worked a bit,
trying to find words as he gazed downstream, watching the
approach of a familiar figure. An old friend.

The major turned momentarily to the Irishman. "D-Done-
gan?"

Seamus snorted back some dribble at the end of his nose.
"Major?"

"Remember that book you found among Liam's things?"
"Oliver Twist?"

He took a moment to answer. "Bring it to me . . .
please."

Donegan could not remember scrambling so fast out of the

pits as he did at that moment. Snatching the leather-bound volume, rushing back to hand it down to Forsyth.

The major painfully shifted his position, dragging both bad, bloody legs across the sand. He opened the Dickens novel, shuffling to a page near the end of the story as he turned his back on the approaching horseman.

Seamus sensed the clutch of something hot in his chest, knowing that Forsyth had never been prepared for this moment. As much as it had been anticipated, none of those men on the island had truly been ready for what they were suddenly made to feel. Yet still the major held his composure, as he had for long, long days of agony and waiting.

It appeared George Forsyth had become suddenly fearful that he would break down in front of the men he had held miraculously together through battle and starvation. Perhaps most afraid to look upon the face of his old friend from the Shenandoah campaign.

Donegan and Grover edged back, waiting, watching the drama. Three horsemen drew close, two white, one buffalo soldier. The white soldier in the center motioned for his lieutenant and the corporal to halt while he came on, alone.

The captain halted his pawing horse at the edge of the bloody pit where Maj. George A. Forsyth lay in the light of a new sun. On one side the temporary grave of Lt. Fred Beecher. On the other the resting place of Dr. John Mooers.

Beyond the circle others milled and swirled in a loud, profane celebration, soldiers and scouts and the rescued dancing, hollering, reveling in the approach of Fitzgerald's ambulance, surgeon and his driver bouncing on the plank seat. Fitzgerald's dog yapping at the spinning wheels.

Capt. Louis H. Carpenter finally slid from his saddle, dropping his reins to the sand, staring down at his old comrade-in-arms. For the longest time, he looked as if he did not know what to do. His shadow eventually moved across Forsyth.

The major slowly closed the book on a finger, as if to mark his place. Then turned, gazing up, squinting into the light in a shiny corona behind the commander of Company H.

"S-Sandy?" Carpenter croaked, unable to believe his eyes, to say anything more from the appearance of the scene. He yanked a bandanna from his pocket and snorted into it, attempting to regain his composure.

"Captain Carpenter . . ." Forsyth began formally, then bit his lip a moment.

Carpenter saluted, tears streaming unrestrained now. "Reporting for your relief . . . as requested, Major!"

"Lou——" Forsyth choked on the word, holding his hand up to his friend.

"Sandy!"

Carpenter tumbled down the side of the pit, taking Forsyth's hand, falling to his knees, hugging the major all at the same time. Both of them blubbering like young classmates at the academy.

"Mr? Mr. . . . Donegan?"

Seamus turned at the call of his name. Seeing the approach of a Negro soldier, the corporal. The hat he wore shadowed most of his face as he slid quickly from his lathered mount. From the looks of every one of the mounts, Donegan could tell the rescuers had charged the last few miles in.

"I'm Donegan," he answered, weak and limping toward the soldier. "Do I know you?"

The soldier ripped his hat off his head, a solid layer of brown dust plastered against the damp, black face. "Don't probably remember me."

"Waller? That you, Reuben Waller?"

His dirty face brightened, his smile cracking the dust. "You . . . you 'member me?"

" 'Course I do," Seamus replied quietly, dropping his carbine at last as he surged forward. More moisture suddenly stinging his eyes. He enfolded the buffalo soldier in his big arms, squeezing and pounding. Waller struggled to free his arms so he could return the embrace. Then they were bouncing together, laughing and crying as one.

"Gawddammed right I remember you, Reuben Waller. By the Mither of Saints, it's a blessing to see your ugly face!"

The main trouble for the ambulance was not in negotiating the sandy riverbed, but in steering clear of the gaunt, wolfish men who swarmed over it once told it carried rations.

Major Forsyth had ordered Sergeant McCall to see to it that no man wolfed down too much at this first sitting, as he knew of the sickness caused by so much food after so long a period of starvation.

Carpenter could not believe the stench of the place. But at his first mention of it, Forsyth realized he no longer noticed the decomposing animals, the rotting, maggot-infested wounds.

"Let's get you and the rest off this island, Sandy."

"Over there. That plum thicket—some good shade."

By the time Carpenter's thirty had transported the last of the wounded off the island, Banzhaf's teamsters had whipped their mules into the valley. In a matter of moments, the entire company of brunettes was attacking the wagons, pulling out tents, mess-gear, readying surgical equipment.

Lifted onto a canvas stretcher, Forsyth was carried beneath the shade of the canvas fly surgeon Fitzgerald would use as his temporary field hospital. The doctor hovered over the folding table, inspecting both leg wounds. More so the shattered leg than the ugly thigh.

"You did that surgery yourself, I'm told," he mentioned gruffly, peering over his spectacles.

"I did, Doctor."

A hint of a smile crossed his face. "Not bad for a novice, Major." He sighed. "Trouble is, the left leg is filled with infection."

Forsyth felt the hot, midday breeze that rattled the canvas overhead as the surgeon settled on a camp-stool.

"What are you saying?"

"Major, I'm suggesting amputation."

Forsyth gazed down at the left leg, cursing the bullet that had shattered his leg. Cursing as well the man who had dropped him on the leg, driving bone from the skin.

He swallowed hard. Looking back at Fitzgerald, he asked, "If I choose to keep the leg, what . . . what are my chances?"

Fitzgerald scratched his cheek absently. "Seventy–thirty, Major."

"Against me?"

He nodded. "Against you. And with your fever spiking like it is, I don't think we have much time to wait."

Forsyth turned to Carpenter. "Lou, pour me another dram of that brandy, will you?"

He threw the hot alcohol back, wiped his lips, then gazed at the surgeon. "Doctor, I'll take those short odds."

"I must advise against wait——"

"You have my decision. I refuse the amputation."

"I don't think you understand. Your life's worth more than that damned leg of yours."

"Dr. Fitzgerald," interrupted Captain Carpenter, stepping to his elbow, "the major's made his decision."

He pressed his lips in exasperation. "Then let it stand for the record that if we wait, Major—tomorrow will in all likelihood be too late."

"Understood, Doctor," Forsyth replied, his head sinking to a canvas coat-pillow once more.

Fitzgerald stood. "Short of amputation on that leg, I must perform some surgery . . . draining it before I set the bones . . . tenting the wounds——"

"Do what you must . . . to save the leg," Forsyth said.

Fitzgerald turned to Carpenter. "Captain, I'll need your men to chop down that small cottonwood at the end of the island."

"What in heaven's name for?" the major asked.

He turned back to Forsyth. "A splint. For that leg. It's the only thing around here big enough, yet not too large."

"Perfect," Carpenter replied. "The right length of it cut, chopped in half, then hollowed."

"We'll pad it with some cotton field dressings I have, Major."

"I'm ready . . . when you are, Doctor."

"I don't really know any words," Reuben Waller said self-consciously, rolling the brim of his hat in his big, black hands.

Seamus looked down at the fresh soil they had tamped down in a long scar at the top of the slope, the new earth drying out beneath the hot sun late on the afternoon of this twenty-fifth day of September. The other fresh graves had been spread out. Those who had died on one end of the island were buried near the places they had fallen.

Across his arms the Irishman had carried his uncle up this umber and red slope before he turned a shovel of dirt.

"That's all right, Reuben," Seamus replied finally. "I think quiet is good for Uncle Liam. We'll just stand here for a while . . . and let the wind blow across this place."

Later, Seamus turned to the soldier, throat burning. "Smells good up here, don't it?"

"It do at that . . . Seamus." Reuben grinned a moment, self-conscious. "Still can't get used to calling you by your Christian name."

"You'll get used to it. It's what my friends call me."

The wind that caressed this jutting finger of land overlooking the valley of the Arickaree sang no mournful song as had that cruel wind slashing off the Big Horn Mountains when Carrington's men laid eighty-one of their own to rest. Instead, this wind whispered only softly spoken words at his ear, foretelling of winter-coming.

Bringing with it remembrances of cold walks across the heath with his uncles. Coming home at the end of the day, to a house where his mother lived. Steaming kettle a'boil in the moss-rock fireplace, fragrances like strong perfumes he would likely never forget. The sound of those strong, male voices in that house after the death of Seamus's father. There for him until the uncles sailed away to Amerikay.

Now there was one. Gone west, Liam said. Yet not to California.

He felt empty again, like someone had gone and sprinkled alum on his insides. No longer filled with the hope that had guided him since leaving behind the forts of the upper Bozeman Road a year gone by. Liam in the ground. Ian O'Roarke somewhere, out there.

And Jennie.

He remembered the fragrance of her hair after she had a chance to wash it. Remembered the play of light on the water droplets that clung to her freckled, ivory flesh in the Little Piney.

"Were that love be stronger than need," Seamus whispered. "Needing to know."

"What's that you said?" Waller asked quietly.

"Just remembering some poetry, Reuben."

"I don't know any poetry, Seamus."

"Most of what I know is Irish. And I'm thinking on one written by a man from Balbriggan:

"A growing youth—I was timid of tongue,
And never trysted with ladies young,
But since I have won into passionate age,
Fierce love-longings my heart engage."

"Sounds like you said that for a woman."

He smiled, eventually, and nodded once. "Yes, Reuben. Were it not for love of a woman, I would not have come to Amerikay . . . nor joined Forsyth's scouts. And were it not for the love of another woman, I don't believe I would have lived to see this day of rescue."

Reuben was silent for a long time, leaning on his shovel, staring at the sun settling on the far, far mountains. Then he finally turned to the Irishman. "Would you tell me some more of your poems . . . Seamus, friend?"

Donegan grinned, cutting his dirty face with soft lines. "Yes, my friend.

"The white bloom of blackthorn, she.
The small sweet raspberry-blossom, she.
More fair the shy, rare glance of her eye,
Than the wealth of the world to me."

And with his whispering those words above Liam O'Roarke's resting place along the nameless river, Seamus Donegan knew why he had survived the nine days with Forsyth.

Epilogue

"You figure that's the Confederate?"

"What the Cheyenne left of him," Seamus answered Sharp Grover's question. "Look at that scar high on the neck. The Confederate who killed my horse had a scar like that."

"If that's his hand," Grover said, pointing, "the one with no fingers on that left hand . . . it was the fella who signed on calling himself Smith."

Beneath this falling sun on the twenty-sixth, Donegan wore a clean bandage on his arm, the bullet wound purged at last of maggots and infection. He and Grover had left the plum thicket where Carpenter's men had established camp upwind from the stench of the island. With a handful of scouts the pair had wandered far upstream, hoping for a look at the ground where the Cheyenne and Sioux villages had stood during the bloody siege.

To their surprise, young Sigmund Shlesinger had discovered the butchered body in the middle of what had been a huge camp circle.

"Bloody good at this, the bastirds are," Seamus commented, long moments later as he had fought his belly down. Emotions roiled within him, like a stew coming to boil: anger, disappointment, sadness, and, above all, the awe of not fully understanding the great hand at work in the affairs of man.

"I take it you seen this kind of thing before?"

Donegan nodded. "Fetterman's dead. Lodge Trail Ridge. Just . . . just like this, Sharp."

"No hands and feet?" Shlesinger asked.

This time Seamus wagged his head, once. "No hands and feet."

"They cut 'em off after the Confederate was dead?" Slinger asked, still innocent of man's brutality after nine days on the island.

Donegan glanced at the youth. "No. Likely this time the Cheyenne hacked his hands and feet off while the bastird was still breathing."

"And peeled the skin back on his chest?"

"The whole flap of his hide," Grover replied. "While he lived. It's more fun for the Dog Soldiers and their squaws to do it when the victim is alive."

"What'd they do to him . . . there?" Shlesinger said, pointing. He stood over the remains, holding his nose.

"Seems they built a little fire on top of his manhood parts."

"He live through that?" Donegan asked.

"He'd pass out . . . if he was lucky," Grover replied.

"You figure his name was Smith? Like he told us?" Shlesinger asked innocently.

Grover and Donegan glanced at each other. The old scout answered, "Doubt it, Slinger."

"We oughta bury him," the youth suggested.

"I don't think this one deserves a decent burial," Grover said, turning his back on the grisly remains.

Seamus scratched a hairy cheek. "Leave him be, Slinger. Eventually feed those wolves what've been howling round us the last few nights."

Donegan had enough. Nothing more he could do but swallow down his unrequited rage. With Grover, he turned away from the circular rings of trampled grass that marked the many lodge-circles, each with its dark fire-hole. Slinger trotted up behind them as the trio walked back to join the others.

"Shame of it is," Seamus commented quietly, "I'll never know his name. Never know now why he tried to kill me . . . when he was so friendly at the start of this goddamned bloody march."

Grover eventually gathered the rest of the souvenir hunters, scouts and soldiers alike, all scouring the campsites for moccasins, weapons, or clothing left behind in the Indians' haste to leave. With the sun hugging the far mountains, it was time to start back to the tent-camp Carpenter had established that morning of his arrival, where the captain had been joined early on the twenty-sixth by two more relief columns.

Just before noon on that day, Colonel Bankhead had rolled in, accompanied by I Troop of the 10th Negro Cavalry, in addition to detachments of the 5th and 38th Infantry. The long, dusty-blue columns trotted up behind guide Jack Stillwell. His return had created a real stir of excitement among the scouts, many of whom had feared Stillwell's death on the prairie. A renewed celebration seemed in order as the survivors crowded round young Stillwell, each man pounding Forsyth's youngest messenger in their happiness, welcoming him back to their motley fold. Having arrived with Bankhead, Dr. Turner joined surgeon Fitzgerald in preparing the wounded for transport.

Less than an hour after Bankhead's column had showed up, Maj. James S. Brisbin of the 2nd Cavalry rode in with an advance contingent of Colonel Luther Bradley's command, also hurrying to Forsyth's aid. Galloping down from Fort Sedgwick, Colorado Territory, Bradley had received the news of Forsyth's siege in a wire telegraphed from General Sheridan.

Less than an hour after Major Forsyth had refused amputation of his leg, Dr. Jenkins Fitzgerald had removed the decomposing leg of Louis Farley, badly wounded in that first charge of their first day on the island. Surgeon and patient alike shared hopes of saving the scout's life. The old man had cussed his share, and when he wasn't praying, the gruff curmudgeon Farley called for more whiskey during the surgery on his gangrenous leg. He had held on to consciousness as long as he could, talking with his son, Hutch, before he passed out midway through the amputation.

Young Farley explained that the reason he and his father had both joined Forsyth was to even a score. Only the year before, the old man had seen his wife killed during an Indian raid.

Wrapping the blackened, smelly limb in a blanket, Hutch buried his father's leg in a small grave of its own.

Sometime before dawn that next morning of the twenty-sixth, one of the buffalo soldiers had awakened surgeon Fitzgerald, with the news that the old man was no longer breathing.

Fitzgerald found young Hutch Farley weeping silently, standing vigil beside his father's body as he had for the past ten days of siege. At sunrise, Carpenter's brunettes scratched a new grave out of the sandy ground, placing both body and leg together for that last trip far from this bloody riverbed, far beyond eternity itself.

Above that newest grave of the island dead stood another small cross crudely fashioned from tent-pegs and swamp-willow by Sgt. William H. H. McCall. As was his duty, he had carefully printed the name of each man on a page torn from his roster book before the slip of paper was rolled and stuffed into an empty brass cartridge Carpenter's soldiers hammered into the top of each crude cross.

By sheer grit, Major Forsyth survived without amputation of his leg, all to Fitzgerald's amazement. It did not surprise Capt. Louis Carpenter that his friend had pulled through, however. Sandy Forsyth was known, above all things, for having some bottom, a soldier made of sand and fighting tallow.

Just before dawn on the cloudy morning of the twenty-seventh of September, 1868, the major finished penning his official report of the island battle and nine-day siege. He wrote that although most of the scouts accounted for many more Indian dead, he himself could only claim counting thirty-five bodies.

Forsyth laid down his pencil, drinking the last, luke-warm dregs of coffee from his tin cup before he reread the final lines he had just scratched across the pages in his memoranda book:

A fitting close to the hardest-fought battle to date in the annals of Indian warfare would be to mark this place with a name befitting the type of man who here struggled against the mighty warriors of this great land.

In honor of the finest young officer I have had the pleasure of serving with under fire of arms, I respectfully request the army to officially designate this hallowed ground as:

Beecher's Island.

"Slinger, Major Forsyth and me wanted you to have these," said Sergeant Billy McCall as he stopped near young Sigmund Shlesinger, a pair of army boots in hand.

Slinger looked down at his civilian boots, the same pair he had worn out of New York City, holes worn in their soles and sides cracked so badly the youth's thread-bare stockings poked through.

"Who those, Sergeant?"

"Lieutenant Beecher's," he replied, seeing Jack Stillwell come over.

Slinger swallowed, not sure how he should feel at that moment. Nine days of growing. Nine long and bloody days that meant there was no going back.

He looked again at his own old boots, then at the good army half-boots that had belonged to Forsyth's courageous lieutenant. Finally he gazed up at Jack Stillwell. Together with young Hutch Farley, the trio had been the youngest scouts recruited by Forsyth. Nineteen years old when they left Fort Hays. Years older now.

"You need 'em, Slinger," Stillwell prodded.

"Major and me thought they might be about your size," McCall explained, trying once more to hand the boots to Shlesinger. "Lieutenant isn't going to need them no more. And, we both figured . . . well, Beecher would want you to have 'em . . . seeing how you did more than your share to keep the rest of the men alive. Especially, how you kept the major going."

"I don't know, Sergeant. 'Bout wearing a dead man's——"

"Just take the boots, Slinger," McCall pleaded. "It's right."

Shlesinger noticed the moisture gathering in the soldier's imploring eyes.

"Awright, Sergeant." He took them from McCall, watching the sergeant walk off, snorting loudly to cover his tearfulness. "What I do about these I got on, Jack?"

"Leave 'em here," Stillwell suggested, plopping to the ground beside Slinger. "Time was while I was walking out there on that prairie, I'd give my left arm for your pair of raggedy, old boots. Now that you got Beecher's, I figure it's fitting for you just to leave yours over there . . . in your pit . . . on that island."

Slinger gazed as the new day's sun emerged off the prairie, spreading pink on the sandy riverbed this twenty-seventh day of September. He sighed, resolved.

"That's a fine notion, Jack. I'll leave my old boots on the island. Where each man of us is leaving behind a lot more."

Stillwell nodded. "I figure some of us, you and me, are leaving a boy behind in this place."

Shlesinger smiled, feeling the warm glow of a camaraderie burn in his breast, something born together between men under fire.

"Some ways, it feels good to leave that boy behind, Jack. Some ways I don't feel so good about it. Sometimes, I get to thinking—that I want that boy back. But, I know I ain't ever gonna be the fella I was when I rode out of Fort Hays behind Major George A. Forsyth."

Jack slapped an arm around Shlesinger's shoulder, hugging him as tightly as he dared, sitting there in the sandy grass of dawn. "Ain't none of us ever gonna be the same, Slinger. As long as any of this bunch lives—no man who rode with Forsyth, Beecher, and McCall . . . can ever be the same again."

Col. Bankhead and Capt. Carpenter bid their farewell to Maj. James S. Brisbin at dawn on that twenty-seventh day of September.

The faces in Brisbin's company of the 2nd Cavalry were all new, including Brisbin's. Men recruited to fill the need of a post-war, frontier army. Sad that most of the major's soldiers had just shaken their heads when Seamus Donegan mentioned names, hoping to find among the 2nd a face from those years of war on horseback.

At last the Irishman was beginning to realize this was a

different army. Sent out here to the West with a different task.

Bankhead pointed his men south that morning sunrise. Back in the narrow-wheeled ambulance, the seriously wounded had earned themselves a jolting ride over the rocky, sandy, sage-dotted plains.

That afternoon of the return trip, J. J. Peate led the columns past the hilltop scaffolds bearing dead warriors. Seething anger and frustration finally boiled over as scouts and soldiers alike knocked over the burial platforms, scattering across the ground those items buried with the Indians they did not claim as souvenirs or the spoils of war. Even the white lodge at the bottom of the ravine suffered the final indignity of their pent-up rage, plundered and cut apart for leggings, for any man a useful item of apparel on the high plains.

When the weary scouts reached the limestone walls at Fort Wallace on the twenty-ninth, Bankhead ordered the seriously wounded bedded down in the post hospital, while the slightly wounded were given one last medical examination before reassignment. Those scouts who chose to remain in the service for which they were hired were sent by wagon to the railhead at Sheridan, Kansas, two days later. From there they would ride the Kansas Pacific back to where Forsyth's march had all begun.

There at Fort Hays, the proud brigade of scouts was undergoing reorganization under a new commanding officer, Lt. Silas Pepoon of the 10th Cavalry.

Major Forsyth remained at Fort Wallace for several weeks, recovering from the effects of both his serious wounds and severe starvation. On October 1, Gen. Philip H. Sheridan sent a wire stating that he would visit the major later in the month, as he was accompanying George Armstrong Custer, who was preparing to lead a punitive winter expedition into The Territories, a massive campaign that would take Custer's 7th Cavalry south to the Washita River.

In the same wire, Sheridan informed Forsyth that he was recommending his friend from the Shenandoah campaign for the brevet rank of brigadier general. Awarded with Sheridan's highest appreciation for the gallantry, energy, and bravery displayed not only by Forsyth himself, but by the men who had served under Forsyth's command.

"Seems you're always bound to go off and do something foolish . . . when you've got the high, the low, and the jack against you," Sharp Grover commented, as he stood alongside the tall Irishman on the pre-dawn parade at Fort Hays, Kansas Territory.

Seamus buckled the cinch, looped and tucked before he dropped the left stirrup on the Grimsley saddle. He gently patted the big mare the Fort Hays livery sergeant had given him to replace The General, without one word of squabble. Then Donegan turned to Grover with a faint trace of a smile. This morning he had labored at shaving for the first time in weeks. Scraping the whiskers from both cheeks, resolute in keeping his short Vandyke beard and curly mustache.

A chill wind swept over the stockade, something with a bite that warned winter was not far behind to batter these Central Plains. And man be warned.

"I best be going, Sharp," he replied, not wanting to talk about his decision to leave the scouts and push north into Nebraska Territory. "Gonna try to cover some ground today, before the storm that's coming shuts the land down."

Sharp tugged up the collar of his own coat, snugging it round his ears. His old eyes peered out beneath the brim of his well-worn felt hat. "No sense trying to talk you out of it, getting you to stay on here with the rest of us for the winter?"

"God knows I wasted one winter already, waiting for Liam." He sighed. "When I should have been holding a good woman who needs me."

"You figure to find her in Nebraska, you say?"

"She wrote me before she left the Bozeman Road," he said, yanking on the thick, leather gloves. "Said she was going to a place near a town called Osceola. On the Blue River, near the Platte. I'll find her, Sharp. No matter what or how long it takes . . . I'll find her."

He swung into his saddle as a pale, buttermilk sun crept over the horizon, its light struggling against the icy, gray overcast just then threatening to spill its undergut on the land.

Seamus held down his big hand. "You meant a lot to me Uncle Liam, Grover. And . . . in them nine days on that bloody island, you come to mean even more to me. I'm going to miss you, old man."

"Till we see your dust again, Irishman," Grover replied as he stepped back, watching Donegan until the horseman's back disappeared in the murky light.

"I'll find her," Seamus whispered as he put the horse into an easy lope beyond the stockade of Fort Hays. He stroked the mare's neck, pointing her nose north. Thinking on Jennie.

"Pray to God . . . I find her."

HERE IS AN EXCERPT FROM *BLACK SUN*—
THE NEXT VOLUME IN TERRY C.
JOHNSTON'S BOLD NEW WESTERN SERIES
—*THE PLAINSMEN:*

Prologue

*A*s bad as the whiskey was, it proved the cure.

By the fourth splash of its liquid fire he had thrown against the back of his throat, Seamus Donegan sensed the tension easing long the cords in his neck. Not to mention tension seeping from those great muscles in his back which bore the scar carved there by Confederate steel. He was loosening like a worn-out buggy spring after a long haul of it over a wash-board road.

It had been some ride for the Irishman whose great bulk now sat hulking over the small glass all but hidden within the big hands. Returned from the dead he was again, and working steadily to pickle himself even more than the last.

Back from the grave that had tried hard to swallow him at Beecher Island.

In the space of the past three weeks, Donegan had returned with Major George A. Forsyth's band of civilian scouts to Fort Hays where the survivors of the bloody, nine-day island siege were promptly reorganized under Lt. Silas Pepoon. Yet without a look back, the Irishman decided he had himself enough of the plains and Indians, enough of blood and sweat and death to last him for some time to come. Seamus pointed his nose north, aiming for Nebraska. He had started there once before—a year gone now.

Nebraska. There in the Platte River country near Osceola, the widow Wheatley had promised she would be waiting for him to fetch her.

But Donegan's quest for Uncle Liam O'Roarke had pulled

him for a time off that trail to Osceola and Jennie. That, and the Cheyenne of Roman Nose.

Seamus was too late getting out to the Wheatley place.

He angrily threw another splash of hot liquid against the back of his throat, remembering the old woman's eyes as she glared up at him in the late afternoon light from beneath her withered, bony hand.

"No, mister. Jenny took herself and the boys back east. Dead set on getting back to her own folk, she was."

"Ohio?" he had asked, numbly, staring at James Wheatley's mother.

She had nodded, her eyes softening, perhaps recognizing something cross the tall Irishman's face. "Ohio."

He had thanked her, crawled into the saddle without feeling much and reined toward the south. Kansas and Fort Hays.

Nursing his grief and anger like a private badge of passion he alone could wear.

For some time he had looked forward to this moment. Promising himself all down that long trail from Osceola he would sit here and drink the night through if he had to, until he decided where next to go and what next to do. Having no clue worth a tinker's damn where he could find his second uncle, Liam's brother, Ian O'Roarke—was he cursed now to wander aimlessly searching the west coast where Liam had hinted Ian would be found?

Now that Jennie Wheatley had moved on after a year of waiting for a restless man.

"Maybe t'is better, after all," he murmured, bringing the chipped glass to his lips once more. "Better a woman like that has her a man who can work the land and stay in one place. I could never give her kind something like that."

Over and over in his mind on that long ride south a scrap of Irish poetry had hung in his mind like a piece of dirty linen. John Boyle O'Reilley's words reminded him most of her.

> The red rose whispers of passion,
> And the white rose breathes of love;
> Oh, the red rose is a falcon,
> And the white rose is a dove.

> But I send you a cream-white rosebud
> With a flush on its petal tips;
> For the love that is purest and sweetest
> Has a kiss of desire on the lips.

Too much of an unquenched burning inside him yet. Unanswered yearnings. Better for everybody now that Jennie moved on without him. Seems she needed something more than he could give, and he sure as hell needed more right now than any one woman could find herself giving him in return.

The whiskey seemed to soften the harsh edges on things, especially the noise of this dimly-lit Hays City watering hole. Soldiers and wagon-bosses, teamsters and speculators all shouldered against one another at the rough bar. A growing cloud of blue smoke rolled slowly past the smoky oil lamps that cast dancing shadows on the murky canvas walls and muddy plank floor each time the door swung open to admit some newcomer and a cold gust of October wind.

He would need something to eat eventually . . . hell, it could wait until morning now. Perhaps if he wasn't careful, he'd end up spending the night right here at this table near the corner where the smell of old vomit and dried urine could make a strong man lose his appetite for anything but whiskey. Perhaps if he kept drinking until he passed out here, Seamus would not need to fill the gnawing hole inside him with one of the pudgy chippies working the half-dozen cribs in the back of this place. Lilac-watered women came to ply their trade in the flesh-pots that followed the army and the railroad west.

"I wouldn't've gambled a warm piss that I'd find Liam O'Roarke's favorite nephew hugging up to a bottle of saddle varnish here in Hays City ever again!"

Through the late afternoon light sneaking past the few smudged, smoky windowpanes, Seamus immediately recognized the face of Sharp Grover. Major Forsyth's former chief of scouts strode across the crowded room, directly for Donegan's table. Abner Grover—comrade in arms from the stench and hell of Beecher Island.

"If it ain't Mother Grover's ugliest son!" he cheered,

momentarily eyeing the younger man who came up on Sharp's heels. "Sit, gentlemen!"

"You're in a better humor than when I found you here in the Shady Rest end of last winter," Grover said, scraping a wobbly chair close.

"And you a goddamned scout, Abner. You're supposed to know where to find me." Seamus held up his cup of amber whiskey to them both, then tossed it back.

"You're drinking alone again?"

"Till the two of you sat down."

"You going to invite us to drink with you?"

He glanced at Grover's young blue-eyed companion with the long, blond bantam tuft sprouting from his lower lip, then answered. "I never enjoyed drinking alone, Sharp."

"Get us some glasses, will you, Bill?"

Grover's companion nodded and rose from the table without a word, shoving into the milling crowd at the bar.

"He's a big one," Donegan whispered.

Grover agreed. "Almost tall as you, Seamus."

"He a scout for you . . . riding with Pepoon now?"

"No. Bill tells me General Sheridan's wired him orders to sit here until the Fifth Cavalry comes through."

Seamus went back to regarding his whiskey glass as Bill came back to the table with two more glasses and another bottle of whiskey. "Didn't figure you'd still be hanging 'round Hays, Abner."

"We're getting ready to hove away for Fort Dodge soon enough, Seamus," Grover replied. "And you could go, too. It'll be good winter's wages—riding with Pepoon's scouts."

"Where you heading this time?" he asked, watching Grover's young companion pour two glasses of the whiskey from the new bottle.

"Word has it we're marching with Sheridan himself—down into The Territories."

"Right into the heart of it, eh?"

"That's right, Irishman. Them young bucks been busy since late last summer."

"Don't we know it, Sharp? Penned up like we was on that island far out in the middle of hell itself."

"No," and Grover shook his head. "This is something different. The Cheyenne been raiding up on the Solomon and

Saline Rivers. Burning, raping, killing stock. Carrying off white women and children."

"Sheridan's going down into The Territories to get them women back, is it?"

"He's called Custer back to do it for him."

That struck him like a chunk of winter river-ice thrust at the middle of his chest. Seamus leaned back in his chair, fingertips playing with the chipped lip of his glass. "Custer, you say? I heard he was serving out his year away from the 7th—for having them deserters shot."

Grover hunched over the table as he glanced about quickly. "This is Custer country, Seamus."

"I damned well know that."

"You're aiming for a fight of it?" Grover asked.

"If one steps up, I won't back away."

"Best keep your voice down in this town when you're speaking your mind about Custer."

"I'm touched you care so much about me spilling me blood, Abner."

"I do, you thick-headed Irishman," he said, slapping Donegan on the shoulder to show all was forgiven. "Best you know—Custer's already back with his regiment."

His eyes narrowed and he felt his windpipe constrict. "Here?"

"The 7th's marched on to Fort Dodge, where they're training for the coming campaign. Custer's already there with 'em."

Donegan's teeth ground with disappointment.

"You were hoping to meet up with the boy general, were you?" Bill asked, speaking for the first time.

Seamus looked at Grover's companion. Then smiled. "We, we just go back to the war, let's say."

"Never fought in the war myself," Bill admitted. "Too young. But I have heard all about Custer's part in Hancock's campaign last year. Sure glad I wasn't no thirteen-dollar-a-month private . . . living on beans and dreams of whores—following that curly-headed bastard. I worked 'round some of his soldiers last month. Out to Fort Larned."

"Larned is some way from here," Seamus muttered.

"Bill here just come in from one hell of a ride, Seamus," Grover said.

"First job I had for the army, Lieutenant Billy Cooke signed me on the ninth of September to re-sack forage for their mounts. Then on the fifteenth, Cooke finally hired me as a scout."

Seamus regarded the young man more carefully, recalling the youth of Jack Stillwell who had handled a man's job and more during Forsyth's chase after the Cheyenne. Donegan looked down into the amber of his glass. "The fifteenth, eh? . . . Sharp and me was less than two days from that God-forsaken island."

"Bill here is the kind what could have held the muster for them nine days on Beecher Island."

Seamus studied the young man. "Sharp says you had quite a ride in from Larned."

"Over sixty miles," Bill accounted. "Bringing word that the Kiowas and Comanches finally broke out. They're joining the Cheyennes on the warpath."

"Bill gave Sheridan that report at Fort Hays—the sort of news that the general had to send out to the other posts as well. Seems Sheridan asked around for a horseman to ride down to Dodge." Grover shook his head a moment. "But too many been killed on that route lately. No one wanted to carry Sheridan's dispatches what with the Injuns rising up."

Seamus watched the young man's eyes hold the table. He figured Bill for being a bit self-conscious. "You told Sheridan you'd go?"

Bill looked up a moment. "I told the general I'd ride, nobody else having the balls to take the chance . . . what with the Kiowas and Cheyennes both jumping off their reservations."

"At Hays Bill got himself a bunk and slept for five hours, before saddling a fresh mount."

"Stopped at the road ranch down at Coon Creek for another hour shut-eye on the way," Bill said, starting to warm to the story of it. "Rode off on a new mount from a troop of cavalry bivouacked there . . . come on into Dodge without seeing nary a feather or war-paint."

"But it wasn't the end of it for you," Sharp said, smiling as he poured some more whiskey in their glasses. "Bill grabbed himself a few more hours sleep, then carried dispatches from the commander of Fort Dodge over to General Hazen at Fort Larned."

"How'd you end up back here at Hays?" Seamus asked before throwing his whiskey back. It had ceased to burn his tongue.

"Hazen wanted Sheridan to have the latest word in from his scouts—the Kiowa villages all running south of the Arkansas."

Grover nodded, smiling widely. "Ain't that just like him, now? Phil Sheridan's a man who wants to know exactly where the Injuns are every minute."

"Seems fitting, it does . . . especially after Sheridan and the rest of them didn't have an idea where Roman Nose and his bunch was when we run into 'em last month, eh?"

Grover swallowed hard on his whiskey, sputtering slightly as he watched the sour grin fade from the Irishman's face. "I figure the army learned a hard lesson there."

"Army learns a lesson—it's for sure the poor sojur be the one to pay." Seamus poured more whiskey in his own glass, offering some to the blond-haired youth across from him. "And you, Bill—have you had enough of riding for the army for awhile?"

"No. Pay's good. Seventy-five a month and found. Better that than scratching out hardscrabble this winter."

"How 'bout you, Donegan?" Sharp Grover turned fully toward the Irishman. "You got shet of what's eating you and ready to ride again?"

"With you?"

"With Pepoon and me, Seamus. We're heading down into Indian Territory with George—by God—Custer."

His beetled eyebrow twitched. "That would be something, wouldn't it now? Me riding scout for the man what stole me stripes back in the Shenandoah?" He hung his head, brooding on it, staring into the dancing ripples of his whiskey. "No. I'd better not tempt the fates again with Custer."

"Then Seamus Donegan will ride with me, by damn," the youngster said.

He looked up at the hard, gray-blue eyes again, seeing there some strength he had not taken the time to notice before. "Ride with you? Just where in hell would we be riding?"

"With the Fifth Cavalry."

"And what the divil would you be having to say about me riding with the Fifth?"

He gazed back at the Irishman steady and long. "I suppose I'd have everything to say about it. Sheridan's just commissioned me chief of scouts for the Fifth."

He nodded, approvingly, then raised his glass in toast. "To the chief of scouts." Seamus tossed it back, then licked his lips. "So . . . tell me just where this Fifth Cavalry of yours is heading."

The young man leaned close over the table, drawing the other men in as he whispered in husky tones. "We're going south and west . . . then turning east toward The Territories."

"You're going to Injun country too?" Grover asked.

He nodded eagerly, the ready smile cutting his young face. "We're serving as beaters to drive the villages and war-parties toward Custer."

"Sounds like winter's work," Donegan said.

"You're damned right," Bill answered. "We'll likely face a blizzard or two and freeze our balls before we're done. If you're not up to riding into the jaws of winter itself, I'll understand."

Seamus sat back, smiling himself as he sloshed some more amber into his glass. He held it up again in toast. "All right —you've got yourself a scout for the winter. Here's to riding with you, Bill . . . Bill . . . ?"

He grinned widely, thrusting his big hand across the table at the Irishman. They shook.

"Bill Cody, Seamus. My name's Bill Cody."

DON'T MISS *BLACK SUN*—
BOOK 4 IN THE EXCITING
PLAINSMEN SERIES!